The Memory of Stones

Reviews of *The Naked Song & Other Stories:*

'This collection of stories about the old South Africa, the new South Africa, struggle South Africa and exiled South Africa should have significant impact. It certainly deserves it.'
— Barry Streek, *Cape Times*

'I had a royal time enjoying the fresh breeze that Langa's anthology blows into the literary creation of post-apartheid South Africa.'
— Professor Nhlanhla Maake, *Sunday Independent*

'… character development and an easy, undemanding narrative quality … Amid the pain is a wry, self-mocking humour.'
— *Business Day*

'… a gritty, urban humour coauthors his perspective … Langa's personal experiences – as a political prisoner, an exile, a novelist and cultural activit … are wide and deep. He draws on all these perspectives for the fictional purposes of this collection, with expecial intensity, compassion and wit.'
— Ingrid de Kok, *World Literature Today*

THE MEMORY OF STONES

Mandla Langa

DAVID PHILIP PUBLISHERS
Cape Town • Johannesburg

First published in Southern Africa in 2000 by
David Philip Publishers (Pty) Ltd,
208 Werdmuller Centre, Newry Street, Claremont 7708,
South Africa

Published in the United States of America in 2000 by
Lynne Rienner Publishers, Inc.
1800 30th Street, Boulder, Colorado 80301
www.rienner.com

and distributed (non-exclusively) in the United Kingdom by
Lynne Rienner Publishers, Inc.
3 Henrietta Street, Convent Garden, London WC2E 8LU

ISBN 0-86486-408-6 (David Philip)
ISBN 0-89410-866-2 (Lynne Rienner)

Printed and bound by CTP Book Printers, Parow, Cape Town

Library of Congress Cataloging-in-Publication Data

Langa, Mandla, 1950–
    The memory of stones / Mandla Langa.
        p. cm.
    ISBN 0-89410-866-2 (pb. : alk. paper)
    1. Natal (South Africa)--Fiction. 2. Women in politics--Fiction. I. Title

PR9369.3.L33 M4 2000
823'.914--dc21

                                                                00-022413

British Cataloguing in Publication Data

A Cataloguing in Publication record for this book is available from the
British Library

Acknowledgments

This novel is a product of the many journeys that my political and social compatriots have taken with me, across all these lands – 'all that water' – until we collectively took the steps to break the cycle and returned to the native land. Some of the people, on whom a few of the characters are based, are no longer alive, and it is therefore in their memory that this is written. This novel was written as an act of exorcism, for my family to come to terms with the death of my brother, Ben. He was shot dead in May 1984, in an act of supreme political irony. Those who had labelled him an enemy agent and caused his death turned out to be handmaidens of the Apartheid State.

The idea for this book was conceived in a collaborative screenplay that Andy Metcalf and I started writing in London. The film was never made although I sincerely hope that it comes out one day. I wish to thank Andy Metcalf and Gillian Slovo for their ideas. Many thanks also to Mary Slack and to the Arts and Culture Trust for their support. There are many more that breathed their lives into the text. There's Ilva, who stood by me during the writing, a long hour of insanity.

Many thanks to President Thabo Mbeki, who gave me a chance when he appointed me to the task group on government communications, which allowed me space to write.

For
Ben Langa,
on what would have been his birthday on 24 August
and Ntsiki Anderson- Mackay and Linda Mackay- Langa,
my daughters, who saw the Promised Land

One

Rumour had it that, when Zodwa first saw the light at birth, on May 21, 1964, she refused to cry. Perplexed by this unheard-of development – and recoiling from the reproachful eyes of the villagers who hold that the new-born exhibiting such peculiar traits are issues of an evil spirit – Nomonde, in whose womb this stubborn girl has nestled, consults the holy men in the vicinity of Ngoza.

Maintaining that this is a private matter and still placing a great stock in prayer, Baba Joshua accepts his daughter's silence as the Almighty's secret way of testing his faith, just like Job. Although Nomonde can't say it, she shrinks at the thought of surrendering her pink bundle to Catholic Church priests. The liturgies intoned in an incomprehensible language lack the strength to address what might well be spiritual possession. Nomonde is equally unhappy with the charismatic Baptist churches to which Joshua belongs and from whose humble pulpit he sometimes preaches to a largely indifferent congregation. Their zeal for the laying-on of hands is unsuitable for one of soft bones. Likewise total immersion, which can prove fatal for lungs which still have an undetermined capacity.

After enduring five days of silence from the crib, Nomonde quietly goes above Baba Joshua's head and confides in an ageless inyanga called Nozizwe. No one, except Nduli the herbalist's apprentice, knows what happened in Nozizwe's hut where the little girl was taken. People talk in hushed tones about fumes whose pungency assailed salivary glands, a sign of the brewing of very powerful herbs. On the May night when the temperatures dance near the freezing mark – when the only clock on the belfry tower of the Anglican church in the town of Ngoza chimes the midnight hour – the village releases its collective breath on hearing the wails of the infant. The tone and unusual timbre mean that Zodwa will grow into a strange child of silence.

★　　★　　★

Thirty-one years later, on a day of turbid rain, vaguely aware that a certain mystery surrounded the circumstances of her birth, Zodwa determined to get the full story out of Nduli. When the villagers of Ngoza were scattered to the four winds, Nduli had trekked to the Eastern Cape where he had relocated to one of the rural slums which filigreed the surface of the Cape like acne on a diseased skin. Zodwa had kept a symbiotic relationship with him, bailing him out when he was broke and taking advantage of his transport. Today was Thursday. On Saturday, she was celebrating her thirty-first birthday with a group of friends on campus – and this was as good an age as any for all to be revealed.

She and her friend Ayesha had risen early to take a lift with Nduli from Alice to King William's Town to buy supplies. Her party would also become a graduation celebration. She just prayed that no drunken gatecrashers would stray to the women's residence – for their sake, really, because, even though she knew there were festivities ahead, it wasn't past her to give a thorough dressing-down to some slobbering mother's son. Now that they were due back, the rain was coming down – and Nduli was still ensnared in negotiations with meat suppliers somewhere in town. Nduli's bargaining strategy entailed wearing down the opposition under a welter of words. It was no accident that, as a young man, he had substituted his apprenticeship in an inyanga's practice for the church. The latter provided him with ample opportunity to convert unbelievers. Accepting that there was no way to prise Nduli out of a situation where an argumentation was at full throttle, Zodwa and Ayesha waited. There was also no prospect of alternative transport. And, of course, the downpour was not the type to be braved.

In the vast, shifting light of a noonday sun, under the raging curtain of dancing raindrops the size of pomegranates, Zodwa closed her eyes and primed her ears to see. Their transport back to campus announced its approach through a full-throated shake, rattle and roll, all the way from the main market on Hunter Street. She heard it drive past the small wooden bridge which was positively ageing under a canopy of leaves, a remembered piece of scenery which had the beauty of a postcard picture. Then the van shuddered and spluttered as if whatever held it together would finally give and scatter exhausted car parts all over the hitchhikers' spot. She heard rather than saw loyal Ayesha gathering their shopping bags, the wet rustle of plastic and polythene. Their heads covered with sections of the *Daily Dispatch*, the two young women dashed off from under the sheltering tree across the puddles on the corrugated ground to their lift: a rattletrap bakkie on whose side panels was the illegible name of the owner's construction company in intaglio script. Since it was raining in buckets, Zodwa knew that only a handful of die-hard shoppers would venture out from the University of Fort Hare campus to King, as this little Eastern Cape town was affectionately known.

Inside the bakkie, listening to the rain drumming on the roof, Zodwa bantered with the driver, a rachitic alter ego of his own vehicle. 'When are you going to get a new car, Mr Nduli?' she asked. 'This one has seen better days …'

Ayesha joined in. 'Perhaps a BMW, Seven-series …?'

Nduli laughed, shifting to engage the car into second gear, his bat-blind hand brushing against Ayesha's fleshly thigh under the coarse nylon fabric of her soaked leggings. He was as bald as an egg, with a high forehead and clear, almost baby-like eyes that alternately seemed to miss nothing and everything. Nduli took a deep breath as if his lungs were about to succumb to the close air in the cab. Still, he seemed comfortable, as if this was where he really belonged. Nduli swathed in an old army greatcoat and

Ayesha in her duffel coat effectively combined in bulk to squeeze Zodwa against the door. Since it was a weekday, Nduli had shed his white-and-green Zionist Christian Church cassock, his raiment of sanctity, which came with an embroidered mitre-like cap. He seemed awkward, a bad military intelligence officer at a loss in mufti.

'This car can tell you all the stories you wish to hear,' he said. Then he paused, looking at the roiling greyness ahead. 'As for getting a new one, I'll wait for a signal from Joshua. He's back home in Ngoza now. He has called all the families back, except mine.' The last was a pure statement of fact, laced, however, with the beginnings of a reproach. Zodwa wondered whether the old man's exile in the Eastern Cape wasn't made all the more painful from a forced adoption of the isiXhosa linguistic peculiarities, where his tongue now sailed smoothly over the 'ndi-' personal pronoun instead of the 'ngi-' of his mother tongue, isiZulu. Mr Nduli, she concluded uncharitably, was not so much homesick as bereft of his gerunds. He was fated to display a certain crudeness whenever in the presence of *amakhwenkwe*, the great unwashed and uncircumcised.

The rain had dashed all possibilities for Zodwa to indulge in her favourite pastime: taking pleasure from the scenery. Yet, beyond the wiper blades which unsuccessfully squeegeed the water from the windscreen in slow metronomic movements, she got a glimpse of the vegetation and the fields, some fenced-in, some not. The pastel colours of the houses in Dimbaza were even more muted, invested, as they flashed past, with the quality of colour prints from a poorly developed negative. There was a little more colour in Middledrift, the small town's shopping centre buzzing with people braving the downpour or, more likely, with no other alternative. Middledrift took her mind back to Ngoza, her father's Promised Land. She thought of Joshua and her mother, Nomonde, and felt an insupportable urge to see them, just for one long moment. She refused, however, to put this down to nostalgia.

*　　*　　*

In her mind, Ngoza could be reduced to abstract terms, a place that was caught up in the maw of contending forces. This was where the might of the government – *their* government, she mentally corrected herself – had removed the inhabitants to make way for white progress. She was very young, in June 1975, when it all happened. The memory of it all was very unreliable. But she could still remember the shouting and the carrying on, the sound of trucks, her mother's dull eyes as she watched Joshua remonstrating with a burly police officer who seemed bored and detached, his own eyes under the peaked cap as soulless as cut glass.

*　　*　　*

It is perhaps in the eyes of the people involved in the drama that she can take a reading of the situation. Joshua's eyes dart from face to face, resting, briefly, on Zodwa, as if trying to determine whether or not the little girl could fathom what is happening. And if she does, what can be the effect on her, now and in the overcast future? He looks at his son, Jonah, who at thirteen is two years older than Zodwa. He has adopted a rigid stance, as if everything inside him, the bones, muscles, fibres and fluids, have congealed into a taut steel spring. Zodwa expects him to jump and hurl himself against the edged weapons of the men, but he merely stands there, his eyes doing all the talking. She has never been so frightened in her entire life. Most men cannot look the women in the eye even though theirs blaze with impotent hostility. The womenfolk, who risk being clubbed down with batons and rifle-butts, are more demonstrative, hurling abuse and household missiles at the police contingent. Some of the younger black constables are shamefaced as if participating in an obscene ritual, but they have to stand firm and continue to bring the dwellings down to the ground. The eyes and ears of the older constables are more attuned to the commands of their bored superior. They don't need any orders before wading into the villagers with their weapons. Their eyes belong to clay figurines:

black coal against a field of muddy white. Years later, Zodwa would still wonder whether those eyes ever closed in sleep or in a moment of passion.

Nduli is among the men who bear the brunt of the police contingent's brutality. He stands his ground, like a barnyard bantam, blocking their entry, holding out a hymnbook the way Zodwa will later see film exorcists confronting the Evil One. But by this time the invaders have had enough. A lateral swing from a rifle-butt catches Nduli against the jaw. While blood gushes out of his mouth as he falls, the pages scatter out of the ancient hymnal. Zodwa helps collect the pages while the men tend to their fallen friend. One of the pages, bearing the muddy impressions of a constable's boot, speaks of someone's father's house that boasts many rooms. At eleven years of age, the irony of their circumstances does not escape her.

★   ★   ★

The memory of the scene made her smile. Guiltily, she turned towards Nduli, realising that he had been watching her during her reverie.

'Whatever happened to the other people?' she asked. 'Like Nozizwe?'

'Nozizwe left with the rest of the villagers,' Nduli said. 'But she was one of the first to return. All her shrubs and herbs are in the fields of Ngoza. She wouldn't know how to deal with the world without them.'

★   ★   ★

Nozizwe, an ancient crone once Ngoza's premier inyanga, has been feared by some of the strongest men. At first Nduli dismisses her as a charlatan until one day when she proves her worth by succeeding where Christian prayer had failed, to exorcise spirits out of Thabitha, a young woman who had fled into the settlement of Ngoza from the faction fighting in Bergville. It is said that one of her admirers bewitches her by calling her name at midnight, invoking the magic of the herbal calabash. On the day she is cured, exactly at the moment when she stops screaming and thrashing about, her tormentor, a fellow refugee called Lobethe – a corruption of Robert – immediately goes stark, raving mad. The suddenness of the young man's transformation from an insufferable braggart into an empty-headed wretch, who counts flies as they buzz past, fills the whole settlement with awe. Some of the men who have reason to fear Nozizwe start a campaign of silent murmurs. Maybe having a resident inyanga who is also a witch isn't such a good idea after all. The women, of course, cheer and ululate, their whole attitude saying, One man down! When Lobethe's brand of lunacy overshoots the bounds of propriety and he takes to exposing himself in public – sometimes in full view of small children – Nozizwe reaches into her depthless bag of spells and calls up one which renders him a deaf-mute. Living alone with all that yawning silence inside his head thus cures Lobethe of his fascination with secret powers, which certain men employ to insinuate themselves on young women.

*   *   *

'A person who seems to have disappeared', Nduli said, 'is Hodoba. Remember him?'

She cast around in her head – mainly because she had trained herself never to remember Hodoba – trying to find a physical association with the name. Gradually, like a progressive appearance of a film image in a developer's tray – Hodoba's face materialised before her, accompanied by that of Mbongwa', her uncle. Mbongwa – always present when the going was good. Never around in times of trouble. She remembered that he had acted as if he really liked her, his niece, but there was always something about him which spoke of distances – a preoccupation with flight – which discouraged intimacy. She had read about people pointing to specific moments in history, such as when they wondered where someone was when John F Kennedy was assassinated or, much later, when Mandela was released. For her, even if it hadn't been such a big moment in her life, her whole connection with history, and the players in that

7

singularly depressing drama, was through the faces that had grimaced as they howled in reaction to the removal from Ngoza. She could recall that Hodoba had been a permanent source of uneasiness amongst the people. While Nozizwe had been a healer, it was held that Hodoba spoke to the dead and indulged in unnameable midnight rituals in his cave dwelling. His disappearance, then, portended trouble, and, for some unknown reason, Zodwa knew that it was trouble that she would have to confront one day. The journey from King William's Town to the University of Fort Hare was suddenly transformed into a holding action, an agency to delay the possibility of her coming face to face with memory.

'I remember him,' she said in a tone she hoped would change the subject. But she was dealing with Nduli, an old man – and old people, she had seen, would always pick on those things which were a cause of discomfort for the young. It was their prerogative.

'When the police had left,' Nduli said, 'we collected our things and went to the cave. Nozizwe directed us to lash together all the artefacts of remembrance for each family. We stored all these in a shrine. Hodoba came later and challenged your father, remember?'

'Sounds like a charming fellow,' Ayesha quipped.

'A nasty piece of work,' Nduli agreed. 'But Joshua was diplomatic about it. Indulging the animal.' He shook his head. 'Joshua believed that the meek shall inherit the earth.'

'Not a very popular philosophy nowadays,' Zodwa said.

'Nor a practical one.' Nduli was a believer, but he was not a fool. Before she could respond to what amounted to a criticism of her father, they had arrived at the arched gates of the campus. Because Nduli didn't wish to engage with the guards who would have required him to sign the visitors' log and taken down his name and the registration number of his van, he dropped the women off. Fortunately, the rain had let up.

'I will see you Saturday,' he said, helping them with their

shopping. Then he got into the van and reversed onto the road leading to the town of Alice. He wouldn't know that the guards were aware of his van and could identify its rattle a mile off. They dismissed Nduli with the distant, affectionate contempt reserved for the dangerously innocent.

'Thank you, Nduli,' Zodwa said to the memory. She watched the vehicle, the man behind the wheel, the road that stretched into another culture, another life. Just then – as if it had been conjured up from somewhere within her – she heard the sound of the ground hornbill. Walking ahead quickly and not stopping to answer Ayesha's question on what was going on, she knew from stories she had heard in her childhood that the sound of the fateful bird foretold disaster. She sensed that the disaster would somehow involve her father and wished she had the power to bring Jonah, her brother, back to life. But Jonah was gone.

*   *   *

For some reason which escaped her, the memory of Jonah became a memory of the community and her family's exile from Ngoza. As if responding to a remembrance triggered off by the strains of forgotten music, Zodwa relived the long night she had buried under layers of concentric circles in her mind. She senses the moonlit night and its rhythms, the foliage breathing, suffocating. She hears the plaintive howls of dogs left behind. No matter how attached the people are to their pets, the animals would prove burdensome in the long walk to God-knows-where. There are no cats. With their heightened instincts for survival and restlessness among losers, felines are the first to sense the tensions in the air. They are no different from their prey, the rats, which jump ship at the first sign of trouble. Moreover, villagers are loth to keep cats, which are associated with witchcraft. With Nozizwe and Joshua heading the procession, the people walk in silence.

Even though the faces of most of the men are unlined by age, their gait and carriage belong to older men. Their squared shoulders speak of the burden they already envision carrying in the land of the white man. It is as though they are breasting the buffeting winds of the future, which lie in town and city. With the rising of the wind, her brother Jonah walks alongside Zodwa. As if wishing to deny her the warmth his presence gives her, he occasionally traipses over to his age-mates, snot-nosed louts created by God for the sole purpose of tormenting small girls. Zodwa has had a set-to with some of them, and has clawed and spat like a cat, the only way of earning their respect. To hit back at her, they once in a while sidle up to her best friends with the aim of weaning them from her influence. Not infrequently, her friends, seduced by the prestige of being taken seriously by the royal fellowship of male adolescents, do turn against her, giggling behind their hands. It is this grasp of the fickleness of companionship that has decided Zodwa that friendship will henceforth be on her own terms. She would laugh and touch a person but has no intention to feel. Feeling is but a step away from hurt. Today, though, the boys are in a more accommodating mood. With the removals in progress, they won't have to trudge two miles to dreaded school where the teachers are quick to punish latecomers. Because they have to herd livestock and milk the cows before sun-up, the boys are invariably late for the morning bell.

Zodwa knows that she will miss the school with its morning chaos before assembly, where children sing hymns in unison under the proud gaze of the principal. It is not so much the singing which engages her as the opportunity to enjoy a quiet laugh at the self-importance of the teachers. There is the choir conductor who tries to seduce secondary school girls, blithely unaware that his bad breath has the power to stun an insect in mid-flight. There is Miss Zikode, who insists on wearing a sun-bonnet to preserve her complexion. This happens in the dark days when skin tone is still a measure of people's distance from or proximity to whiteness and social acceptance. There is the principal himself, bursting with the flatulence of his own importance. He is the only man who has ever seen Durban and won't let anyone forget it. He is wont to start his sentences with, 'In Durban, this is how we see it …' like a governor invoking imperial authority. There is her class teacher, Miss Shelembe, quiet, passionate, and tall and as black as ebony, with a sculpted face which seldom smiles. It is she who reinforced in Zodwa the attitude which is already second nature to the little girl: the wisdom of silence and the prudence of speaking up against wrong. 'Don't say a word unless you have to,' she once advised. 'Men are suspicious of silence, and it's part of your arsenal to keep them guessing.' Miss Shelembe refers to men as if they come from another planet. 'But if anyone steps on you, scream!' Encouraging the girls to dream, she would say: 'You must dream what you wish to achieve, but remember it is only those who dream who know nightmares.' Zodwa would miss her.

Jonah comes back and takes her hand in his. 'What do you think?'

She shrugged. 'I don't know,' she replies. 'Do you know where we're going?'

'The caves.' Jonah knows everything. 'Baba and Nozizwe are leading us to the caves.'

Before Zodwa can compose another question, he hurries her along into the throng marching into the cave. The temperature has dropped even further here and Zodwa feels the chill begin at the soles of her feet, to rise and engulf her whole body. The foliage is already glistening with frost which, caught in the pale light of the moon, looks like grains of sugar sprinkled over black-velvet cloth. A few of the men and children carry flares, which flicker futilely against the darkness inside. To fight the dark, she shuts her eyes, eliminating the feverish bursts of light, allowing the darkness to possess her, becoming one with it so that she can overcome it. Still holding her brother's hand, she reopens her eyes and is rewarded with a passably clear view of the cave and the people milling about.

It is not so much a cave as an old, disused mine out of whose uneven floor jut stone pillars to the chest height of the tallest grown-up. Here and there are signs of ancient industry: a wheel-barrow rots in the close air; old digging implements lean against the rock; gumboots lie on the side as if awaiting the warming feel of their owner. It is a place of work, which has been arrested by the blast of a whistle, where the dust-laden men once waited patiently to be paid, and then filed out to join the world outside. The air is rank with odours of organic material, despair and neglect. The low ceiling is supported by timber which, illumi-nated by flares, seems old and brittle, raising in the little girl's imagination the spectre of all that ground and rock crashing down on their heads. The debris, which has collected through the ages, has been piled to the edges of the sloping cave, a cairn of ancient stones, ineffable, so that Zodwa has an impression of moving inside the ruins of an old place of worship. As her eyes grow more and more accustomed to the gloom, she can make out a rude table hewn from rock, an altar on which the villagers' prized belongings are arranged in neat piles. People have formed themselves into a circle around the altar. The light in the centre seems to pull the community towards it like a magnetic force.

Joshua comes in sight as if from the light itself and is trans-formed into its source. He lifts his hands, calling for silence, although the chatter in the chamber has already decreased to a whisper, as if the villagers appreciate the irony of their situation. Underground, forced into an existence of moles, they squint to make sense of the shadowy shapes thrown by the light. Clasped to clutch the air, Joshua's hands strive to pacify their appetite for anger and, perhaps, ameliorate the sense of defeat. At forty-one years of age, he is already an old man in Zodwa's eyes. She takes in his army greatcoat over a threadbare black suit whose fibres are held together by nothing more than dignity, and rough boots appropriate to the miner's domain. Nomonde stands watching, catching each word that drops from Joshua's lips. Zodwa has a sense that her mother is perhaps awkward in the knowledge that Joshua is no orator, and can make a fool of himself before the assembled village.

'It hurts me to my heart to see you like this,' he begins, 'underground, like rats, homeless. The whole thing, though, is no longer in our hands, and we can lose a lot of time wallowing in self-pity.' He stops and gazes at the farther recesses of the cave, as if searching for a source of strength in the shadows. 'The most important thing, however, is how we shape our future. How we make it livable for our children, our children's children and ourselves. Because, the white man has come and touched all the things we hold sacred and dear and has taken away our dream. In doing so, he is building a future for himself and his children and – he hopes – for his children's children. But the future cannot be built on a lie, because the dispossession of others is a foundation of lies. A bird that builds on the nest of others must be endlessly ready to defend itself. This is the fate that the white man has called upon himself and his children's children. Whether or not he has come to terms with reaping this whirlwind is not our concern. Our concern is the future, which is buried in the ruins of our past, in the dwellings razed to the ground and in how faithfully we preserved the memory of the time when we were human beings. We shall move and seek work and carry out orders on the terms set by those in power. We shall be cold and hungry and bereft of all the support which has nurtured us through the ages. But we shall return to this land which was given to us by our forebears. What matters, then, is how we conserve our energy to ensure that we do return.'

Weaned on silences, Zodwa has a great mistrust for words and their power to hide meanings. She, however, feels drawn into the orbit of her father's spell. He speaks haltingly, pausing, not so much for rhetorical effect as to tease out of the tangled threads a skein to best articulate the incoherence roiling inside his head. As her father touches on the many unknown journeys people are about to undergo, the light, unaccountably, seems to glow brighter, banishing the shadows. Dancing above his head, it bounces off the receding hairline, flattening the broad forehead, creating shadows under his high cheekbones and sculpting his lips. A heretical and uncomfortable thought takes hold of her. Did these lips ever touch her mother's in a kiss? She has already learnt, from the school grapevine and picture books smuggled into class by the more knowledgeable of girls, what adults do in nocturnal rituals of regeneration. Was this how Jonah and I were brought onto this earth? she asks herself, looking at her brother, who is watching the old man with an intent, strange and proud smile on his face. Her mother sidles off, to tend to some of the injured, whose groans can now be heard above her father's speech. One day, Zodwa thinks, I'll sit down with her and ask her what it means to be a woman.

A stronger, almost sexless woman has now taken over from Joshua. Nozizwe is small but gives an impression of being larger than life. Even though she is an inyanga, and is expected to dress according to her calling – bands of blue-monkey skin adorning her wrists, phials with *muthi* strung around her neck – she has chosen a gingham frock which accentuates her frailty, her bony shoulders covered by a shawl. Enacting a rite that is familiar to the villagers, she asks them to produce family totems, which she then stores in each family's bundle on the table. Somewhere in the distance a baby squalls and is shushed by a mother. The representatives of households file past the table, as grim as mourners viewing a coffined body, and tender artefacts symbolising their birthright. 'We who are pure at heart,' Nozizwe intones, 'who have not colluded with the enemy, will come back and make the claim.' She repeats these words. The words become the only living thing in the vast cavern. At eleven years of age, Zodwa starts understanding that an infinitely dire fate lies athwart the path of those who work against the collective will of the people.

★   ★   ★

She must have nodded off on her feet, like a horse. Becoming conscious of her surroundings, Zodwa sees confusion around where her father was speaking. A scuffle breaks out where the villagers sweat from the effort of restraining a huge man whose whole attitude is threatening, as if he wants to strike her father. Hodoba. A deep, rasping bass – reminiscent of nails dragging across a galvanised iron surface – booms throughout the cave. 'You, Joshua, how dare you rule that I'm not part of this community?'

His arms folded against his breast, Joshua regards Hodoba as if a great abyss separates the two of them. 'Hodoba,' he says calmly, 'you forfeited your right to this community. You took it upon yourself to trample on every rule we set. I know that you and your men have been snatching young women into the caves. We don't need you.'

Nozizwe nods. 'Yes,' she agrees. 'Those who'll return here are the faithful and the pure.'

Hodoba laughs. The sound sets Zodwa's teeth on edge. 'Faithful and pure? What nonsense is that?' He turns to Joshua. 'You let this old crone menstruate all over us ...' Pulling himself up to his full height, he spits. 'You have not heard the last of this. Your son will wander the Four Corners of the earth. His own kinsmen will devour him. As for your daughter, she will go and return, and my men and I will feast on her flesh!'

He strides out, a ball of fury, followed by a chilled silence.

Mbongwa pushes his way past the phalanx of men fronting the altar. He is also a big man, but his is the protest of corrupted limbs and organs, a distension of the epidermis against internal excrescence. Dressed in a black suit, a white shirt and a bow tie, Mbongwa resembles an undertaker. The shaven back of his neck folds and unfolds like a concertina. 'S'bali?' he says, 'My brother-in-law – how can you do such a thing?'

'What thing?' Joshua regards his brother-in-law coolly. 'You mean Hodoba?'

'Yes, the man is after all your supporter.'

'That support we don't need.' He pauses. 'Tell you what, if you feel so burnt up about it, why don't you follow him?'

'I don't have to follow him, but I still think you're wrong.'

'*Wrong?*' Nomonde has come back. 'Wrong? The man threat-

15

ens your own flesh and blood and that's all you can say? *Suka lapha wena,* Mbongwa, get away from here!'

Zodwa half-expects her mother to strike him. Mbongwa takes a step back, this retreat from his sister's wrath eliciting hisses of derision. Shooting sharp glances at the faces glowering with barely held contempt around him, he too shuffles out of the cave.

Zodwa has heard the girls at school make fun of Hodoba, sometimes calling him a cannibal. His enormousness has spawned a legend that he clips his nostril hair with a garden shears, and that, generally reported to suffer from scrotal elephantiasis, Hodoba supported his genitals on a wheelbarrow whenever he took long journeys. But right now, Zodwa is in no mood to entertain jokes or gossip. She heard his words and they rang like a curse. Shivering, she turns to her brother for some sort of affirmation that what she has just heard is not a figment of her imagination. Jonah's face betrays no awareness of Hodoba's denunciation. Soon enough, the people prepare to leave. Having made an uneasy peace with their past, they now have to face the future.

*   *   *

Now as the van receded into a dot on the dusty horizon, she cursed herself for having neglected to ask Nduli to fill in details surrounding her birth. Hers was not a case of egotism, she just wanted to separate fact from fiction. Ngoza villagers were past-masters at weaving fantasies, a strategy to kill time and deal with humdrum existence in an unforgiving region. Zodwa had also meant to garner certain information relating to her brother, which would have perhaps helped her understand him more, even in his absence. But that would wait until Saturday. In any event, a confidential conversation would have been impossible with Ayesha around. The child, she thought with affection, is a right royal blabbermouth. She proceeded to pack her supplies in the room. Watching the light play on the window that looked out on the flowerbeds, Zodwa wished that Ayesha had been with her on the night they left Ngoza. When they crossed the river.

★   ★   ★

It stands there, unmoving, this black silver snake of treacherous depths. She has been on the riverbank, innumerable times, to draw water or help Nomonde wash clothes, but never at night. Her father, who has baptised some of the believers in the same water, crosses first and, with the help of Joachim and Nduli – whose head bandage looks like a turban – they secure a rope around a sturdy tree. The people cross, women and children first, followed by the infirm, and then the men. Crossing the river saves them the time involved in going the route past the New River settlement, which has degenerated into a slum. Short cuts, of course, are never without discomfort. Zodwa, a child at last, holds onto her mother's hand, and takes a step into the water. The current is surprisingly strong, and deceitful in its silence. The cold water comes up to her neck, some of it entering her mouth, tasting of Hodoba's curse. Remembering the reassuring darkness in the cave, she closes her eyes. From that moment of isolation from the accumulation of fear and rage thrashing around her, Zodwa finds the rhythm of the water. Releasing herself from her mother's hold, she walks with a sureness of foot that comes from second-guessing an adversary. The water, she knows, always destroys what it cannot heal, and she is not about to die, not yet. Neither the dripping expletives of policemen nor Hodoba's violent augury has the power to disturb her ride on the water. In her mood of resistance to the predicament facing her and her family, Zodwa almost misses seeing the Humiliation Tree, which stands hulking, like something ineffable just emerged out of the water, perhaps an ancient craft or an ark. She knows stories about the tree, which, she sees now, consists of a number of trunks, like a mangrove, out of which grow sturdy boughs that support a series of rope-like creepers that form a hammock. It is an ideal location for a tree house, but no sane child would ever play here. This aversion to the aura surrounding the tree introduces an instinct, which strangles for expression inside her mind. It tells her that her life is undergoing an irrevocable change, and that the starting-point of her growth from childhood into adolescence would be determined by the exact moment she lands on steady ground. Minutes which felt like hours later, safe and trembling on the other side, she watches Jonah's progress as he glides like a seal, laughing with another boy, his teeth glinting, leading Zodwa to understand the terrifying beauty of love.

TWO

The gong summoning the faithful to prayer sounded far-off, muffled, not quite breaking the quiet of the evening. For a while, Joshua listened to the soft notes trailing off and fading outside into the dark. Speaking to him in the secret language of creation, the sound became the only thing he wished to hear. It carried the language of birds, stubborn growth, babbling rivers and the wind among the leaves. Where other people's ears were attuned to the silence of the interval between notes, his heard a multitude of tongues which explained for him the path to take on his seventy-year-old journey.

Conscious that he was nearing the journey's end, Joshua suffered a sudden attack of immodesty, where he couldn't envision his absence from Ngoza: this vast expanse of scrub and rock, a terrain he and his followers had reclaimed. Grudgingly, he accepted that, with him gone, there would still be the silence carrying words to guide the elder who would step into his shoes. But, this evening, the silences portended strife. Where their sound had in earlier times raised his spirits, he now experienced uneasiness, an absence of calm. This he attributed to the discordant notes he had heard in a recurring dream which foretold turmoil. Groping inside his head for details of the dream, he failed to assemble the frayed ends and wisps of images into a coherent picture.

He left off writing, rose from the low stool and stretched, preparing himself for the evening prayers. For as many months as he cared to remember, he had sat down and entered into his lined executive notebook the events of the day, a log he hoped would speak for the settlement long after his bones had turned to dust. His gaze took in the interior of the tent, illumined by a paraffin lamp: the rough table and chair, an inflatable mattress on which the grey army-issue blankets were folded in a severe military style. Strewn across the table, the papers were the only lapse in orderliness. He thought of arranging them, but decided against it, confident that Naomi, the young deaf-mute woman who worked in the settlement, would come in and leave the tent in apple-pie order for his return. He then joined the groups of believers walking slowly to the community tent, their voices subdued under the light of a pale moon. The night air was restless with the fragrance of freshly turned soil, frangipani, jasmine and jacaranda. This mingled with the smell of earth baking in kilns and new-sawn timber.

Joshua responded to the greetings of the believers without putting his mind to them. He wrestled with the meanings of the dream, in which the ancient dead came to life and, with eyes blazing condemnation, cautioned him against taking rash decisions. What decisions? he asked himself. Hadn't it been they, the ancestors, who had charged him with the responsibility of developing the settlement? Of delivering all these lost sheep from mire onto steady rock? Now they were bothered with rashness: he wanted to howl at the injustice of it all. How could he tell them that the water pump had broken down? That the ground was stony and stubborn and discouraged cultivation? And that the drought would kill them all? Ancestors were notoriously impatient with detail.

Still anxious, he concluded that something was wrong here and someone was responsible. A piece of machinery couldn't just break of its own accord. The believers were a motley lot, consisting in the main of people beyond reproach, but there was no ruling out a bad apple in their midst, someone probably in league with Johnny M and his henchmen.

He visualised Johnny M in his big car and expensive suits; he even wore a hat, like a plantation foreman. What was inescapable was that Johnny M represented new money and power; the white farmers bought their supplies from his trading-store. When the residents of Ngoza were forced to move some twenty years ago, Johnny M had joined forces with the authorities. They gave him an empty plot and allowed him to build a modest two-roomed store, with the proviso that he didn't compete for profits with Police Chief Arnold Grey. Like the proverbial camel which first stuck its nose in the tent and progressively displaced the owner, Johnny M wheedled more concessions out of an increasingly unstable local authority, to the point that Grey – who owned other businesses and was said to be infinitely corrupt – formed a partnership with him. Now they jointly owned the funeral parlour and a bottle store and had minority shares in the adjoining hotel. When Mandela was released on February 11, 1990, and there was a scramble by property owners to include blacks in their enterprises, Johnny M was not short of white people who would enlist his name in their books. Single-minded to a fault, he saw no reason to spend sleepless nights over being used as a front for white businesses. The shift in the balance of power brought forth by the new dispensation had allowed men like him to wiggle themselves into the juicier parts of the national cake. Like maggots wallowing in a rotten carcass.

Joshua shook his head to banish the offending image, which had become as familiar as the evils he had escaped in the Other World. But Johnny M's oily face stamped itself into his memory, like a wrinkle marring the smooth surface of fine wood. This will take the edge out of my sermon, he thought. Are we realistic in assuming that we can annul the legacy of our past? He was interrupted from dwelling on the implications of his own question when he heard someone call him from behind. He turned round.

'What is it, my son?' he asked a young man also dressed in the regulation blue robes. Joshua was glad to see Joachim. He was a lad with a great future who had made his sacrifice. In the Other

21

World he had been an artisan plumber. Before Joshua's only daughter Zodwa disgraced the region with her romance with that white lawyer two years ago, Joshua had marked Joachim for a prospective son-in-law. Now Zodwa was gone. She had left the village for Johannesburg and thence to Alice. He wondered when she would come back. Even though he still smarted from the humiliation she had visited on Ngoza, she was his daughter – and she was much more intelligent than most people thought. She would have been vital in the negotiations with the Land Claims Court.

'Baba Joshua,' Joachim said, his voice choking, 'look at my hands. . .' He stretched his arms, hands cupped as if accepting a bowl of gruel. 'They are full of blood.'

Baba Joshua gazed down at Joachim's hands and regretted the younger man's unnecessary statement because, even under the moonlight, the blood stains looked fresh and vivid. Since blood was taboo in the settlement, he understood the reason for the younger man's trepidation. 'What happened?' he asked, his earlier anxiety reproducing itself.

'I was in the kraal,' Joachim said, 'to check if all the sheep were in. Then I heard the bleating of a lamb suckling. Since it was getting dark, I immediately got a lantern and counted the animals. Two ewes were missing. A number of lambs were gathered around a ewe, which lay on the ground. I thought it was ill, so I lifted it up, only to find its throat had been sliced from ear to ear.'

Joshua made a sound as if someone had kicked him under the heart. He asked the question, already dreading the answer: 'And the other sheep?'

'It's gone, Baba.'

Joshua stroked Joachim's shoulder. He remembered the feel of stubble on his own son's face. Jonah was dead now, shot in those political struggles of the Other World. He had loved him beyond endurance and could still hear the keening wail of his girl-friend Dudu, when the body was brought home. 'Go to the ablution trough,' he told Joachim, 'and clean up.' He watched Joachim disappearing into the darkness. 'I'm glad that you told me first,' he said to himself absently. 'No knowing how panicked my own flock would be.' He wondered what this fresh abomination meant. Blood called for blood, which was why it was anathema in the settlement. The believers raised livestock, but these would be sold to the farmers and the owners of abattoirs where the ways of the Other World still held sway. In Baba's sect, the Temple of the New Jerusalem, the devoted never touched meat; a law had been passed, which forbade men from sharing the bed or table with women who were menstruating. Now, he thought grimly, the blood is returned to claim us. Whichever way he handled this, there was going to be a struggle with his brother-in-law, Mbongwa, who was not above challenging Joshua. Mbongwa believed that there was merit in using ways of the Other World when the settlement was menaced. Shrugging, Joshua hastened to the large canvas tent where the congregation waited with a song.

It was in their singing, which Joshua and the council of elders encouraged as part of the holy ritual, that the believers could tell the story of how they had been delivered from violence and strife into their New Jerusalem. All the believers wore blue robes; this set them apart from the choir, clad in white, standing at the centre of the circle, singing a hymn of redemption. The choristers' faces looked so pure, these faces, their voices untouched by alcohol or nicotine, their brown bodies glowing with health under a generous light of countless hurricane lamps. Above them, on the rude platform, a dozen elders sat, their solemn faces bespeaking the responsibility of creating a new order. It was a responsibility urged by the believers' acquaintance with the world they had left behind. They had repudiated all knowledge of the past, which had been typified by treachery, shame and a potential to diminish hope. The choir sang of the glory of the new land, this Garden of Eden, now and in the hereafter, where the horizons that had been denied, the springs and summers of harvest to which they had been barred, would be made tangible and accessible to the children of the blasphemed.

★   ★   ★

Joshua visualised the beginning of this movement back to ancestral lands. Three years ago, the government that has ruled without mercy for five decades finally crumbles, leaving behind
chaos, scepticism and rage. The black people, who moaned under
the heel of oppression and cried for emancipation, are now masters of their own destiny. They now carry the onerous weight
which freedom brings. Their hearts groan under the awesome
load of crimes and unforgiven injustices. The perpetrators of
atrocities, who strut as if they are the wronged ones, write in the
newspapers that their deeds were sanctioned by their love for
their children. After a great celebration lasting weeks, where firecrackers light the skies, letting loose a shower of fiery benedic-
tion down on the people, the workers return to the factories and
the children to school. The hurricanes and drought come to him
in a dream, and he sees multitudes wandering without aim, looking for a leader to decipher for them the meaning of liberation.
Soon enough, the seekers turn into beggars, looking for alms. In
this confused roaming, the forces of state are set loose on the
people. The hungry workers, who expected more, organise
strikes and the country plunges into confusion. Those who took
the mantle of liberators find themselves staring at the people
from across a great chasm. In this narcotised state Joshua sees a
seraph with diaphanous wings emerge from the clouds. With a
voice of a timbre of God's trombone, the angel appoints Joshua
the chosen one. He has to lead the people from the land of strife
to the unclaimed ancestral plains of Natal. The followers would
have to eschew all connections with the Other World and build
the Temple of the New Jerusalem, whose sole purpose would be
the glorification of the living god. Joshua wakes up in a cold
sweat, knowing that his life has changed and he has a mission. He
visits a dressmaker on Commercial Road and asks her to fit him
with robes similar to the angel's. Resigning from the tyre factory where he is a shop steward, he uses his savings to travel

through the length and breadth of the country, agitating, cajoling and pleading with the leaders of charismatic and fundamentalist Christian church groups. He meets resistance from some elders of the Zionist churches. He manages, however, to wean off a few followers who form the core of his sect.

They pitch tents wherever they can find space in the townships. This is a miracle in itself since all clearings are a lacework of squatter camps. Here they preach the gospel, calling upon the populace to turn their back on the futility of political life and wage labour. Joshua teaches a new order where people, not beholden to any boss, would work the land, raise livestock and live by the sweat of their brow. Township dwellers, weary of glib preachers and false prophets, scoff at this bearded charlatan in outlandish garments. Others, though, disenchanted with noble notions and sophisticated schemes that can't keep the wolf from the door, derive some comfort from Joshua's prescriptions, never mind that he resembles a runaway scarecrow. There are large defections by adherents to Lekganyane and Shembe. Joshua's only problem now is to convince the initiates to wear the new raiment of sanctity designed in heaven. The masses might be hungry and disgruntled, but the preacher isn't exactly a model of sartorial elegance. Another source of worry is the propensity for violence on the part of the preachers whose flocks are diminishing with increasing regularity. Another vision comes to Joshua and he is ordered to organise able-bodied men and women into self-defence units. During training in unarmed combat, he cites the text in the Bible where Simon Peter cut off Malchus's ear with a sword. But he cautions against the spilling of blood or taking of life, which run counter to the tenet of the Temple of the New Jerusalem.

Even as they sang now, Joshua listened to the cadences, the staccatos and stutters that defined the origins of the believers. They had experienced untold hardships as they made their great trek into the sleepy village of Ngoza. But Joshua was resolute that he would do everything in his power to fulfil the mission that had been ordained from above. As the song died, he stood up and raised his hand.

'People of God,' he began, 'we are all gathered here, on the fifth year of our arrival in this holy place. I remember how many of you who in their fervour for upliftment trudged with their humble bundles across this bleeding land. You were no different from those men and women of yore, who traversed the hills and valleys, through rivers and mountain passes, in search of a land where they could be free. But their freedom was faulty, a hollow sacrifice, because it was not inspired by God or his angels, but by a greed to enslave, which beats in some people's hearts like a pulse. Our freedom has nothing to do with dispossessing others; we are here to hearken to the voice of God, to praise him and submit ourselves to his will.'

As he spoke, Joshua became aware of a slight disturbance at the back. First, he saw the hat, then the face of Police Chief Grey; he was dressed in his usual blue suit and an open-necked shirt, the holster visible beneath the jacket. People exchanged smiles of unease, shifted and made a place for him along the bench. Grey sat down and looked up at the preacher. Unaccountably, Joshua wondered where Naomi was.

'As soldiers of the Lord,' he went on, 'this struggle is just beginning. We have moved from the Other World outside, where clouds of darkness hover above a people steeped in hatred and fear. We call ourselves free because there is no power which can claim to rule over us. Not in these times.'

He paused, remembering the journey that Jonah had taken. Before leaving home to join the armed wing of the African National Congress, Jonah was transformed by passion, where he spoke like a recent convert extolling the virtues of a new religion. Returning a little more than a decade later, his eyes shot with blood, his head turned completely from the path of mercy, Jonah recounted how his compatriots had betrayed him. Jonah had disobeyed an order from a commander, where he had been required to transport an unstable would-be guerrilla across the border into exile. That had made him a marked man. By the time he was felled by the assassin's bullet, Jonah had long made a covenant with death.

'The world we repudiated', Joshua said, 'wants to return and wishes to grip our successes with its cold hand of death. There are men out there, who want us out of this land. The water pump has been sabotaged. Animals are being killed. Perhaps we're coming to a pass when we have to listen to the call from on high to defend the glory of God.'

There was anger abroad when Jonah was buried. Other people – some had been his boyhood friends – could not attend the funeral of an *impimpi* – an informer. Even when all allegations were proven false, Joshua was still avoided like a leper. He would wonder, then, what people knew of loss. It was very easy for them to bandy labels and point fingers, but what had they endured? Did they know the feeling a father experienced on examining the shattered face of a son in the government mortuary? Or how death transformed loved ones and burdened memory because, in the parents' recollection, their offspring would remain whole, full of life? It was even worse when one of the killers was captured and executed by the government. There were memorial meetings where the assassin was hailed as a hero of the people. Which people? Knowing that he was dwelling at length on an issue he had promised himself to forget, he tried to cast the offending thoughts away. I have a congregation to lead, he told himself.

He sat down and the baffled congregation broke out in a song. Another elder stood up to allocate the tasks for the following day. The choir struggled through a hymn,

'Tis me, 'tis me O Lord,
Standing in the need of prayer.

And Joshua led the procession of elders outside into the cool evening air. Hands pumped his and patted his shoulders. He made his way through the throng, his eyes resting on each face, trying to read in the eyes of his people who might be the traitor. He saw the policeman standing with his back to the tent.

'Chief,' he said, 'what brings you here? I was just saying to myself I need to go and see the authorities.'

'Oh,' Grey said carelessly, 'thought I might come for some spiritual sustenance myself.' He grinned and fell into step with Joshua. 'You have no idea what it's like trying to keep order nowadays, especially now that everyone is equal.'

'Why? You miss the good old days, Chief?' Joshua's eyes twinkled in the dark. Some of the stragglers from the revival meeting were still humming the hymn, beating time with their hands on their bibles. Joshua imagined he detected a note of levity in some of the voices. He directed Grey to his tent.

'It's just that', Grey said, 'before all this bloody confusion, people knew their place. I knew where I stood with you people. Now …' He let his voice trail away and gave a shrug.

'Now things need to be defined once more.' Joshua did not want to seem to be disrespectful to the white man. Even before truth was revealed to him, when he was a shop steward, Joshua had marvelled at the way people like Grey played with power, not understanding that it possessed its own inner logic and momentum. Those who wore it around themselves, who flaunted it and caused people to cower, were themselves preyed upon by the same power. It claimed them and had them dangling, like marionettes, at the end of a string. Moving to this wilderness, albeit at the urging of the Holy Ghost, had crystallised in Joshua's mind this unalterable fact. The sons and daughters of the masters of the land found that maintaining their own version of Eden exacted a heavy price. They were there, every day, searching for people they could confide in, for arms to hold them. As children, they had nestled on black bosoms, but now that this was impossible, they were enraged and bewildered. But he could not say this to Grey. On reaching the tent, Joshua, suddenly not wishing to hear what Grey wanted to unload, stood with his back against the entrance. Grey took out a cigarette and stuck it between his lips.

'You said you might have wanted to see me,' he said. He lit the cigarette, the flame flickering and creating shadows under his eyes. 'What's it about?'

Joshua stooped when entering his tent. Grey followed. The Elder was relieved that Naomi was not inside for he wished to keep her away from people like this tormented policeman. He was irritated that he was smoking in the tent, a deed of such insolence it bordered on the profane. He stood supporting himself on the table, his whole manner reciprocating Grey's lack of manners. But Grey, oblivious to Joshua's disapprobation, or choosing to ignore it, blew a cloud of smoke in the preacher's direction.

'So,' he asked, 'what's bothering you, Baba?'

A donkey hee-hawed somewhere in the distance. Joshua made a mental note to ask Joachim to arrange fodder for the dray animals who tended to be forgotten. There was also a need to plant more shallots around the tents to repel the snakes. The area was infested with adders and cobras. Scorpions and large spiders crawled out of the nearby rocks. There was a dagga field nearby which needed clearing. The animal's feeding on hemp might have occasioned the braying of the donkey. Remembering Balaam's ass, he suppressed a chuckle, imagining a donkey in the grip of a benevolent hallucination.

'Strange things are happening here,' he said gravely. 'And I have no doubt that Johnny M and his people are involved.' Swallowing, he met the white man's level gaze, seeing as if for the first time the blue eyes in a face that strove towards affability, the large fingers which squeezed the cigarette clamped between thin, bloodless lips. Something about Grey triggers off a memory of an earlier encounter with Johnny M.

★   ★   ★

It is five years ago on a cold morning in June 1990, when the first lorry load of new settlers arrives in Ngoza. Joshua alights and supervises the unloading of building materials. The terrain is rough, stones and ruins jut out of the sparse bush, like jagged teeth on diseased gums. The old church that also doubled as the only school stands roofless, the rafters bent and collapsing; surely a dangerous place. The once-white walls show the effects of the elements; but pockmarks from bullets worsen their state. When they lost Ngoza, twenty years earlier, the government allocated the area to the army.

The men roll up their sleeves, spit into their palms and heft picks and shovels and start clearing the terrain of stones, rusted corrugated-iron sheeting and two decades of military waste. The twenty-four odd members of the advance party strip to their shorts or roll their overalls down to the waist; by now the sun is up and the wind refuses to rise. Birds accustomed to the sound of gunfire chirp from scraggy mimosas in counterpoint to the grunts and work songs. The unit starts with patching up the broken stones of ancient graves, weeding, their iron implements ringing against stone.

Joshua hears the sound of the car before the vehicle emerges out of the dust on the dirt road. The driver and his passenger sit and watch the men working, cigarette smoke curling around them and shielding their faces. Presently, the door opens and the two men come out and walk towards the workers. They are dressed in city clothes, their shoes gleaming in the morning sun. The shorter man walks up to Joshua, while his partner leans against the car, puffing at his cigarette, his eyes hidden by the brim of his hat.

'What are you people doing here?' Shortie asks, not bothering to greet.

Joshua, normally polite, balances on the pick handle as he regards the interrogator. He is about to tell the man to mind his own business when Joachim, his torso glistening with perspiration, puts in. 'We're digging for gold,' he says. 'What does it look like to you?'

'You don't talk to me like that,' Shortie snarls, advancing with his fists doubled. The other diggers tense up and trail their implements behind them, ready to strike. Other men form a shield between Joshua and the new aggressor.

'Fakude!' the taller man calls in a voice full of his importance, throwing the stub on the ground and mashing it with his heel. 'Take it easy.' He comes up to where the men are standing. Wrapping an arm around Fakude, he whispers something in his ear. Then he turns to Joshua. He owns a pair of eyes that can no longer be surprised by anything.

'You're the leader of this group?' he asks, his eyes on Joshua.

Joshua nods. He has a feeling of meeting a malevolent beast in the loneliness of a forest. Something tells him that the battle to reclaim the land from the whites was but a rehearsal for this. He hesitates as the man extends his hand.

'I'm Johnny M,' the man says. 'This young man is my assistant. Only he gets hot-headed, you know how it is, when strangers trespass in your land.'

'Your land, Mr Johnny M?' Joshua asks, wondering distractedly what the 'M' stands for – possibly 'murder'. But he wasn't going to be frightened off, not now, or ever. 'Forgive me, but this is our land. We have got it back from the government.'

'Ah, the government.' This causes Johnny M to smile. 'Let's say maybe the government made a mistake this time, you know how governments are not famous for brilliance.' Fakude joins him in laughter. 'So they just bundled you people here and told you to come and farm and raise your chickens?' Johnny M shook his head at the injustice of it all. 'And they never told you that this part of Ngoza is under my jurisdiction?'

'They didn't need to tell us anything,' Joshua puts in. 'You see all these men? They were born here. Then we were all removed, years ago, probably before you were born.'

'Well,' Johnny M says, 'things have changed. Land costs money and since you want to build here, it's me you have to talk to. My boys will be coming to collect the levies.'

Joshua remembers the moment of the first removal. The trucks. The police prodding people with *donkiepiele*, the billy clubs. The women weeping silently and the children wailing. The

31

livestock carted off to white farms, the anger and the impotence. The long years of exile where people waited to tend to ancestral graves. And now this.

'I'll ask you and your. . . assistant to leave us in peace,' Joshua says, softly, almost inaudibly. 'We don't owe you anything, Mr. Johnny M. This is our land.'

'We'll see, old man,' Johnny M says. He signals for Fakude to get into the car. 'You'll be hearing from me. Very soon.'

Joshua and his men watch the car driving off, a swirl of dust in its wake. They later take a break. It is already dusk when they pitch the first tent. They build a fire and drink coffee and look at the stars. The chirping of cicadas and the croaking of frogs in a nearby pool break the quiet of the approaching night. After prayer, they sleep, taking turns to guard the equipment. In the morning, accompanied by Joachim, Joshua will inspect the squatter camp three kilometres away. 'God is great,' Joshua thinks before falling asleep.

*   *   *

Joshua told Police Chief Grey what had happened with the pump and the sheep. Grey listened without interrupting, now and then nodding. 'Why would Johnny M want to do that?' he asked.

'Who knows?' Joshua replied. 'The land is fertile, maybe some people feel that it is wasted on us.' He thought of the dagga field. Maybe that is Johnny M's crop growing out there. But he didn't volunteer this piece of information to Grey, a representative of the law, even if it was the law of the Other World, and Johnny M needed to be brought to book. Grey must also have known about the levies imposed by Johnny M on the squatters. Grey must somehow find nothing illegal in that. The thought dismayed him.

'So what do you expect us to do, Baba?' Grey asked. 'I thought you people had your own ministry of law and order.'

'We can only punish sinners amongst ourselves. We have no right to pursue people from the Other World.'

'The Other World, hey?' Grey's tone was laced with contempt. 'Do you really believe that this little *besigheid* will succeed?'

'We are in the service of the Lord,' Joshua put in. 'We also believe that when you are in doubt, it is better not to mock.'

'I'll remember that,' Grey said. He backed out of the tent. Joshua followed him outside. 'In the meantime, you'd have done me a great favour if you gave me a list of all your people. The men, specifically. Might be some infiltrators in your little party. Ta-ra!' He touched his hat and soon disappeared in the gloom. Gazing at the darkness, Joshua felt that Grey hadn't quite explained his visit. He could not trust this unbaptised white man.

Going back to his writing, tired, wishing that Naomi would bring him a cup of tea, he found the words on the paper became mere scrawls made by mocking insects. Looking up, resigned, he wondered whether his failure meant he hadn't really made peace with the past.

★   ★   ★

The full weight of the exile is felt in KwaMashu, where he lives with his wife, Nomonde and two disgruntled children, Jonah and Zodwa. Everything goes wrong here. The water is brackish, and has to be fetched two kilometres away. Following rains, running rainwater mixed with sewage becomes a river separating, isolating, the houses. Each day, he trudges to the station, to take a train to town, where he works at a rubber factory. Some of the men from Ngoza are unemployed, and they look to him to help out. Others die slowly from poverty and despair, taking to the grave the memory of condemning eyes of loved ones. Nozizwe seems to survive on air and herbs, consulting with him every weekend, urging him on even when Nomonde has lost all hope. It is this lack of will to survive which makes her weak and susceptible to colds. The people she works for on Musgrave Road – undoubtedly a kindly family – still have to let her go. In the loneliness of the house, while the children are at school,

Nomonde sees visions, Hodoba in all his ugliness standing over her in her bed. On the day Jonah gets on a moving van to Johannesburg, Nomonde dies. Joshua is disconsolate. Nomonde is buried in a cemetery in KwaMashu. Two weeks later, all of Baba Joshua's dreams are about Ngoza. Then he starts to see visions. It is then that he embarks on the task to collect the scattered people with an aim to return to the place where his umbilical cord is buried.

Three

On the day Mpanza left Johannesburg, a city awash with signs, for Natal, the papers crow over the first anniversary of independence. Banners on which optimism was emblazoned in loud colours fronted the city buildings. Streamers and pennants fluttered from street-lamps and wrought-iron gates guarding driveways leading to hallowed halls of power. Tacked to almost every lamppost was a placard for the people to register for the local government elections. Progress in the registration drive had been slow. There was concern in many sectors that, since the public relations company that had been given the government contract was Saatchi & Saatchi, who, commentators remembered, had spearheaded the National Party's election campaign, there was a possibility that the messages for registration would only address the NP constituencies, to the exclusion of the black majority.

The traffic wound its way with a maddening slowness, the blast of horns in counterpoint to the laryngeal industry of traders at the Noord Street market. In the parks and squares, where statues glorifying the pioneers of the discredited regime had presented an insolent challenge to the populace, scaffolding and hardboard sheeting covered the graven images that would be in line with today's impulses. Birds, not given to political correctness, hovered above, ready for the unveiling when they would deposit their hoary loads.

It was when Mpanza was packing that he realised how meagre his belongings were. The two pairs of jeans and some shirts and underwear, books and a pair of trainers, all fitted snugly in his suitcase. The saxophone beckoned to him from its stand in the corner of the room. He couldn't remember when last he had played it. Suppressing an urge to lock himself in and blow until he dropped, Mpanza dismantled the instrument and laid the pieces carefully inside the case. He didn't know whether he would get an opportunity to practise his scales where he was going, but the saxophone had been his trusted companion that had never let him down. While packing and checking the weight of his luggage, something about the mustiness of the room, the drone of traffic outside, the knowledge that he was doomed to be forever on the road, brought his mind to Luanda, Angola.

★　　★　　★

He has finished his military training and is waiting to be given his mission when he is assigned to the Amandla Cultural Ensemble of the ANC. Its repertoire consists of music, dance, poetry and theatre. Jonas Gwangwa, the director, looks at him and says: '*My laaitie, jy's so klein en jy's klaar 'n* terrorist – you're so young and you're already a terrorist.' The other members of Amandla laugh at this; for the first time in his life, Mpanza knows that he is going to enjoy being here.

They perform to rapturous receptions in the Luanda theatres of Miramar, Atlantico. On May 1 they are part of the Workers' Day celebrations organised by UNTA, the national trades union, usually on the Primeiro de Maio Square. Home is where the music is.

★　　★　　★

He looked around the Hillbrow flat, hearing the shouts from the street, everything filling him with sadness and a savage joy. His live-in girlfriend, Thembani, had long left for a nursing job at the Pelonomi Hospital in Bloemfontein. She was still in love with him, but she could not handle his drinking and the irresponsibility. 'Maybe if I go,' she had said, 'you'll find space to grow up.'

Well, he said to himself as he went down the steps, Natal sure has wide spaces for a man to grow up, Thembi. He felt no rancour, just a cold disgust with himself. I'm fucked.

This emotion is not dissimilar to the one he experiences, six months earlier in October, when he leaves his wife and two daughters. He is a little drunk after the farewell party some officers threw for him on his discharge from the army. When he gets out of the car and walks up the paved path to the house, Khethiwe is already standing, looking at her watch. Oh, oh, he thinks. Trouble. These scenes have become commonplace in their marriage. Khethiwe hates his drinking with a passion. Mpanza has had to use every ruse in the book to cop a *dop*. The children and a vague loyalty born of companionship have up until now held their marriage together. But now Khethiwe has found a well-paying job with Transnet. Armed with some form of economic independence, with its implications for her ability to support the kids, she never lets him forget that the South African National Defence Force is paying him peanuts. Now he has got his discharge, albeit with a full pension. The very fact that he's expected to join the ranks of the unemployed is certainly going to add to Khethiwe's shame. She is a very proud woman, pretty and confident. For her, life is not to be squandered away. She has tried to interest him in studying so that he can increase his chances of landing something cushy in the private sector, but Mpanza has been adamant that he is a military man. He has no intention of swelling the ranks of what he contemptuously calls the patriotic bourgeoisie.

'So,' Khethiwe says, 'you've been fired.'

'Not fired,' Mpanza replies. 'Discharged.'

'It's the same thing, isn't it?' Khethiwe says. 'And you're drunk. What kind of example do you think you are setting for the kids?'

'Don't bring the kids into this, Khethiwe. The army had to rationalise. . .'

'And the first backside the boot of this rationalisation lands on, of course, is yours. You've turned out to be a real winner, haven't you, Mpanza?' Khethiwe asks, turning and entering the house. 'You can't worship two masters or, in your case, four. Work. Family. What you call "my music". And liquor. You can't.

Something's got to give, and, I suppose, liquor has come up trumps.' She clicks her tongue. 'You're pathetic.'

This discord, expressed with the venomous disgust that has accumulated over a long time, is the last straw. Without thinking about it, Mpanza strides off into the bedroom and starts packing his suitcase. That's it, he says to himself. I'm out of here. In the middle of his packing, Thandi and Busi, his daughters aged eleven and six, come into the bedroom and watch him.

'Are you going, Papa?' Busi asks. He is closest to her. Thandi takes after her mother; her accusing eyes are also a bequest from Khethiwe.

'Ja, Busi,' Mpanza says, gathering her in his arms. 'I'll be gone for a long time.'

'How are you going?' Thandi asks. 'You don't even own a voom.'

'I'll go, all right,' Mpanza says. 'When I was born, I didn't have a car.'

'But mummy has a car.'

'Yes. Mummy has a car.' He tries to make a joke. 'You see, she was born in an ambulance, got a taste for petrol fumes from small.'

The girls don't find this particularly funny. Later, as he stands with his suitcase on the threshold waiting for a taxi, Khethiwe gives him a long, lingering look, her face unreadable. 'Go on,' she says, 'run. That's all you ever do. *Hamba, juba, bazokucutha phambili* – Go, pigeon, they'll pluck your feathers wherever you are.' He wants to cry, knowing how he will miss the children, but masters himself. It wouldn't be him crying, Khethiwe is sure to say. Drunkards cry all the time.

★　　★　　★

Mbonambi, the old night watchman, was inside his cubicle in the foyer. He looked up from his racing-forms when he heard Mpanza approach. 'Hey, Mpanza,' he called, 'taking the midnight train?'

'Yes, Mbonambi.' Mpanza said, handing him the keys. 'This

time it's really goodbye.'

Absently consulting his form, Mbonambi asked: 'Do you think Persian Prince has a chance at Turffontein tomorrow? I hear he's an odds-on favourite.' The last word was pronounced as '*mfivilithi*'.

Mpanza shook his head. 'I'm probably the only person in this city who knows absolutely bugger-all about horse-racing.' He paused, pondering. 'Which is strange because I used to be a good rider in Hungary.'

'In Hungry?' Mbonambi asked. 'Isn't that a funny name for a place? Where's that?'

'In Europe. In what was called Behind the Iron Curtain.' Mpanza remembered Budapest, the coach journeys from Batthyany Ter to Szeged or Szentendrei. How when he got on a horse it was as if he belonged there, the animal beneath him bounding over short cherry-plum trees, the orchards red like anger, the colour of fallen leaves. It was a memory that was almost insupportable. And then Mbonambi interrupted his train of thought.

'*Uyaphi* – Where are you going to?' he asked.

'Natal. Zululand. Where you guys carry kieries and spears,' Mpanza said, 'and stick plugs in your ear-lobes.'

'Well,' Mbonambi said, 'you'll meet some real women there.' Giving a low whistle, his hands drew an outline of a bosomy, broad-backed figure in the air. 'Women with melons in the front and pillows in the back.' He grinned, exposing bluish gums.

Mbonambi stood up from the desk and came out of the cubicle, supporting one leg with a stick. He had taken a bad fall during a jolly night out. He walked Mpanza down the two stone steps to the concrete path leading to the street. Taxis vied for space, displacing crowds; the vans and trucks rushing to the marketplaces of the city fought each other for the right of way. Men and women toting bales or pushing carts laden with merchandise struggled to weave through the wall of humanity and steel.

'All these years,' Mbonambi said, 'I've heard nothing but the noise of this city.' He paused to look at the frightened faces and listen to the drivers swearing at the tops of their voices. 'We came here to reinforce our clansmen who were being attacked by the Msinga people at J H Isaacs and Geshen. To avoid being ambushed, we crept into various hostels at midnight and fled at the crack of dawn. I thought that with the new government now in power, we would be done with this kind of thing. But, just look at all that...' He shook his head at the sight of a burly drunk knocking a woman to the pavement. 'Whatever it is that's causing your flight from here, consider yourself very lucky.'

Mpanza could not tell him that he was leaving the city in disgrace. In his mind's eye, his descent into ignominy was outlined so clearly. He had striven all his life to whittle self-pity out of his system, to admit that most misfortune is invariably self-inflicted. Take the drinking, for instance. Mpanza knew that liquor didn't agree with him. Apart from the harrowing hangovers that lasted days on end, it made him thoroughly unstable. But this knowledge did not discourage him from taking a sip, which he knew would lead to more sips until he was spinning out of control. It was the taste; the slow warm glow that took charge of the throat, coursed down the stomach and sent recycled fumes to the brain – which was what made his days interesting. And the conversation: he would feel the words rolling out of his mouth crackling and brightening up a shebeen or bar, the people laughing at his wit, the women's teeth glistening like alabaster against the foreground of soft red lips, which God hadn't created merely for the act of smiling or eating or sipping drinks.

That was another problem: women. Despite all the years of political education where the pernicious effects of sexism had been drummed into his head, he regarded women as pleasure zones. It had become so bad that he couldn't look a woman in the eye without imagining what she did, or the changes that came over her, in a moment of ecstasy. Many a time in the company of a woman, he would get lost gazing into her eyes and lips as she talked, taking in the smooth and vulnerable curve of the neck, the angled chin and the contoured shoulders, until the woman, disconcerted, would say, 'What?' And he would apologise, feeling like a fool or a rapist and plead absent-mindedness. In this, he knew he was no different from most men, only he acknowledged the problem. Returning from exile, he was struck by the proliferation of young limbs that seemed to sprout like mushrooms after a thunderstorm. He fell in love with as many women as he encountered, seeing in one qualities complementing those of the other. Mpanza wondered endlessly whether this weren't a medical condition. It certainly possessed the qualities of a mental one.

What was puzzling was that in the camps, he had never been obsessive about women or alcohol since both were out of immediate reach. Mpanza had learnt to do without them, the way an amputee adjusts to the loss of a limb. Where some of his comrades made forays into the settlements outside Kamalundo or Ndalatando in Malange, looking for women, *caproto*, dagga or some combination of the three, he found retreat in his underground dwelling where he practised his scales. It was not so much a case of discipline as a rejection of transient gratification. Drinking was a serious undertaking, no *manga-manga* business, where he sought a guarantee that he could go on and on, without let, whereas camp life didn't provide for that. Ditto with women: they had to be accessible. He was suspicious of dagga or any narcotic and steered clear of them. Getting drunk was different in style from the loss of control imposed by a drug, where the mind could take a long, returnless journey to oblivion.

The years in exile had been hard, but there had been a purpose. The military camps had been characterised by comradeship, song, courage and tears. A commissar of the last platoon to leave Angola, Mpanza lived with the unforgettable moment when Cubans withdrew for Havana. There were the tear-eyed farewells as the joint Cuban and Fapla (*Forças Armadas Populares de Libertação de Angola*) troops staged the last parade. MK soldiers toyi-toyied as they raced across the Primeiro de Maio Square,

41

holding aloft the black, green and gold colours of the ANC. This was shortly before Namibia's independence.

★   ★   ★

Before he can leave Angola, however, Unita launches a series of offensives against the ruling MPLA, and in the east in Cacuso an MK garrison falls under attack. At this time, convoys transporting supplies, fuel, arms and ammunition to MK camps in Caculama have to pack ZG-U anti-aircraft artillery pieces to repulse ambushes. Fapla and MK troops have taken some casualties in the firefights. Mpanza and his section find themselves in the battle zone, where they have to conduct reconnaissance deep in Unita territory. For a week nothing happens. They are asleep when Mpanza hears Jonah, their commander, commanding in Portuguese. 'Wake up! Now, move, pronto!'

The guerrillas who sleep in full combat gear, scramble out of their sleeping-bags and take positions, weapons at the ready. Jonah looks resplendent in his Fapla uniform, the bill of his cap turned sideways. 'The *bandidos* are here,' he says, his face stern.

They crawl for about twenty yards. The whirr of nocturnal insects and the croaking of frogs in a nearby stream punctuate the silence. There is the louder buzzing of blue flies that commute between the latrine downwind and the men. The stench rises like steam and wafts over them. Boy, the shit of starving peasants sure smells bad! A few minutes later, the sentry in the lookout post signals a false alarm, just a peasant going for a shit. There have been many of these lately, and people are jumpy. Guerrilla warfare against a conventional force is different from hunting other guerrillas – even if you called them bandits – since they are equally conversant with waging a war of nerves.

The other members of the section are young, the oldest must be about twenty. Jonah and Mpanza, commander and commissar respectively, are much older. While crouched, looking at the darkness and the stammering sky, Mpanza puzzles over the meaning of it all. Why are we here? Why are we tracking down a bunch of bewildered Africans when we should be fighting the

42

Boers at home, thousands of miles from this stinking shit-hole? As if on cue, mosquitoes descend on them, singing and stinging.

One of the comrades, Josh, goes back to the tent and returns with a packet of Populares. The men light up and cup the glowing ends of their cigarettes in their palms, a useless precaution, really, because there is no way for them to camouflage tobacco smoke. Convinced that they won't be engaging the enemy this time around, Jonah allows this breach of security.

The enemy. Mpanza is intrigued by the idea of leaving the enemy in his own backyard to go in search of enemies in foreign territories. As he inhales the acrid smoke, feeling it bite his tongue, he looks at Jonah – whom he hardly knows – sitting with his back against a baobab, his PKM machine-gun pointing upwards. Does he have memories? What does he think of the journeys they have taken?

Mpanza has a feeling that Jonah is quietly contemplating the darkness beneath a sky that is just above their heads like something they can reach up and touch. The trees that have been silent now release an amalgam of odours that recall the concoctions of healers. Everywhere is the smell of the tropics, pungent, straining to overcome the rank odour from the latrine. They sleep again, with one eye open, feeling the richness of the forest engulfing them like scented vapour in a massive bathhouse.

At dawn, their section security, Jimi leaves and doesn't come back within the regulation two hours. Trouble. A villager runs through the forest, crashing against the branches and snagging his tattered clothes on the thorn bushes. In the typical Kimbundu expression of infinite grief, he laments loudly as he beats himself about the head, telling the story of the horror he has witnessed. Josh and Spokes rush him and escort him to the glade where the section assembles. Glancing fearfully at the guerrillas, the man becalms himself somewhat and addresses Jonah.

'*Chamo-me* Joaquim,' he introduces himself. '*Voce e camarada chefe?*'

'*Sim*,' Jonah says, nodding. 'I'm the commander, Joaquim.'

'*Esta bem*,' Joaquim says, satisfied now that he is dealing with authority.

Jonah asks him what the problem is. Mpanza can only decipher snatches of the exchange, babble about no *compreendo*, *desculpe* and *camarada Sul Africano* and knows that they are discussing Jimi.

'*Onde esta uma camarada?*' Jonah persists. 'Where is he?'

Joaquim doesn't answer the question, switches from Portuguese to Kimbundu and into some other yammering none of the men understand. Josh, who shows signs of an incipient breakdown, sidles into the circle and, without warning, strikes Joaquim with the butt of his AK–47 assault rifle across the face. '*Falar, filho da puta, falar!*' he screams at the prostrate man, still as if scared to even writhe in pain. Jonah grabs hold of him and shoves him aside. Mpanza has never seen him this angry before. Jonah's face has darkened, like clouds about to unleash a storm, the neck muscles and veins bunched into ropes as if the blood pumping within was on the verge of shooting out in a violent crimson flood.

'Comrade,' he says, 'you don't come here acting like a fucking bandit. We're supposed to co-operate with the locals here, for fuck's sake, not abuse them.'

'Sorry, *kommandir*, but this man. . .'

'Shut the fuck up!' Jonah snarls, glaring at Josh for one full minute as if ready to shoot him on the spot. Then he sighs. 'Just let me handle this, okay?'

But the blow seems to have succeeded where diplomacy failed. Joaquim is now talking slowly and lucidly, with much waving of hands, indicating to Jonah where he last saw Jimi.

'Okay,' Jonah says, 'we'll follow you.' Leaving Spokes and Simba with last-minute instructions to guard the post, he leads the section of guerrillas, a couple of steps behind a Joaquim who must now understand the quandary of being between a rock and a hard place. Mpanza keeps the regulation three steps behind Jonah, the rest of the men taking up the rear. There is an unstated suspicion that Joaquim might just lead them into an ambush, each tree menacing, a perfect cover for a sniper. They march on, scanning each copse, weapons on automatic fire. A rustle from the underbrush ahead; the men hit the ground, muzzles trained into the shadows. A wart-hog trots out, surveys the scene and trots back into the bush, snorting. Mpanza catches a whiff of fresh faeces; Joaquim's pants are stained. Poor devil. I'd also shit myself with all these guns on my back.

Jonah slows down and lets Mpanza catch up with him. Their footfalls bring a scurrying of field mice which dart from bush to bush, like well-trained guerrillas. Beetles, red ants and termites climb up stalks and rotting timber. The rain, which fell earlier in the morning, has left a rank odour of growth and ruin. Jonah clears his throat.

'So,' he asks, 'what do you make of this situation, Commissar?'

'I think the man's shit scared,' Mpanza replies.

'Don't need to tell me that. I've got a nose.'

'You were a little hard on Josh. Might create morale problems among the men.'

'Well, he can't go around hitting people. This is not the taxi rank on Noord Street.'

They talk about landmines, the fact that Unita's supply comes from South Africa, the irony of losing a foot here and bleeding to death. Where the trees break, Mpanza gets a glimpse of the rolling hills and realises that they are, paradoxically, in one of the most scenic parts of Malange. It is also the deadliest. He concludes that Angola, being such an ideal country for ambushes, was forever doomed to be an arena for unwinnable wars. Already hundreds of thousands have died, and many more maimed by bullets, machetes or landmines. It is not so much a country as a geographical scream of pain. The peasants, who conduct their lives with humbling dignity, must prefer something different from the existence of jackrabbits thrust upon them by warring parties. He is seized by another existential crisis: what the fuck are we doing here?

45

'I don't expect that question from a commissar,' Jonah chides. Mpanza has actually voiced the question in his head. 'Although I must say I have also wondered. Then I think of my sister, Zodwa, back home, and my parents. Then I know I'm doing this for them.'

'She must be very special, your sister.'

'Believe you me, she is.'

Larger baobabs. Jonah tenses. 'How long is this trek going to be, then? Peasants have no sense of distance. They tell you that, oh, that place is just over yonder, and they mean fifty fucking miles!' He laughs. Mpanza smiles.

That brief moment of naturalness vanishes when they come into a glade where villagers had slashed through in search of fire-wood. Cashews and mubanga thorn trees have all but disappeared; their stumps bring to mind amputees with mobile eyes in the Luanda hospital. Jimi lies in a pile of freshly cut wood, as if he had surprised gatherers and then been shot. His eyes open, there is no blood where the bullet entered the forehead. When Jonah turns him over, brain tissue oozes out of the hole in the back of his head, like scarlet yoghurt from a cracked gourd. Blood trapped by the position of his neck spurts out, once, twice, like a small geyser. Mpanza feels his gorge rise, swallows and forces himself to look. Turning away, he knows, simply means delaying coming to terms with violent death.

Not knowing what has possessed him, he removes his cap, hunkers down and scoops the brains, feeling the shattered head under his fingers. The warm, fruity and salty stink of death in his nostrils, Mpanza cradles what remains of Jimi, until the other comrades join him. They carry the corpse to the side and fash-ion a stretcher from branches and saplings. Joaquim supports himself against a baobab and retches, the exercise all the more desperate because nothing comes out. He must have been very hungry.

They carry Jimi back to base and bury him under the shade of the largest tree. Jonah says a few words about being a soldier, the essence of struggle and the vows they have all taken to defend the struggle. Some of them, he says, will pay the supreme sacrifice, but it is a dream to imagine that the Pretoria regime has the power to kill the people's resolve to be free. Then, with fists raised, they sing, *Hamba kahle, Mkhonto*, and the lone villager listens with his head bowed. Although unfamiliar with the lyrics, Joaquim intuits their loss. His own lips move in supplication. A redemption song for his own fractured land.

★ ★ ★

The snarling of traffic breaks Mpanza's chain of thought. Turning to give the block of flats one last look, Mpanza knows that he would never come back. In a small way, leaving Johannesburg – even in disgrace – has relieved him of a burden. Mentally, he made a roster of his failures. He hadn't been a good guerrilla. He didn't count himself among brilliant musicians. His marriage was on the rocks and he had deserted his kids. His relationship with women during his stay in Hillbrow had been a disaster. Hey, he thought, I'm normal. He would be more normal once he got rid of Jonah's ghost, which sat on his back like an albatross. Here, he felt particularly angry that, when the ANC made a submission to the truth and reconciliation commission – and Jonah's case was discussed – he hadn't been brought in. Why, they didn't even consult him. On several occasions, he had gone to the ANC headquarters in Shell House, on Plein Street, declaring his wish to appear as a witness, but for some reason, this fell on deaf ears. Or got lost in some bureaucratic shuffle. It was as if no one had faith in the testimony of a washed-out drunk. He was aware that people were ignoring him, pretending he didn't exist. It was only when he really lost it, spun out of control that the full weight of the organisation's disciplinary structures descended on him. Like cops, they were never there when you needed them; when you didn't, they came in bunches.

His breach of discipline was small beer, really, when looked against the backdrop of serious infractions committed by some comrades where people actually lost lives. What had he done?

47

Booze, that's what. It was uncanny, he thought. The moment you make up your mind to go on the straight and narrow, you suddenly amass a battery of friends who want to treat you to a drink. After one extraordinary binge, Mpanza threatened to shoot the proprietor of a shebeen. The man was a known collaborator, but was now the most vocal proponent of the government's social and economic programmes. For some reason, the hypocrisy stuck in Mpanza's craw, and he pulled out the gun, just to scare the man, really, he didn't mean him any harm. In no time, the Movement structures were in Mpanza's flat where he was told that it had been decided that he leave Johannesburg. He was known there and had made many enemies. The popular wisdom was that he would find a possibility of cooling off in KwaZulu-Natal, anywhere in KwaZulu-Natal.

His return to civilian life was strewn with thorns and glass shards. Comrades he had known had become career politicians; they had their eye on the elections. Where idealism had once shone in their eyes now gleamed a single-minded resolve to survive on terms which had nothing to do with the revolution. The very word 'revolution' had become something close to a swearword; it caused uneasiness in dinner-table conversations. He watched his friends rising in the ranks through climbing on the shoulders of others. A good number found employment in the private sector. The problems of homelessness and unemployment, the poverty and its concomitant of violence were codified in the secret language of statistics. In no time they were speaking corporate language, their suits and BMWs declaring the distance between them and the bush. Mpanza had a feeling that the memory of the bush was beginning to become a source of national embarrassment. Former enemies were being courted left, right and centre and there was a collective impulse to refrain from rocking the boat. Still, there were those comrades who were bonded by the pledges they had taken at the camps, who believed that this transition was but a holding action for something more meaningful to evolve. They trusted some sections of the leadership, knowing that they were hard-pressed to compromise with the enemy and start the process of reconstruction. Mpanza knew that these leaders were also wrestling with their personal demons, the same way he was, still, with the corpse on his back. It demanded to be laid to rest.

Even as he made his way to the taxi rank where the transprovincial mini bus taxis called Zola Budds plied a brisk trade, he harboured a suspicion that perhaps some of his superiors secretly hoped that the random violence which sometimes characterised KwaZulu-Natal would sort him out. Yes, he thought without joy, KwaZulu-Natal would be cool, like a grave.

Mpanza was still lost in thought when he heard someone calling his name. Tsepo Nkoane came from behind a billboard advertising Bright 'n Lovely beauty cream and ambled towards Mpanza. He was a young man in an older man's body, prematurely balding while his belt supported a rounded belly. Wheezing, he stopped beside Mpanza.

'Been trying to catch up with you,' he said, 'since you left the flat.'

'Didn't know you're still shadowing people, Tsepo,' Mpanza said. 'What's up?'

'Heard you were bound for the *bundus* and thought you might do me a favour.' His eyes searched Mpanza's face. 'Do you have a minute?' He didn't wait but started walking away from the taxi rank. Night-time trade was going in full swing. From the stalls came the heavy, bass-dominated sounds of *mbaqanga*, Mahlathini and the Mahotella Queens.

The song recorded the goings-on in the area. Live pickpockets moved in twos and threes, their fingers working convulsively, making no effort to hide their intention, causing the milling throngs to give them a wide berth. Tsepo led Mpanza into a dark doorway; they went up the stairs to another corridor that was banked by numbered doors. Jazz music issued from the inside of the door they entered. Formica-topped tables supported quarts of Castle Lager and miscellaneous mixers and spirits. Men and women sat in the gloom, drinking. Their eyes turned to appraise the new entrants, like quarry sensing a hunter in the bush. Tsepo waved airily, muttering greetings; the tension subsided.

Having found a corner table, Tsepo beckoned to the waitress, a large lady whose lipstick accentuated the abundance of her lips. Dressed in a glittering dress of crushed velvet, she hovered above the men, a pencil in her hand. 'What'll it be, gents?' She had a voice of deep, masculine timbre that reminded Mpanza of tubas in a military march.

'Sis' Maggie,' Tsepo said, 'how come you never smile for your faithful customers?'

'Smiles are expensive, Mister,' she said. 'What will it be?'

Knowing Mpanza's drinking habits, Tsepo ordered a half-jack of fast-move. Maggie brought back half a bottle of Smirnoff vodka, a litre of orange juice and two glasses.

Tsepo paid her and, when she was out of earshot, cursed, 'God, this place is a dump.'

'You didn't bring me here to talk about shebeens, Tsepo,' Mpanza said. He took a sip of his drink, felt the liquid coursing warmly down his stomach. He remembered that he hadn't eaten. When he next looked up at Tsepo, at the bland, shaven face, the weak chin he associated with weak men who strove to be liked, Mpanza could not conceal his distaste for him. Seeing grey tufts of hair on Tsepo's Adam's apple also nettled him. Although Tsepo was dressed in a clean grey suit, a laundered shirt and a gaudy television presenter's silk tie, Mpanza had a feeling that there was something unwholesome about him. Since Tsepo was still connected to the security department, it occurred to Mpanza that the man was privy to hideous secrets. Raising his glass in a half-hearted salute, Tsepo peered at Mpanza from above the rim. 'The boys back at HQ are still on a nostalgia trip,' he told Mpanza. 'And if we know what's good for us, we'll have to play ball.'

Mpanza didn't know what the hell Tsepo was alluding to, but he imagined that it had something to do with a mission in

KwaZulu-Natal. He was feeling too relaxed with the liquor mellowing him. Moreover, he wanted the satisfaction of turning Tsepo down flat, see how they would deal with that at HQ. 'You mean Security?' he asked.

Tsepo looked round quickly, his furtiveness causing Mpanza to smile. But he nodded and traced a long finger across his nose. 'There are our people working in Natal, but they are spread thin on the ground.'

'You know that the Military and the Security will never see eye to eye, Tsepo. What with you guys acting like you call all the shots.'

'That was in the past.' Tsepo seemed to be listening to something outside the shebeen. 'Now, you're off to Natal for something different, we feel you could tell us a little bit about some people there. There's a certain development.'

'Officially?'

'Don't be silly,' Tsepo snapped. 'Nothing is official.' He took a sip, seeming to think this over. 'And then, everything is official.'

'You know I wouldn't offend Security for the world, Tsepo,' Mpanza said. 'But I've seen you guys at work. I am familiar with the victims. I know that I'm being shanghaied to Natal because I'm a security risk. No,' he continued, raising a hand when Tsepo opened his mouth. 'Don't interrupt. This vodka is all right, and thanks, but no.'

'We want you to keep an eye on Jonah's old man.' As far as Tsepo was concerned, Mpanza hadn't raised any objection. 'He's running an operation down in Ngoza. People feel he might be fronting for the counters.'

Mpanza knew that 'counters' was a collective term for enemies of the new state, and this applied to a wide spectrum from the white extremists, through the black traditionalists to the black far left. He saw that he had under-estimated his comrades. They knew his weaknesses, how the killing of Jonah and the burden of guilt had scarred him.

'No,' he repeated and made to stand up. Tsepo leaned forward and laid his hand on Mpanza's shoulder. 'Get your hands off me, Tsepo.'

'Look,' Tsepo said. 'We all make mistakes. But we have to take the big picture into account. Rosie was a fuck-up.'

Mpanza regarded him, anger building up inside him. 'Rosie was a fuck-up, you say. But it was Security which vetted Rosie and gave him carte blanche over the Natal military machinery. I got an order that we should eliminate Jonah. That he'd become an askari. I was the commander, when we shot him. With Stanley.'

'Sure, Mpanza,' Tsepo persisted, 'but you also know how infiltrators work. Granted, comrades in Maputo should have checked that the command came from the right structures. Rosie was fighting his little war, and you guys were used. But this doesn't mean that you should spend the rest of your life wearing remorse on your sleeve, like a fucking badge. You have to learn to live down ugly memories.'

'How come I wasn't briefed earlier?' Mpanza could have hit Tsepo. 'It's never been officially said to me that Jonah was a mistake.'

'You mean before your own personal cock-ups? People had to be sure that you'd be willing to go to Natal.' Tsepo nodded his sympathy. 'But when I saw you at the taxi rank, with your case, I knew you were on your way.'

Mpanza put his glass down. He stood up and picked up his case. 'Just go and tell those HQ people to go fuck themselves.' As he made his way out of the shebeen, he heard the scraping of the chair and the footfalls behind him. Tsepo caught up with him outside.

'Problem is,' Tsepo said conversationally, 'HQ might send someone completely unsympathetic to the old man. And you'll have yourself to blame if shit happens.'

'Fuck off, Tsepo.' Mpanza braced himself to strike. 'Just get the hell out of my face.'

Tsepo retreated with a smile. 'Don't forget to send us a card, bro.'

Mpanza hurried to the taxi rank. Touts called out for passengers; beneath the clamour, he heard soul music, sweet and low, the story of his life. Inside the minibus, Mpanza was squashed between two women. It was fast getting late.

★ ★ ★

He managed to sleep, being woken now and then by the erratic motion of the minibus to peer through the window, seeing the snatches of scrubby acreage rolling past. Somewhere flames on the side of the highway spoke of earlier barricades. Inside the taxi, a couple of passengers passed around a carton of sorghum beer, the ripe smell of fermented grain almost overpowering in the close atmosphere. Someone attempted to light a cigarette and was shouted down by the women. The driver fiddled with the tuning dials of his radio, eventually zeroing into a station, Radio Metro. An announcer who spoke as if his mouth housed a hot potato rattled off the latest racing scores; it wasn't quite clear whether he was talking about Turffontein or Greyville. The transmission scattered in a crackle of static. Mpanza recalled Mbonambi and his Persian Prince.

'True's God,' one of the drinkers was saying from behind, 'Zulu was crushed by the knowledge that his son resembled the lodger from next door …'

'Ag,' his mate put in philosophically, 'if we worried ourselves about fatherhood, there'd be a lot of madmen on the streets. It's only the women who know.'

'And the children. You'd be surprised how quickly they learn who their real pappy is.'

The men laughed, bonded by their uneasy relationship to their offspring. Mpanza turned to look at them, fascinated by their subject. The man who had spoken first now readied himself for sleep, his jaw already slackening. His friend, who still cradled the beer carton in his arms, looked back at Mpanza with eyes that seemed doomed not to know rest. Wordlessly the man extended the carton to Mpanza, who demurred, shaking his head.

'Maybe you prefer something with a stronger kick,' the man said. He rummaged into his plastic carrier bag and extracted a bottle of Sprite. Unscrewing the top, he took a sip. His lips twisted and, eyes closed, he gave a satisfied, if pained, belch. The smell of home-made gin, *gavini*, wafted over to Mpanza. When the man offered the drink this time, Mpanza accepted the bottle, wiped its mouth with his palm, and tasted. The liquor burned down his throat, but he managed to take a few sips. Handing the bottle back, he also made the appropriate sound: a mixture of awe and appreciation. 'Ha! It burns hot!'

'The waters of immortality,' the man quipped, 'older than the Queen of England.'

Listening to the hum of the engine and the rasp of tyres against the road and hearing the wheels spitting out the gravel, Mpanza thought back to his own parents. His mother and father had died while he was in exile; now he had a few uncles and aunts and brothers and sisters who had carved themselves a different existence in this big slice of political transition. He had visited his kinsfolk as irregularly as possible, there being an unwritten law that a returned exile was more trouble than he was worth. He felt, moreover, that he made them uncomfortable, in the same way they made him feel like a poor relation. When his comrades and friends were nominated into the election list, his absence from the hub of electoral activity had stigmatised him as a possible future dissident, a counter. What was strange was that they had not shown any enthusiasm for the struggle; but now that there were benefits to be reaped, they tended to weep louder than the bereaved, their celebrations more and more vulgar. Mpanza felt that he really didn't know them. But, now, this exile to Natal, their stamping ground, might mean his bumping into them. He didn't look forward to it.

He thought of Ntombi, his younger sister who worked as a laboratory assistant at the University of Zululand. That would be a person to visit, seeing also that she was married to an accommodating sort of fellow, Roger Zindela, who lectured in Geography. They lived at eSikhawini, a sprawling township that serviced the university. It was set then, he told himself. When I hit Durban, I'll scout around a bit and then take a bus to eMpangeni.

'What's the job situation around?' he asked his new-found friend. The man was smacking his lips after another satisfying swig from the bottle.

'It's bad,' the man told Mpanza. 'There are openings in construction, or sweeping the parks for the Municipality. I suppose they'll need more men to cart the old statues to the quarries for rubble.' He laughed and extended the bottle once more. 'Funny how the more things change, the more they remain the same.'

Mpanza didn't want to pursue this field of country. He was content with the little information the man had given him. He had a driver's licence and was a mechanic, thanks to the patience of old comrades in Lusaka who had tinkered with the Movement's vehicles. But that trade would certainly mean operating in the urban areas, a sure-fire recipe for colliding with relatives. He wanted to work with his hands, do something mindless that could promote forgetfulness, where he could maintain anonymity.

It was early in the morning and still dark when the minibus pulled to a stop at the bus and taxi rank at the bottom end of Queen Street. Mpanza bade his drinking buddy goodbye and sauntered to the shelter offered by shop awnings. People slept in the doorways, bundles covered in dirty blankets and greatcoats, all posing like victims of an execution. Boys and wide-eyed girls scavenged in the garbage bins where mangoes and guavas, leftovers from the nearby market, had been discarded to give that corner of Durban a rank odour of fecundity and defeat. Slight autumnal drizzle quickened the pace of early risers who rushed to queue for transport to God-only-knew-where. Mpanza wished for some coffee, but all the cafés were shuttered down.

He walked towards the Victoria Arcade where not-so-young

women with faces ravaged by skin-lightening creams were setting up their stalls. Within an hour, he knew, the place would be
a hive of activity. Already, an enterprising soul was lighting a
Colman burner, the pot of offal on her side. Mpanza was fascinated by her collection of long forks and spoons, which were
carefully arrayed on a newspaper. He was composing a greeting
in his head, thinking that she might have coffee in her Thermos
flask, when someone tapped him on the back. He turned, figur-
ing that it was a little too early for this to be a mugging.

'Excuse me, *Mfowethu*,' a thickset man in bib overalls said. 'I
need help with my truck. It just won't start,' He gave a nervous
giggle. 'I'm beginning to think that the damn thing's been
bewitched.' He led Mpanza along the stalls, the smell of cooking
now taking over from the earlier odours. The truck stood on the
other side of the street; on its side panels was the name of the
firm, Atlas Foods, registered at eMpangeni.

'Are you sure the battery's okay?' Mpanza asked when they
approached the truck.

'It should be okay. I re-charged it only yesterday.'

Placing his suitcase on the running-board, Mpanza motioned
him inside. He opened the bonnet and checked the battery ter-
minals. Sometimes these went loose and people went crazy, but
these were secure. He went round into the cab and opened the
fuse panel; the smell of burnt electrical tubing told him immediately what was wrong.

'Get me some foil,' he ordered. The driver ripped off his cigarette packet and extracted silver paper. Mpanza scraped the
burnt fuse endings and inserted strips of foil, all along the panel,
isolating the blown fuse. He gestured for the driver to start the
truck. After two or three false starts, the engine ignited. The man
smiled.

'Shit, this makes me feel bloody stupid.' He extended his
hand. 'I'm Bheki. I don't know how to thank you.'

'No problem.' Mpanza introduced himself. Then he made his
decision. 'Say, Bheki,' he asked, 'you wouldn't be passing through

eSikhawini by any chance?'

Bheki had a few deliveries to make, but could drop Mpanza off at Dlangezwa. Although he and his sister weren't that close, Mpanza hoped that she wouldn't mind him dropping in on her. Ntombi was a decent person, and so was her husband, but it would be unrealistic to expect to live indefinitely on their welfare. He would tell them that his luck would change and that he needed a few days to get himself straightened out; then he would seriously look for a job, maybe with a freight company. Or join the timber workers at Hunt Leuchars & Hepburn, who were always looking for able-bodied men. He would stop drinking and strive to pay back whatever he might borrow from his sister or his brother-in-law.

He had a vision of Ntombi teasing him about his bad luck with women. Here he was, forty years old, without anything to his name. But his luck would change. The period of transformation, he determined would be long and there would be temptations. But he would return to his comrades, whole, and make them feel guilty for the high-handed manner in which they had treated him. But now, it was his turn to show the driver his appreciation. 'Ngiyabonga, bro. Thanks.' Collecting his case, he hopped on board.

Four

'Well,' Benedita Venter said, 'here we are, and I still don't know if we're doing the right thing.'

She and her husband Jannie Venter were sitting under a mdoni tree, in the yard of their new house. It was early, around ten a m, but Venter was already on his second whisky. Having had first-hand experience of the destruction wrought by alcohol, Benedita disapproved of this early drinking. She disapproved of drinking any time, but this was her husband, her personal albatross. At the same time, she was entranced by the novelty of Ngoza, where the sun bore down on you at six a m. Like a mother delighting in her children during a rare summer outing, when offences normally punishable back home are tolerated, Benedita felt a need to indulge his weaknesses and get into the swing of things. Aware that she had begun mothering him, she determined to criticise his less and lead by example. To this effect, she chose to made a ceremony of pouring into the glass and drinking her iced lemonade.

'It's the best thing for us,' Venter told her. 'Otherwise, I'd go crazy, eating myself up, when I knew that I could do something.'

★   ★   ★

A fortnight earlier, Detective-Sergeant Jannie Venter wangles a transfer from the Brixton Murder and Robbery Squad. The going is hard, as the transfer meant taking a cut in the salary, and he doesn't have the stomach for the endless quibbling over insurance and other benefits. He doesn't mind, for police work here has lost its lustre. The new regulations governing police activity insist on frustrating paperwork. Shoot a suspect, then you end up filing so many reports you might as well write *War and Peace*. The Security Directorate approaches him, but even here most police stations and offices are in the thrall of pervasive demoralisation, this time for different reasons. Each time you open a newspaper, some former member of covert operations is blowing the whistle on his erstwhile buddies. Since the changeover from apartheid to a limping democracy, most police officers find themselves in some sort of official operational limbo. The lines of command have been diffuse for a while. New codes have to be worked out, what with more darkies now in commanding positions. To be fair, experienced white officers still have a lot of pull.

It is exactly this pull, where abuses are possible, which prompts Venter to seek a transfer, although his reasons are personal and refer to wounded pride. Even though married again, he still hears whispers behind him. Even women officers laugh at him behind their hands. All because of Cynthia and Grey. In the parlance of the squad room, Cynthia has been passed from man to man, like a goblet of sweet wine. When Grey is transferred to Ngoza, Venter knows that he has to follow him, settle the account. Grey is under suspicion and Venter's private mission is to put Grey behind bars. Millions of rands disappeared under the rubric of operational funds, moneys for covert operations against the terrorists. Now that the terrorists are running the show, heads are beginning to roll. Benedita remembers that the rot started earlier, with Captain Dirk Coetzee's crossing over to the other side.

'But do you think that Grey will co-operate?' Benedita worries because she imagines the man to be ruthless. 'You're the one told me that, before his transfer to Ngoza, he was responsible for your assignments to border missions, all the time hoping that you would be killed. All the while he was diddling Cynthia.'

'He doesn't have to know a thing,' Venter says. In thinking about Cynthia, he can't help comparing her with Benedita. Venter and Benedita share a secret. Although she looks white in the eyes of white South Africans for whom such things matter, she admitted to him that she was not. Even though Benedita is not white – could, in fact have been classified Coloured if such a system still operated – she comes from abroad, that mysterious terrain which feeds the inferiority complex of most whites who've never been outside the borders of this country. Benedita's father was a black South African seaman who had disappeared soon after Benedita and her brother Steven were born to a Scottish woman in Glasgow. Benedita, formerly a staunch member of the British Anti-Apartheid Movement (A-AM), left London in 1992. The journey to South Africa had as much to do with the emptiness left by the release of Mandela as finding a connection with a lost father.

*   *   *

On a lonely afternoon of February 1990, Benedita fears that she might be heading for a nervous breakdown. There is exultation mixed with a sorrow among the members of the anti-apartheid movement. A ban spanning three decades on political parties inside South Africa has been lifted, and it is clear that the regime is floundering, looking for a face-saving measure to release Nelson Mandela. Mandela is a myth, a man who could have been dreamt up by the magical fictions of a Gabriel Garcia Marquez. Many of the activists know Mandela is behind bars, but the Pretoria authorities have effectively banished him from the public with the result that he lives only in the imagination. People ask questions: on his release, will he be the same fiery revolutionary whose popularity rose in direct proportion to the number of years in prison? Knowing how South African intelligence works hand-in-glove with Mossad, past-masters at suborning incarcerated adversaries, how long will it take before Mandela sells out? A bigger question roils in the collective head of the A-AM: what is the price to be paid by a people who have invested all their hopes in one man, if he turns out to be another quisling? What will the children do?

She walks the long and busy Kilburn High Street, absent-mindedly admiring the market stalls where you could buy almost anything, and realises that the fortunes of London are irreversibly intertwined with those of the developing world. On display are fruits and vegetables from all over the globe, imported from the former colonies, the seasonless bounty peddled by strangers who transform London into a tropical storm. Crossing the street, she enters the foyer of the Tricycle Theatre, hoping to buy a ticket for August Wilson's 'Joe Turner's Come And Gone', and finds that the play finished its run last night. Damn! That's how she missed seeing the Amandla Cultural Ensemble at the Hackney Empire. The story of my life, she thinks grimly. I'm one gene short from being white; one from being black. She laughs at this observation, causing an old man to give her a quick look. Another one, she knows he must be thinking, on the way to or just coming out of a madhouse.

As the wind rises, the afternoon light loses its harsh edge and changes into dusk. She pulls up the collar of her jacket, realising that this February, although unseasonably warm, is still a winter month of suicide. As her head begins to crowd with unwholesome thoughts, a bus rolls up and she jostles her way to the upper deck. Black jackets, polo shirts, skirts that barely cover the groin, black or charcoal-grey jeans, scuffed Doc Marten's boots constitute the official uniform of the hour. Here and there is a splash of foreign colour, saffron or crimson, but black rules the day. It is peculiar to her how blacks, a minority, have also succumbed to the seduction of fashion magazines – these black people whose forebears come from climes of bursting colour.

A West Indian bus conductor walks along the aisle, issuing tickets, inspecting bus passes, his eyes refusing to communicate what goes on in his head. When he returns after a round to the front, he gives Benedita a look which says, I see you, sister. It is an exchange more meaningful than a handshake, something familiar to people thrashing against going under. Benedita regards the white people in the bus from the vantage point of a mediator. They have moulded the world in their own image, she muses, but the power of despots has excluded them from the secret strategies blacks have developed to maintain survival and dignity. Don't these people feel an urge to understand what another section of their population endures? Wasn't it curiosity that had occasioned Voyages of Discovery? It is strange that, after the discovery, there is a compulsion to obliterate from living memory the implications of what has been encountered.

As the bus rolls on, there's a sparkle of Christmas lights, which haven't been pulled down. On leaving the more fashionable parts of the city, the street lights change to the dour amber. At King's Cross, Benedita sees the cluster of women in short dresses and fishnet stockings, braving the early evening chill, their shadowed eyes probing for strangers who seek a salve for their loneliness. More doomed men and women mill in front of the station, before the plate glass fronting W H Smith's and Burger King, swigging hard brews from cans and bottles. Policemen walk in twos and threes, like zoo masters keeping watch on their unpredictable charges.

She turns round to look as a young black man in jeans and a dark windbreaker comes and sits across from her. The conductor greets him and asks him why his face looks like thunder. 'You can't believe these people,' the young man says. He is addressing himself to the conductor, but it is clear that he wants the whole bus to know and take responsibility for what has happened. 'I just parked my car to rush to the cash-point,' he says, 'and when I come back, they're busy towing it away. I tell the cops that, hey, this is my car, man. Know what they say to me, Joe? This fucker, he says: Tough tit. *Tough tit.*' He shakes his head in wonderment. 'Now I have to shell out eighty fucking quid to get my wheels back. I feel so mad I ought to spit at somebody!' The other passengers, who might have taken an interest in the young man's tale, decide that they have no wish to be spat upon. There is a rustle of paper as noses bury themselves within the sports pages of the *Evening Standard*. The conductor, who must have seen it all, tells him to cool it. 'Cool it?' the young man asks, his lips twisting into a sneer. 'That's the fucking problem, isn't it? Cooling it.' He looks across at Benedita. 'What this country needs is a fucking Nelson Mandela.'

She is still pondering the young man's plight when the bus stops alongside the Brixton underground station. She gets out and weaves her way through the massed bodies of mainly black people. The radios blast a mix of hip-hop, calypso and scratch music, the sound seeming to influence the walkers' rhythm. There is everywhere the smell of food cooked or fried in too much oil. The vendors in front of emporiums shove watches or trinkets up her nose. Two young men in dreadlocks and oversized jackets, baggy jeans and high-top trainers amble towards her. One of them catches her eye and, without seeming to stop, whispers, 'Business?' For a moment, Benedita toys with the idea of copping a bit of the new drug, Mother's Little Helper, but then remembers her own modest stash of hash in the flat. She hurries on towards The Village, past the Ritzy cinema, which seems closed, not that she feels like taking in a movie.

The street corners whisper their own brand of menace. The walls are daubed with scrawls detailing unfulfilled desires: 'Hip hop on a cop', reads one. On Railton Road, the starting point of the 1981 Brixton riots, there is a more celebratory sentiment: 'Darryl, you luvly thing you.' Along this street, which is where she lives, are signs of ongoing construction. Skips are overloaded with debris and furniture, the paraphernalia of a people in the grip of rampant consumerism. Cannibalised television sets squat atop the heap. Mattresses whose coiled entrails show through the urine-soaked ticking sneer at a populace that will always sleep but will never know rest. Here and there dogs and cats chase each other, snarls and mews punctuating the still night. Walking up her paved path, she opens the door to hear her phone ringing upstairs.

'Hello?' she answers, out of breath.

'Hi, Benedita?' It is Mark, from the office of the A-AM in Camden Town. 'Have you got a minute?' He sounds breathless.

There is a crackle of static in which Benedita imagines Mark's intense face. 'Just got it from a reliable kabash,' he says, 'that there's an announcement concerning Nelson Mandela tomorrow on LWT.'

She hangs up the phone, more out of fright than discourtesy. Feeling as though something had entered her most private world and introduced a strange order, she goes about cleaning her flat, starting with the Zimbabwe Ruins of the dishes on her sink, scouring the bathroom and ending up arranging the avalanche threatening to roll down her bookshelves. But the flat proves mutinous and Benedita gives up after suppressing an urge to smash everything into pieces. First putting on a record on an ancient turntable, Miles playing Jack Johnson, she rolls a joint and dulls its edge with a glass of vodka and orange juice. She takes a sip of her drink, her taste buds separating the rye from the oranges. Smoking, Benedita hears the trumpet wailing as if trapped somewhere inside her skull. She feels displaced, outside of herself, the buzz in her head allowing her to watch herself, this woman of dubious parentage who is on the verge of a nervous breakdown. She falls asleep on the settee with the record playing, John McLaughlin sending the guitar into inspired spins, occasioning psychedelic pipers from the highlands.

The morning comes, as strange and intimidating as the first day of creation. Dissolute and disjointed from the rhythm of the day, Benedita feels the heaviness of the room pressing down on her. She has a sense of something as unanswerable as Judgment sitting on a throne, watching her trying to ignore the importance of Mark's call. She comforts herself with the remembrance of the general disbelief that met the Pretoria government's legalisation of political movements. Could this be another item in F W de Klerk's bulging bag of tricks?

Time flies. The blue-red-and-white LWT logo flashes on the television screen and Benedita increases the volume. The newscaster announces a special news flash. Through a haze, Benedita sees De Klerk in a still photograph standing next to Mandela. He has the grim, tight smile of someone uneasy in the presence of an ineffable power. In a grey suit, Mandela looks vaguely oriental; his grey hair combed back. In that instant, Benedita remembers the photo with Henry Kissinger and Le Duc Tho, joint winners of the Nobel Peace Prize at the end of the Vietnam War, a graphic juxtaposition of arrogance with humility. De Klerk then comes into life and declares that the cabinet had met and saw no reason to hold Mandela any longer. The prisoner, who still has to be released, does not get any air-time. De Klerk adds that the prized prisoner, a reluctant apotheosis of resistance, would be released. The exact, named hour of freedom is three p m.

Something with the weight of a boulder snags in Benedita's throat. Her chest bound by a band of steel, scalding tears roll down her cheeks and drop like rainwater to the floor. The tears are not for Mandela. They are not for all these blasphemed years of men watching stolid walls for decades. Benedita cries for herself, for the loneliness, and for the coming moment when she would come face to face with herself.

Alone among the multitudes in front of South Africa House on the Sunday Mandela walks free, she watches his fist punching the air in a self-conscious gesture with which his wife, Winnie, is more familiar. The crowds on the pavement of the embassy are jubilant yet derisive of the Bobbies who try to maintain order, who are seen as defenders of an edifice of shame. The policemen are mostly young, and Benedita has a feeling that they might have preferred to be elsewhere today, perhaps walking hand-in-hand with their loved ones, the way Mandela is walking with Winnie. ANC members are also watching, and it occurs to her that, perhaps for the first time in their lives, they are looking at the six thousand miles separating them from Cape Town. Written on the dirty Cape Town sky is the message that, from now on, events would flow with the inexorable logic of a river in flood. Benedita wonders if her people have worked hard enough to come to terms with all that water.

Beneath this realisation throbs the knowledge that – even

though she was a member of a progressive movement – she has never really subscribed to the ideal of African liberation. Hers has always been a case of human rights. That the people at the bottom rung of the racial totem pole are African is always balanced against a subliminal admiration for the progress with which she credits white involvement in Africa. She is surprised that it takes Mandela's release for her to admit that she doesn't really care how Africans deal with power, just as long as it doesn't set the country ablaze. As for Mandela being an African – and thus inflecting her ideas with an unutterable irony – she rationalises that Mandela, whatever he and his followers think, is a world figure. And world figures fall outside any ethnic or racial classifications, like deities who straddle the universe. It matters so little to the world community that Gandhi, the Dalai Lama, Mother Teresa and most of those who represent the finest in humanity are not children of the West. Africa, Asia and Latin America, she reasons on that memorable afternoon, have a way of announcing their importance. This is mostly achieved through a programme that spans many years. In given cases, they influence cataclysmic changes without warning.

*   *   *

Benedita has long perfected the art of living alone inside her head. Venter finds this thoroughly exasperating for it means there are certain moments when she effectively cancels him out of her life. But there's something more – and this heightens the tension between them – which points to the restlessness of the blood. She travels everywhere with a camcorder, interviewing people about everything from what it means to be a South African to the economics of inner-city crime. Venter has a feeling that, since she doesn't have a clue to the buried layers of this country's thinking, she could endanger herself. She dismisses his concern. 'I've been around the block,' she would say. Her block was of course Govan in Glasgow, Brixton or the East End in London. On a mission sponsored by the BBC in December 1991, she went to Rio de Janeiro to the studios and sets of the Globo television network to study their *telenovelas*. Although she never tells Venter, he knows – he can sense the wistful smile in her tone – she fell in love with a dancer from Bahia and returned to London with a broken heart. London, she once said, has the highest per capita count of the broken-hearted. This cosmopolitan city spawns a constellation of political and cultural groups and individuals whose changing fortunes determine their return to their native lands or to neighbouring states whence they launch their struggles, leaving behind a trail of tears.

Venter doesn't know that the love of her life was Jacobo, an exile who had learnt Portuguese in the ANC camps in Angola before being posted off to the diplomatic mission in Rio. The distance from home and the uncertainty of exile led to his collapse. Jacobo graduated into a *nega maluca*, a crazy nigger, to be found in the slums, blind drunk from *cachaça*. Or dancing the *gafieira* in Copacabana, consorting with the *mulheres da vida*, as they called prostitutes in those days. In the veins of Benedita's own mother runs a mixture of ancient Celtic and Brazilian bloods. She had named her daughter after Benedita da Silva – a working-class organiser, feminist, parliamentarian, and defender of street children – who had transcended her poverty as a little girl from the *favela* to senator despite her African ancestry.

To a people of Pretoria eternally fascinated with ancestral lineage – although unable to bear a close examination of their own tangled family trees – Benedita's entry into their small community is edifying. Venter's exotic acquisition becomes a high point of dinner conversations among his peers. He knows that even though his kinfolk despise the indigenous blacks, a point of view he shares, a beautiful, olive-skinned, thoroughly foreign woman with a South London accent elevates him in their eyes. Marrying her has however not quite managed to exorcise Cynthia's memory. It lives, cackling from the wings, making unscheduled appearances on the theatre of his life.

In Benedita's London writhing with the pain of confronting itself after Mandela's release, she finds it somehow easier by day to deal with the wide-open spaces inside her. Because she feels the magnetic pull of the African continent, she strives to demystify it through exploring its secrets, myths and legends, which hide complexity in child-like simplicity. Reading through the poetry collections, she encounters not only literary works employing contemporary themes but also insights into societies which once owned healing balms against the plunder of civilising forces. Nightly, the abstractions contained in the written texts, become transmuted into flesh and blood in her dreams. Scared of the dark and the ghosts and their secret societies, Benedita usually spends the whole night reading, leaving the light on until she is woken up by an elegiac score, the signal tune of Breakfast News. It is when she finishes Nurrudin Farah's *Maps* in a single sitting that she accepts the need to seek help.

Her entry into medical care is, however, not voluntary. She lands in hospital following her collapse outside Holborn underground railway station on Kingsway Road. She has just returned from a meeting with a BBC radio producer of Focus on Africa at Bush House. Meaning to commission a short film feature on Ali Mazrui, the producer has swollen Benedita's cache of research material with audiotapes where the eminent intellectual speaks on his book, *On Heroes and Uhuru Worship*. Benedita tries to reconcile Professor Mazrui's veneration by Western academia with the bad blood between him and African political scientists. It is exactly at the moment that Benedita recalls Mazrui's confrontation with Ghanaian writer, Ama Ata Aidoo, when everything suddenly goes dark before her.

She regains consciousness in a ward, ironically enough, of the University College Hospital, a stone's throw from the School of Oriental and African Studies, where she got the books and mimeographs on Mazrui. The doctors and nurses are pleasant enough, but are unable to get to the root of her problem. For three days, they wheel her from her bed to a warren of cubicles, where men and women in white coats poke and probe at her body internally and externally. They start giving her curiously exasperated looks as if she were part of a conspiracy to show them up. Samples of her bodily fluids are stored in some jars somewhere, to be further examined under microscopes. On the afternoon of the second day, an African doctor she has never seen before installs her on a rigid chair and looks at her via a light shining out of his forehead.

'Have you been to the tropics recently?' he asks.

'No,' Benedita says. 'Why?'

'When you came in here,' the doctor says, 'you showed signs of cerebral malaria. Then it was something akin to meningitis.' He stares at her. 'Are you sure you haven't been to Africa? Asia? Latin America?'

The Third World, she thinks. 'I was in Brazil,' Benedita says. 'Almost one year ago.'

The doctor seems to find this information interesting. Then he calls for a nurse and writes out a prescription and tears it off and hands it to her. 'Make sure', he instructs, 'that she takes her medicine three times a day.' To Benedita: 'I want you to take your medication. I'll find out what's wrong with you if it kills me.'

Rather you than me, doctor, Benedita reflects in bed that night, as she hears the distant growl of traffic outside. She feels weak and useless. Life goes on outside, in the university, on the Tottenham Court Road cinemas – something new must be showing. She has a friend at the British Film Institute, just round the corner. The West End is a walk away. Suddenly, in this confinement, she starts to appreciate freedom. After taking one of her pills, she falls into a deep sleep.

It must be towards midnight when she wakes up to voices droning above her. When she opens her eyes, the ward is dark, the only source of light a dozen candles forming an incandescent ring around her. Within this circle of light, stands her mother next to the doctor. Both of them are naked. Around them, Benedita's doctors and nurses are singing something sorrowful and nostalgic, like a medieval madrigal. Mary lifts her head and faces the doctor, and the two look like lost children or slaves on an auction block. There is a sign from one of the senior doctors, and the song segues into an upbeat blues that is as familiar as it is strange, inflected here and there with a salsa tempo. There is a sound of drumming, punctuating the singing, which has dropped into a chant. This seems to urge the naked couple to dance. Horrified and spellbound in equal measure Benedita watches Mary, her mother, doing a parody of the bump-and-grind routine of night club strippers, her hands caressing the doctor's body. There is something natural about the scene, reminiscent of kids cavorting in the rain; but Benedita is simultaneously revolted and fascinated by her mother's nakedness. It is then that Benedita finds her voice.

'Ma!' she says. 'What are you doing?'

Mary laughs. When she turns to look at her daughter, her face is covered with whitish pustules of someone with eczema. Without being told, Benedita knows that her mother is going to die. When Mary opens her mouth to speak, there is a small bed of aloes in the place where the tongue should be. Benedita screams, frightened of the dread disease that her mother might transmit with a kiss. But the doctor, who is now shrouded in a white sheet, takes Mary's hand, as if to take her pulse, and raises the candle-flame to be level with her lips. Snuffing it out, Mary breaks free and starts running, her high heels beating a staccato on the wooden floor. The other members of the medical team extinguish their candles and, without a word, all run off into the corridors. Benedita wakes up in the morning with birds pecking inside her head. A nurse takes a reading from her chart.

'Who's the doctor who was here yesterday?' Benedita asks.

'Dr Sibiya?' The young nurse is puzzled. 'Why'

'I just wanted to know,' Benedita says. After a pause, she asks: 'Where's he from?'

'You like him then?' the nurse asks. 'He's from South Africa.'

'Yes,' Benedita says. 'I thought so.'

Later, when Dr Sibiya comes into the ward, Benedita finds herself disturbed by his presence and debates with herself whether to ask him about her dream. But, what is there to ask? The man is a medical doctor, stupid, she tells herself, not an obeah doctor. But still, she can't keep her eyes off him. She strips him naked in her mind, trying to see if he fits the proportions in her dream. But the doctor is all professionalism, his dark face showing no sign of having taken part in the dreams of his exotic patient.

Once discharged from the hospital, she phones her mother. 'How are you?' she asks.

'Funny that you should call,' Mary says. 'I had this crazy dream last night.'

'What about?' Benedita's mouth has gone dry.

'Have you been ill?' Mary asks. 'I dreamt you were in hospital.'

'Don't bullshit me, Ma,' Benedita says. 'Someone must have told you that I was in hospital. Three days ago.'

'I'm not turning you around,' Mary says. 'I was away the whole of last week.' She pauses. 'What did they say was the matter?'

'They couldn't find anything wrong,' Benedita says. 'Rest is recommended.'

There is a long silence. Then Mary says. 'In my dream, I'm to tell you to go and find your father.'

'Who told you?' Benedita asks, dreading the answer, because she knows it already.

'A doctor. Your doctor,' Mary says. 'The African.'

There are a few people who can prescribe a cure for something that finds its origins in anxiety. Plagued by thoughts of suicide, Benedita confides in her mother that something is wrong. Mary refers her to a friend in Clapham Common who knows someone who could perhaps help her. Ever since her collapse in Holborn, within the trendiest square mile of the city, she is suspicious of the Tube. But she musters up her courage and takes the train and gets off at the station milling with black men who stare at her with smoking eyes. Although it is cold and there is slight drizzle, most of the people are dressed for a summer's day. The men are in T-shirts and the women wear shorts. Only their children are in duffel coats and heavy jackets. The whole community, from grannies to toddlers, wears trainers. What is it about black people, she asks herself (for almost all the people here are black) and trainers? A young woman some feet ahead of Benedita pushes a buggy and from behind Benedita can see the knitted colourful bobble hat. Walking abreast of the young mother, Benedita sneaks a look and, yep, Baby's wearing trainers! She finds the address without difficulty. It is a dingy flat at the end of a long and narrow street whose name she strives to forget. As she knocks on the door, she feels the eyes of the people peering at her from behind drawn curtains.

A little black girl of about eight opens the door and looks up at Benedita. Just as the visitor composes her face into an appropriate smile, she recoils as the little girl screams: 'Ma! There's a honky lady at the door!' She tries to slam the door, a reflex perhaps from unwanted intrusions by social workers, but Benedita has jammed it with her shoe. From inside the house she hears the mother scolding the girl. 'Din' I tell you never to call people that?' There is a sudden sound of a hand-clap; a palm striking a cheek, followed by a shriek which momentarily drowns the mother's footfalls.

Benedita is surprised by how young the woman looks. She had expected someone eccentric, old, ministering to the needs of the unhinged from a divan or supported by a Zimmer frame. She is small and very light complexioned, with full lips and wondering brown eyes, like an anorexic Sade. Although she smiles at Benedita, the latter has a feeling of being judged and condemned as another white girl in trouble. 'I'm sorry,' she says in a tone that's not at all apologetic. 'My daughter goes barmy at the sight of white people.'

'I'm not white,' Benedita says. She is suddenly angry at her own defensiveness.

'I know that,' retorts the woman. 'That I trust, is your trouble.'

'I don't know what you mean.' Benedita feels herself redden.

'Come on in,' the woman says, leading Benedita along the dark hallway into the lounge. The place is cluttered with old furniture, settees, which must have been salvaged from skips or second-hand shops, unstable chairs and a table that must have been hewn out of exotic, ancient wood. In the close atmosphere of a lounge where the dominant odour is that of cat piss, several ginger cats stare at Benedita with such malevolence that she recoils. They only leave the settee after the woman has shooed them off. 'Tea?' she asks.

'No,' Benedita demurs. 'I'm fine. Thank you.'

'Please yourself,' the woman says. She gazes at Benedita. 'I'm Alina. You don't have to tell me yours until I ask you to.' Going to the window, she draws the curtains. 'I see that you're annoyed with me. That doesn't concern me. We're not here to make friends.'

'It's just that —' Benedita starts. Alina stops her with a gesture.

'You don't need to explain yourself to me,' she says. Picking a spot at the corner of the settee, she takes out of her frock pocket a small tobacco pouch. A pipe, in whose bowl she tamps strands of tobacco, carefully, ensuring that nothing dropped on the bare floor follows this. She looks up as she lights the pipe.

'I was very small', she begins, 'when my father left us. My mother's English and my father is Nigerian, as I'm sure you must have noticed. All the time he was with us, my father was the most considerate man you've ever known. He loved my mother, I'm sure of that. Then he left. Went back to Lagos. After a few weeks, he sent for us. When we got there, we found that he had another family. Several wives and a battery of children. My half-brothers and -sisters.' A light from a passing car catches Alina's face and Benedicta sees in her eyes a conflict of ironic sorrow and regret. 'My mother went crazy. Lost her mind completely. Back here, I knew one thing. My father had ceased being our father. He'd become an African.'

As Alina recounts her bleak tale, Benedita listens to the sounds

73

of the approaching night. Beneath this, she hears something dragging itself across the floor and she imagines it must be the recently punished little girl crawling towards her to wreak her revenge. She almost jumps out of her skin when she sees a tortoise plodding leisurely towards her. She has never seen a beast this ugly before. Although she knows it is harmless, there is something grotesque about the short, stubby legs and the shell whose hard edges are softened by the lighting. It is however the eyes that get to her. They are black and full of great sadness, an incalculable capacity for suffering. Sensing Benedita's terror, Alina scoops the animal into her arms and places it on the table. 'Don' be frightened,' she says as much to the animal as to her visitor. 'This tortoise might have answers for you.'

'How?'

'I will ask it questions and it will guide me.' Alina finishes smoking and empties the contents of her pipe into an ashtray. Looking at the animal, she starts singing something sweet and slow, in a tongue totally alien to Benedita's ears. Her tortoise's attentiveness gives it a scholarly look, as if it is listening to a fascinating though complicated lecture. Then it pulls its head back into the shell. 'You tell us your name first.' The tortoise brings its head out, gingerly as is testing the atmosphere for noxious gases. It opens its mouth and chews on something that Benedita cannot see. 'My name is in a strange tongue and it means a blessing,' Alina says.

Benedita. A blessing. Big deal. Whoever her mother's friend is, she must have told this Alina Whatshername who she is. There's no mystery about that. Summoning up all her reserves of scepticism, Benedita feels strangely elated that this is another smoke-and-mirrors performance. Ho-hum. What next? 'Who's grandpa and grandma?' The tortoise goes back inside the shell. A clock somewhere in the house ticks Benedita's impatience away. Time seems to drag. Maybe the bloody thing has died inside the shell, she thinks. But the tortoise's head reappears.

'The old geezer comes from the North, where he lived in a

snow-bound hamlet for many of his adolescent years. He did not marry the woman who becomes the mother of the two children. The boy dies after a short illness on his thirtieth birthday and the girl survives them all. The mother is a beautiful woman, as pretty as summer flowers. She comes from warm places and has a shared ancestry with my own people who pray to Shango in Yoruba.'

Allister McMurty and Tereza Cardoso. Benedita's heard starts to spin and she fears she will collapse in this strange woman's lounge. Overcome by discomfort, Benedita watches from the edge of her seat as Alina and the tortoise conduct their strange routine of divination. The information, she feels, is still deliberately vague and could make up the histories of any number of families. At the same time, there are details which Mary only could have told the woman, or her friend. But, Benedita wonders, would Mary have so brazenly disclosed such intimate family secrets?

Shamans can only take their cue from information communicated by the sufferer's gestures. Their capacity to read and interpret body language arms them with awesome power, where they are then seen to unearth the secrets, which are writ large on the map of the human body. From her readings on South Africa, Benedita knows that *izinyanga* and *izangoma* are less psychics than psychotherapists. Sometimes they delve into the realm of interpreting dreams, but all this is based on rudimentary psychology and a dependence on the testimony of the dreaming interviewee.

Alina then recites Benedita's more immediate family history. 'Your mother', she says, 'is of humble origins. Unlike most women here, she not only prayed for love but also was courageous enough to get it from a stranger. Your father was not just a seaman; he'd fled the country after someone had died. A white man. And he would have been hanged.'

Benedita starts realising that this woman is, in the language of the streets, the business. Her mother never talks about Solomon

Beukes. Never. 'Is he still alive?'

The tortoise researches its library. Comes out. 'Yes.'

'Where will I find him?'

'You know the answer to that one,' Alina says. 'You will have to find him in his country. He is not well. He also pines for you and your brother.'

'What about my mother? Doesn't he want to see her?'

'Your mother betrayed him. He cannot live down that knowledge.' Alina's eyes mirror her tortoise's sadness. 'As for you, my dear,' she goes on, 'remember one thing. Whatever happens to wherever you're going, just be careful about the kind of guy you marry.'

'Why?'

'Your granny's blood', Alina says solemnly, 'is crying for expression.'

★   ★   ★

Right now, Venter cries silently for deliverance from a throbbing headache, a condition that he associates with the memory of Cynthia. Boy, she really fixed my wagon. As he stuffs his police manuals into a satchel, he knows that he will only excise Cynthia from his book of life the day Grey ceases living. But, meanwhile, he has to bite the bullet and cosy up to the man if his investigation is going to succeed. 'To him, I'm just a whipped cuckold, a ball-less wonder.'

Benedita trails a finger across his stubbled jaw. 'You don't have to take this personally,' she says. 'Do you hear what I'm saying, Jannie?' She pronounces his name the Americans way. *Jahn-nee*.

'I really hate it when you ask that question,' Venter snaps. 'Of course I hear what you're saying, I'm not deaf. As for this thing being personal, of course, it's bloody personal.'

'That will be your downfall, my friend,' Benedita tells him. 'That and the booze.'

'Ag. I can handle the old whisky any old time.'

She feels a sense of regret that they are now leaving their Pretoria home. So many memories, on the streets, on the air that was clean – rarities in Johannesburg. The jacarandas are in their bloom, the lavender petals colour the tarmac. The neighbours who are mostly police families, the guarded camaraderie. There had, of course, been instances, when one of the neighbours became disparaging of her origins without seeming to be. Mrs van Vuuren once asked from across the fence whether Benedita didn't consider herself lucky that she had married such a nice white man. Before Benedita could compose a cutting retort, Mrs van Vuuren complimented Benedita on her garden and her clean house. She was not, Mrs van Vuuren maintained, like the other 'Coloureds'. 'Do you know', she asked, 'that at school we had this expression, *So dronk soos 'n kleurling onderwyser* – As drunk as a Coloured teacher?' Stung by this barb, Benedita watched Mrs van Vuuren rearing her head and hooting with laughter, the sun highlighting her dark-brown tresses, deepening the curls at the roots and the swarthy neck. 'But I hear', Benedita offered innocently, 'that some white people, especially the Afrikaners, have some black blood in them?' Mrs van Vuuren's spasm of mirth was cut short suddenly as if a light had been switched off. The look she gave Benedita could have stopped dead a stampeding herd of bulls. 'Where', she asked, 'do you get such arrant nonsense?' Turning, she waddled back to her white house where she raised white kids, never to speak to Benedita again.

*　　*　　*

The one and only blight on Benedita's peace is that the house was once Cynthia's domain before the divorce. Benedita had to insist that they burn or give to charity anything that once belonged to her. Even as they prepare to leave, she finds trinkets, a ring or artefact, which still carries traces, real or imagined, of Cynthia's smell.

In Pretoria, she observes, you seldom worried about crime. But that is soon coming to an end, what with all types of unsavoury characters, including crime syndicates buying chunks of prime land in the Midrand. This is the advance detachment, opening up the possibility of setting up bases in the Pretoria suburbs. When that time comes, Benedita knows, gone will be the glory of the Union Buildings, the State Theatre and its grand operas. Although she hasn't visited any of the cultural houses – Venter regards opera and theatre a waste of time – she appreciates the buildings for their connection with a history which might have been unkind to her people, but which enabled human beings to enter the realm of grace.

And, she asks herself, who are my people? When she arrives in South Africa looking for her father, an ex-seaman who was known as Absalom Beukes, part of her claims his people, but her whole upbringing shrinks at the powerlessness he represents. Benedita reaches this conclusion after a long hour of soul-searching. She sees the potential political power in the hands of the blacks, but that is all. Here and there they've climbed the economic ladder, but their footing is unsure and the rungs are slippery. I am black, she tells herself repeatedly, but this is accidental. Here, she remembers the conundrum faced by James Baldwin, the black American writer who found no connection with Africa. The palpable poverty of Africans – for whose cause she braved the winter chills as she stood at picket lines in front of South Africa House near Trafalgar Square – horrifies her. It is not lost on her that she is also a victim of a curious form of self-hatred. Her education and training and exposure to the best institutions of culture have given her tools with which to analyse the world.

It is exactly this sense of being cultured person, which entraps her. She enjoys the company of her husband's kinsmen, but she cannot abide their coarseness. And they are so unattractive, with those moustaches that resemble City Council brooms. Even though Venter's people cannot be said to symbolise civilisation, they haven't sunk so low as to kill peoples the way blacks do. But these are private thoughts, because she cannot express that she fears the blacks, not so much for the intelligibility of their tongues as the randomness of their violence. For them, it is not so much a matter of killing a person as how thoroughly you mutilate them. She knows, as these thoughts crowd in her head, that a time is coming when she would have to make choices. She prays for a stay of execution.

★   ★   ★

Benedita got up and entered the kitchen, the screen door banging behind her. She sincerely hoped – prayed – that this place, Ngoza, would offer something different, if only because she knew how Venter had suffered in Johannesburg. The break-up with his wife had been messy and had left him emotionally scarred. Benedita conjured up an image: Venter must have been a tow-headed young man, built like a scrum-half in his earlier police days. He must have driven the police van with reckless abandon, scattering papers on the streets and sending clouds of dust into the air. Much later, he married Cynthia and moved to Johannesburg, where he began his graceless descent into self-hatred. He would sometimes be seized by fits of unreasoning rage, and he had started using his fists on Benedita and stopped only after she threatened to leave him. That Cynthia was a real bitch, Benedita remembered bitterly. Wherever she is, I hope she chokes on the knowledge of the harm she left behind. What kind of woman could be nicknamed Suction Pump? Unaccountably, she started crying.

She was rinsing her face in the kitchen sink when Venter came in and wrapped his arms around her and nuzzled her neck. She felt his stubbled jaw and took in the whiff of whisky on his breath. The room was filled with the sound of insects; light entered through the window and splashed on the sink, like a golden liquid. She loved the feel of Venter on her and had long made up her mind to work towards his healing. But he had to know that she hurt, too. And she needed reassurance that they would be safe.

'*Ag, skat,*' Venter purred, kneading her shoulders, '*Moenie huil nie* – Don't cry, love.'

Benedita felt stupid being comforted by someone who needed comforting. But then the stubborn thought came to her. To

79

hell with this! Men revel in acting like babies and being treated like babies. Women were to blame for this, always massaging the fuckers! Why couldn't she just lash out and claw at him and tell him that this shit had to stop?

'I'm going to quit, Benny,' he said as if reading her mind. He always shortened her name as a preface to springing an unpleasant surprise. 'Benny?'

She steeled herself. 'Yes?'

'I might have to be on the move a lot,' Venter told her. 'It comes with the job.'

'You've been out loads before, so why tell me this time?'

'Because the periods away are going to be longer.' He paused and tried to swat a fly in mid-air. 'And dangerous.'

'But I thought your work now meant keeping tabs on Old Greyhound.' Benedita wanted to see an end to this investigation, or whatever Venter called it. It had gone on far longer than necessary. 'What's this thing you don't want to tell me about?'

'There are range wars in Msinga,' Venter said. 'I have to be there to make sure the *munts* don't slaughter each other. Venter loved the Rhodesian Selous Scout slang.

Benedita flinched as if she had been slapped. 'I told you not to use that word here!'

'*Ag*,' Venter said airily, 'things might have changed, but those baboons haven't, *my ma hoor my*.'

So, Benedita thought, he isn't about making peace after all. How she had misjudged him. She felt this sharp taste of disappointment in her mouth; the piquant flavouring to the joke was that she would be left alone in a strange place, in a country still struggling to define itself. Honour, duty and single-mindedness she knew and agreed with, but this was ridiculous. And they hadn't even unpacked the bags. Was she so hidebound with rules that she would not even use female wiles to keep him in the straight and the narrow? Men wanted to play cops-and-robbers, inhale all that outdoor air, drink themselves to a standstill and support the government of the day. Fun. That entailed watching men butchering one another. It was expected of black men, they would do that, with greater sophistication, well into the next millennium. But, she told herself, white men had slowly joined the fellowship of the primitive.

'When I come back,' Venter said, 'we'll work towards that baby.'

Recalling Alina's warning, her heart sank. After their encounter, and when Benedita's mind was made up about South Africa, she had slept like a baby. Her female instincts told her that the present would be a good time to get pregnant, but she was not sure how Venter would react to a caramel-coloured baby. Probably throw a major wobbly. But, right now, his mind was on the mission to Upper Ngoza.

'We'll work on the baby,' he repeated. 'Very soon the gods will smile on us.'

With their false teeth, she wanted to add, but fighting was useless. 'When will you go?'

'Soon. They'll give me a sign.'

'Quite,' she said bitterly, 'like Noah. No more water, the fire next time.'

'Is that a curse?'

'No, love. It's my little mantra. Keeps me going when the world gets a little loopy.'

Venter went outside to pour himself another drink. From the distance, the cowbells tinkled and the insects chirped with renewed vigour. Benedita rinsed her hands and wiped them on her skirt. It was going to be a long, hot day. Normally she would have been at the shops, picking up the vegetables; now that they were here, she would have to grow her own. Although the soil was dark and fertile and showed great potential, there was the little problem of the drought. She thought lazily of her camera and whether she shouldn't go to the settlement and film the activity there. She knew, though, that what she needed was a pair of extra hands to help her transform this place into her little haven. But she checked the thought, sensing that a new equation was in place: Africans might not take kindly to being approached for casual labour, or any labour for that matter. The ground had shifted subtly from under the feet of white people. Knowing that she was as condemned in the minds of Africans as were white people, Benedita identified with their loss. Their sun had set. Without warning.

Without warning. This was how she could characterise her life with Jannie, her lovable bundle of contradictions, who was decisive, yet scared of the implications of his decisions. For example, the movement towards KwaZulu-Natal came while he had been investigating the possibility of settling in Mafeking. This was where he waxed lyrical about nature and had inculcated in her a love for border towns. He spoke longingly of the rolling mountain range separating South Africa and Botswana, the sisal which grew in stubborn abundance, and the albinic grass, the swathes of black land where the grassland had been set ablaze.

*   *   *

One afternoon they drive from Mafeking via Lichtenburg to Tarlton. The gnats commit suicide by dashing themselves against the windscreen. Benedita drives because Venter has had too much to drink over lunch. Although feeling the onset of a familiar migraine, Benedita enjoys the quiet moment behind the wheel. While Venter lies slumped and snoring on the seat, she takes pleasure from the throb of the engine, the snarl of the tyres against the asphalt, the sight of grassland spreading ahead.

As the sun sets, an orange orb against the leaden sky, she experiences a pang of nervousness. It will be dark soon. The workers in the maize fields climb onto the trailers of tractors. Sitting forlornly on fallow ground is a green insect-like harvester, its driver having called it a day. Black women field-hands hasten homewards; scarves covering their faces against husks. At dusk, oncoming traffic flashes a warning, at the most dangerous period for driving, when visibility is compromised in the battle between darkness and light.

It is quite dark when they reach Tarlton. The light has hardly died but the small town looks ready to crawl under the blankets. She takes the fork towards Krugersdorp and drives for thirty minutes before Venter stirs beside her. He asks her to pull up. She guides the car to a halt on the shoulder of the road and kills the engine.

'How long have I been asleep?' He wipes a trail of spittle from the corner of his mouth

'Long enough for you to start driving,' she says, stretching, groans. 'I'm whacked.'

He opens the door, letting in the sounds of the night. The overhead electric wires hum and crackle. In the dark, Benedita gets a whiff of the grass and freshly turned soil, growth, something which takes her to the stretches of meadow on the five-hour rail journey from London to Glasgow, to meet her mother. From where she stands, she can see a line where the land meets the sky. Giant trucks trundle past, causing their little car to shake. She gets out of the car and comes up to Venter, who is smoking quietly. Without word, he takes her in his arms, holds her close until she can feel the outline of his rib cage, his heartbeat.

'I love you very much,' he says, throwing the cigarette stub. 'Do you know that?'

She takes her time answering, looking at the cigarette stub arcing like a lazy tracer and disappearing in the grass. She imagines the field catching fire. She senses that Venter must also be scared. Do I have it in me to allay his fears, she asks herself. This, for her, is what love is, sharing the feeling of being vulnerable with a loved one.

The darkness claims them as they stand. More traffic whispers and thunders past, transporting people burdened by their own fears. There are many more black people owning cars now, German cars. This is their hour. She remembers visiting a friend at the Africa Centre in Covent Garden. Imruh was a film-maker with whom she shared most insights. He showed her books in the upstairs store while a disco rocked in the floor below. A jacket cover where an angry, bearded black face stared out at her entranced her. She read the unpunctuated poem by the African–American author. What was his name? Baraka. Amiri Baraka. The name itself rubbing it in.

> *the day will not save them*
> *and we own the night.*

The lines prophesy something savage and true.

'I love you, too, you drunken oaf.' She suddenly wishes that men would get out of their shelter and weep, let it all out. Once this happened, they would find redemption.

★   ★   ★

Now, Benedita went into the lounge, marvelling at the expanse of space. Whatever misgivings she had, this place could be transformed into a small paradise. Immediately, her eyes went to the wide windowsills where she would place her boxed plants. It was a good season for gardening. Her windows looked out on the ample acreage, her field, the trees and the hydrangea, which snaked over the wrought-iron gate. Her brother, Steve, for ever in search for enchantment, could easily take to this place. Where was he, now? Benedita still had his letter in her handbag, postmarked Barcelona, where he was having a royal time, probably with another lover. In the letter, he had been matter-of-fact about leaving Tim. You see, he wrote, Tim merely wanted to turn me into his personal Agony Uncle. Benedita had at first been shocked beyond words when she got to know of her brother's sexual inclination, worried that it would kill their mother who constantly complained that people were out to rub her face in it. Steve and Venter wouldn't see eye to eye. When Steve comes back, Benedita told herself, I'll invite him over. Give Venter something to think about. She was cheered up somewhat by this thought which smacked of subversion.

Five

Zodwa considered herself lucky that her dormitory at Elukhanyisweni Hall was on the fourth floor. Were it any closer to the ground, she most probably would have dived down to grab some luckless son-of-a-bitch by the scruff of his neck. Were it any higher, she would still have jumped, but for a terminal reason this time. So, the fourth floor suited her fine. Now, four stories below her window, a group of male students, whose rumpled yesterday's clothes and hoarse voices evidenced a marathon carousal, were bantering with women, wolf-whistling and laughing as some of the female students indicated their reluctance to indulge in fun and games.

Zodwa knew that the carnival scene would soon turn ugly, it being a truth held universally by most males that when a woman says No she actually means Yes. She was tired of the immaturity shown by her university colleagues. This sullied Fort Hare's reputation as a liberal institution, the alma mater of illustrious sons of African politics like Mandela, Tambo, Mugabe, Kaunda or even of that Kenyan dickhead Njonjo, who balked at getting on a plane until assured it was piloted by a white man. But the glorious legacy of the university did nothing to elevate male students. Even those doing legal studies seemed oblivious to the fact that sexual harassment was an indictable offence. But Zodwa's anger was specifically directed at her female associates – her sisters, in the idiom of that hour – who seemed to delight in this benign molestation. It was insulting. She could hear them now, chirping away like mynas, offering perfunctory protests to being groped while giggling like adolescents. Zodwa resisted an urge to stick her head out of her window and give them all a thorough tongue-lashing. She had a bad reputation as it was and had narrowly escaped being sent down for loosing a volley of expletives at a Law History professor.

Even now, she still bristled. The man really was a sanctimonious asshole, and she had endured three full years of his asinine bullshit. Still, she couldn't afford a suspension. In twenty-four hours she would formally graduate, pack her bags and take the first transport the hell out of Alice.

Zodwa donned her tracksuit and running-shoes and went down the stairs. As she progressed to the glass doors, faces came in the opposite direction. There was a polite exchange of greetings; this formality was tinged with excitement and sadness. Students knew that they were coming to the end of the term. For many, there was trepidation, since this rupture with their home from home would mean joining the real world that snarled outside the university precinct. Others, of course, who had been seconded to the institutions by their companies, were going back to fatter cheques, expense accounts and a sedentary life and the early clotting of the arteries.

Even if Zodwa were uncharitable towards the female students, she felt a grudging pride at the way they carried themselves. They were mostly trim, their bodies charged with the tropical sensuality of ripening fruit. A couple in short tennis skirts murmured secrets of their dreams. One of them laughed. Her teeth, flashing against the backdrop of strong red gums and a chocolate-brown skin, seemed whiter than her skirt. Zodwa would have liked to know the source of their merriment.

She walked on, admiring the flower arrangements; the discarded leaves of the wild agapanthus on the paved path resembled wood shavings. In the middle distance, down below, rose the whitewashed walls of the Christian Union building, the venue where parties and a pagan, fleshly worshipping crowned late Saturday's activities. Towards the east, a latticework of scaffolding appeared ghostly silent without the lecherous workmen whose task was to construct a new wing to the ever-growing administration block. On the road leading down to the stadium, Zodwa recalled the countless confrontations between students and armed authority, which had raged in this field of unkempt turf and rotting pavilion timber. Those days were past, thank God, but her rebellious spirit craved for an opportunity to throw a rock at a helmeted white face.

But still – her conflict with male students was undermined by her ease in the company of men. They were wild and infinitely infantile, but they could also be disarmingly honest. Their gratuitous fibbing was forever operating within an unswerving truth. While engaging, the men could be as unpredictable as tropical weather, evincing, unexpectedly, a great propensity for random violence. There was, for instance, talk that the boy who had been found dead on the steps of the administration building had been sodomised. While this appalled her, she did not know what to make of a man who found gratification in sexual contact with another man. She had seen transvestites, *ongqingili*, in Wentworth and Clairwood. Maybe she was just being naive. However, she was in no great hurry to find out why the beast in men could be unleashed against members of the same sex. She rebuked herself for the direction in which her ideas were heading, at the implicit acceptance of male violence against women.

There were other disturbing stories, which made her thank her stars she would be leaving the university. Strange men who were neither students nor workers were reported hanging around on campus. In fact, the assistant registrar noted that, in the morning, there was always traffic away from the campus; who were these people and where were they going? If people didn't take matters in hand, blood would flow.

She was still thinking of blood and eruptions when Khaya, one of her homeboys, came shuffling towards her, holding up his loose trousers with one hand while absently swinging a cane walking-stick with the free hand.

'How's the going, Zodwa?' Khaya asked.

'My friend,' Zodwa said, 'things are just fine. They'll be finer once I leave this place.'

'Any news from home?' Khaya looked her up and down and gave her a vacant smile. 'Hear there's trouble back there.'

'There'll always be trouble, Khaya.' She sniffed the air, catching a whiff of oranges. Outspan had come and launched a big promotion in the week, giving each house a few bags of oranges. At this rate, she supposed, many people were going to die of good health. Regarding Khaya walking beside her, like a faithful dog, she admitted to herself that she found comfort in his presence. With most members of the male breed, she was always on guard. Zodwa knew she had a reputation as a hard-case, but tougher women had been plied with liquor and 'test-matched' in the wooded area called Miami around the Tyume. A woman had contacted Aids after the gang rape. Zodwa could, however, relax with Khaya and get snippets of information as well. Contrary to popular belief, men were the worst gossips. 'What have you heard?'

Khaya drew on the sand with his stick. 'Oh,' he said, 'the usual stuff. Your old man is still herding the holy hordes, but your uncle would still like to be top dog.'

'Why are people so concerned with meaningless things?' Zodwa asked, more to herself than Khaya. 'What's there to be top dog about in Ngoza? The squatter camp? The road leading nowhere? The peasants trying to make a living? Papa's followers are just so pitiable I could scream.' She laughed. 'Reminds me of the Polisario Front and the Moroccans: people fighting over a barren desert.'

'It's their land, Zodwa. Their shrines and their memory.' Khaya regarded her. 'What would happen if they wanted you back there?'

'Not on your life. Me, I'm a city woman, give that smoky bundu to someone else.'

'No. Seriously.'

'I'm also serious.' Zodwa looked at him as if seeing him for the first time. 'Those people treated me very badly, Khaya. I'm in no hurry for a reunion with them.'

'They're still your people.'

'So what?'

'Just that.' Khaya sent a can skittering across into the bush. 'Your father did a great thing, getting all those people to return to Ngoza. You're your father's daughter. And, don't forget that you were not totally blameless yourself.'

'It's not my brief to drag people into the twentieth century,' Zodwa said tartly, stung by words of someone she might have despised. 'I have made my life out here. Tomorrow I'm graduating. Then I'm working in Jo'burg. Get a car, a house, a man, possibly not in that order, but organise my life anyhow.' She swallows. 'I have great admiration for what my father did, and I love him a lot – but I also love me a lot.'

★   ★   ★

On thinking about it, Zodwa could not say why she had adopted Johannesburg as the city where she would work. It had something to do with her father and his people's exile. When they were moved from Ngoza to be scattered in the different townships of KwaZulu-Natal, Baba Joshua regularly visited the families, exhorting them to keep the faith. Zodwa and her brother Jonah were born in Ngoza but grew up in KwaMashu Township, south of Durban. Like children of exiles, they quickly adapted to their new surroundings and turned their backs on their father's desire to return to ancestral lands. The parents' obsession with past territories where people had been free to run their lives aroused certain restlessness in the young minds. On her repeated visits to Johannesburg, where she saw the hustle and bustle and heard the many languages on the streets, Zodwa felt somewhat at home. The promise of anonymity appealed to her. Jonah had left South Africa for political reasons. But Zodwa suspected that it also had something to do with escaping the stultifying effects of Durban.

Durban also held memories of her mother's death. While her father worked at Dunlop on Sydney Road, Zodwa's mother worked as a domestic servant for a Jewish family on Ridge Road. Nomonde hated the work although she put a brave face on it, never showing her dissatisfaction with her lot. Her employers treated her with consideration, allowing her to go on leave on Christian holidays, giving her cast-offs and paying her more than other employers. But she was sickly and spent long periods in hospital. Her illness, Zodwa thought, had something to do with being removed from her original home. She couldn't stand the life in the township: the small houses and the lack of space, the squalor, the brashness and the violence. On her deathbed, she made Joshua promise that he wouldn't bury her in the township graveyard but would take her body to Ngoza. Joshua promised, but the reality of the situation defeated him. She was buried in a plot in KwaMashu, near her son who had been shot. For Zodwa, Durban had become an area of unfulfilled dreams.

When Joshua moved to Ngoza, when the Land Claims Court had ruled in favour of the community occupying their ancestral lands, Zodwa was happy. For her father. She was already in the Eastern Cape by this time, at Fort Hare. On her second December at Fort Hare, Zodwa decides to fly to Durban.

★   ★   ★

The city has changed. The airport bustles with a new clientele: blacks are no longer an insignificant minority here. Even the sweepers and attendants behind the food counters reflect a city coming to terms with itself. Delegations, mainly political leaders, mill about, their cases guarded by men whose suits were not tailored to accommodate shoulder holsters. Zodwa feels a pang of pity; Durban is hot and humid, and these people have to wear these suits. They cannot take off their jackets. In the first year after the release of Nelson Mandela, people are nervous; they can no longer trust that their hands alone can protect them.

The airport bus takes her to the centre of town. The streets are teeming with holidaymakers in revealing dress. Zodwa cannot bear to think about the amount of exposed flesh at the nearby beach. A cool wind wafts from the Indian Ocean. Even though she is suspicious of the feeling Durban evokes in her, she enjoys the respite from the brown earth and tawny bush of the Eastern Cape. Real trees front buildings here; it is as if there is a perennial struggle between concrete and timber. She smells the salt in the wind and she looks up at the clouds rolling across the sky.

Walking down Smith Street, now a one-way street, Zodwa encounters progress in motion. Black people now walk with a strut – a toe-to-heel bounce – their shoulders squared and heads held high. Even the poorest of the poor exhibit a shabby pretence to dignity. But then, there are those who stand on street intersections, bullying motorists with mendicant messages on cardboard placards. A man bumps into her. Zodwa halts and glares at him, expecting an apology, but instead he sneers, calling her by a rude name. She watches him loping off and disappearing inside a crush of bodies. Despite herself, Zodwa laughs, shaking her head, the nerve of that guy! She sobers up and mutters to herself: 'What has happened to us, that we treat one another with such callousness?' She's uncertain if her father has finally managed to instil a sense of community among his followers, all power to him really. South Africans, she concludes, are a terrible, terrible lot. This observation is validated by the way people drive, the foot on the accelerator and the hand on the horn, an aggression without bounds. And impatience. Cars give throaty revs as if attempting to induce traffic lights to change, then shoot forward, scattering pedestrians tardy enough to be crossing the street as the light changes.

Confusion reigns at the taxi rank on Lorne Street. There is a cacophony of sound as touts steer customers into the minibus taxis. Pickpockets slouch about in dust-coats and dirty trainers, their slender fingers twitching involuntarily at the presence of so many fat handbags. A pair of ageing twins in top hats and tails cavort to the *mbaqanga* beat from a *gumba-gumba* on a grass mat. The twins' stylised ecstasy causes people to stop and stare and little children to titter and point. Women hunched by loads that would intimidate a dray horse remonstrate with young men trying to squeeze them into overloaded taxis. Scrawled beneath one taxi-driver's name and address on the side panel of the minibus is the legend: FATTIES PAY DOUBLE. Zodwa thanks her ancestors for her trim figure.

After much shoving, she finds herself wedged in between the driver and a sweaty, middle-aged man who looks like an out-of-practice insurance salesman. The driver, in whose thick lips an evil-smelling panatella has assumed the dimensions of an insult, curses under his breath, promising mayhem if a rival taxi company continues poaching in his territory. He wears a cap with the letter 'X' on the front, the bill turned sideways. Something hard repeatedly chafes Zodwa's side. She gestures to him that she feels uncomfortable. 'Sorry, Miss,' he says, smilingly transferring his 9 mm pistol from the waistband to an ankle holster.

'Lessgo, driver,' a woman commands from the back, 'our chicken wings are crying to be eaten at home.' There is a general titter, followed by the driver's comment: 'I'll have a nibble of your chicken breasts, and legs, any old time you invite me, lady.'

'Ah, sharrup!' Then they are on their way.

*   *   *

This exchange takes Zodwa back to the days of her youth. Her mind latches onto a moment when she did Standard VI at the Isilimela Higher Primary School. The boy who came from nowhere and terrorised the whole school. What was his name? – Yes, Mbazo. What was peculiar was that he was never kidded over his name, seeing that his head resembled an axe. Mbazo's rage came from another source. During an English comprehension lesson, their teacher, Mr. Mpinga, snapped at Mbazo when the boy gave a wrong answer: 'Mbazo, you glow-worm, when are you going to get your head straight?' This was cruel, of course, but the kids laughed, and the word 'glow-worm' became analogous to dumbness. Ah, don't tell me about so-and-so, he's a glow-worm. It was like that until Mbazo put a stop to it.

★   ★   ★

After a week of sniggers, Mbazo arrived in class carrying a worn satchel. Clara who imagined herself the life of the school party, piped up: 'The glow-worm has a new bag —' doing a James Brown routine; and that was it. Snarling, 'Sharrup!' Mbazo vaulted over the desk and gave her a slap that sent her spinning to the floor. Zodwa and her friends had seen people being slapped before, but Mbazo's variant, called the 'take-five', was in a league of its own. It was sharp, hard and loud. So effective that Clara – who was a feisty enough girl – was quiet throughout the morning, another miracle since her incessant chatter could uncurl shavings in a Carpentry class. Sporting for a bloodying fight, Mbazo returned after lunch, now accompanied by a brace of known township *tsotsis* who arranged themselves in the back. Before the teacher arrived, Mbazo took out a tomahawk and brandished it. 'Listen you fools,' he said. 'If anyone of you as much as whispers the word "glow-worm", that person will be food for worms.' His tsotsi friends went further. They warned the class against saying any word that contained the letter 'w'. 'It's an insult to our friend.' To prove a point, they ganged up on boys with names like William, Walter or Welcome. Township school teachers, a breed well-known for self-preservation, acted as if nothing were amiss.

The educational and linguistic patterns of Isilimela Higher Primary changed from that day on. Students cut classes in droves, especially on days of English poetry recitals. The attempts by teachers to encourage proficiency in English, whereby kids had to speak English the whole day, crumbled. There was no problem of avoiding the letter 'w' in Zulu; in English it crept up on you unawares, with painful consequences. Those with copies of Shakespeare or Wordsworth prudently kept their books covered with brown paper. Other kids transferred to Thandukwazi or farther afield in 'K' Section, where Mbazo's reign of terror had no

93

jurisdiction. It took some delicate negotiations by a group of students for the letter 'w' to be reinstated. 'Glow-worm', however, remained embargoed until Mbazo left school for greener pastures in the criminal fraternity where his methods of persuasion were in demand.

Zodwa wonders what happened to her schoolmates? Many, she knows, got married to pot-bellied men who pumped them full of kids. Others became professionals. Many more entered the church and scaled greater heights of self-delusion. A good number went into exile, to return with tales of triumphs, travails and tears in foreign lands, sometimes accompanied by an exotic matrimonial acquisition, and children unfamiliar with African languages. Some of these are in government, one of them a minister.

*　　*　　*

One passenger is telling a story about witchcraft; Zodwa pricks up her ears because the story is set in Bergville, the birthplace of her uncle, Mbongwa. The man says that Bergville is famous for two things: dagga plantations and faction fights. This was where two fellows were charged with murder, and there were dozens of witnesses who were ready to testify against them. The brothers had one court-appointed lawyer, but it was clear that they wanted to conduct their own defence. The storyteller chuckles. 'What happened,' he says, 'really changed my thinking about the existence of other powers in our lives.'

'What happened?' another curious passenger asks. Even the driver, who has been muttering imprecations while singing a bawdy tune under his breath, stops to listen. Zodwa is thankful for this timely intervention.

'The accused stood in the dock,' the man continues, 'facing the magistrate. When asked to plead, they said, "Not guilty, *makhosi*" – and that was it. As soon as they had spoken, the magistrate looked uncomfortable, and there was suddenly this smell of fresh shit in the courtroom. The magistrate was seized by a hectic bout of diarrhoea, true's God. The case was adjourned.'

'*Unamanga?*' titters the lady who has chicken wings waiting for her at home. Not so much sceptical as egging the storyteller on. The driver construes this to be a put-down aimed at a brother who has a good story to tell.

'*Heyi wena*, Chicken Wings,' he booms, 'don't come here and start accusing my customers of lying …'

But Chicken Wings is not to be out-done. '*Thula, wena,*' she retorts. 'Just drive your *s'korokoro*, you black thing, you, that does not even have a driver's licence.'

'Whose car are you calling a *s'korokoro*, you washerwoman?' In a fleeting second, the driver's deep-brown skin tone is transformed into Sudanese ebony. His bloodshot eyes against this field of unrelenting black resemble live coals, the bill of the cap quivering like a beak of a giant predatory bird ready to strike.

'Hey, hey, hey,' Zodwa cuts in. 'What's all this? We're listening to the man telling a story and all of you are suddenly jumping up and down!'

'Tell them, *suster,*' someone pipes in from the back. Then, to the storyteller: 'Go on brother. What happened?'

'Well,' the man says, 'we thought this was a one-off. But no. Each time the magistrate faced the men, his stomach started running. They brought in a replacement from the factory where they manufacture these monsters, a Boer from Vryheid, as thick as a brick. Same thing happened. I mean, I was in that courtroom everyday for two weeks and they couldn't hold the trial. At the end the case sort of lapsed and these men are walking freely as we talk.'

'Maybe there was a virus in the region,' the first man suggests.

'Yeah,' the becalmed driver drawls. 'A virus which only attacked magistrates.'

'The moral of the story being,' puts in one joker, 'if you're in trouble, forget about lawyers – get yourself a trained shit stirrer.'

Zodwa looks out of the window, hearing the passengers' guffaws, suddenly distant from it all. As they drive on, the landscape undergoes a subtle transformation. Gone are the city buildings;

they are replaced by rondavels, which soon give way to decrepit structures, lean-tos that characterise a rural slum. The foliage has also changed dramatically from sparse scrub and thorn bushes into sturdy evergreens and swaying saplings. Here and there are glades on which people's rickety dwellings will in time change into shacks. The hills start building up some seventy metres from the side lane; they rise in green waves until they reach their full height as Mveli Mountains.

The shadows have lengthened by the time they reach Ngoza, the setting sun the colour of burnished copper. Looming suddenly before them is a collection of whitewashed buildings: an old hotel, a trading-store, a police station standing flush against a squat flat-roofed building, which houses a small clinic and a mortuary. Three or four dead cars line the street. A few passengers, among them Chicken Wings and the storyteller, alight and bid the others goodbye. Zodwa asks the driver the way to the new settlement. Eyeing her up and down, he informs her that it would be too far to walk. To the scowls of the remaining passengers who are headed farther afield – something that is quickly silenced by a scowl – he makes a detour to a side road, if it could be called that, which is grooved by wagon wheels and hooves. This degenerates into a tract of squidgy earth; wheels hit the flooded hollows and splash into the tall grass. Zodwa holds onto the sidebar of the minibus taxi, looking at the squatter camp flashing past, fast and slow like a search sequence in a video playback. Women carrying loads and men walking with their sticks cradled under their arms stare at the passing vehicle. Children wave and make funny faces, some shout with joy. God knows, Zodwa muses, what is so bloody cheering about a place like this?

When they start their ascent, they come upon another spread of a village slum, huts made of straw and twigs and hessian sacking. Little children stand watching, thumbs stuck in their mouths as they suck in the hunger that has bloated their bellies. An old woman walks behind a burdened donkey, a stick in her hand. The way she walks without turning her head even as she hears the minibus taxi pulling up behind, bespeaks a life of drudgery and a preoccupation with survival. It occurs to Zodwa that many of the starvelings could be her grandchildren. A troop of monkeys plays in the trees, swinging and catching branches, making strangely human faces.

'There it is,' says the driver, pointing. In the middle distance rises a tent village, the grey canvases seeming like so many bundles of clothing, alongside timber supports that look skeletal in the approaching dusk. Men that are like brown ants work; hammering, sawing and pushing wheelbarrows to and fro. The minibus taxi can't go any farther because the dirt track disappears abruptly as the wall of stones stands athwart the car's path.

'Okay, sweetie,' the driver says as Zodwa gets off. Then he regards her with something approximating genuine fondness, which, to her, was akin to being appraised by a penitent hyena. 'You don't know how glad I am that you was on my taxi today. Because I'm going to dream *lekker* tonight. You see, I share a dormitory in the hostel with a couple of red-eyed men. Were it not for you, I swear to God, I'd have gone to bed and dreamt of lions gobbling me up.'

'Why, thank you,' Zodwa says, walking away.

'No,' says the driver, '*I'm* thank you!'

For Zodwa, if there is one person who represents the absence of malice, a belief in the undying goodness in mankind, it would be her father. She finds him among the men, holding court, flitting from one group of workers to another, dispensing advice. From the patient exasperation on the younger men's faces, she knows that he is doing more than is required, that, in some instances, people hear him out just to humour him. But there is no doubting that the people hold him in high esteem. She remembers one of Kurosawa's films where a patriarch leads his community from adversity into prosperity but has to be banished when he reaches senility. An idea suggests itself to her: will this happen to Baba Joshua? For the first time since her arrival, she experiences a pang of anxiety.

But Joshua stills her fears, guides her round the settlement, introducing her to the men and women, the pioneers. Many remember her as a young girl, and they marvel at how she has grown. This is a moment of awkwardness. No one wishes to be reminded of their childhood days, which are invariably moments of nakedness, when they were vulnerable. It is in its own way a remarkable dilemma, because human beings always hanker for that memory when things took place and they were too young to reflect on them. Life, being an eternal process of putting pieces of the jigsaw puzzle on the board, is experienced through memory. Zodwa then hugs and takes in the smells of the people, remembering. It is a heady mix of joy and sorrow. Her uncle, Mbongwa, a burly, bullet-headed man given to premature balding, embraces her and calls her 'my sister's child'. She casts around in her mind for the reason why Mbongwa fills her with revulsion; surely the man aims at being pleasant – so, why did she feel uncomfortable around him?

At sunset, an hour before evening prayers, Joshua asks for Joachim to accompany them to the caves. 'This is something you have to see,' he says.

'You sound like a tourist guide, Baba,' Zodwa says, happy that she has found him.

'We have had our share of that breed,' he says. 'Tourists of all stripe, descending upon us as if we were animals in a zoo.'

'Next time they come,' Zodwa quips, 'do tell me, and I'll sort them out.'

'We might need you much sooner than next time.'

She lets this ride, pretending not to hear the gravity and longing in his voice. Joachim, who has been trailing behind, catches up with them. Zodwa is amused. In her father's eyes, she sees how highly he regards the younger man. Which means that this little walk-about has more to it than a mere excursion to the caves. She envisions what Jonah would have made of this little arrangement. He had been a city boy, as headstrong as the old man. She hasn't thought about her brother in a long, long time. This apprehension suddenly fills her with an urge to be alone with Joshua.

But she knows, also, that her father must have good reason to trust Joachim. The settlement is new and there looms a possibility of trouble. She feels instantly resentful, upstaged, understanding at the same time that this man represents her father's dead son. Her brother.

'Do you hear anything regarding Jonah's case?' Zodwa asks.

Joshua gives her a sidelong glance. 'Nothing. The people from the Movement came and told me that it was a mistake – and that I should understand. That was all.'

'It was difficult for me,' Zodwa says. 'There would be commemorations for people who died in the struggle. I would be present – and even receive pamphlets – in meetings where Jonah's killers were canonised as heroes of the struggle.'

'It doesn't make sense,' Joshua murmurs. 'But then again, it makes too much sense.' He lowers his voice even more. 'I went to Lusaka, paying my own way, to ask people there what had happened. I met some of the leaders. The impression I got was that they could not find it in themselves to admit that some of their more trusted people could have been enemy agents. I felt bad, especially because I had trusted them with the life of my only son – and they blasphemed it.'

★   ★   ★

A year after leaving Ngoza, when Jonah is fourteen, he leaves his father's temporary residence in KwaMashu township for Johannesburg. Exactly at this time, in June 1976, the whole of South Africa reverberates from the killing of schoolchildren in Soweto and elsewhere. Many of the young people leave for exile. Some stay in Botswana and Lesotho and are integrated into the political structures of the ANC. In 1977, Jonah travels from Gaborone, Botswana to Maputo in Mozambique and thence to Angola, where at fifteen he is among the youngest of MK recruits.

On the first night in Viana, the transit camp in Luanda, which is a stone's throw away from the Swapo refugee camp, Jonah sleeps on the floor, on a sponge mattress. A senior comrade occupies the bed. It is very late, and he is gripped by anxiety to sleep peacefully. Jonah wakes up after a dream and looks under the bed to find grenades, small pineapples, and an AK47 assault rifle fitted with a magazine to which is lashed another curved clip, the 7.62-mm cartridges shining in the gloom. It is the first time he has been so close to weapons. When he eventually falls asleep, he dreams that the grenades are rolling off towards him and he's warding them away. In the morning, his arms are sore, as if he spent the entire night wrestling with a phantom.

It is early evening, a week later, when Jonah and forty other recruits find themselves on the back of the Graz trucks, where they sit watching their new home coming alive, the knots of barefoot peasants walking, the roundabouts where Fapla soldiers demand the *carta transito*. Inability to produce papers during the curfew could have dire consequences. Someone points out the hospital, residences and factories. On another roundabout, past the square, they see in a fenced-off area the South African tank captured in 1975, standing as monument to apartheid aggression. The traffic consists mainly of military vehicles, which drive on the right side of the road and seem in a great hurry. They are now on the bridge of the northbound highway, and Jonah has a crazy notion that, at this speed, they're likely to careen across the railings and plunge into the gaping darkness below. They drive for another two hours, now in the hinterland, the bushes girding the dirt track looming dark, before they reach a checkpoint manned by the elite Red Berets. After a rapid-fire exchange in Portuguese with the drivers, the Red Berets wave them through, into Malange. After forty-five minutes of wrenching bouncing up and down in the vehicle, they reach the gates of Hoji ya Henda, a camp named after a hero of the Angolan revolution.

Above the roar of the engines as they enter the gates, Jonah hears a hum which seems to come from millions of bees. The singing. It is like something he has never heard before, something which blasts him with its power and quivers in that corner of the heart where the deepest secrets are stored. It comes from the square, in the centre of the camp beneath lights that attract moths and mosquitoes. Two detachments of men and women sing in unison, their voices as clear as a trumpet on the river bank. Jonah looks down at a bearded, wiry man who leads the singing, his free arm punching the air while the other cradles his assault rifle. The song stretches into the dark.

> *Sobashiy'abazal'ekhaya*
> *Saphuma sangena kwamany'amazwe,*

They sing, and something happens in Jonah. He hears in the singing all the things which have waited to be expressed but were snuffed out in the villages, towns and cities of his native land. What he hears has been suggested in snatches in the hymns of the holy celebrants or in the curses of the hard-eyed women in the dark corners, complaining about being short-changed by their clients. This singing has been there all along in the dirges sung at funerals – where the preacher intercedes for the spirit of the departed; it is there in the syncopated rhythms of women rejoicing at the entry of a new life into this world. Jonah has heard it rasping in the whisky-scarred voice of the derelict lying in the gutter with stab wounds, still asking for more liquor. It was there in his mother's tone when she made love to his father and in the old man's groans when he failed her. It has been in the eyes of children witnessing the humiliation of their heroes. It has been in the young men dreaming dreams, declaring with steel in their hearts that the country would change and the evildoers would get their come-uppance, and the people would remember everything and forgive nothing. It is as if Jonah has waited all his life to hear these voices raised, not in despair but in an affirmation that is as enduring as fire.

*   *   *

The first four months of training are the hardest. Waking up at dawn, Jonah dons his tracksuit and trainers and falls into step with other trainees – called *kursants* – to the exercise yard, which is an old colonial tennis court. It being dark, the instructors have a hard time ensuring that, during press-ups, people's bellies do get off the ground. With the first light above the mountains, the trainees wash and put on their khaki combat uniforms. A timetable is tacked to the bulletin board, detailing the training schedule of the day. The men and women read and groan whenever there are two lots of *fisico*. Tough instructors who never seem to tire make physical training all the more strenuous. Running ahead, they execute the toyi-toyi dance favoured in the ZAPU campaigns in Zimbabwe.

'You run, my friend,' an instructor yells, 'and bark like a dog!' And the trainees bark, exhorting their lungs to see them through this stretch of terrain, the mind registering nothing, the body screaming for deliverance. The trainees curse and will their muscles on, knowing that any show of weakness is surrender, selling out. Sometimes an instructor deviates from the usual track and leads them into a bush of tangled vines, lianas and undergrowth, urging them on, screaming: 'Cover!' Just when they are flat on their bellies, copping a rest, 'Up and run!' until the trainees cursed God and his angels and the fucking Boers who've made this torment inevitable. They curse the people of South Africa for having left this apartheid fuck-up for so long. They curse their mothers and fathers and sisters and brothers, their lovers probably living it up in some smoky shebeen, or writhing in the arms of strangers. During these sessions Jonah paraphrases the training manual. Memory can screw you up. Everything about this place, he concludes, is aimed at fucking up your mind. Shit. There are wasps whose stings carry an electrical charge. There are red ants. Once, a snake slithers into a hole. All these conspire to turn you as neurotic as a two-headed hamster.

But all these thoughts disappear when the platoon dances its way back to base. There is a spring in their step as they pass the familiar landmarks that give them an idea of the distance covered. The Angolan villagers, a species that can no longer be surprised, stare; now and then a pot-bellied toddler chewing a stick of sugar-cane waves, and someone grins. The mothers shoo their charges indoors. The goats and chickens, unused to tremors caused by the soldiers' hard tramping, scatter. And the trainees dance and sing, weapons at the ready, itching to engage the enemy.

There is a law, however, definitely respected throughout the history of conflict, that the enemy strikes when least expected. The truth that will stand the scrutiny of the sun confirms that the enemy comes in many guises. It comes to some cloaked in the smothering cloth of loneliness, where men thrash and groan at night, sometimes to wake up in the morning with the blankets stiffened by their own seed. It comes to many more via cerebral malaria, where people writhe like worms on a hot plate, their bodies burning and their minds having taken a long journey to oblivion. For others, the bug of madness overtakes them and they ramble on and on, with staring eyes.

The training is hard here. Belonging to a platoon called Mbelebele, famous for composing new revolutionary songs, Jonah knows he has to acquit himself well here, if he is to be given a mission to go back home and fight. He masters topography, firearms, *fisico* and tactics, leading the camp administrators to promote him into the special platoon leaving for the German Democratic Republic. There, he studies military-combat-work (MCW), more firearms, engineering and returns to Luanda two years later a fully-fledged fighting machine. Then he is sent to Cacuso, to fight Unita bandits. Much later, the Chinaman picks him – MK jargon for a mission back home – where he finds himself in Maputo. He is hardly a week there when he is transferred to Lesotho. This is when his troubles start. The small aircraft develops a problem in South African airspace and has to land in Bloemfontein, where South African security officials await Jonah with open arms. For two months he is in their cells, being tortured and interrogated. The ANC invokes international law and Jonah is released. Statutorily a South African citizen, he is allowed back into the community. There follow unsubstantiated rumours that he broke under interrogation and betrayed the Movement. Although aware that he was under a cloud of suspicion, as a political animal, he enlists in the United Democratic Front in 1985, and helps set up community defence structures. Leading a normal life for a few years, he becomes a victim of intrigue in Swaziland, involving Rosie, his erstwhile commander. Comrades who had been in his platoon in Cacuso shoot Jonah dead in early 1990.

★   ★   ★

Zodwa despairs for her father, knowing that he is left with nothing but his memories. She watches him turning his head and grabbing his nose between thumb and forefinger and blowing snot onto the stony ground. Then he wipes his fingers on the seams of his overalls. Zodwa remembers him as a fastidious man, therefore this unclean habit disgusts her, deepening her sorrow.

As they labour up the hill, Joachim rummages in his rucksack, unstops a gourd and hands it to her. Refusing to imagine what is inside, she proceeds to drink. Water has a slightly brackish taste, but it cools her, letting her understand the depth of her thirst. 'Thank you,' she says. Joachim wordlessly returns the gourd into the rucksack. Up the narrow sandy path they meet a man leading a mule cart laden with wood. He greets them, stops to let them pass. As he walks past with his animal, Zodwa catches a whiff of a feral odour, leading her to suspect a possible shortage of water in Ngoza.

'What happened to Nozizwe?' she asks her father. The old medicine woman had been a regular visitor at her father's house in KwaMashu, and Zodwa had taken a liking to her. There was something infinitely honest and engaging about Nozizwe.

'She's probably up in the mountains, gathering her herbs,' Joshua answers.

'Is she still okay?'

'That woman is like an oak tree. She'll outlive us all.'

'And uncle Mbongwa – what's his story?'

'Mbongwa is still part of us,' Joshua says. 'At the same time, you can say that he has his eyes on the future. And the future in this country means a lot of money. So, he's always carrying on about how we can modernise the settlement. He has dreams of turning it into a tourists' paradise.' He pauses and concentrates his gaze on a grasshopper labouring up a stalk. 'I've seen enough of paradise to know that's not what we want for this place.'

They arrive at last before a clump of dying thorn bushes, which front a cluster of boulders. Joachim steps forward and dislodges one of the stones; the rest collapse with a crash onto either side, leaving open a low and narrow entrance into the cave. When Joachim takes a torch out of his bag, Zodwa remembers a childhood photo-story hero, Chunky Charlie, whose khaki overcoat hid all sorts of contraptions to confound the villains. She suppresses an urge to ask him what else is in his bag of tricks. Crouching behind her father, she follows Joachim who, using the fickle light for Zodwa and Joshua's benefit, walks inside the cave with a practised familiarity.

She starts when bats fly forth from their roosting and buzz round their heads. Following the torch-light in the near absolute darkness, she feels the smoothness of the floor beneath her feet; when the beam shines, it gleams, burnished stone tended by caring hands. She imagines villagers hunched over the floor, polishing, never being distracted by newspapers and rumours of peace, finding a simple pleasure in thankless tasks. Zodwa, her eyes now accustomed to the darkness, makes out configurations, shapes of things that rest on a stone table. She sees mountains of shields, spears, kaross wraps, earthenware and gourds – all showing age. These artefacts are lashed together into bundles by leather ropes. The cavern curves, stone glistening with condensation, the air close.

'When the police removed us,' Joshua says, 'these are the things we salvaged. Each item represents a family.' He sighs. 'We wanted to be able to remember something of ourselves that was left behind.' Zodwa senses rather than sees him shaking his head.

'Many people died in the long exile. We have a duty to bring their bones back here.'

Suddenly, her father is no mere champion of people returning to their ancestral lands; he is also their spiritual leader. The responsibility on him must be overpowering. How do you keep together a people once scattered through the four winds of the land? How do you create favourable conditions for families that have imbibed other influences, some inimical to the vision of Joshua and the Elders. What is their vision?

She gets to hear Mbongwa's vision later that evening. He is a big man with a generous paunch. Looking at his face, Zodwa marvels how closely he resembles Nomonde, whom she wishes were alive. An epitome of avuncular congeniality, Mbongwa organises some beers from a shebeen in the squatter camp; then he breaks out with a dusty bottle of Chivas Regal. As he pours the drinks, conspiratorially since his brother-in-law frowns on worldly indulgence, he confides in Zodwa that town developers see great potential in turning part of the land into a golf course. Zodwa knows that when people confide in you, they make you an accomplice in some dubious scheme. Non-committal, she hears him out, enjoying the whisky.

Alone in quarters provided for visitors, she senses that she is being sucked into something that is beyond her. Remembering that she just wants to become a lawyer, Zodwa determines to return to campus. The collective vision of the people who have returned is the least of her worries because, she knows, understanding implies taking some measure of responsibility. Her spirit on campus and the cities of the country, as well as the route to her chosen career, cannot be nurtured in this land of symbols and skins and the stammering memory of stones.

★　　★　　★

A dog barking around the administration block interrupted her reverie. She caught up with a group heading into town. Purchases for graduation party had to be made, and the Victoria Hotel sometimes ran out of liquor stocks. To offset a disaster, which would mean a drive to King, a woman had to be early. Or make do with sweet wines that the locals drank in large quantities. Zodwa was partial to scotch, no imitations.

'Ready for the big day, hey, Princess?' one of the male students quipped.

'Piss off,' Zodwa said. She hated being called 'Princess'. The name had stuck after reports appeared in the newspapers about her father's return to Ngoza. She didn't need any of the bullshit. She just wanted to party and forget – and get out of Fort Hare.

Six

Much earlier, before the release of Nelson Mandela from twenty-seven years' imprisonment, the more desirable section of Ngoza had been occupied by whites and, in a few instances, by the few black families who had the means. Since this section was nearest town, it had been called Central, one of the leafy suburbs insulated from the unrest and violence wracking the outlying parts of Ngoza. But much later, white people, for whom the rumours of a drastic and devastating change were becoming unbearable, started streaming out. Estate agencies, which were mostly located out of town, recorded major losses because there were few takers willing to pay hundreds of rands for dwellings where murder and mayhem reigned supreme. The great trek took the previous residents out of Gehenna to the more sedate Eden of Durban where the only black people they saw were gardeners and maids in their employ.

For some black and homeless people, an interchangeable condition, this was a jackpot. They moved in, tentatively, some burdened by an undefined notion in their heads that they were participating in a betrayal of sorts. Younger members of families became disgruntled because, even if the shacks were squalid and dangerous, they still offered the kind of diversions not found in suburbia. Most families kept their new residencies quiet, expecting the knock of policemen and removal trucks. But not so with Johnny M. Not content with relocating into a plush suburb, he also put his own stamp on the split-level, pleasant, four-bedroom residence. The formerly whitewashed facade was painted flamingo, an outlandish pastel colour which, impregnated with a magnesium-based chemical, became luminous at night. The swimming-pool at the back was generously supplied with lamps, which gave the weekend parties a surreal effect, where the revellers and swimmers glowed like neon lights in motion. The stereo system inside the house was hooked to giant speakers, so that when the music played, everyone in Ngoza had to know that Johnny M was having a party. The people then started calling him Gatsby, after F Scott Fitzgerald's sybaritic hero. Possibly reinventing himself to complete the effect, Johnny M took to gracing his parties resplendent in bleached calico suits, spats and a matching snap-brim Fedora with a black headband.

But this Friday afternoon, Johnny M was not in a party mood; in fact, he was downright angry. And when he was angry, he didn't just brood about it – someone had to pay. Since he was not the kind of man to dirty his hands, he cast around in his head for the right man to administer a swift but meaningful corrective measure on those who had crossed him. These were legion. The residents of the Two Rivers squatter camp had defaulted on their monthly levies for three months running now, their excuse being that they had no money. Well, there was no money everywhere, so what else was new? A person just had to find the cash or relocate elsewhere, that was about the size of it.

He pulled down the shutters fronting his trading-store and put up a sign reading, CLOSED FOR LUNCH. COME BACK AFTER TWO. Since some drunk had tried to burgle the store in the small hours of one morning, Johnny M had appended 'P.M.' with a felt-tipped pen. Just so no hobo misread the sign. Right now, he would welcome someone trying to break into his store; he would break their hipbone for them, such was his anger.

He got into his Datsun panel van, shielded his eyes from the sun and started off. He wished he were cruising in his other car, a souped-up burgundy Chevrolet Impala with a V-8 engine. But it would wreck his baby's chassis, since the roads were in an appalling state. His anger now directed itself to another target,

Mac Maharaj, the minister of transport. Even though he dismissed the ministers of government as unimaginative jerks, he had hoped that Maharaj would move mountains and ensure that the roads were repaired and tarred. Maharaj or Jeff Radebe, his homeboy, who had also seen the inside of a prison. But then, he thought philosophically, you do get these disappointments in life, don't you? Just like the people who were supposed to pay the levies. What did they take him for? A *moegoe* – a jerk, that's what they thought he was. An image of a defaulter flashed across his mind, the man bowing before him in a servile fashion, crushing a felt hat in his calloused hands, saying, 'Ah, Mr Johnny M, I've just had a bad month … couldn't sell any crops …' Well, he was also having a bad month. As for crops, fuck that. This time, he would crack some skulls, no more Mister Nice Guy. His calabash of milk of human kindness was empty. He was Johnny Mbazo, the axe-man. He owed no one, well, maybe a little something was due to Grey, a sweetener; that he could fix that up, no problem. The only man he could say he was beholden to was Shakespeare, the bard who had seen him through the long prison years.

★   ★   ★

Johnny is seventeen years old, freshly arrived from the Magaliesberg *stoutskool*, a reformatory that was as close to prison as anything. Some of the friends he had at Isilimela Primary give him a wide berth because he now has a reputation as a bad boy. He still shoots dice and uses the money to better his appearance. His parents warn him to keep in the straight and narrow, or he'll wind up in a real prison or at the back of a black limousine.

Much as he knows that the endings prophesied by his parents are real, the streets have their own imperious allure. For one, no one wants to tangle with him because, it is known that reform schools teach inmates a familiarity with knives. Moreover, to be feared gives him great pleasure. Knowing that a knife could prove useless against hordes, Johnny saves up for a gun. When an itinerant plumber steals his hoard that he keeps in a cistern, no less, he takes the advice of one of the street fellows and joins a karate club.

He jogs each morning along Ntombela Road, fascinated by the smell of dew on the leaves, the crunch of gravel under his trainers. The KwaMashu sky is grey, except during summer when you cannot see the sky for the rain. But still he runs, exerting himself, feeling his calf muscles bunching up from the strain. During working hours, he visits the cinemas of Shah Jehan and Raj, where he watches the picaresque adventures on celluloid, and dreams. In the evenings, he again jogs to the dojo in 'D' Section, which is run by two no-nonsense second-dan black-belt instructors, Lameck and Themba.

Each time he is in the gym, the streets and the dagga and the knives and the brown, voluptuous thighs of street sirens are banished. Young men and women, kitted out in white canvas suits, the *gia*, and belts denoting their ranks, go through their *kata* sequences, rhythmical and disciplined. There is no sound save for the knuckles smashing against the *makiwara*, or the percussive grunts of combatants parrying, striking or leaping – our people could fly! – into the air like winged dancers. Looking at all this grace, smelling the sweat, discovering the confidence, savage charm and disciplined power, Johnny cannot help but wonder why the authorities hadn't bothered to set up gyms in the reformatories.

As months go past, he comes to terms with his environment. The garbage cans overflowing onto the pavements become reminders of things that need cleaning up in the township. Where the women on the streets had caused him sleepless, thrashing nights, they now become a breed which can be channelled into meaningful action. Even his parents, who, while mortified by his former hellish ways, are mystified at this spectacle where their son seems like a recent convert into Jehovah's Witnesses.

It is the Black Witnesses, however, a street gang which hangs out at the shopping centre at 'F' Section which claims him. It all happens in one day, a Monday afternoon as he walks Mumsie, his girlfriend, home from school. Johnny has been aware of the knot of young men seated atop a wall, legs dangling while their sneakers beat a pattern against the graffiti-scrawled wall, but their presence has never become a source of his disquiet.

'*Ek sé, wena s'febe,*' one of them calls. '*Zingila hier.*' It is Vusi, whose liver-like lips can hurl the most hurtful insult, calling Mumsie a bitch, ordering her to come over.

Discipline, Johnny tells himself; then we'll be out of range of these louts. He tightens his fingers around Mumsie's little hand. He feels that she is shaking. He is also shaking, but for different reasons. They walk on, quickening their step. As they progress, diverting from the main road onto a paved path, past dogs barking behind fences and chickens squawking in their fenced-in runs, Johnny hears the footfalls of the gang on the gravel, their breath coming out in short, expectant pants. He knows that he should run, get out of their sector; but the idea of flight is unthinkable. Fleeing is one way of ensuring thorough excommunication from the royal fellowship of the township.

When he turns, he sees that behind the four young men, knots of people are running, hoping to see some action. A fight holds some fascination for lots of people in townships; KwaMashu is no exception. Already some snot-nosed urchins are yelling, '*Pera! Pera!*' – slang borrowed from the Indians for 'fight'.

Johnny hands Mumsie his bag. 'Just keep behind me,' he tells her. 'And when I say run, you'd better do just that.'

Mumsie nods. 'Okay.'

More than twenty years later, she still tells the story in hushed tones, how Johnny whirls and whirls, the wind stilled as if in expectation, leather colliding with bone as Johnny executes his awesome kicks. The fists going *thwack!* against flesh. Vusi's lips split by hardened knuckles. The other men picking themselves off the dust and running, scattering into the throng, their knives abandoned. It is over in an instant, and Johnny hasn't even raised a sweat. A paunchy man in a Trevira suit of electrical colours, tan brogues and a wide-brimmed hat, known to all as Big Papa Dee, steps out of his Ford Biscayne and approaches Johnny, who still looks stunned. Ushering Johnny and Mumsie into his car, he drives them to 'E' section where they drop Mumsie.

'I'll see you later,' Johnny says.

And that is the last time she sees him. Later he runs errands for Big Papa Dee, delivering packages and collecting money from customers. He is given his own car, a white Valiant, which he drives with his right elbow resting on the window frame, style in motion. The crooks and normal citizens of KwaMashu know that, when the Valiant stops in front of your yard, Big Papa Dee's boy has come to collect.

As happens all the time, Johnny's popularity in the underworld soars in direct proportion with his disgruntlement at being someone's boy. He imagines that he can run these operations without Big Papa Dee. Who was he, anyway? Just an old, over-the-hill gangster with bunions. Johnny starts cutting some of the dagga, finding his own customers and pocketing the change. That goes on for a while until he sells to a customer who works for the police. In no time he is again standing before a magistrate – and this time it is no longer reform school but real prison for big men.

Point Prison is known throughout as one of the harshest correctional facilities in the country. Convicts come in for petty offences, get burnt in the prison crucible and end up doing nine-to-fifteen, or, in some not-so-rare cases, life imprisonment. Johnny meets members of the Big Fives, whose speciality is assault, and whose store of strategies for disabling opponents is legendary. Then there are the Twenty-sixes, smugglers, poisoners and procurers of *abafana* – young male inmates who were routinely sodomised. Their rivals are the Twenty-sevens, specialists in robbery and rape. The major obsession of Twenty-eights, convicted murderers doing terms from fifteen to life, is escaping from prison.

Johnny Mbazo fights, knowing that, if he succumbs, he is done for. But the odds are against him, the desperation of the men greater than his resolve to maintain his dignity. A combined assault of the Twenty-sixes and -sevens leaves him weakened and bloody, his mouth and anus bruised in a gang rape. 'You're now our woman,' they inform him, 'and you'd better not forget that.'

While Johnny is spitting out blood and semen, feeling the fabric of his trousers glued to his buttocks, Peter, one of the rapists, gives him soap and perfume, and the *Collected Works of William Shakespeare*. 'I want my cunts to remain cultured,' he says. To keep his mind off the humiliating touches of the men, Johnny immerses himself in the fantasy world of kings and heraldry, heroism and ancient treachery. In Macbeth's world he sees a little of himself, how things could have turned out differently if he had played it straight with Big Papa Dee, whom he is now suspecting of having set him up in the first place. When he is released three years later, by now having found Peter's touch as familiar as a lover's, he knows all the *Works* by heart. Much as he owes Peter something for the education, he knows, too, that if he sees that man, he will kill him, slowly, agonisingly, with joy. If I catch him once upon the hip, I will feed fat the ancient grudge I bear him. He saw himself stuffing a stick of dynamite up Peter's wide arse, lighting the fuse …

★   ★   ★

Enlivened by imaginings of revenge, Johnny M regarded the grass growing on either side of the road, the people walking, a squad of workers out on lunch, some hurrying back to the plywood factory some few kilometres beyond the perimeter of the Two Rivers squatter camp. There were many that loitered, the unemployed. His enterprising mind was already conjuring up ways of using these men when he heard the news item on the car radio. David Horwitz, a constitutional law expert, had successfully fought for the incorporation of Two Rivers and Dameni into Ngoza. Which meant that a new local authority would soon be in place to improve the situation in Ngoza.

Well, Johnny M thought, that does it. Where the fuck was Grey when all this was being hatched? And who was this Horwitz? Probably another Jewboy out to make money on the backs of blacks. God, he hated them, the white people. They thought they had suffered, but wait until he got his hands on them. They are as sick that surfeit with too much, as they that starve for nothing. This was just another trick to take bread out of his mouth, by the Jews and holy Jeremiahs in the settlement. He'd have to do something about that too.

The beauty of the land assuaged his anger. In this section of Central, the creaky buildings were covered with creepers, ivy perhaps, and were fronted by hedges of bougainvillaea and wild flowers whose hues dazzled the eyes and brought about yearnings for unknown things. Some farmers had earlier on planted kikuyu grass, meaning to fence off hundreds of hectares for a game park. The project had been abandoned when the few game brought in from Hluhluwe were killed off by dogs and poachers. But the grass remained, growing stubbornly white against the dappled dark-green of the gum trees and wattle and weeping willows at the edge of the stream. Above the fences and hedges, he could see the tops of palm trees which the Jews cut for their annual holiday Sukkot; here, in this afternoon stillness, the crackle of electrical wires was the loudest sound. A flock of birds soared soundlessly into the sky, unconcerned with terrestrial contention over land among men.

He recalled how he missed the sight of greenery at the Point prison, where the attributes of the terrain were exaggerated in his imagination. Now that all was before him, he rejoiced in the knowledge that he had the power to own land. He had in harness many people who would ensure that his dream came true. In his mind's eye, Johnny M saw bulldozers levelling off shacks and abandoned houses, making room for the cattle ranch or the casinos of his dreams. A rabbit hopping across the road took him back to the urgent matters at hand.

Reaching the circle where three roads converged, he took the left fork and headed towards the Two Rivers squatter camp. By now there was no tar, the road had degenerated into a dirt track. He saw a team of oxen hitched to a wagon, the hatted driver, Reuben the Collector, absently lashing at the beasts with a switch, his attitude so distracted he could have been warding off irksome insects. Reuben also owned a mule-drawn cart for wood and odds-and-ends. Johnny M determined to own that too, the driver and his beasts. It stood to reason that he was destined for greatness, and the smallholders and their property would finally get a better deal by getting into his employ. It was on this principle that the Barnatos and the Oppenheimers had scaled the dizzy heights of greatness. It had nothing to do with altruism or becoming weak-kneed at the plight of the common man.

They passed an agglomeration of shacks, lean-tos and adobe houses whose rusted zinc roofs were held down by boulders and drying pumpkins. Here and there a rondavel hut, the thatch bringing to mind the elaborate braided patterns on the heads of city women, backed a shack. Farther up, sat a two-storied shack that some proud owner had finished with hoarding from a Marlboro cigarette advertisement. Should charge him double, Johnny M thought, amused. The world was still full of gentle surprises.

He turned into an even narrower path where rainwater had cut furrows on the ground, like wrinkles on an old woman's face. A knot of people lined up behind a solitary communal tap, their vessels clanking as they pushed and shoved to the front. To the left stood the shack owned by the Two Rivers Women's Collective; they had schemes to appropriate some land which they would cultivate. Already, there were tables in the front where seeds were drying in the sun. Potted seedlings with colourful identifying sachets stood on the ground, the prices written on cardboard tags with a ball-point pen. The women gave him stony stares. These were going to be a headache, Johnny M knew. Once women organised themselves into some collec-

116

tive, there would be no end to their demands. He put this information in the vault at the back of his mind.

Queen Nerissa's shebeen was where he found the men. Fakude was holding court on some obscure philosophical point, thoroughly losing his audience, which consisted of Nerissa, Jomo and Victor. 'White people', he was saying in between sips from a tall glass, 'will never understand the African concept of time.'

'That's right,' Nerissa supplied. 'Because Africans might have rhythm, but they sure don't have the sense of time.'

'That's where you're wrong,' Fakude persisted. 'You see – I read this somewhere. When you come across Africans lying under a tree, what's the first thing white people think? That they are lazy – right?'

Victor could not bear this any longer. 'And they'd be correct in thinking like that.'

'That's where you're wrong. When people are sitting under a shade, or *blomming*, as some of you might say, they're waiting for time for things to happen.'

'Waiting for time?' Jomo screamed. 'Waiting for which fucking time, Fakude?'

'Don't get your jaws into an uproar,' Fakude said smoothly. 'It just means that people are waiting for things to happen before they get into action.'

'That's about the craziest thing I've ever heard,' Victor said. 'Nerissa, are you sure it's just beer or has he been smoking that funny tobacco from Jamaica again?'

'Look,' Fakude pressed on, 'if you check out the Batswana …' He stopped, remembering. 'Boy, that's a hard place to have someone owe you, Botswana. You travel miles under the sun to collect, and you get into this village and you ask where's So-and-so, and this sleepy oke says he's not here. When did he set out? *Maloba*. Which is really helpful since it means anything from a couple of minutes ago to back to the fucking Anglo-Boer War. When's he due back? *Gantele*. Indefinite future. Don't let no one from Botswana owe you, man. It'll just break your heart and kill your faith in human nature.'

'Can't imagine you in Botswana,' Jomo said. 'What were you doing there?'

'Cars. We were taking hot cars there, just after the black-power kids left the country in 1976.' Fakude paused. 'That was boom time, man. And we were cool about it, never got into this trigger-happy hijack shit that kids are pulling today. We just took cars that were parked. Or raided car factories, and it was great. That is, until some greedy cretins started selling hot Jaguars to the Batswana. Imagine an E-type zooming up the dusty trail from Mochudi to Molepolole. Some thieves have no imagination. No timing.'

'How did they pay you – in cattle?'

'No. Real money, the pula. The only headache was changing that into rands. We were better, though. Do you know that the Zambian promoters paid Osibisa in bags of dagga?'

'Now I know,' Jomo said, 'why you have to be stoned to hear Music for Gong-Gong.'

'And while we're on the subject of payment,' Johnny M said, emerging from the corner, 'what are you guys doing here, getting pissed when there's work to be done?' He turned to Nerissa. 'What did I tell you about supplying them with booze during working hours?'

Nerissa's nostrils flared. 'Look, Johnny, I'm running a business here. These men might be working for you, but to me, they're customers. They're over twenty-one, and they have thirty-two teeth in their heads, and they can vote. If they're not supposed to drink, then that's their decision, not mine.'

'Are you finished?'

'Yes. But it's you who told me that a shebeen is the corner-stone of South African economic prosperity.' She rolled her huge eyes as if saying, Can you believe this shit?

'Are you finished, Nerissa?' Johnny M's tone was soft; he could have been addressing the annual convocation of the Housewives League.

Fakude, his rational mind telling him that the boss was angry but alcohol speaking in tongues, stepped forward and placed a placatory hand on Johnny M's arm. 'Cool it, Boss,' he said. Without seeming to move, Johnny M's foot unhesitatingly lashed out once and caught Fakude on the crotch. He gave a belch, doubled up and tottered, upsetting the drinks table, going down with the table-cloth in his hands. Then he started retching, gouts of stale beer mixed with remains of the morning's breakfast and bile spreading on the carpet. Jomo, Nerissa and Victor sprang back to avoid the vomit splashing on their shoes.

'*Sies!*' screamed Nerissa. 'What you do a thing like that for? Look at my carpet. It's ruined.'

'You're looking at the state of your future face,' Johnny M threatened, 'if you don't shut that bitch mouth of yours and do what I pay you for.' He wanted to round off this outburst with something smart, cutting, maybe a fitting quotation from Shakespeare, but inspiration and anger were incompatible. He turned to Victor and Jomo. 'Get that piece of garbage into the van and let's go. You,' he said to Nerissa, 'I'll see you later tonight.'

Nerissa cursed under her breath as the men walked out of the door. She watched them through the window, half-dragging Fakude and installing him in the back of the bakkie. Already a group of curious onlookers were assembled, pointing. What got her goat was that her place was increasingly getting a bad name. Anyway, she sighed, a woman's got to do what a woman's got to do. The van moved off, splashing some of the rancid water on the onlookers. Serves them right, Nerissa thought as she turned away from the window.

She set about mopping the floor, scowling at the food remnants. Men, she thought bitterly, they're so inelegant. No timing, no style, puking all over her fine carpet. But she was scared; she had never seen Johnny M so furious. She had to watch her step. For a woman who placed a big premium on her looks, it wouldn't pay to have a face resembling a compound of scrambled eggs and stale beer. So much for a discourse on African time.

Hearing Reuben's ox-wagon labouring outside, she opened the door and called him in. She handed him a wad of notes and instructed him to get some liquor stocks. Johnny M had said something about throwing a party, and he really hated it when stocks ran out. As Reuben got into the seat of his wagon, Nerissa waved at him, wishing that his luck would change. She remembered her own humble beginnings in Mthunzini, where people knew one another and greeted each other warmly. But, she thought, here we are in this place where people have grown claws, where the weak are prey to the likes of Johnny M.

This was his place. He owned everything in here. Come to that, she was also one of his assets. She imagined him filing his tax returns, adding Nerissa as part of tax-deductibles. You might own me, Mister Big Stuff, but you'll never touch my soul with your grubby hands. And, one foolish day, I'll pay you back in spades.

Seven

One extraordinary feature of eSikhawini was how the upheavals of the past decade had left no visible mark on it. The houses in the middle-class section called Kwamazakhele – Do-it-yourself – were all intact, testifying to the status of the occupants. Since this was during school holidays, the scrubbed youngsters walking in twos and threes or playing quietly on well-tended lawns didn't look like the type that would fashion Molotov cocktails. A fashionably dressed couple piled golf bags into the boot of a shiny Mercedes, the woman haughtily beautiful and her partner, balding and paunchy, seeming satisfied with the government of the day.

Looking at the scenes of everyday life, Mpanza felt out of place. What was Khethiwe doing at this exact moment? He wondered. And the kids – would they ask after him? He was certain that Khethiwe would take him back if he pledged to work towards a Mercedes, a big house with manicured lawns, access to exclusive clubs where the well-heeled clientele practised their swings and closed business deals. Still imagining their ease with the world, he was narrowly missed by a passing armoured personnel carrier.

'Fucking Casspir,' he cursed, watching the squat, ugly armoured car rolling past. Some kids snickered, enjoying the discomfort of an adult. He ignored them and trudged on.

Mpanza had noticed these Casspirs trundling along the main road. It was usual for them to stand like sentinels at intersections. These insect-like APCs had become so much a part of the landscape that their presence had become a township habit, the armed troopers accepted with the same resignation some adolescents regarded acne.

The houses had at one time been the regulation four-roomed structures before the owners built on them, setting up other wings and, in a number of cases, even complementing the original bleak design with another floor. All the houses he passed had high fences; where he could look through the gates, he found that the driveway led to a garage for two cars.

He found his sister's house without difficulty even though the directions he had were vague. Although it was a well-to-do section, it was still the township, and only a blathering idiot lost his way in a township. The wrought-iron gates were open; two children, a boy of about eleven and a girl who must have been nine, were playing, hitting a tennis ball with ping-pong paddles. They stopped their game and watched him with adult eyes as he came up. Still eyeing him carefully, they mumbled responses to his greetings, their stance now indicating a readiness to flee. 'Is Ntombi here?' Mpanza asked, placing his cases on the paved drive, suddenly feeling very tired. The fact that his nephew and niece didn't know him left him with a strange sense of not belonging.

Without taking her eyes off him, the girl shouted: 'Ma? There's an uncle out here who wants you.'

As if on cue, a pair of small puppies of dubious pedigree – one of them limping and favouring the injured led as it leapt – came yapping from the direction of the closed garage. The boy squatted and, gathering them in his arms, he stroked their ash-grey heads, murmuring endearments. He looked up at Mpanza. 'My dog's hurt. Do you know anything about dogs?'

'All I know', Mpanza said, hunkering down, 'is that they frighten me.' But he proceeded to inspect the leg; it had an ugly gash above the front left forepaw. 'What happened?'

'Some stupid kids from across were teasing Sooty,' the boy said. 'Then when he went out to chase them they hit him with a stone.'

'You'd better get your Ma to apply something on that,' Mpanza advised, feeling impotent that he had no healing powers. 'She's a nurse, she should know how to do these things.'

'My Ma is not a nurse,' the girl protested. 'She's a Nursing Sister.' The way she proudly stressed her mother's occupation, Mpanza could almost hear the capital letters. Two strikes out, he thought. Can't heal the bloody dog and then this kid is teaching him a thing or two about getting people's professions right. And he hadn't even brought *umngenandlini*, a homecoming gift – what kind of uncle was he?

But Ntombi, who had quietly stepped out of the house, saved the situation. 'Khulu? Zandile?' she chided, 'did you greet Uncle Mpanza?'

Zandile looked Mpanza up and down. 'Is he the one who was a gorilla?'

'Not gorilla,' Khulu said authoritatively. 'Guerrilla, stupid.'

'Don't call me stupid, Fat-cake!'

Ntombi, hugging her brother while separating the young warriors, gave Mpanza a look which said: See what I have to deal with? But there was no doubt that she derived a lot of pleasure from her children. 'Take those mongrels to the back and make sure that the gate is locked. And wash your hands, then hurry on back inside.'

He watched her as she preceded him into the house; she was heavier, perhaps a little sadder, but she was still his younger sister. He remembered wrestling with her, she unyielding, refusing to give him the satisfaction of seeing her cry. He mulled over all the things that would make her cry. Was she happy? There were just too many questions, the ground to cover as wide and stammering as the Sahara.

In the lounge, he installed himself on the settee and stretched his legs. His tiredness was real, starting from his toes, up the calves, to rest in the small of his back. While his sister pottered about the kitchen, he paged through a photo album. When he

123

saw the pictures of his parents, he experienced a great sense of failure. They had both died while he was in exile. He had not been able to come back and bury them. When their eyes stared back at him, they were filled with accusations. Our son, the eyes said, why this monstrous betrayal? He tried to imagine how Jonah's parents must have felt when the news reached them that their son was dead. It was something he couldn't bear pondering. But the scene returned, like a demon refusing to be exorcised. I was a soldier, he thought. I'm a soldier.

*   *   *

It starts in the shebeen. Every fucking time something must start in the shebeen. Stanley is pissed. It was a bad move to allow him so much alcohol. What was the name of the shebeen again? Rowena's in Rockville. Rowena carrying on about a son of a cleric, who had just come back from America, full of shit. 'I'd just like his father to leave me with him for one day,' Rowena vows, 'then I'd show him what being a darkie means.' Rowena of the big, flouncy breasts, two cushions you could bounce on from here to eternity. Stanley picking on the cop, saying he is going to buy him liquor if he sings a song. Journalists who know that the policeman is a killer file out one by one. They are here to cover stories, not become news themselves. Which is what they'll become once the cop draws his gun.

Somehow, Stanley cools it. It could be the music. Bix Beiderbecke. Cryin' All Day. The notes coming out of the speakers of the stereo, fluid, hovering in the air and shimmering like honey. Memories of Hungarian kids in the bus – *zsia, bácsi néger!* hello, black uncle. Magyars not being racist, just being friendly. Waving his hand as the Ikarus bus rolls down Margit Hid, the Danube snaking sinuously, glowing like an inspired saxophone solo. Man, why go to all these places when we are going to be haunted by memories?

Moving out of the shebeen. Dark nights, the blues in the people's veins – we people who are darker than blue – screwing up the cluster lights. The kids riding on Converse or ProKeds, see-

124

ing you from a distance, already counting the change in your pockets.

'Stanley? Where's the car?'

'Huh? What?'

'Where's the fucking car, Stanley?'

'Fuck knows. You were driving.'

'Shit!'

Special Ops told you to be resourceful, now, the car you hot-wired on Jeppe Street has been stolen. Damn tsotsis don't know when their antics are downright unpatriotic. What do you expect from the tsotsis? People so slick they steal your television set while you're watching a replay of Muhammad Ali and Foreman in 'The Rumble in the Jungle'.

The other cars on the streets are either guarded or simply not worth stealing them. And Heidelberg would be the unfunniest city in which to get stuck.

'We'll take the train.'

'What?'

'The train. Ah, forget it!'

★   ★   ★

'Hey, hey,' Ntombi said. 'Wake up.'

Mpanza looked wildly around him, orientating himself. 'How long have I been dozing?'

'For a while. I thought of letting you sleep on,' Ntombi said, 'but Roger will be here soon – and I didn't want him to see you like that.'

'Did I snore?'

'Like a runaway steam engine.' She studied him. 'Come to think of it, you were mumbling something about a train.' Placing a tray with tea things on the low, glass-topped table, she continued looking at him. 'You're not in some kind of trouble, are you?'

'What do you mean?'

'You know what I mean. You're here without Khethiwe and the children. You've got that wild look about you I remember as a kid when you'd got yourself into some stew.' Ntombi paused.

'Do you want to tell me about it?'

He studied the lounge, the soft colours of the furnishing, the drapes and the pictures on the wall, everything so orderly it was a strain for his turbulent mind. And Ntombi. She was his sister and he loved her. He hated introducing into this house all the negative things from outside, from the jungle. At the same time he knew that it would be unfair to keep things from her, especially because the streets had a tendency to break into the most cloistered of surroundings and touch them with their soiled hands. She would know anyway, sisters always ended up in possession of the unvarnished truth.

'Khethiwe and I have split,' he said. 'It could be temporary, it could be permanent, I don't know. We'll devise an arrangement for me to see the kids. I have no great wish to see them now. Not while I'm in a weak position.'

'But that's not all, is it?' Ntombi asked. 'You've separated before, it's nothing new. But something else is bothering you.' She poured out the tea, the steam swirling to her face. 'Something that happened when you came back a few years ago?'

Mpanza nods while absently stirring his tea. 'It's not very easy to talk about it.'

'Consider me a grown woman,' Ntombi persisted. 'In my life, I've seen the unspeakable. As it is now, I also get involved in mediation between the ANC and the IFP. And it's not *pap en vleis.*' She raised her head and her face had a faraway look. 'It's not easy, hearing the testimony of people preoccupied with removing others from the face of the earth.'

★   ★   ★

It is in the safe house in Lusaka that he is told to go to Maputo and thence to Swaziland. Already the Swazi authorities are enforcing the Inkomati Accord which Samora Machel signed with P W Botha. The hearts of the comrades are heavy because the Swazis are arresting anything that smacks of involvement in the ANC. It is this accord which prompts a saddened Oliver

Tambo to lament that Samora has chosen to embrace a tiger.

In Swaziland, the instructions are clear. The underground Natal Machinery has asked for the removal of certain people suspected of working for the enemy. Its commander, Rosie, is in Swaziland to get help from the Special Ops people in the assassination squad. Stanley and Mpanza are chosen. Furthermore, they know who the target is. Word has also come from Pietermaritzburg that Jonah had refused to organise transport for an operative, leading to the fellow's arrest, what more proof is needed that Jonah is an enemy agent?

After stealing across the border, Stanley and Mpanza finally make their way into Johannesburg. They hot-wire a Toyota Cressida along Plein Street, hoping it doesn't belong to an operative gone for a quick pee in the men's lavatories. Maybe, he thinks, MK cars should carry stickers with the legend, This vehicle is on official MK duties, avoid stealing at all cost! They get their weapons, two Makarov 9-mm pistols, extra ammunition, and F1 and RGD-5 grenades from a dead-letter-box near Phefeni. The strain of infiltrating into the country, the years of living underground like a mole, begin to tell. Mpanza relents when Stanley suggests that they visit a *smokkie* and catch a *dop*.

And Stanley's knowledge of watering holes is phenomenal. For him, the issue of DLBs poses no problem; nor does he employ double-steps, azimuth or reference points for directional bearings. He is wont to say: 'Oh, I know that area. Between Gwala's settlement and the Tugela Ferry there are so many bottle stores ...'

But it is at the shebeen where things go wrong and Stanley loses it. The car is stolen. Mpanza debates with himself whether to hijack another car, but shrugs off the thought. A hijack comes with a lot of headaches, with the cops setting up roadblocks, it's not worth the trouble. They take a train. In the train, Stanley gets into an argument with another tsotsi and it takes a supreme effort to dissuade him against using his gun. Finally he sleeps and they reach Durban Station without incident.

They wait for Rosie to lead them to the target but he is nowhere to be seen. They sleep in an all-night club in Umlazi before taking a minibus taxi to Pietermaritzburg. To conduct their own investigation, they steal a Toyota Corolla parked near the Swallow Road police station, just to prove a point. Finally Mpanza finds a young man, Zitha, who knows Jonah's habits. Jonah is a jazz fanatic, frequenting the music bars on Calder Street. For two days they follow Jonah, debating whether to take him on the street and deciding to wait for a more opportune moment. On the first night they shadow their quarry but are stopped by the presence of a woman, someone they later establish to be Jonah's sister, Zodwa. Finally, they travel from central Pietermaritzburg through Peterson Street to get to John Gilbert Drive heading north. After crossing the motorway, they take the left turn into Longmarket Street, then right into the student residences of Burlington Square.

Since it is Saturday, most of the students are out on the streets, carrying record albums, black, white and brown summer bodies displaying a startling vitality. They wait in the car with the engine running where Zitha and Stanley bolster their courage via neat shots of gin. At the entrance to Jonah's flat, they enjoin Zitha to knock and announce himself. That done, Jonah opens the door; behind him, Mpanza can hear John Coltrane's mantra:

> *A love supreme*
> *A love supreme …*

And something flickers in the man's eyes; he looks from Zitha to the men behind. As he takes in what is going on, Jonah tries to close the door. That is when Mpanza draws his pistol and shoots him in the neck, sees the target stepping back under the blast, the face ruined, to fall against the stereo system and stretch out, all light out of his eyes.

★   ★   ★

'Stan and I parted ways,' he told Ntombi. 'He got arrested in Chesterville, something stupid to do with booze, a woman … a gun. There was a trial – and he was hanged.'

Mpanza retraces his steps, takes the route back to Lusaka. He is interrogated and spends some months in Malange, Angola, doing menial jobs in the camps, disarmed and somewhat disgraced. It is much later when Rosie is discovered to be the enemy agent that Mpanza's case is reviewed. And there follows a presidential pardon.

'I have just been told that Jonah's father is in Ngoza,' he said. 'I don't know whether it makes sense to try and see him.'

'See him and do what?'

'I don't know,' Mpanza said. He didn't tell her about Tsepo and Security. 'In any event, Reuben is there. Might as well go and check on him.'

The afternoon dragged into evening. Roger, Ntombi's husband arrived from work and the two men drank a few beers. Mpanza took in this domestic scene, Ntombi happy with her children and Roger playing the genial host. It occurred to him that any talk about money or an extended stay would shatter the peace the family enjoyed. He cursed himself for having ventured here in the first place. What had he hoped to achieve? Later, around seven p m, Roger said he had to go out to a meeting. Mpanza went to sleep. In the morning, his sister drove him to the taxi rank.

'Sure you'll be okay?' Ntombi asked.

'Don't worry,' Mpanza said. 'I'll write you a nice long letter.' Then he kissed her goodbye. 'But, seeing that the kids are burning down the post offices, I'll probably have to send you a smoke signal.'

'*Suka, lapha,*' Ntombi laughed, disengaging herself. 'Do give Reuben my love. Tell him that he should open his rag-and-bone business here, there's scope.' Then she waved, got into the car. Mpanza watched her small car driving off until it disappeared in the morning traffic. Then a thought that had been nagging him, as elusive as a tadpole in water, came back to him. Jonah had a sister. He remembered seeing her face in a newspaper photo. How old would she be now? And where was she? Where were all the sisters?

The morning workers emerged out of the mist like ghosts, people walking, hurrying to work, to make some change which would alter the meaning of their lives. He applied his mind to this thing called work. What was it for? Okay, Karl Marx and his buddies had insisted that labour had brought about development in society. Development and then what? And at what price? Here he was and he had worked for the Movement; he had even worked for the new government of national unity. What had it brought him?

The people who were conspicuously not working – they were the ones who seemed to be inheriting a lot. Or, maybe you needed to have spent a long time on Robben Island – then you could get a cushy job. He remembered a child who once asked Mandela whether he had gone to prison to learn how to be a president. Out of the mouths of babes. There were some people who found themselves in prison for reasons that had nothing to do with changing the political face of the country. Then there were some in higher councils who deserved to be in prison. Mpanza couldn't really tell what was happening.

The taxi, still shy of passengers, waited. We've been waiting for such a long, long time, Mpanza thought. One day we'll get there. Soon enough, three passengers came and the driver, a young man with a bee-bop haircut, started the vehicle and they were off. The driver hit the PLAY button on the tape deck, and the interior was flooded with nostalgia.

The morning people headed for work, or to seek work, were mostly quiet. Like Mpanza, others were grappling with the meaning of the future, what it had in store for them. Listening while not really listening to the music playing, he felt irredeemably lost, unanchored. All the things that he had hankered for – peace, joy, a possibility of enjoying his children – receded further and further into the horizon of his mind. For the briefest moment – something he quickly banished – he focused upon the possibility of Jonah's ghost returning to haunt him. We were taught against obscurantism and fantasy, he thought. He looked out the window, the land spreading and flaunting its greenness, emphasizing the reality of life, and nature's creation.

The vehicle turned away from the main road onto a narrower trail. Crossing a bridge spanning a stream where, on the west bank, farm labourers were turning the soil or cutting the yellow grass with sickles, the passengers looked eastwards at the hallucinatory stretch of a viridian golf course, unattended, the players still catching the last winks before getting up to practise their swings. The stream wound its way farther west, the banks so heavily overgrown that it was inconceivable that a path existed. A few hundred metres on, the woods gave way to bamboo patches, which seemed to usher in fenced houses. Smoke billowed lazily out of chimneys; here and there, standing on a doorway, was a man, woman or child, all looking at the passing vehicle as if witnessing a miracle. Some of the toddlers grinned and waved.

The stream, which had grown into a small river, followed, supporting on its banks a stubborn growth of eucalyptus trees, whose smell wafted into the taxi, heady and earthy. A group of hadedahs and herons walked as if self-consciously, following food trails along the banks. From an outcrop of boulders emerged a brace of black duck, headed for the water. A few minutes later, the boulders became a common topographical feature.

'*Chama stesh*, driver,' called one of the men from behind, irritating Bee-bop with this request to relieve himself. Bee-bop craned his neck, slowing down, to appraise the passenger. 'We're near Ngoza,' he said. 'You mean you can't hold it?'

The passenger who wanted to urinate was young, perhaps in his twenties, in an oversized lumber jacket. Something about his eyes disturbed Mpanza. He was cross-eyed, with the disconcerting habit of looking somewhere else while addressing you. 'Mister,' the passenger said, 'would you rather that I flooded your taxi?'

'Ah, okay,' the driver said, pulling up against a constellation of

Cosmos flowers. The sliding door rattled open. The man got out and was half-hidden in the bushes. Mpanza heard his stream splashing the dew-ridden foliage. Two other men followed suit, discharging their hoses. Mpanza had a vision of a younger self where he and his schoolmates competed over whose yellow stream could climb the highest. Just as he was debating whether to go, too, the passengers came back, Lumber Jacket trailing behind.

Then it happened, suddenly. Lumber Jacket raced round to the driver's side and pressed a pistol against Bee-bop's head. 'Give me the keys.' When the driver looked at him nonplused, he struck him across the face with the gun-barrel. Grunting in surprise, the driver collapsed across his seat. Lumber Jacket leaned forward and removed the keys from the ignition. Then, opening the door with the gun hand, he dragged Bee-bop out and roughly bundled him onto the roadside. Then he got into the taxi. Turning, waving the weapon whose muzzle looked like a hole of death, he shouted: 'Okay, all of you, give me the money.' Training the gun on Mpanza, he barked, 'You, Stone Face, come on, collect the money!' He tossed a cloth cap at Mpanza. 'Here. Make like it's for the Holy Ghost.'

Mpanza complied. He turned to the passengers behind. 'You heard what the man said.' He stretched out his arm and coins and rand notes plop-plopped into the cap. 'Those who've paid, get out!' the hijacker ordered. He sounded as if he was beginning to enjoy himself, this was so easy, a breeze, really. As soon as he said that, Mpanza knew that the robber would take him along, possibly as a hostage. And that prospect didn't appeal to him.

The travellers, eager to be done with the gunman, deposited their money and hurried out, almost tearing the door off its railings in their haste. Soon, Mpanza was left alone with the robber. He surmised that the hijacker was banking on Mpanza's anxiety that he be not taken as an accomplice by the passengers who'd been forced to disembark. Lumber Jacket started the minibus, the gun still pointed in Mpanza's general direction. 'Here's the money,' Mpanza said. Possibly sensing something in Mpanza's tone, the hijacker turned to look at him, the focus of the eyes elsewhere until Mpanza had an impression that the muzzle did the seeing for him.

'You're not about to try something, are you, Stone Face?' he asked Mpanza. 'I mean, you look intelligent, not like those *moegoes* back there.' He started laughing. 'Boy, did you see the way they scampered?' The eyes examined a spot to the left above Mpanza's head, the muzzle winked at his midriff.

'Maybe you can put the gun away,' Mpanza suggested. He hoped he sound agreeable. Hijackers were a very petulant lot. He imagined the irony of surviving exile and its hazards and getting snuffed out here in his native land. It wouldn't be funny.

'It's making you nervous, is it?' The hijacker pondered his own question. 'Tell you what. Come up here and drive. I have a feeling I need to watch you.'

'Drive where to?'

'We'll see,' the robber said airily. 'Anywhere. Around here. The land is beautiful, might even take in a little scenery, appreciate God's creation.' He made a big thing of looking at the grassland and shrubbery drifting past, then turned sharply, hoping to catch Mpanza grabbing for the gun. 'I'm an okay fellow, once you know me. My name is Zamani.'

'I'm pleased to meet you, Zamani,' Mpanza said. 'Only thing I don't know is we'll drive around and then what?' He was certain now that this man was going to shoot him dead.

'Then nothing,' Zamani said. There was now an edge to his tone. 'Now, be a good boy and do what I ask you. True's God, I won't hurt you.' He then gave over and let Mpanza replace him at the wheel. 'That wasn't so hard, now, was it?'

Mpanza agreed that it wasn't hard, all the time thinking about how to get out of this predicament. He saw through the corner of his eye that the gun was a .45 Astra automatic. He had to be very, very careful. Lots of youngsters carried guns with scant knowledge of their destructive capability. During his training, he was told of how the Rhodesian security forces could identify guerrillas in a civilian setting. Just fire into the air and see who takes cover. Because civilians just scatter like confused sheep. Like the passengers earlier on.

'What are you going to do with the minibus?' he asked.

Zamani seemed to debate with himself. Then, remembering that he was travelling with someone who would be a corpse quite soon, he answered: 'This taxi belongs to my brother,' he said. 'He was hijacked and killed by Johnny M. They made it seem like a political killing, just because there was *udlame* around this area.'

'Who's Johnny M?'

'Someone you wouldn't have liked to meet,' Zamani said. He was unconscious of the underlying meaning of the future conditional tense. 'A bad egg if ever there's one.'

Mpanza heard the tractor coming in the opposite direction before he saw the crossbar on which the vehicle's horn was secured. Then, across the gulf made wider by the dust, the body emerged, then the outsize wheels. It moved erratically, compensating for the weight of the loaded trailer articulated to it. As he drove on, Mpanza was aware that Zamani was staring at him, possibly weighing up the situation. He heard Zamani cocking the gun, a message that he should drive carefully and perhaps live a few more minutes.

In the depths of his panic, something churned in him, a cold hand which clutched his insides with icy fingers. He knew then that he wanted to live, if only to redeem himself in the eyes of his children. As for Khethiwe, there was nothing there, not now not ever. He understood something that had been the philosophy of Special Ops comrades. That, to fear death was the surest way of bringing it near to you.

'Careful of that *gandaganda*,' Zamani said softly.

'Okay,' Mpanza told him. 'Okay.' Then, when the tractor was about twenty-five metres away, he changed from second to third and stepped on the accelerator – let's see how you like eating an ancient machine! – and shot straight ahead. When two metres away, praying that the tractor driver would have the presence of mind to apply dead brakes, he turned the steering wheel one hundred and eighty degrees, heard the wheels protesting while the vehicle turned, and its left side smashed against the trailer. There was a deafening crunch of metal, the soft pop-pop! of disintegrating glass.

But Zamani, though shaken, was still resolute. As he brought his arm up to fire, Mpanza lunged at him, deflecting the aim. There was a loud explosion and Mpanza felt a searing pain across the jaw. With his free hand he gathered the cap miraculously still holding the reluctant donation, bunched it into a cosh and started hitting Zamani around the face and the neck. When the latter weakened, Mpanza prised the gun out of his fingers. For one long moment he contemplated emptying the magazine on Zamani, but decided against it. Hefting the weapon, he lashed out, again and again, hearing the soft crunch of cartilage breaking underneath. In some distant, perverse way, he found that he enjoyed what he was doing. He felt alive, as if with this maiming, he was reclaiming something for himself.

'Hey, hey!' a voice called out. Then someone grabbed Mpanza from behind. He allowed himself to be pulled out of the minibus. The tractor driver, a small, wizened man in khaki overalls raised his arms to show that he wasn't fighting. When Mpanza explained what had happened, the old man said he didn't want to get involved. The tractor wasn't damaged, just a scratched surface. The minibus's left side would need panel beating, something that Johnny M – whoever he was – would be sure to organise.

The tractor rolled into the bush before turning into the road, the driver ramrod straight on his seat. He didn't even once look back. Mpanza had an impression of an old man who had encountered a wild animal in the middle of the forest. Getting back into the taxi, he pulled the gunman out, took off his jacket and put it on him again, this time back-to-front, and fashioned a strait-jacket where the gunman's hands were secured with his own belt. Then he pulled his trousers down to his ankles and tied the laces of both shoes together. That done, he carried Zamani to the back seat and laid him out, face down. Pocketing the gun, he went back to the wheel and reversed the minibus.

Some of the men who had been robbed and forced to vacate the minibus, seeing the tormentor's vehicle bearing on them, scattered into the bush, flushing out a flock of river ducks which squawked raucously away. Mpanza sounded the horn before people started venturing, cautiously at first, then more confidently when they saw him waving. Six missing, but Mpanza wasn't going to scour the veld for them. Piling a bleeding Bee-bop into the taxi, the passengers thanked Mpanza, and resumed their journey. They were so grateful they didn't even broach the subject of their money until Mpanza handed them the blood-stained cap with an instruction that they take what belonged to them. He pocketed the change belonging to the six escapees who had disappeared.

He drove the limping minibus taxi towards Ngoza half-listening to the conversation going on behind him. When he reached the town, he was assaulted by the brutality of something old and dying strangling to give birth to newness. Squalor resided cheek by jowl with attempts to shabby respectability. The Central police station stood next to a whitewashed hotel, the only structure standing more than two stories high.

The drive had left him tired, and a little anxious. Bee-bop was conscious now and he could speak, albeit with some difficulty. Zamani was quiet in the back, where he was trussed up like a Christmas turkey. The passengers took turns sitting on him. Now and then Mpanza heard a percussive fart followed by the smell of rotten eggs.

'If this man suffocates and dies,' someone observed, 'Satan will first have to fumigate that place where he fries the sinners.'

Mpanza didn't join in the nervous laughter. He wondered how Zamani was taking all this, seeing his nose was at the epicentre of these gaseous eruptions. Villagers, he thought, certainly have their own imaginative ways of demonstrating their displeasure. He remembered one of the renegade MK tsotsis, Carlos, who sold stolen cars to the Mozambicans. These vehicles had been smuggled in through Swaziland and were supposed to be used by the Movement in underground work. Then Carlos started playing games with the customers, demanding cash but never delivering. When they got wise to his game, they sought him with guns and machetes. The last that was heard of him was that he had stumbled into a village where the inhabitants were notorious for their special form of retribution. They locked you up in a barrel crowded with snakes and scorpions.

'Here comes the boss,' Bee-bop mumbled. He sounded very nervous.

Johnny M advanced to the minibus across the litter of disemboweled oranges and squashed cardboard. A truck, possibly from the orange packing plants had left its calling card. The urgency of his gait meant that he foresaw trouble; he went round the side where Bee-bop, visibly in pain, sat. He gave the vehicle a brief inspection before peering in.

'What happened, Sipho?' he asked.

With great difficulty, Sipho summarised the earlier events and how Mpanza had disarmed the hijacker. 'There he is, at the back,' Sipho recited.

Johnny M gave Mpanza a long, quizzical look. 'Thank you very much,' he said, offering his hand across Sipho's lap. Mpanza and Johnny M shook hands. 'I'm really indebted to you.' Then he gave a shrill whistle and two uniformed policemen, followed by Grey, emerged from the police station. Johnny M hurried across and went into a huddle with the trio and then they all walked back to the minibus. The policemen opened the door and hauled Zamani out. Mpanza watched Johnny M's appraisal of the scene, the restraints on Zamani. He motioned for Mpanza to get out of the minibus.

'Say,' he put in conversationally, 'what did you say your name was again?'

'I didn't say,' Mpanza replied and proceeded to introduce himself.

'What brings you to these parts?'

'I've got an uncle. Reuben.'

'Oh,' Johnny M said, brightening up. 'I know Reuben. I always regarded him as another lean unwashed artificer. Thought he didn't have any relatives.'

Since this didn't call for a response, Mpanza studied Johnny M's face. He smelled of after-shave, and Mpanza disliked men who wore after-shave. There was always something questionable about them. 'He's my uncle. I don't know whether that answers you.'

'Will you be staying long?'

'I haven't decided,' Mpanza said. 'It all depends.'

'Well, I could use new people in my business,' Johnny M said. 'There is a tide in the affairs of men, which, taken at the flood, leads on to fortune. So, if you ever need a job, look me up.' He turned and pointed at a cluster of buildings next to the hotel. 'My store is over there, and you can always leave a message with the girl.'

'Thanks,' Mpanza said. He was ready to go. His suitcases felt heavier. He would have to find a quiet corner and examine his saxophone; he prayed it wasn't damaged.

'By the way,' Johnny M said casually. 'What happened to the gun?'

'What gun?'

'What did Sipho say? Did the man hijack the taxi with a banana then?'

'Oh, that gun,' Mpanza said. 'Honestly, I don't know. The situation was confused. It might still be in the taxi – or in the veld where the struggle took place.'

Johnny M studied him with a small smile. 'You don't strike me as the confused type, Mr. Mpanza. But I'll take your word for it. We'll need the weapon for the case, you see?' He shrugged off the importance of this piece of evidence. 'With luck we'll find it.'

'Goodness, I hope so. Guns are dangerous.'

'You're telling me!' Johnny M grinned, his eyes as blank as kidney beans. 'Well, it was great meeting you, and thanks for saving my boy.' He turned and walked to the knot of people crowding the taxi. He turned and waved. 'Don't forget about the job – or anything.'

'I won't,' Mpanza said. As he started off to look for Reuben the Collector, he wondered why he hadn't been asked to make a statement. Johnny M had offered him, a total stranger, a job without bothering about credentials. Things sure work differently here. He saw the off-licence nestled beneath the Castle Lager sign. Collecting must be a thirsty business, he thought as he purchased beers, and Reuben would appreciate a little libation.

Eight

The news of mass slaughter in Upper Ngoza filtered into the settlement and made everybody nervous. Most of the men had predicted that violence was coming; some had moved their families to Joshua's sanctuary, casting their lot with a dispensation they felt was somewhat manageable. Even though people were unhappy about venturing into the unknown, the prospect of gritting their teeth at the sounds of screams and gunfire did not appeal to them. In moving, they left their kraals and their beasts. It was well worth it.

Joshua had called a meeting of the Elders. The settlement had grown with the arrival of new refugees. He had spent an exhausting morning visiting the makeshift clinic where some of the children were having their dressings changed. It was unnerving to look at such young people who had sustained burns and injuries. The Other World is still with us, he thought, and hurried to the fields where his happier kinsfolk were celebrating the bountiful fourth October anniversary harvest. They had solved the problem of the broken water pump; some of the newcomers had worked in Boer farms and had the necessary expertise in setting up functional irrigation sluices. That some of them had their own peculiar ways was something he had come to expect. He knew that, come nightfall, not a few of the men would beat a path to the shebeens in the squatter camp. Joshua had long eschewed the responsibility of spiritual leader. The flesh takes care of its own, ran his philosophy.

But now the boy Horwitz had come in his battered car and

reported that the settlement had been the first to be considered under the provisions of the Restitution of Land Act. This meant that the Land Claims Court – which Joshua had been sceptical of, as he was of any court in the land – had finally, irrevocably, ruled in the settlement's favour. But what did it all mean? Horwitz would brief the meeting of the Elders. Joshua didn't like the young lawyer. Horwitz knew his law but he had other things on his mind – such as seducing his daughter. That was the thing that had almost led Joshua to lose the respect of his peers. Much as people understood that there were changes in the government, that the Immorality Act had been scrapped, his people still couldn't accept that black and white people could have a friendship that had sexual implications. Since she was his daughter, people looked upon him to instill order for, in their eyes, there was nothing more anarchic than a liaison across the colour line. And, then, what had Zodwa seen in the boy? Scrawny, sloppy, chain-smoking. And a real drunkard as well. He couldn't bear imagining Zodwa kissing the boy's bearded face. Anyway, they were somewhat beholden to the man. If Jonah had been alive, maybe he would also have become one of those hot-shot lawyers who spoke English as if wasps had taken occupation of their tongues and who drove big cars. Zodwa was soon going to become a lawyer, but her heart was in the city, in Johannesburg. She had told him as much.

Naomi brought him lunch and he chewed distractedly, knowing that the word would be transmitted to the women who had washed and prepared the new vegetables. Although a deaf-mute, Naomi was the most expressive woman he had ever met. Since he had long stopped eating meat – the oracle had forbidden him – he was known as a connoisseur of vegetarian foods. And here it was now – pumpkin, freshly roasted corn, spinach and potatoes, sprinkled with spiced tomato-and-onion sauce – and he was not interested. Shoving the half-eaten plate away, he washed his hands and wiped them on a towel.

Naomi gave him a look of disapproval before carrying the

tray covered with a doily back to the kitchen. She brought back a mug of lemonade, sweetened as usual, and he drank, gulping it down.

Before venturing to the main rondavel where the meeting would be held, he stopped over at Nozizwe's tent. He found the wizened old woman bent over a grindstone, pulverising an evil-smelling mix of herbs, sweat running down her face. Nozizwe stopped grinding on hearing Joshua's footfalls. Turning round, she left off the work and greeted the visitor.

'What have we, lowly ones, done to deserve this visit?' she asked.

'I thought I'd look you up before the meeting,' Joshua said. 'How's Selina?'

'She's quieted down somewhat. That boy must be using some really strong *muthi*.'

Selina was one of the settlement's beauties who had left the troubles of Msinga. Her suitor had vowed that he would get her back. Nozizwe said that the man was calling her, using the calabash in the midnight hour. When a man called a woman like that, she was sure to get into hysterics, screaming, '*Ngiyekeleni ngiye kuyena* – Let me loose, I am going to him!' It would take several strong men to restrain her, so strong was the imperative to go. Joshua had ruled that women only should handle such cases since some men's hands tended to slip and touch parts that caused them to sigh and moan.

'So,' Joshua asked, 'how are you going to solve this one? I'm sick to death hearing that woman shrieking at night. She'll soon bring the police in here.'

'Don't worry. I'm brewing something that will rebound on the boy.' Nozizwe walked to the corner and returned with a canvass bag. She reached into it and showed Joshua what looked like a handful of wood shavings. 'This is *umbola*, which I collected in Zimbabwe. Mixed with bits of *ichithamuzi* and a little of my *makhathakhatha*, the woman will boil it and cover herself with a blanket to steam herself. Then I will take the used mixture and put it in the calabash. Then Tabitha will recite after me: "*Wena, s'thutha sakwaSibanibani, ngikhohlwe*" – You fool, son of so-and-so, forget about me!" If he wakes up tomorrow morning still knowing his name, then I will have failed.'

'You mean he loses his memory?'

'All of it.' Nozizwe was certain. 'His head will be full of nothing but blankness.'

'Isn't that rather extreme?'

'If a man is in love, he should do the right thing,' Nozizwe put in gravely. 'When a woman says, "*Angisakufuni* – I don't want you any more," then he must accept. If he doesn't and keeps on pestering the woman, then I apply my stop-*nonsonso*.' Then she laughed, showing a ragged row of teeth. It was not hard for Joshua to suspect that the old nyanga was again pulling his leg. Stop-*nonsonso* my foot!

'Can it work on a white boy?' he asked, suddenly remembering a deserving candidate.

'*Ja*,' Nozizwe replied slowly. 'It's worth a try. Problem is, if it's the white boy I think you have in mind, then he might forget all the legal details which we need for this place.' He gave his friend a long, speculative look. 'And you wouldn't want that, would you?'

Joshua laughed for the first time that day. 'No,' he admitted, 'it certainly wouldn't do.'

'I thought as much.' Nozizwe picked up a shawl and draped it round her bony shoulders.

As the two elders stepped out of the hut, she asked, 'How's my little girl?'

'As headstrong as ever,' Joshua said.

'She's good.'

★   ★   ★

'You're no good,' he says to her as she returns from town, smelling of liquor. 'On your first visit to this place you decide to shame me!'

'Baba,' Zodwa pleads, 'please understand.'

143

'Understand, heh?' Then he looks beyond her, notices the ramshackle of a car in which the white boy is sitting, his hands on the steering-wheel. 'What's he want here?'

'Baba, I met him at the hotel. And he promised to drive me back to Fort Hare.'

'And? It's two days you were supposed to go. Has he been driving you all that time?'

'One thing led to another, Baba. I couldn't take this place. It's so heavy.'

Joshua spits. 'You slept with him?'

'Do you really want to know?'

'No. Just go.' He turns and enters the tent. She doesn't follow him. The thought that she might have slept with the white boy upsets him.

In the weeks that follow, Zodwa is on everyone's lips. People whisper when they see Joshua. Only Nozizwe tells him that he is courting a stroke. 'Zodwa is a responsible girl.'

★   ★   ★

'Maybe I should write her,' Joshua said. He had written to his daughter long letters which he never posted, where he told her how sorry he was that things had soured up between them. 'It's not good for a girl to be out there among the sharks when she could be of service to this place.'

'Would you like her to come and take care of this place?' Nozizwe asked; it came out so effortlessly that it was clear she had been wrestling with the thought for a long time.

'That's my lifelong wish, Nozizwe.' Suddenly feeling a great urge to embrace the medicine woman, Joshua checks himself. 'We are old now. Our bones are brittle, and this battle has just been joined.'

'Zodwa will come,' Nozizwe said. 'She has a good head.'

'You won't try your mumbo jumbo on her, will you?' Joshua asked, smiling.

'Not on your life,' Nozizwe vowed. 'Not unless you instruct me to.'

144

'No,' the patriarch said. 'We're late for the meeting. Let's hurry up.'

Joshua and Nozizwe came into the meeting just as Horwitz was expounding on the Restitution of Land Act, tracing the history of legislation that had dispossessed Africans. He looked and sounded nervous as if uncomfortable in the presence of so many dour black people. From where Joshua was sitting, the boy looked pale, the light that came in through the latticed slats made his audience formidably black. But other people were listening intently. Joachim, interpreting, had even put on a dark suit for the occasion. I bet he wishes Zodwa were here to witness his hour of glory, Joshua thought.

'This legislation which is designed to roll back the effects of grand apartheid', Horwitz said, 'was approved by parliament when the Land Act was voted onto the statute books.'

The decision meant that South Africans who were forcibly removed from their land since 1913 could lodge claims for the return of their land. Dlamini, one of the Elders who fancied himself a legal eagle raised his hand.

'Yes?' Horwitz asked, a trifle irritated. Question time would come at the end of the briefing, but he couldn't alienate anybody. 'Do you wish to say something?'

Dlamini got to his feet. He turned first to look at the Elders behind him, as if saying, Just wait and see how I'm going to mesmerize this upstart! 'Isn't it misleading for you to say "South Africans" because,' he asked, 'as far as I know no other people except Africans were ever forcibly removed? Why lump everybody together?'

'Indian and Coloured people – and some whites – have been removed,' Horwitz said. 'Perhaps there was a difference in the method for different groups. And for different reasons.' He looked at Dlamini. 'That satisfy you?'

Dlamini sat down. He was not quite satisfied and the wind had been taken out of his sails by other Elders who, instead of appreciating the acuity of his mind, were muttering, suggesting that he stop wasting their time and sit down. 'I'll come back to the issue later,' he mumbled, scowling darkly.

'Land Affairs Minister Derek Hanekom introduced the legislation,' Horwitz continued, 'in the National Assembly. He said …' and here Horwitz consulted his notes, ' " … Through the restitution of land rights and by enabling uprooted communities to re-establish themselves where they belonged, the Bill gives meaning to the process of reconstruction, economic empowerment and development." And, also, that claims to state and private land can be lodged with the Commission on the Restitution of Land Rights within three years. The commission will settle claims through mediation and negotiation.'

In the case of Ngoza and the settlers, Horwitz recited, people were lucky in that they had foreseen the process and staked a claim with the Court. 'My presence here, then,' he went on, 'is simply to tell you that your claims – thanks to Baba Joshua – have been acceded to. This means that you, yourselves, have claim to Ngoza and Upper Ngoza, Two Rivers and the area called Central. What has to be worked out is setting up structures for local governance. In the meantime, you have traditional authority over said area.'

'What about Johnny M?' Joshua asked. He wasn't going to raise his hand like a schoolboy. 'Doesn't he have any claim?'

'As things stand,' Horwitz replied, 'the little fiefdom which Johnny M and his cohorts are running is nothing short of mythological. It doesn't exist.'

'Are you certain that there's no loophole they can exploit?'

'Absolutely.'

Well, Joshua thought, someone ought to tell Johnny M. Read him the Act that is in black and white. He felt a mixture of joy and sadness, as if what he had worked for had finally come to fruition but was blighted by the possibility that trickery and violence would follow. He suddenly felt hot and short of breath, aware of Nozizwe looking at him, saying something inaudible. A commotion up in the front. Then he felt a fist hammering at his heart; the figures in front of him misted. 'Call my daughter,' he said. Then he fell into darkness as turbulent as that mysterious moment before the baby's first cry at birth.

Nine

It was mid-spring when Benedita Venter decided to take control of her own life. Throughout her stay with Venter in Ngoza, she had let Jannie dictate the pace of things. Her brother had disappointed her and postponed his visit for another six months. Steve's preoccupation with continental Europe got on her nerves. She had her fill of postcards from snow-bound addresses where the sevens were crossed and the fours looked like a profile drawing of a sharp nose resting on a stick. It occurred to Benedita that Steve's visit would have provided an opportunity for him to be shown how far his sibling rival had advanced. She had a house that she had furnished to her own taste whereas Steve was still rudderless, being thrown hither and thither by exigencies outside his control. To be denied a possibility of gloating rankled. Benedita knew, though, that her brother's chosen path was a way of affirming his freedom. When he comes over, Benedita thought, I'll show him how thoroughly unfree he really is.

Still she wasn't satisfied with the arrangements in the house. This discontent had become expensive when she arranged for the tiled floor to be ripped open and parquet flooring laid. Heavy drapes had given way to louvered shutters and bamboo blinds, which effectively screened the hot sun. The lounge was a wildness of colour, batiks, and African prints with hunting motifs and gingham toiles covering the large, comfortable sofas and chairs. She had replaced the coffee table with side tables, covering the middle of the room with coir matting. The wall tapestries depicted animals and scenes of Africans with expressive faces.

Venter had observed all these changes without comment until one afternoon when he came back from the ranges. It was clear that something had upset him and, fortified by whisky, he charged into her.

'What's all this supposed to prove?' he had asked, his arm embracing the transformed lounge.

'I don't know what you mean,' Benedita had retorted.

'This place. It's getting so fucking poncy,' he had lamented. 'I feel like I'm living in someone else's house.' Clicking his tongue, he had continued. 'Look at all that. I deal with *these* people everyday, I don't have to bring them into my home.'

'You don't like it, then?'

'I don't like it.' Then, relenting: '*Ag*, but what the hell!' Then he had stormed out and enfolded himself within the hammock beneath the mdoni and the mango trees out on the yard. What in God's name is eating him, she had wondered, but, by this time, she had stopped probing; he would tell her whenever it suited him. This was where Benedita started understanding that men's problems stemmed from their inability to communicate what was bothering them. When lambasted by elements outside, they brought their baggage back home, and sulked. One reason for Venter's foul mood could have been the bureaucratic snarl-up affecting his salary; if he had known how much all this refurbishment had cost, he would have thrown a fit.

Venter's grudging compliance was a small victory for Benedita. But it also made her very angry. He could have asked, for instance, how she had managed to engineer this transformation single-handedly. Benedita would have told him that a month earlier she had been going into the settlement, hiring casual labourers, and paying them by the hour. Contrary to a widely held notion, she found the men hard-working and unthreatening. And they hadn't lifted a cent or anything of worth from the house. She had set traps such as leaving a folded ten-

rand note behind the sofa, but found the money placed carefully on the mantelpiece. Added to all that, the workers received
their due with gratitude, accustomed, as they were, to being
swindled by other employers.

They had dug up the garden and removed the stones, which
seemed to increase in number with each digging. Benedita
would be there, pointing, directing, and subconsciously hoping
for an excavation of an ancient crypt hiding artifacts of antiqui-
ty. One afternoon the men dug up the remains of a dog, its skull
looking strangely well preserved. The workers were not pleased
with this discovery. Concluding that their reluctance to handle
the blackened bones might be connected to some ancient taboo,
Benedita elected to bury the bones herself. It was later borne in
on her that after her demonstration that she wasn't above soiling
her hands, the African honorific of 'Madam' was said with genuine respect.

She marvelled at her bird garden, something she had created
without putting her mind to it. Twenty-five metres from the
edge of the southern hibiscus hedge was a scattering of bushes
and small trees. Knowing that birds feed on insects, she had
planted some fig trees whose soft fruit was a delicacy for insects.
Warblers, robins, orioles, cuckoos and shrikes fed themselves silly
on fat caterpillars, spiders and praying mantises. The trees and
shrubs, a legacy of the last spring, growing in wild, stubborn
abandon, were now flowering. From where she stood, looking at
the spectacular profusion, and hearing the worker bees buzzing,
the smell of nature became something she could not separate
from her own existence. Red velvet, pale mauve, deep yellow,
colours which attracted sunbirds were, for her, much more
meaningful than talk about the Rainbow Nation she was
increasingly hearing. While deep in thought, she heard the gate
opening.

Thinking it was a peddler, Benedita took long, urgent strides
to the old woman who was struggling to secure the latch. The
woman, in a shapeless gingham dress, a man's hat and sandals,

carried a canvas bag slung over her bony shoulder. She gave up on the gate and turned to her when she heard Benedita clearing her throat.

'I'm sorry to disturb you,' she said. 'My name is Nozizwe. I've been going around the area looking for a certain *intelezi*.'

'*Intelezi*?' Benedita was confused. 'You don't mean Buthelezi, your Zulu chief?'

'No, madam. *Intelezi*. A plant,' Nozizwe explained patiently. 'One of the men who worked here told me you have it growing in your garden.'

'You're not looking for dagga by any chance?' Benedita asked, remembering that this weed which Africans euphemistically called *umthunzi wezinkukhu* – the shade for chickens – was indigenous to these parts. 'Are you, Mama?'

For the first time a cloud of irritation flitted across Nozizwe's impassive face. She took a deep breath and Benedita inwardly regretted her flippant remark. The old woman turned her mournful eyes to her. 'It's for our leader. He's dying.'

'I'm awfully sorry,' Benedita said. 'I didn't mean —'

'*Kulungile*,' Nozizwe said, putting her at ease.

Benedita grasped – and this knowledge left her strangely disturbed – that she had lost ground. The old woman had entered her yard and asked her for permission to dig up her garden for God-knows-what plant. But, from the way she stood surveying her as if from a great height, she might as well have ignored her and gone ahead and taken what she wanted. It was this knowledge that impressed itself in her mind that Africans only interacted with white people to the extent it served their immediate purposes. When done, they would bid their sponsor a polite *sala kahle* and retreat into their dark, unknown world. For some reason, Benedita suddenly found this unacceptable.

She knew very little about black people and could therefore not claim to be an authority. The books she had read which had added up into an unfinished film script had not prepared her for the existential reality of living in a country where black people were the majority. In London, she had been part of them, an exotic cabal, which shouted its blackness as if from the dizzy heights of the Telcom Tower. The little she knew about black South Africans led her to the conclusion that the way they conducted business could easily be construed as selfish. But it was not selfishness in the classical sense because, she knew, they were giving when it came to their own communities. They had a support system; the difference between the 'haves' and the 'have-nots' was always lessened by this kind of solidarity. What got her, though, was that in their preoccupation with supporting their own structures, they enclosed themselves in a shell which no outsider could penetrate. She was an outsider. The woman came, asked for what she wanted and would be gone as soon as she had finished. That Benedita was a human being who might have been having problems was the least of her worries. She would not appreciate the colour schemes, the arrangements in her garden. In fact, she might even resent the fact that the digging up had been done by her brethren. Benedita could imagine her thinking, We are just your tools; we are the labour that brings beauty to your lives. She would have liked to share the beauty of the garden with someone. Venter was now as effectively cut off from her concerns as these people with impossible names were.

'I would like to call on your sick leader,' she surprised herself by saying, when Nozizwe came from the garden holding what looked like a clump of sedge in her hand. 'Is that all right with you?'

'I am certain there would be no problem,' Nozizwe said, wiping her hands, which were sticky with black mud on her dress. Taking her time arranging the straps of the canvas bag over her shoulder, she regarded Benedita as if registering her presence for the first time. 'Why do you want to see him?'

'He has been kind to me,' Benedita said. 'He allowed your people to come and assist me here when he could well have refused. I mean,' she went on, 'you do have a community to build.'

'Baba Joshua is not like that,' Nozizwe said. She looked up at the sun and, as her gaze lowered, she caught sight of shiny red apples in a grass bowl on a rough-hewn table near the entrance. Benedita followed her gaze.

'Would you like one?' she asked, glad of a chance to offer something.

Nozizwe shook her head. 'I could say yes,' she said, 'and taste your apples which must be very sweet. Then, tomorrow, I'll think about them, remember the sweetness, but they won't be there. If I came here again, it'd be because I wished to appease the memory of apples – and you might not be here. Your man with a gun might be here. And, who knows, accidents happen.' She nodded. 'I don't cultivate a taste for that which I can't have.'

The logic of self-denial was unassailable. Another round lost. But Benedita quickly recovered from this. Quickly plucking apples from the tree, she handed them to Nozizwe in a plastic bag carrier. 'They're not for you,' she said. 'They're for the dying man – and his children.'

Then, pushing her luck, she took two apples from the bowl, gave Nozizwe one and took a bite of hers. She tasted the sweet juice, wiping her lips.

She followed Nozizwe out of the gate, fell in step with her as if it was the most natural thing to do. Suddenly she remembered her walks with Jacobo, where they would stand at the entrance of the Rebouças Tunnel in Rio de Janeiro, waiting for a break in the traffic. To every motorist's annoyance, Jacobo would step out of his car and walk to the fruit vendors and come back with a harvest which he dedicated to her. 'Seize the time,' he'd say, his teeth crunching into an apple.

The memory of the brief time with Jacobo triggered something else: a remembrance of her many breakdowns and the fear that they might return, unannounced, like a thief. Throwing caution to the wind, she sought the right words to tell Nozizwe what had happened to her. On her part, Nozizwe listened attentively, now and then throwing in a question, seeking clarification over a statement obscured by the dividing gulf of language.

153

Nozizwe's eyes narrow imperceptibly when Benedita touched on the encounter with Alina.

'Where was she from?' Nozizwe asked.

'London. Lagos.' Benedita found it almost hopeless to convey the meaning of her experience with Alina and her tortoise. The more she tried to explain, the more she wondered whether the shaman hadn't been a figment of her imagination. 'She was a strange one,' she added lamely.

'But she was able to stop the bad dreams?' Nozizwe prodded. 'This strange woman?'

'She was,' Benedita agreed. 'It could have been that I was so shocked by the episode with the tortoise, it blocked out all my other dreams.' She wanted to add, using the analogy of a computer, where a programme overrode the data of a previous application.

'And you haven't seen you father?'

Benedita paused; would it be possible that of the many old men she cad come across one was her father? She shook her head. 'No,' she answered. 'Right now, I'm not very sure I actually want to meet him.'

'Why?'

'Perhaps it's better to leave some things well alone.'

Nozizwe stopped and picked a stalk of grass. She drew patterns on the grass, the activity aiding her to collect her thoughts. 'The thing that happened to you,' she said, 'we call it *ukuthwasa*, when the ancestors pick you out for a special healing task.' Nozizwe paused, her eyes full of the kind of authority which seemed to say: We're in Africa here, and these are the things that happen. 'Women who've had your experience are rare,' she continued. 'And most of them, if they listen to the call of the forefathers, become *isangoma*.'

'How does that happen?' Benedita asked. 'How do they know they've got the call?'

'Illness is one sign,' Nozizwe said. 'With others, they are discovered from an early age, where they become posessed. It

154

becomes difficult to treat them until they accept the call.'

Benedita had no intention of becoming an isangoma. 'What, happens', she asked, 'if they ignore the call?'

'They go mad,' Nozizwe said simply. 'Stark raving mad.'

Hoo, boy!

Uniformed children from the recently built neighbourhood primary school spilled onto the main road, chattering excitedly. They seemed to be readying themselves for a ceremony, the boys fooling around with drums and bugles, and the girls goose-stepping while they twirled batons, their legs looking ashy and ungainly in the short gym-dresses.

'What are they going on about?' Benedita asked.

'They are going to the sports grounds yonder, to rehearse for the funeral ceremony,' Nozizwe answered.

'Isn't that rather odd? I thought Africans never prepared for a death until someone was certified dead?'

'These are new times. With new symbols.' There was an edge to Nozizwe's voice. 'There may be some Elders who wish that things were done rapidly. For some of us, this is unseemly – an affront, but then, people who hold views similar to ours are fast disappearing from the stage.' There was no note of regret in Nozizwe's voice, just a matter-of-fact acceptance of an immutable truth.

Although Benedita had recently visited the settlement, she had a feeling now that she would get lost if she undertook the excursion back there on her own. From the main, unpaved road, a track widened out and became several paths worn by people walking between the developments of Central on both sides. A small spruit ran the length of the myriad of paths; it stank from the waste from the squatter camp. The camp itself rose, noisy, squat and stammering with rage, to disappear behind head-high reedbeds. It would meet them again some half-a-mile downstream at the spread of grassland which had become an informal bird sanctuary. White-winged widows displayed themselves in the reeds; Benedita was startled by a flock of longclaws bursting out of the thick grass at her feet. Nozizwe watched her with a small smile on her face.

'I hunted in this area when it was just a wild forest,' she said. 'Warthogs. Buck. But I remember feeling bad whenever a bird got caught up in a snare.'

'Did you release them, then?' Benedita asked. 'The birds?'

'We ate what we could eat,' Nozizwe said. 'But we were not proud.'

They were not proud, she thought, but there must have been joy. Not like what she and Nozizwe shortly encountered when they entered the gates of the settlement. Around the community hall that also served as a meeting place, men and women clustered about, speaking in muted voices. The tents were fewer now, having been replaced by rondavel, adobe or brick-and-mortar structures. There was here, again, the co-existence of the young and the old, much like what was happening in town.

Benedita felt like an intruder and cursed her impulsive nature when the people stopped and stared at her with undisguised curiosity. Trailing behind Nozizwe, she saw how the people greeted her with deference. Nozizwe, however, seemed ill at ease with her people, her gestures communicating that she was aware that the courtesy was not so much for her skin as for her being a stranger. Strangers from foreign lands were thought to be representatives of power.

Someone who exuded real power, however, came out of the main tent. It was a young woman, a few years younger than Benedita, in an olive velour blouse fastened with gold studs to her long neck, a dark serge skirt and brown leather boots. Her hair, although covered with a scarf, trailed down in braids; large hoop ear-rings dangled from her ears as she spoke animatedly to a thickset man who bore a certain resemblance to her. They seemed to be arguing over some point, the man seeming angry while the woman chopped the air with her hand while making a point in short, deliberate deliveries.

'Who is that?' Benedita asked.

'That is Zodwa, Joshua's daughter,' Nozizwe said. 'She arrived this morning from the university.'

'And the man?'

'The man is her uncle. There's no love lost between them.' Nozizwe didn't attempt to hide the pride in her voice. 'Come,' she said, 'let us go and greet her.'

Before they took another step, Zodwa had turned away from her uncle and hurried down to Nozizwe and Benedita, arms outstretched. She embraced the old woman. Then, looking over her shoulder, she murmured: '*Gog'uNozizwe*, I see you're still bringing us different herbs ...' Then she laughed, rearing her head, exposing the long neck and the gap between her upper incisors. Her lips were softened by something she had applied '... And this time you've honoured our humble settlement with an import from the other side ...'

Benedita felt herself flush, but she composed her face, maintaining a quivering smile. Knowing that Nozizwe's introduction would be awkward, she offered her hand. 'I'm Benedita Venter. I'm sorry about your father.' She knew, even before she touched the other woman's hand that Zodwa didn't approve of her.

Benedita gathered that Zodwa had recently graduated at the University of Fort Hare and now had a law degree. Her eyes were puffed from crying or lack of sleep, Benedita couldn't tell what. But as she bantered with Nozizwe, there was no hiding her calm though effervescent nature.

'So,' Nozizwe was saying, 'you'll be the one defending us, then?'

'*Ja*,' Zodwa put in carelessly. 'I'll look for the most difficult cases, just to prove a point.' Then she turned her eyes to Benedita. 'Nozizwe tells me that your husband is a policeman. What do you do, yourself?'

'I studied film and was some time back a member of the Anti-Apartheid Movement in London,' Benedita said, words cascading out of her mouth. 'But now I could say I'm just looking for what to do around here.'

'You don't strike me as the type that's content with doing housework?'

'There's very little to do around here,' Benedita said, 'except tend to my plants, watch something mindless on TV and take care of my man.' Then she looked beyond Zodwa and Nozizwe and saw someone coming over, an 'uh-oh' look on her face. 'Speaking of which, here he comes. My husband.'

Even from the distance of the gate where Venter was negotiating his way through the brace of people, Benedita could see that he was angry. She knew that being in such close proximity to so many black bodies further fuelled his anger. Dressed in a felt hat, a ranger's bush jacket, khaki trousers and *velskoene*, he looked like a character out of a film inspired by Sir Rider Haggard's stories. The effect was further deepened by Venter's obvious bewilderment, looking much like a little boy lost in the jungle. He was lost all right, Benedita thought, somewhere in the jungle of his mind. As he approached, Zodwa gave him a long, speculative look.

'Why didn't you tell me where you're going?' Venter demanded, completely ignoring the people with Benedita.

'I was going to leave a note,' Benedita explained lamely, 'but—'

'She remembered you can't read,' Zodwa chipped in.

'What?' Venter couldn't believe his ears. 'What did you say?'

'You heard what I said,' Zodwa responded. 'It's only dumb, uncouth people who act like you. You come here, you don't greet, and you don't even know the people your wife's talking to. Is that a way to behave?'

'Jannie. . .?' Benedita started, placing a hand on his arm. Venter shook it off.

'You keep the hell out of this,' he snarled. Turning to Zodwa, his fists doubled, he said: 'The last time someone talked to me like that they swallowed their teeth.'

'You obviously don't know where you are and who you're talking to,' Zodwa said evenly. 'This is my father's place. And these', she went on, the swing of her arm covering the throngs which had swollen since Benedita got there, 'are my father's people. Whether or not you break a tooth where you come from that's another matter. But, here, on this ground, that would be your last conscious act this side of eternity. By then you'd have learnt not to treat women like garbage.'

'Are you threatening me?'

'You bet your white ass I'm threatening you.' Zodwa stared at him, meeting his gaze. Then, in the sweetest of tones, she turned to Benedita. 'Nozizwe says you wanted to see my father. Come with me.'

'Jannie?' Benedita said tentatively.

Zodwa pulled her gently. 'Don't worry about Jannie, he'll cool off.' Smiling, she cocked her head to one side. 'You'll cool off, won't you, Jannie?' Then the two women strode towards the tent, Benedita now and then turning to look back. A stunned Venter watched them disappear behind the flaps. He had a distinct impression that his wife was giggling.

'That woman is trouble,' he muttered to himself. Nozizwe, beside him, quietly mouthed words in Zulu. Venter didn't know the language, although he had taken some lessons at Police College. He found that black people readily responded when spoken to in Afrikaans or English. Otherwise, he told himself, we'd be talking like dogs. You said to a dog, 'Sit,' and the dog sat – or it soon became one miserable mutt. In a lot of ways, knowledge of languages was a matter of a mental attitude. When Kruschev ranted and raved and banged the heel of his shoe on the table at the United Nations, many American college kids thought it prudent to take Russian as their major subject. Now many of them were enrolling for Japanese or Asian studies. You studied the languages and cultures of peoples you loved – or feared.

It left Venter quite introspective then to discover that, even though he might not have understood Nozizwe's words, the meaning behind them was as clear as day: You ain't seen nothing yet.

Ten

It was nearly thirty-six hours earlier that Zodwa was compli-
menting Khaya on his resistance to the effects of liquor. 'I've
been watching you,' she said, 'and you've just polished off what
amounts to one whole bottle of gin. How do you do that? I'd be
dead by now.'

Khaya laughed and flicked at the blades of grass with his
walking-stick. 'Chemicals,' he said, like a lecturer pointing out a
simple fact to a particularly dim student. 'Just chemicals. I've
found ways of countering the effect.' He reached into his pocket and came out with a small bottle containing yellow tablets.
Rattling the bottle, he said, 'I take 500 mg of Vitamin C each
time I go on these binges.' He nodded his head. 'Never fails.'

The drinkers who hadn't benefited from Khaya's corrective
for intoxication now lay scattered and stupefied on the grass.
Men and women, some tangled in pre-coital poses were mainly
dressed in black graduation gowns over their tailored suits, the
tasselled mortarboard caps resting at jaunty angles on their heads.
They looked to Zodwa like a congregation of clerics who had
surrendered to the astonishing power of the Holy Ghost.

In the morning, the solemnity and ceremony of the occasion
had almost overwhelmed her. This was when the guests of honour, all resplendent in black, moved as if on tiptoe across the
wooden floor to their high chairs on the dais. The vice-chancellor, academic staff and administration officials in the lead looked
foreign and sombre and unreachable. Above and around them
stood the university choir, their caftans and dashikis providing

colourful counterpoints to the dominating dark gowns. There were a few white faces she recognised, officials from non-governmental organisations, lecturers and professors, all as grim as hangmen. Behind the graduates rose several terraces of students' faces, the juniors or freshmen far at the back.

It was the singing that got to her, and the young, sprightly conductor, who seemed diminished by his voluminous dashiki, leaping and swaying while he steered his flock, and the volume of a hundred voices raised in song. In the past history of the institution people sang songs which spoke of the splendour of nature, hymns to the glory of God, in metaphors masking the exhortations to fight; but now – although the melodies and cadences hadn't undergone a transformation – the songs were different. They spoke of struggle and victory and the need to carry this heavy load of responsibility. Stammering beneath the lyrics was an understanding that, yes, the political struggle might have been won, but greater obstacles lay athwart the route to genuine independence. It was in the deep bass of the men that she heard the voice of her father, her mind stealing back to a past she had kept hidden in the deepest corners of her heart. She watched the men singing, their necks taut, the muscles outlined as if for a sacrifice. The women testified in soprano and alto voices, in acknowledgement of their deepest desire inside themselves, supplicating, cajoling and surrendering.

> *Thousands and thousands and thousands*
> *Are marching,*

They sang in diminuendo, the voices rasping now as if the choristers could envision blistered feet that marched on and on until something was made real.

★   ★   ★

It is January 1990 and they have been marching and protesting for days. Jonah looks tired, but he still has a word of encouragement for the group. Their theatre performances have suffered a setback with the detention of two members. The remaining members of the troupe march by day and sleep in safe houses at night, knowing that the security police always come at dawn.

She watches her brother saying goodbye to his girlfriend, Dudu, who looks a bit stunned when Jonah kisses her. 'I'll see you later at the usual place,' he promises her. 'For the time being, I have to take care of my sister.'

'Be careful,' Dudu warns and then gets into the back seat of the group's battered VW minibus. As the vehicle pulls off, hooting twice, Jonah and Zodwa stand watching. The late afternoon has transcended so swiftly into evening. The driver switches on the lights and the little corner of Longmarket Street gleams, momentarily, as if illuminated by a flash of lightning and then settles back into a cove of the country's secrets.

'I'll be careful,' Jonah mutters, almost to himself. He turns to Zodwa. 'What do you feel like doing?'

Zodwa yawns and stretches herself. Her muscles are cramped. 'I'm bushed. We could get something to eat for starters.'

'There's a hot group at the Bravo tonight,' Jonah says. 'I've been promising myself to go and check them out.'

As they walk, Zodwa tells him that she has decided to further her studies, and law seems to be a viable route. He looks at her, his face grave and asks her whether she knows what she's in for, whether she has bargained for poring over volumes that merely comment on the base nature of humankind. She assures him, her mouth set in a determined line, that she has the mettle to deal with it. Suddenly, he laughs, the amber lights catch his face, creating shadows, making him look handsome. *The mercy of our masters*, she remembers the lines, *and the beauty of our brothers*.

'What's so funny?' she asks.

'Lawyers,' he replies. 'They start off hustling like us, and then, *boom*! They are out there in Dracula's gowns, riding these very posh cars. You speak to them and they tell you, Can't stop now, *bro* – here's my card. Call me as soon as possible.' He shakes his head. 'Then you get into real trouble and you call the guy. A secretary tells you, No, So-and-so's out on a case in Bloemfontein. Did he leave a number? No.'

'You think I'll become that kind of monster, too?'

'Why not? You're human.' Jonah puts his arm around her while they wait for the light to change. They then cross the street. 'There's actually something quite sick about the black professional. It's like they have to pay lip service to the struggle, giving us hand-outs, but when the chips are down, they only want to rise and show the world how far they are from the sewer.'

'Would you rather we all stayed in the sewer, then?'

'No. People have a right to achieve. But that achievement comes with a price.' Jonah kicks an empty box of matches across the pavement onto the kerb. 'And the price merely means that you can't be true to yourself.'

'What about lawyers who've been killed by the Boers?' Zodwa presses on. 'The Mxenges? Mdu Guma who was killed at Matola – are they sick too?'

'Don't cross-examine me, Counsellor,' Jonah says, smiling. 'Those are exceptions.'

'As are Mandela, Tambo, Duma Nokwe, Skweyiya, Bizos, Soggott, Moerane, Baqwa ...' Zodwa shakes her head. 'So many of them, Jonah. What are you trying to say?'

In the gathering dark, after this question was posed, Zodwa feels irredeemably sad. She has always looked up to Jonah, her beautiful brother, and was willing to accept his word as gospel truth, but now she finds him wanting. She comprehends, now, that, like most young people of their generation, political comprehension resides cheek by jowl with illusions, that there is no strong ideological basis for their campaigns beyond being united in discrediting the white regime. She has seen a hodgepodge of mainly banned literature in Jonah's room. Mao. Lenin. Che Guevara. Eduardo Galeano. There are posters of Carlos Marighella and Angela Davis. While this affinity for romantic – and, sometimes, doomed – personalities on whom he models himself endears Jonah to women and arouses antagonism among men, Zodwa finds it tedious and somewhat blasé. He has reinvented himself through so many people that he doesn't exactly have a sense of his real identity.

It is this search for self-definition, for a political home, which lands him among young ideologues of the black consciousness movement where, owing to his fame in left-wing circles, he is venerated as a guru. Since the death of Steve Biko in 1977, Zodwa knows, the movement has never been the same, dominated, as it is now, by self-styled Marxists, eclectic demagogues and weak-eyed visionaries. Of course there are many young people who subscribe to the black consciousness philosophy who are moved by Biko's clarion call, Black man, you're on your own! Who believe in self-reliance and the unshackling of the mind. Many of these have joined the liberation movement, especially the ANC; others are in the ranks of the newly formed United Democratic Front, a coalition of trade unions, civic organisations, political formations, arts and culture groupings and professional bodies. It is following the arrest of some of the UDF leaders that Jonah and his comrades go out on a march of solidarity.

'Here we are,' Jonah says, ducking under a low awning on whose front the legend, Bravo! is written in blood-red fluorescent letters against a field of blue, to enter a narrow passage leading to a flight of stairs. Flush against the top landing is a table behind which stands a young woman whose practised smile reminds Zodwa of a television presenter. On the table is a curlicue snarl of tickets, which the woman tears off in sections. Her smile widens under Jonah's gaze, hardening when her eyes meet Zodwa's. Without word, she hands Jonah two tickets; he gives her some folded notes. The exchange done, Zodwa follows Jonah and they squeeze past the jam-packed bar to the room. Under the dim lights which invest the chattering crowd with a red hue, Zodwa becomes aware of two men who have entered; something about them tells her that she and her brother are being watched. She turns to get a good look at them.

There is something tentative about them, like newcomers to a strange town. The taller, bearded one is talking to his partner who is a head shorter. He is making a point, but his eyes waver and rest on Zodwa and Jonah. When his gaze meets hers, his eyes quickly shift to concentrate elsewhere. Security police, Zodwa thinks. What a pity that they are now recruiting handsome men.

But Jonah's easygoing manner in this dim place reassures her. He installs them at a table and orders drinks from a waiter. It takes a while before their drinks come. While they sit waiting for the band to start, Jonah studies the menu, finally settling on *pap en vleis*. 'It's not the house speciality,' he says, 'but it's a while since I had something that reminded me of home.'

'You've not been there for ages,' Zodwa says at last. 'When are you going to visit dad?'

'Hell, I don't know.' He sounds sorrowful. He lights a cigarette and, in that flicker of light, Zodwa sees how closely he resembles their father. 'Thing is,' he goes on, 'you get caught up in so many things, and, at the end of the day, you can't tell what you've accomplished.'

'Are you having troubles?'

'Jesus, what a question.' He looks round him, nods at a familiar face, and raises his hand in greeting. 'All of us are having troubles.' Taking a long drag and expelling twin columns of smoke through his nostrils, he waves the cigarette, like a wand. Then he lowers his head, and his voice. 'Some fellows came up to me last month, asking that I drive someone to the border.'

The food comes. Although hungry, Zodwa now feels a little nauseous. She concentrates on her drink. 'Yes?'

'I was given some money and I hired a car,' Jonah goes on. 'I took this guy, Dingo from his place, this was on a Sunday morning, timing myself to reach Jo'burg in the evening. My intention was that we'd spend the day holed up somewhere before driving to Oshoek.' He looks up at her as if trying to see if she is still with him. Zodwa nods her head.

'We reached Jo'burg much earlier,' Jonah says. 'That's when Dingo remembers that he has a relative in Orlando, some uncle. I say to him no relatives as this is serious. He insists, saying that there are a couple of things he has to pick up from there. So I relent – a fucking mistake.'

He makes a stab at his food, scoops a dollop of pap and drowns it in gravy. He chews slowly while looking ahead of him, as if reliving the drive to the township. 'We hit Orlando and we go to the old geezer's place. And what do we find? A whole fucking congregation having a service meeting. It's not just your good old prayer meeting, it's a service for Dingo's safe passage from this cruel world of apartheid to the welcoming arms of Umkhonto we Sizwe. I see this and I say, Dingo, what the fuck are you doing? You told this uncle of yours that we're coming? He says, yes, but his uncle is discreet. Discreet? With the whole bloody Zion Christian Church synod and you tell me it's discreet, come on, and grow up, man. It was when they were laying hands on him and mouthing phrases like "our liberator" and "freedom fighter" that I decided I'm getting out of here, shit. Drove non-stop all the way to Pietermaritzburg.'

'Shit,' Zodwa says.

'That's right.' He takes a sip from his glass. 'I went around looking for the guys who approached me with this Mickey Mouse operation, and guess what?'

'What?'

'They'd all been rounded up by Security.' He shakes his head. 'I had to dump the hired car, knowing that the cops would be waiting for me. I must have a hole in the head, getting mixed up with these amateurs.'

'I thought people were thoroughly briefed before they undertook a mission?'

'Well, I don't know who to blame.' He pauses, glancing at the bandstand where the musicians are beginning to set up. 'But I have a bad feeling about this.'

'What's going to happen? Where's Dingo now?'

'I hear he also got picked up,' Jonah says with a heavy sigh. 'Near the border.'

'The man that God didn't save – what a mess.'

'It's a glorious mess, all right.'

166

Then the lights become dimmer and the conversations stop. Musicians install themselves within the blazing circle of light on the bandstand. Like most jazz combos, they don't just come out and play, but move about, introducing an air of informality, patting one another on the back, laughing self-consciously, and stubbing out the last cigarette. They allow brief bursts from their instruments; in this way it would be impossible to know, until one was firmly hooked, when exactly they had started on a tune. It occurs to Zodwa that they, too, are aware of the terrain in which they operate. That is why musicians conceal their weapons in music cases, their cultural weapons. It is a matter of survival.

A smooth-faced black man, whose broad belly stretches and bells out the shirt over the waistband, approaches the microphone and rattles off a few jokes. 'Talking of money,' he says, 'there's this Zulu window-cleaner on the sixth floor of the Carlton Centre in Johannesburg. He sees something shiny way, way down in the parking lot and he says to himself, *Hawu! nang'uzuka* – That is a sixpence. Being quick on the draw, he takes a short cut and dives for it. As he clears some floors, the size of the coin increases, and he says to himself, It's a shilling, it's half-a-crown. More floors: It's a crown, until, just before he hits the concrete, *Hawu*, it's a dustbin lid. . . ' There is polite laughter, which sums up what people think of the joker.

'Ladies and gentlemen,' the impresario says, tapping the mike. When certain that now has everyone's attention, he introduces the musicians. Zodwa hears the names, some of which have been written in lights in the marquees of the city. There is a pianist, a drummer, a bassist, a lead guitarist, a trumpeter and a saxophonist who looked spooked, the instrument dangling in front of him an onerous weight.

Taking a sip of her drink and looking up at the bandstand, Zodwa confronts a truth that is as simple as it is complex. The musicians are isolated from the darkness; the radiance above their pomaded heads is their light. Since they take possession of it at that moment, and the moment claims them, they are the primary source of energy. It seems to her that since music is never heard but felt – and feelings are heightened in the dark – it is logical that music should be experienced in the private darkness of the listeners. She recalls that most jazz record titles derived their creative sustenance from the idiom of darkness – 'Mood Indigo', 'Blues in the Night' – where the solitary soul wrestles with pain and fear.

The music starts, continuing from the earlier banter, becoming a statement freighted with grave meanings. It segues from simple piano riffs to arpeggios, where each man communicates with a spirit through an instrument. It is no different from a religious service where sinners testify and the believers stand outside the circle of light and await the intercession of the Holy Ghost.

The audience listens, their silence emphasising the rasp of brushes against the nerve endings of brass cymbals. The men play without seeming in any great hurry to reach the moment of resolution because, it is clear, the road to resolution is long and strewn with glass shards, and they can't trust themselves – not yet – to reach that promised land. The piano, which sounds like an ancient harp, leads them across the marshes, coaxing them out of their dark skins to hold on until they can find steady ground. The pianist seems to be listening for something, a corroboration that would signify the sighting of a friendly zone. The trumpeter, a short balding man whose eyes are perpetually closed, licks the mouthpiece and lets loose with a spurt of warm notes that bring about memories of fire. It is as if the men are saying, There is fire everywhere, and we have to burn first before we can conquer it.

As the men tell their story, which is also the story of the listeners, a mixture of joy and sorrow descends on the room. The drinkers pause with their glasses halfway to the lips. Lovers holding hands hold on tighter, or disengage from each other, allowing solitude to touch them. The drummer, who seems in torment, lashes at the drums – *boom-boom-bah!* – beating a subterranean message to the trumpet. The saxophonist stands, head bent, left foot tapping to the beat, listening. He also, it seems, is waiting for the moment when his own story can be told. The men on strings pluck, pinch and tyrannise their guitars, causing a roar reminiscent of an ocean to rise up in the room. There follows a silence that indicates that there is yet a tough tale waiting to be told. The musicians look at the saxophonist and the light above wavers as if in deference to a shadow. Then the man takes a step forward and starts telling his story with his horn.

It is a story of generations, something which South Africans, black and white, cannot bear to hear. He speaks of the land and the beauty and the ugly weight of blood on the shoulders of the children. He speaks of a sadness that has taken hold of millions of people, of the workers and their bosses, of the mineshafts where men toil like moles in the bowels of the earth. He reminds the listeners of women without hope and men who prey on helplessness. On a higher register rings the piano's harp, reminding the tenor player that, somewhere, triumph lies waiting, throbbing like a pulse. Would he listen? No, he seems to say, straddling the saxophone and riding it in an act of savage coupling, screaming, No, no, leave me alone!

Then he starts his climb, his calf muscles bunched as exertion taxes his limbs. Sweat pours out of his brow and rolls down his face. Tears spring into the man's eyes and he appears to pray for some form of deliverance. Come with us, the other players suggest. This is our mess and we have to deal with it. Rearing like a maddened bull, the saxophone bellows, and the piano peals assent, Yes, and they all begin their journey home. Someone sniffs and Zodwa knows that her brother is weeping in the dark.

★   ★   ★

Someone else was weeping, somewhere in the back rows, and it was not clear to Zodwa whether the emotion-packed graduation ceremony was the cause, or that the student – for it must have been a student – was simply overcome by alcohol. Where she sat, the fumes were akin to a blast from a brewery, even though people had been warned against excess, since there would be visi-

169

tors. She saw Khaya swaying towards the close of the ceremony, as the assembly sang 'Nkosi Sikelel' iAfrika'. Another patriotic soul amidst the faculty members started singing 'Die Stem'. There was a confused, ragged rendition which ended, abruptly, when one of the choristers raised his fist and shouted, '*Amandla!*' There followed a throaty affirmation, '*Ngawethu!*'

Later in the evening, Zodwa sat at the edge of the settee in Khaya's room, watching the party animals having a ball, drinking still more whisky and pondering the events of the day. There was a mixed crowd of about twenty people squeezed into the room, those who had graduated still hysterical with relief that it was finally over. Loud music blared from the stereo player hooked up and synched to a VCR. The images on the television monitor showed sultry, pouting African–American women singers and dancers in soft-coloured silk costumes; below them, across the screen was the legend, TLC – 'Creep.'

  I'm gonna creep … yeah
  Twenty seconds of loneliness …

And the women students danced, shuffling and shimmying and being sexy, doing seductive routines that seemed to confuse the men. Just when Zodwa was toying with the idea of joining in, there was a loud rapping on the door that was, anyway, ajar. Khaya limped to see who it was and came back with Horwitz in tow. 'The massa's looking for you,' he said and, after giving her a quizzical look, he went back to his drink. Horwitz looked worse for wear himself.

'God, Zodwa,' he said, 'I've been searching for you high and low.'

'Well,' Zodwa said, crossing her arms. 'You've found me now. What do you want here?'

'Can I get a drink?' Horwitz whined. He looked round him. 'Good party.'

'No drink,' Zodwa said. 'You want to know the reason why not?'

'*Ja*, tell me …'

'Seems to me you've been drinking already,' she said, 'and I know that whatever brought you here, you'll still be driving back to Ngoza. I don't see you making it in that state.'

'*Ag*, Zodwa,' one of the male students said, 'let the man have a drink. Here,' he said, handing Horwitz a glass full of amber liquid. 'Drink to the future when the past will be seen in tinted glasses.'

'Thanks,' Horwitz said, and took a sip. 'Mmm, whisky, my favourite drink.'

The student who had offered Horwitz a drink was staring at him with a frightening intensity. 'You believe that the future will be brilliant,' he asked. 'Don't you, my man?'

Horwitz smiled, unsure of his ground. 'Of course. We all have to work towards that.'

'It's a noble ideal, don't you think?'

'Yes, I suppose so.'

'You suppose so? You mean you're not entirely convinced?'

'I'm convinced,' Horwitz said uncomfortably. 'The future is what people make of it.'

'Hey, that's nice.' The student was grinning. 'So,' he went on, 'we made the past for you white people and we now have to secure your future too. Don't you think that's a little unfair? I mean,' he said with vehemence, jabbing his finger against Horwitz's breast, 'when are you white fuckers going to *suffer*?' He hurled the last word, like an insult.

'Hold it!' Zodwa said. 'David? Let's get out of here.' She shoved David Horwitz gently towards the door. As they left the room she found herself humming, 'Creep … yeah.' Outside, she felt the blast of the breeze from Hogsback Mountains. 'What is it?'

'It's your father,' Horwitz said. 'He's very ill.'

'How bad is it?' Zodwa learnt on the doorjamb. I'm a strong woman, she told herself, and I shall not collapse. My father is ill and the music is playing, Creep … And they sent this creep to tell me, oh my God.

'It's bad enough. I was told to come and get you.'

'How are we going?' she asked. 'Don't tell me you're driving, not in your condition.'

'Don't worry about it. Nozizwe and the elders organised a chauffeur.'

★   ★   ★

Here she was, now, with her father lying still on the bed, the strange white woman watching. She thought of the drive, how Horwitz had declared undying love for her – and she had been immovable. She was angry at his indiscretion, knowing that the stone-faced man driving them would report everything to Nozizwe, word for word. Horwitz was a dalliance that had cost her dearly, something she wished to wipe out of her memory.

'I brought someone to see you, Baba,' Zodwa said. She motioned for Benedita to sit on the edge of the bed. 'He hates people standing over him,' she explained.

'I see,' Benedita whispered. The inside of the tent was well ventilated, but beads of perspiration had appeared on the tip of her nose.

'This is my father, Benedita,' Zodwa said, 'and he went through the length and breadth of the country to make a home for us, back here in these stony plains. He had a dream. Only this fucking country cannot deal with dreams and visions, did you know that?'

'You mustn't curse,' Baba Joshua, whose eyes were now open, said feebly from his bed. 'My daughter,' he said to Benedita, 'I'm happy that you came to see me.'

'I'm honoured, sir,' Benedita said. She gazed down at her lap and fiddled with her fingers. 'I'm just so sorry that you're indisposed.'

'I'm glad you're here,' Joshua said, 'because I wish my daughter to promise something. And –' he struggled to smile, '– since she's now a lawyer, she knows that there must be a third party to make a pledge binding.'

'What's that, Baba?' Zodwa asked.

'That,' Joshua said, 'when I go, you'll take charge of this place. Help us build.'

'I can't, Baba. I have to go to Johannesburg to start on my articles.'

'Zodwa …' Benedita said. 'He's your father.'

'Of course he's my father!' Zodwa snapped. 'You mean I must just make a promise and not keep it.'

'I implore you, Zodwa,' Joshua persisted. 'For the people.'

'Look, Baba, the people don't know me here.'

'They know me. They know you.'

'They don't even like me.'

'They don't judge, my people.'

'Still …'

'All right.' Joshua was tired. 'For Jonah.'

'That's not fair,' Zodwa said in a small voice. She scanned her father's face and noticed that his skin had taken on a greyish tinge. Small white bubbles frothed at the corners of his mouth. Seeing him in this condition, reduced from a scourge of sinners into a shell inhabiting a treacherous body, she understood that even though he loved her, he wished that his son were present to continue the bloodline. But, Zodwa knew, although he was a practising Christian, who also believed in the Christian ethic of forgiveness, what had been done to his son drove him to invoke choice Biblical texts that turned their backs on forgiveness. Vengeance is mine. She would be the fool to achieve a dream that straddled the grave. She nodded. 'Okay.'

Joshua struggled to sit up. Zodwa propped his back with the pillows. 'I'm going to ask you to leave us for a minute,' he said. 'I need to talk to my daughter. Alone.'

'Yes, of course,' Benedita said, with some relief. She quickly went out of the tent. Outside, the crowds had multiplied. Above the heads of the people, she saw Venter turning to look at her. She ignored him and stood by the tent, feeling, all of a sudden, a strange emotion that threatened to overwhelm her. She had been privileged, allowed a glimpse into the lives of people who,

173

for her and her people, were mere means of convenience. The young woman's strength left her feeling ashamed.

Presently, Zodwa came out of the tent, a little unsteady on her feet. Benedita rushed to her and caught her in a clasp whose strength – or desperation – surprised even herself. Zodwa's face looked ashen, drained of colour, her eyes stunned.

'He's in a bad shape,' Benedita prompted. 'Isn't he?'

Zodwa nodded. 'It looks very bad.' Then she allowed herself to be enfolded in the strange woman's arms. Tears sprung into her eyes, and she thought of all the words of love she should have showered on her father. Before long, she knew, she wouldn't be able to reach him. Already, it felt like the end of a long dream.

Eleven

Mpanza spent the morning washing his clothes and talking to Reuben. At noon Reuben left him to make his deliveries and collect whatever knicknacks were part of his trade. Later, Mpanza hung the shirts, underwear, socks and two pairs of jeans on the clothesline, satisfied that, since Reuben's place was on a higher plane, the clothes would dry quickly. Perched on a rock and stripped to the waist, he watched the activity on the settlement below, people moving like so many black ants. Reuben had told him of Baba Joshua's critical state. This had been something of a shock for Mpanza because he hadn't managed to make peace with the old man. Mpanza had also seen too many of his comrades struck down by strokes and coronaries: he imagined the vessels bursting inside the head, the heart pumping blood and recycling oxygen in its struggle to save life, succeeding in obliterating life. Most people survived, and conducted themselves with care, like dreamers who had been shown the reality of death, but the trauma usually diminished them, where they became shadows of their former vital selves.

The village grapevine had also crackled with the news of Baba Joshua's daughter, who had come in from Fort Hare. Once the relatives of the stricken started visiting, he knew it was time to consult the undertakers. What kind of daughter was Zodwa? he wondered. He remembered her face, when he and Stan had sat listening to music while keeping an eye on Jonah in the Bravo! The memory of it all left him sick.

A short time after noon, he was cooking them some meat and

potatoes on a Primus stove in the kitchen when he heard the sound of hooves on the packed ground. He turned and saw Johnny M dismounting from his horse. Striding towards the cabin, he was fanning himself with his hat while squinting to scan the surroundings. From where he stood, Mpanza wished to advise the visitor to get himself a pair of sunglasses to filter the strong glare. He stepped outside, the more to admire the exquisite animal than to welcome Johnny M.

'*Heita*, Mpanza,' Johnny M said. Without waiting to be invited in, he entered the kitchen, looked around and pulled a stool and sat down. Looking up at the doorway where Mpanza was standing, he said: 'Seeing that I was in the neighbourhood, I thought I might come and look you up.'

'I'm flattered,' Mpanza said, coming in and checking his pots. 'The last time I dealt with a black man on a horse it was a policeman in Durban trying to break up a demonstration.'

'Well,' Johnny M said, 'you might have to ride one, too. For the kind of thing I have in mind for you.' He paused. 'You can ride, can't you?'

The question immediately told Mpanza that Johnny M had made inquiries about him. Because, it was clear, the man knew that he could ride; he was that type of person who checked on everything which concerned people he had dealings with. Reuben had told him of Johnny M's connection with Grey. The wires must have crackled with all the data from Hungary, Lusaka, Angola and the return to the Defence Force. And being demobbed, or retrenched, as Khethiwe might have delicately put it.

'I can ride,' Mpanza said. 'But what is this that you have me in mind about?'

In lieu of an answer, Johnny M stood up. 'Shit, it's a bloody furnace in here. Let's step outside and find some shade.'

Mpanza threw herbs and spices into the stew, closed the saucepan and lowered the flame. Then he went outside and joined Johnny M, who was sitting on a low stool under the shade of a mango tree. Smoke was billowing from cooking-fires down at the settlement. 'You care for a drink or something?' he asked Johnny M.

'No, I'm okay,' Johnny M said, tugging at the seams of his trousers to relieve his knees. He glanced at his horse, which was nibbling at the dry kikuyu grass before turning to Mpanza. 'Some of my guys have been messing up,' he began, 'and I need a thinking person to help me sort things out.'

Johnny M was chairman of the Two Rivers Squatters Development Board. Owing to the confusion deriving from the transition from apartheid governance to community structures, there was a leadership gap. But development needed to take place. Transitional mechanisms were being put in place, but this was a slow process, with the few of the functional community leaders being spread thin on the ground. This meant that the monthly rates of five rands per household were not being collected. Johnny M had discussed the matter with the police chief, Grey, but Grey also had a personnel problem. There were range wars in Upper Ngoza and he felt that this was a sensitive issue, which needed the community to sort out. Would Mpanza help? He would be paid – handsomely – for his pains.

'You want a glorified debt collector, is that it?' Mpanza asked.

'I wouldn't put it that strongly,' Johnny M answered tentatively. 'Fact is, this has to be done. I thought a man with your political experience would see the necessity for community development.'

'What has the Board achieved?' Mpanza asked. 'Those shacks look like. . . shacks.'

'I organised workers to improve the sewage,' Johnny M said. 'There were no toilets, people shat all over the place and there was an outbreak of diseases. Diarrhoea. Typhoid. People died. We got some money together and hired a few fellows. Now', he went on expansively, 'you can even read comics in the loo.'

'But how many families are there?'

'Give or take two thousand units.' Johnny M leant forward. 'I know that the little computer in your head is rattling off figures. Two thousand multiplied by five by twelve equals R120 000 a year. But it's not that simple. Sometimes fires break out, people become homeless – or die. We bury them and rebuild. All that can sometimes mean throwing good money after bad. That's what makes it so crucial that everyone pays his or her dues.'

'But shouldn't that be the headache of the Ngoza administration?' Mpanza asked Johnny M. 'I understand that the squatter area falls under their jurisdiction. That the Land Claims Court ruled in their favour?'

'What do you think can be achieved by a bunch of religious greybeards?' Johnny M countered. 'With a strong traditional lobby thrown in just to screw things up more? Nothing. While some new settlers might look to God or the spirit of Shaka, or both, the people need something done for them.'

'I take it that you're not exactly overjoyed over the Land Claims Court ruling?'

'I won't pretend that I get into rhapsodies over it,' Johnny M admitted. 'It's something that has to be fought until real, strong leadership can be set in place.'

'Meaning yourself?'

'If the people want me to continue getting them what they want,' Johnny M said, 'then I can identify with that.'

'Even if it means going against elected authority?'

'Let's be fair, now, okay?' Johnny M was getting heated. 'Those people wouldn't know how to elect the village dogcatcher if that opportunity presented itself with their breakfast cereal. I've heard all this talk about democracy and accountability. Big words, nice on the tongue, but meaningless in the real world.' He glanced at his wristwatch. 'Damn,' he said, 'I've run out of time.' He got to his feet, brushing dust off the seat of his pants. 'Look,' he said, 'personally, I think you can use the money I'll be paying you. But it's all up to you. When you have decided, get in touch with me.'

Mpanza watched Johnny M getting on his horse. He waved and carefully guided the animal down the stony steep. Mpanza

178

thought it would be nice to be on a horse.

★   ★   ★

'Take the job. Take the money,' Reuben the Collector said, his voice coming through one of a pair of Makonde masks hanging on the wall, flanking the passage. Mpanza had become thoroughly irritated by his uncle's trick – learnt during a stint with a travelling circus or theatre company some decades ago – of throwing his voice. During his rounds, Reuben would sometimes bring some of the Two Rivers women very close to heart seizures when he adopted the voices of their men, and threw them from within somewhere in the house. 'You'll throw that voice once too often,' Nerissa once warned him, 'and when you look for it you'll find it gone.' Recognising that Mpanza was in a serious mood, Reuben now spoke in a normal voice with his mouth full. 'Take the money and run,' he said, spraying his overalls with particles of food. Mpanza wondered despairingly which of the two habits was more disgusting. Reuben dipped a handful of pap into the spiced meat and potato gravy and gesticulated with the greasy hand. '*Mshana*,' he went on, 'this is the new South Africa, all right. For many people, it's also new money. The struggle is over, no-one's going to give you a tickey *bhansela*, true's the living God.'

'But', Mpanza said, 'I have a feeling something's not very kosher here. People are being robbed blind.'

Reuben stood up from the table and rummaged in the cooler. It was then that Mpanza looked at the kitchen, which adjoined the simple bedroom and admired Reuben's building and carpentry skills. He had somehow converted an old building, perhaps an ancient place of worship, where he had knocked off the original ceiling and added two layers of blocks. The crossbeams overhead could have been cannibalised from an old church, sanded and varnished. Occupying a central place on the ceiling was a rectangular skylight, fashioned from the same hard plastic covering the tall window frames. Like the windows, the door was reinforced with gauze to keep out the insects. Even as

179

they talked now, Mpanza could hear gnats and moths attempting to enter with such ferocity that the insects might have been motivated by a need to savage the light. The floors were made of polished sandstone, which gleamed like marble, bouncing off the last light of the day from above. Everything in the two-roomed dwelling, from the wooden spoons to the beds and wardrobe, had either been scavenged elsewhere or constructed by Reuben. He took a dim view of the wastefulness of people, and would have to be coaxed into buying anything he could make himself.

Reuben was a short, small man with big bones and a large head with prominent cheekbones. Mpanza thought that there was something oriental about him, his eyes sloping at the corner, a thin, unnegroid nose, and dark glasses that he wore even at night. 'To spook the spooks,' was his offered reason. Thin as he was, Reuben never ceased to amaze Mpanza by the amount of food he could eat; he also had a staggering resistance to alcohol. Mpanza had never once heard him mentioning a woman in connection with himself, although there were conflicting stories that he had left KwaMashu Township in a great hurry when found in a compromising situation with the wife of a notorious warlord.

Now, he came back with two cans of lager. Opening the can and taking a long draught, he leant forward. 'Seems to me those years in exile robbed you of an understanding of what's going on. *Mshana*, people all look out for number one – themselves. When the white boy Horwitz went to Pretoria to talk about the land of Ngoza, I was asked by Joshua to go with him. Why, I don't know, but he wanted someone else to accompany the *mlungu*. What I saw there opened my mind. Everywhere you go you see white people, secretaries and officials. They walk like they own the place, never mind that the minister is a black person. The people who play the *katara* are white. Do you think that they have any interest in developing us? No. It is for this reason that I believe you must take the job and the money and do something.'

'But it's not doing something,' Mpanza protested. 'It's just continuing with the corruption, and that doesn't sit well with me.'

Reuben clicked his tongue. 'Mmf, don't preach to me about corruption. Is it corruption to ensure that your friend has a bite to eat?'

'No, but ... ?'

'So,' Reuben said triumphantly, 'it's not wrong for ministers to have people of their kind or their chommies in powerful positions, is it?'

'It's wrong if the emphasis is on friendship rather than merit.'

'Merit?' Reuben laughed. 'That's a funny word. What merit? If people were chosen on merit then this country wouldn't be in such a mess.' He looked up. 'Seriously, though, you need to think about how you'll survive. Also think about Khethiwe and the kids.'

'That's a closed chapter, Rue,' Mpanza said. 'Don't bring that up now.'

'It's not me who's going to bring it up,' Reuben said stubbornly. 'It'll come up all by itself, mark my words.'

Later, Mpanza sat alone while Reuben was away again on some errand. He was a strange man, Reuben. And Mpanzal saw how easy it was for people to misjudge him, and undermine him and think he was merely a rag-and-bones man. Reuben was as sharp as a tack. He had taught himself to read and write, later on attending night school to confirm his self-education. Most people, Mpanza judged, couldn't have known this, simply because this knowledge was beneath them. But Joshua had not been fooled by outside appearances, hence his inclusion of Reuben in the delegation to Pretoria.

A truth that was painful as it was damning was that certain sections of black society tended to judge people on their ability to imitate the white man. The closer the pale ghost was to the ways of the masters, the higher he was elevated in people's eyes. He remembered, as a child, when people spoke admiringly of slim, light-skinned women: '*Muhle ungath'umlungu* – She's pretty as a white person.' People said this with a disarming, bland and bluff lack of self-consciousness; for them it was an unassailable fact. As a Boy Scout, one of the greatest infractions that Mpanza committed was suggesting that the Queen of England also used a toilet. It was not surprising, then, that natural, native intelligence counted for naught if it wasn't sanctified by certificates from the white man's institutions – or reasonable facsimiles thereof – of higher education.

He had seen this when he joined the SANDF. Ex-combatants who knew everything about military technique and intelligence, but who hadn't received any formal qualifications, were, during the integration process of the armed forces, downgraded in rank to NCO level – these people who had evolved ingenious military strategies that had confounded the security forces. Years of the bush and years of gleaning knowledge from far and wide didn't count. *What degree do you have?* This was the operational question. In government, people who had spent the years of struggle grappling with *-isms* and arcane and abstruse concepts occupied some of the senior positions. Like the fabled Mau Mau fighters who had waged war against colonial Kenya, returned combatants started assuming the status of pariahs. Those who had lived high on the hog during apartheid years now lorded it over those who had endangered their own lives and careers. The latter had hoped that the new dream would accommodate – as Margaret Walker, the African–American poet put it – *all the people, all the faces, all the Adams and Eves and their countless generations.*

But, Mpanza thought, it is true what they say about the revolution eating its own children. He remembered his own mission to South Africa, where Jonah was killed. He agreed with the strategy and tactics which the liberation movement had adopted in relation to the execution of the armed struggle. The 1969 document, coming out of the Morogoro Conference in Tanzania, outlined that central to the objectives was the liberation of the African people. They were, after all, the most oppressed. The curious paradox, however, was the harshness of measures taken against black transgressors, whether inside or outside the formal liberation struggle. Informers or suspects who were mostly black – and thus accessible – were treated with callousness beyond imagination. But people who were members of the regime's security forces were, in the eyes of many, welcomed with open arms in the new dispensation. Securocrats were part and parcel of the new structures. But, to deepen the confusion, the black quislings, former 'presidents' and functionaries of the bantustan system, were given great responsibilities. It was not difficult, then, to shrug and sigh and ask: Was it all worth it? Or be resigned to the gloating of a businessman who, after the April 1994 elections, summed up the anxieties of white people: Now that they have been given political power, we can concentrate on our task of consolidating economic power.

*   *   *

The visit to the hotel beer garden, which was on the same block as Johnny M's all-purpose store and the police station, made his mind up for him. He was sitting outside on the wire chairs, sipping a beer and listening to people talking about Baba Joshua, when a familiar figure ambled up to him. Mpanza had long forgotten about Tsepo and the structure he represented. But here he was now, walking towards him, politely nodding at the sprinkling of people, mainly whites, around the white tables under umbrellas. Tsepo, in a khaki safari suit and polished brown boots, a small leather bag attached to his wrist, pulled up a chair and shifted his ample upper body into the shade.

'I'm embarrassed,' Tsepo said, 'that my being here doesn't surprise you.'

Mpanza continued studying him. 'I didn't think that embarrassment was within your range of emotions.' He shifted the glass and drew patterns on the table from the moisture from the glass base. 'But I must say, I'm disappointed it's taken you so long to get here.'

'Are you settling in, though?' Tsepo asked, snapping a finger to catch the waiter's attention. 'Because your uncle's place might not be the most ideal location. We could provide you with alternative accommodation.'

'I'm okay where I am,' Mpanza said, knowing that Reuben would be mortified if he heard this conversation. 'Moreover,' he put in cruelly, 'any place you offer would be crawling with all sorts of electronic insects.'

'You overestimate us,' Tsepo said, smiling thinly. 'I wish our enemies thought we were that organised.' The waiter came and he made his order. 'Heard you had a dramatic contretemps with Johnny M the other day?'

'News sure travels fast.' Mpanza was impressed with Tsepo's fieldwork, his busy nose. 'He's offering me a job.'

'How's that?'

'He needs a debt collector. Looks like his regular enforcers aren't up to scratch.'

'Do you feel cut out for something like that?'

Before answering, a thought insinuated itself into Mpanza's mind. His cashiering from the Military Headquarters. Khethiwe precipitating a split. Tsepo appearing and his own sojourn into Ngoza. Suddenly everything felt connected. He hoped he wasn't going to become a victim of his own conspiracy theories. 'I have to do something. I'll probably take it. See where it goes, really.'

'Don't you think it's simply amazing,' Tsepo put in, 'that people now actually *consider* taking a job? In the past, with the cops hauling you into jail for *looking* unemployed, people jumped at the mere mention of the J-word.'

Mpanza agreed with him, remembering the pass raids, the prisons filling up with young men – and women – who'd been endorsed out of White areas. In his mind's eye, he saw the insatiable *kwela-kwela* trucks full of people whose only crime was being born black. However, some of the leaders, alarmed at the rate of crime in the downtown area of Johannesburg, were already calling for some form of influx control, complementing the clamour for the return of the death penalty as a reaction to a particularly horrific murder or rape. How was South Africa going to deal with this singular blight – crime? Carjacking, for example, had reached unacceptable levels. What was an acceptable level?

'We've been keeping our sights on Johnny M,' Tsepo said. 'Having you as part of his outfit might have its advantages.'

'For you, you mean?'

'For us – sure,' Tsepo said, sounding irritated. 'But it's also for the country, you know? There's this little thing called patriotism, Mpanza. It's something that kept us faithful to the cause.'

Mpanza wanted to tell him that patriotism was not his cup of tea, that, like many of his compatriots, he was also looking out for number one, himself. But he thought better of it. 'I'm taking the job, Tsepo. I feel that, having given me two assignments, you people must start coughing up some money.' He paused for the waiter to finish serving. 'What's your reading of Johnny M?'

'He's dealing in something,' Tsepo said, taking a sip from his drink. 'When some of the Right-wingers were here, they left large arms caches. We don't know where they are. In the wars in Msinga and Upper Ngoza, some of the captured rifles come from those stocks.'

'How come you don't just go in and arrest the bugger?'

'Proof. There's no proof. We think that he's in this with Grey. That makes our work quite difficult.'

'Where do the people in the settlement fit into this?'

'I don't think they know,' Tsepo answered. 'At least, we have established that the Old Man knew nothing. His daughter, though, is another kettle of fish.'

'Why?'

'We don't have anything on her,' Tsepo said, 'except that she's one hell-raiser and is quite fond of scotch. Beyond that, her politics leave us stumped.'

'If Baba Joshua goes,' Mpanza asked, 'is she taking over?'

Tsepo shook his head. 'It's highly unlikely,' he said. 'She does-n't sound like the type that would stay here a minute longer than necessary. The grapevine suggests she might join one of the big-deal legal companies in Jo'burg. They are always looking for fresh meat, and she's a juicy prime cut in affirmative action stakes.'

'And your sources have always been spot-on?'

'Indubitably.' Tsepo silently mouthed the word as if entranced by its syllables. 'But then,' he added weakly, 'you never know, do you?'

'Yes, you never know.' Mpanza snapped his fingers. 'Now, about that money. . . ?'

'You never give up, do you?' Tsepo said. Then he reached for his wallet.

Twelve

Exactly at 0345, eighteen hours after Baba Joshua's stroke, Jannie
Venter left the guardhouse to relieve Jim Momberg from guard
duty. Bloody Momberg, Venter thought, always accompanied by
his chattering monkey. Unlike Momberg, who had a companion, even if it were a primate given to percussive farting, Venter
would be alone. He didn't look forward to the task since it was
dark and a torrential downpour reduced visibility to zero. He
had known darkness before, but this was ridiculous. He was
armed with his AK-47, which was not security issue. It was part
of the booty from the military arsenal, which the C-10 unit had
diverted to KwaZulu-Natal, just to keep things boiling there.
Well-stocked with extra magazines and grenades, he felt that the
only thing lacking was a torch. There was a torch in the guardhouse, but anyone on guard duty knew that light was the easiest
way of drawing fire, and he wasn't up to that, yet.

However, he enjoyed the solitude the night gave him.
Beneath the roar of the rain against his hooded waterproof jacket, frogs croaked; somewhere in the dark was the sound of sleepless insects. Apart from that the silence was complete. It was the
silence of an African bush, something that stretched and spread
and became part of the night walker's world. There had been
many such nights, where men became men and forgot everything happening in civilian life – and merged with nature and
the breathing things hidden in the bush. He sincerely hoped that
those hidden things didn't include someone with a sniper's rifle,
because, to die here would be a supreme irony. He had come to

tangle with Grey, take him out even – not to get killed by some scared *munt* with a twitchy trigger finger.

The whole campaign was full of ironies. Here they were, assigned to stem gunrunning and the resultant butchery in which the villagers of Upper Ngoza and Msinga engaged with savage relish. They had met with a measure of success, confiscating large consignments of arms. Yet the truth was that people connected to the security force in the first instance had distributed these weapons. White South Africa, he reasoned, tended to act this way, putting into motion a series of self-fulfilling prophecies. We call blacks jailbirds and then we create conditions whereby they have no option but to resort to crime – and then we lock them up. Philosophical considerations bored him, and gave him a headache. Some of these things were meant to be this way, and it didn't make any sense to try and change them. You just got crushed in the process. Not that he wanted to change anything.

Benedita presented a mule-like obstinacy when faced with this contradictory aspect of her husband's kinsmen. She simply didn't understand. Had she grown up in this country and known the price people had paid, then she would be sure to empathise. She saw things his way, here and there, but on the whole, she felt that he was getting so deep into the culture of brutality that he was slowly but surely sloughing off all decency and becoming one of 'them'. He got stumped when she got all steamed up, not knowing whether 'them' referred to the armed *munts* or the armed security people. She probably saw both parties as two sides of the same coin.

But he had made some gains. Venter was sure that the guns they had confiscated came from an arsenal controlled by Grey. The serial numbers tallied with the numbers in the record book. He had stolen into Grey's office and photocopied the pages. Now the weapons were nicely stashed in the strong-room next door to the holding cells where about twenty captured men and women were held. At first light, Venter meant to assemble the physical evidence, both human and material, and transport it to Durban, where he was sure to meet sympathetic officers who were not tainted. The thought of Grey getting his come-uppance lifted his mood.

With thoughts of an abstract humiliation of his enemy in mind, Venter sloshed through the mud, the whole surface of his skin prickly alert, straining to keep his progress to Momberg's observation post as quiet as possible. But not so quiet that he slammed into a bullet. Momberg was a nervous kid; he wanted out of this detail and there was no telling what would happen if shit really hit the fan. Venter didn't want to know either. He had seen many people die in accidental shootings or, as happened on border duty, someone went *bosbefok* and let loose with a machine-gun, screaming at an imaginary enemy. Reflecting on those dark, dreary moments, he wondered how he had survived those periodic sojourns into enemy territory. He was intact, he reasoned, because there was a bigger and higher imperative that guided him and ensured his continued survival.

★   ★   ★

Seven years earlier, Venter is in a bivouac tent, listening to cicadas punctuating the late afternoon crackle of thorn-bush with their chirping, when Ralph Elgin approaches him and cadges a smoke. Other troopers from the company are in their dugouts, alert in that lazy, contemptuous way which characterises their collective attitude towards the terrorists. They know, now, that the combined forces of Fapla and Swapo have shelled some garrisons, and the troopers have taken some casualties. Intelligence reports have also alerted them to the massing of Cubans. Even though the troopers might be disparaging of Swapo and, to some extent, Fapla, the Cubans are another matter altogether. Simply because the Cubans are crazy and unpredictable. But since Venter's company is equipped to deal with any contingency, there's confidence all round.

The tension of waiting for action – any action – begins to tell on the men. The heat doesn't help. It pounds down and envelops them like a wet thermal blanket. The heat crackles like static, a moving mass of a palpable blast from some celestial furnace. Men, browned by the sun, kid each other that back home, they would run the risk of being reclassified as *darkies*. 'As long as my *pippie* stays white,' one of the men quips, 'my *vrou* will never mistake me for a fucking *houtkop*.' Another wit puts in 'Unless, of course, a *houtie* is busy diddling her right now …' 'In this heat?' the first man cries. 'Come on, man, even *houties* are not that *bedonnerd*.'

Ralph Elgin has been meaning to catch Venter's attention, but Venter can't be bothered. Everyone knows that Ralph is dangerously unpredictable. This is the persona he has built around himself, a self-invention aimed at the army hard cases that once thought him a sissy, just because he was a graduate from Wits and held a respectable job as a chartered accountant in his civilian life. To prove how macho he is – that he is far from being a *banggat* – Ralph draws attention to himself. During patrols where sometimes the troopers have to crawl, he will walk upright or crouch, perhaps meaning to draw enemy fire, until an officer orders him into adopting requisite military conduct. The men are clear that he is beyond the pale, this bright boy who harbours a subconscious death wish.

But today he seems calm, like a malaria sufferer who's just been told that the fever has broken. He sits on a boulder and traces bird patterns on the sand with a stick. Looking up at him, Venter feels that a rambunctious Ralph is preferable to the one before him. Then Venter notices that, behind the thick glasses, tears have sprung into Ralph's eyes, and are rolling down his cheeks; Ralph makes no effort to stem the flow creating trails down his dust-encrusted face. Venter has seen men cry before and knows that it spells trouble. He looks across where other men are lying in their tents underneath the camouflage netting. To stand up and walk away will be a slap in the face, he reasons. Better let the man come out and say what's eating him.

'I hear there was an attack at Vootrekkerhoogte,' Ralph says.

'My brother's dead.'

As if drawn by bad news the way flies are to an open sore, other men approach from the armoured trucks to hunker down beside Ralph. The news is still fresh and will only be official once a bulletin has been released. The men caution against reaching hasty conclusions – how could Ralph know that his brother is dead? Names of casualties are the last to be released for the public. Everything has to be cleared with Headquarters first. Therefore, Venter found this demonstration by Ralph particularly irritating, especially since it might have a negative effect on the troopers' morale.

'What makes you think your brother's dead?' he asks. 'Someone send you a fax?'

Ralph looks at him with eyes that are slightly out of focus, as if dismissing the questioning of something so patently self-evident. 'We are twins,' he puts in simply. 'This morning I woke up feeling very depressed. That only happens when something's wrong with Jerry.'

'But you're always depressed, Ralph. Does that mean your brother's been dying everyday since the beginning of this week?'

The men laugh, not realising that Venter is quite serious. He merely wishes that Ralph could get over his absurd attitude. The other troopers saunter away, possibly to find other company whose prospects are a lot more cheery. Venter, wishing that Ralph would go, slumps back and tries to relax. 'Don't say things until you've really verified them, Ralph,' he admonishes. 'Otherwise you'll get all of us into deep *kak* with your high jinks.'

Chastised, Ralph leaves for his section. Venter closes his eyes and thinks about Cynthia in Pretoria. He loves his wife, but he feels weird, being so far away from her. Something tells him that it is unhealthy, this distance and separation. He can't conjure up in his mind an instance when they really spent quality time together. He goes on these border missions, or, as is happening now, delves deep in Angolan territory. Like most policeman on this tour of duty – and, as soon as he returns to civvy street – he finds himself assigned back again. And when he tells Cynthia about this, she acts all lovey-dovey and convinces him that she doesn't mind the periods of separation. She busies herself with studying as she wishes to advance herself when they leave the police force. Furthermore, she tells him, these assignments to the bush will advance his career; it just shows that Grey and the other officers have a lot of faith in him. 'There's nothing more important', Cynthia advises, 'than people having confidence in you.'

But now, in their encampment some five kilometres from the edge of Angolan swampland, he begins to doubt everything. When he goes home and wants to sleep with Cynthia, she pleads exhaustion, or ever-lasting headaches. When they do make love she doesn't disguise the fact that, for her, this is a chore. One night he catches her watching him in a speculative and hostile way. He files this off and dismisses it as the imaginings of a sex-starved husband. Increasingly, sex starts taking a back seat in their relationship, until such time as he accepts her point of view that sex is actually not that crucial – companionship is. She assaults him with her blue-eyed candour, enlisting his complicity in this conjugal denial. He is then put in a position where he has to be grateful for those small acts of affection, which she dispenses with the economy of a quartermaster in a military establishment beset by hard times. This heightens his tension, setting him on edge, occasioning his bungling when the sexual rations come his way.

The dirty, yellowing sky in the west heralds the approach of night. It is in the night that his failures roam, triumphant and arrogant, taunting him remorselessly. Memory being such a bastard, he remembers a time when he would come back home, like a real soldier returning from war, to the surprises Cynthia would have in store for him. She would wait in the room, her blonde hair cascading down her face, like a dream, under a yellow electric light. Somewhere in the room a record would be playing something soft, muted, like the sighs of lovers, and Cynthia would stand, looking at him, self-conscious in her sweater and skirt – and high heels he loved her to wear. Their love or union would always be characterised by a dependence on fantasy. He accepted the need for make-believe, a spice. She would sit on the settee and kick off her shoes and beckon him with a crooked finger, her painted lips mouthing the words, Come on, big boy! And he would comply, crossing the carpeted floor to cover a distance that would seem as wide as rivers. 'Just to be close to you', the song would go, and Venter would get close to her and take in her fragrance, caress her neck, feeling the corn-silk texture of her hair under his fingertips.

From her remembered touch, Venter knows that she was in control. She shed the skirt, kicking it off, he drinking in the sight of her golden legs, long and seemingly endless, and slipping his hand in the warmth of the inside of her sweater, touching the softness, careful, remembering how she once cautioned him against grasping. 'Men just grab at you, as if you're some piece of meat.' At this moment, he would be unable to ask her which men, the power of speech having devolved to *his* piece of meat, somehow understanding that such knowledge would damn him. Then she would turn from his grasp and pin him against the settee, appearing so slow but actually hurrying, unzipping his fly and nuzzling his tumescent penis with her teeth, murmuring almost inaudibly about his natural taste. The image, here, thousands of miles from home, shatters and dissolves into wisps of memory. He falls asleep still thinking about his beautiful unattainable wife.

★ ★ ★

Later, it is quite dark when Ralph returns, fully kitted out, and asks Venter to accompany him on a walk. Venter mulls over this and decides to join him, why the hell not? Part of his mind tells him that this is against the rules; his other, more rebellious self dictates otherwise. The sound of the birds chirping happily and obliviously from a distance of some seventy metres at the edge of the forest convinces him that everything will be all right. Somehow, he feels that the troopers are in need of something, even nature, that could lift their spirits. The night has always brought a sense of uneasiness; it descends with alarming speed and gives birth to shadows as unreliable as a drunk's memory.

Ralph spins the guard at the gate a yarn; there is the nudge-nudge, wink-wink understanding among the men that too much tension can be as bad for morale as the Wednesday evening Cuban and Swapo anti-government propaganda broadcast in Afrikaans. It was therefore within the context of a gentlemen's agreement that troopers sneaked out to look for some illicit fleshly diversions. They called it sexual healing, after Marvin Gaye's raunchy hit.

The night air carries the smell of the woods, rank emissions from the cassava immersed in water to make *funji* and the muddy mustiness of the marshes. Frogs croak and some nocturnal insects, possibly crickets, chirp. A bird screams in fright or warning, its sound strangely human. Mosquitoes, alerted to the presence of fresh blood, descend on Venter and Ralph; even though the men are protected by regular doses of chloroquine and insect repellent, the bite and the whine of the malaria carriers cause great irritation. Here and there, sometimes hidden behind giant baobabs, is a sign of dwellings abandoned in great haste. Clapboard and corrugated-iron sheeting and adobe ruins comment on the earlier existence of a rural slum. Venter prays that neither one of them steps on a landmine; he has seen what these do to people. The terrorists don't amount to much in a firefight, but they love booby traps. They have a capacity for unimaginable evil, where they devise complex methods to dispose of a person – their creativity surpasses itself when it comes to landmines. You step on an anti-personnel mine rigged to an anti-tank TM46, and your company engineers are destined to scour the dust for pieces of your memory.

This somewhat gloomy train of thought is interrupted by the sound of something splashing in the water. Venter senses that they have detoured towards the river. They come out of the woods, and the water stands there, placid and silvery under the moonlight. Water gives him the heebie-jeebies, but he'll be damned if he would volunteer that little piece of information. There is an unwritten code among the men: if something scares you, it's better to keep that to yourself. The men understand, even if only when they get a whiff after you've voided yourself in your pants.

'What was that sound?' he asks in a whisper.

'That's Hugo,' Ralph says. 'He's got a boat for us.'

'Where are we going?'

'You'll see,' Ralph answers with a touch of irritation. 'What's the matter with you – don't you like surprises?'

Venter stays quiet; he actually doesn't like surprises, but can't say this to Ralph. Might trigger off an unexpected spin, he thinks. The boat is a black slash against the dirty silver-grey expanse of water. Hugo, whoever he is, paddles on noisily. The water, nearer, is frothy, the air rank with the odours of rotting cassava and other vegetation. Breathing it, Venter feels a stab of anger against Ralph for bringing him here; he saves the rest of the anger for himself, for being such a dummy to be coerced into these crackpot jaunts. What the fuck for? he demands of himself. The smell becomes a live thing, which settles at the back of Venter's throat as they wade in the mush, before Hugo steadies the old, rotting wooden craft for them to climb aboard. Even in the dark, Hugo appears to Venter as the blackest man he has ever seen, almost luminous under a bush hat favoured by hunters. He is dressed in unidentifiable battle-dress, although the webbing and sidearm are distinctly SADF-issue. He and Ralph exchange a few words of greeting in Portuguese. Well, Venter thought, remembering something he read somewhere, this is getting curiouser and curiouser.

Despite himself, he finds the boat ride relaxing; the terrorists haven't developed expertise to mine a river. His mind drifts to some of the tricks favoured by black women with razor blades lacing the tubing inserted into their vaginas, who were sent to lure white troopers. Man, he thinks, the memory bringing back the cadence of speech of his *dominee* father, it is a cruelty which passeth all human understanding.

The rippling water laps against the boat, carrying the sounds of the night. Venter is about to trail his hand in the water when the vessel shakes from a series of dull, wet thumps from stem to stern; the sound takes him back to where he is. This is Africa, he tells himself, and African rivers have crocodiles, not just the bitty lizards at the aquarium, real motherfucking monsters. He imagines the big reptile snapping his hand off the wrist. That wouldn't be funny, he reasons. Cynthia already treats him like some kind of cripple – perhaps a sexual cripple. With his arm gone, he is sure, she'd just pack up and go, *Tot siens!* Stay loose, Stompie, he imagines her saying.

It is cooler in the river, the breeze soothing. Earlier in the day the temperature had approached forty degrees, the steaming humidity making things worse. Venter is still thinking about this unwanted bliss, when Hugo whispers something to Ralph. Ralph looks at Venter.

'I trust you know how to keep your mouth shut,' he says.

'No,' he says, 'I'm your regular blabbermouth, what the fuck do you think?' Venter is a bit tired of all this. There's always something fishy when people require you to take vows of silence.

'I'm serious,' Ralph says. 'Because we're nearly there.'

'Where's "there"?'

'You'll see.'

The river flows eastwards into a forest of rushes; this growth creates a lagoon about fifty feet across. Forming a semicircle is a barbed-wire fence whose submerged stakes glow from a fresh application of creosote. Beyond the fence are timber structures, a rough pier, which continues along until it rises up a wooden shed, which looks to be two stories. Camouflage netting hides the shed from above. On either side, resting on stilts are smaller sheds. The area below them is occupied by several aluminium rowboats.

Venter follows the two men after Hugo has secured the row-boat to a stanchion. As the men advance through the water, Venter thinks of crocodiles. Hugo leads them along a round-about route where he helps them negotiate the razor wire; he then beckons them up a short flight of rotted wooden steps. Then they are on a walkway of slatted planks. Venter can see the dark-brown water below and it thrashes with what he suspects to be reptile movement. Eventually, though, he gains confidence, especially as he hears the drone of a power generator. Venter sur-veys the area quickly and finds a wooden watchtower about fifty feet high, partially hidden amid the dense leafage of a baobab. He cannot see the guard, but the sky-grey muzzle of a machine-gun covers the encampment's entrance.

They come up to a sturdy steel door painted green. Hugo knocks and enters without waiting for a response and ushers them into a spacious room where about a dozen men in fatigues and green BVDs lounge in chairs. The battle dress without insignia or rank suggests one thing to Venter: mercenaries. They live high on the hog, the giant refrigerator set in the corner a veritable cornucopia of frosty beers and an assortment of iced goodies.

Nothing is home-made here, deciding Venter that the camp has literally been airlifted into the jungle. The walls, though painted with green and bamboo-coloured tones are made of metal. He reaches a conclusion, with some amusement, that they are inside a cargo container whose internal size has been increased via welding machines. Whilst full of admiration for this little piece of subterfuge, he knows that it makes little sense. If a powerful bomb lands in the camp, this container would be a death trap, the effect much like a sealed motorcar disintegrating in a high-speed head-on collision.

One man scoops Hägen-Daz ice cream out of a tub, in his thirsty haste managing to spill vanilla globs on the floor. The refrigerator door closes with a pneumatic thud. The young man treads on the widening stain as the soles of his boots leave patterns on the floor.

'Hey, Pieter!' a deep bass voice shouts from a corner where a group of men play stud poker, 'what's the matter with you? Are you a pig or something?'

The ice cream gleaner stops and wipes his mouth, leaving a trail of ice cream moustache on his upper lip. He is a tall, gawky specimen with glinting eyes behind his horn-rimmed spectacles, the type that makes the front cover of *True Crimes*. He looks down at the mess he has made, and squints at the direction of the voice, shrugs and makes to go away. Venter has an impression that the man is completely blind, directed to the ice cream by a homing device, or a primeval instinct that guides moles to food. The owner of the deep voice stands up suddenly, upsetting the card table, and slaps the cards on the table to the grumbling of the other players. He advances to Pieter and, without effort, strikes him across the head with his fist. The young man drops to the floor. He gets onto his knees and fumbles for his glasses, which have skittered across the floor to the corner, miraculously intact.

His civic duty done, the burly man proceeds back to the table, murmurs a few words to the other players. He picks up a random set of cards, his whole demeanour saying, Let's play! Some of the other men pick up a bloodied and nearly blinded Pieter, shaking their heads, What the hell's the matter with him courting the big man's anger?

For Venter, there is something fascinatingly unreal about this tableau. Screwing up his eyes, he concentrates his mental sights on this bearded, silver-headed juggernaut in a green singlet. Above his shimmering head is a poster showing Jonas Savimbi haranguing his troops; Venter concludes that it must have been taken in Jamba. One of the players nudges Silver Hair with an elbow and tilts his head towards the newcomers. The man halts in mid-sentence, raises his mane-like head and regards the visitors. He kicks back his chair and strides purposefully to where they stand, involuntarily, at attention. Something about the man commands obeisance. He exchanges a few rapid-fire words in Portuguese with Hugo. The black man smiles and points at Venter and Ralph with a crooked thumb.

'My name is Fenton,' the bearded man introduces himself, smiling, showing a row of even white teeth. 'Sorry about the little hoohah back there, but you have to instil discipline, otherwise you end up running a fucking pig-sty instead of a tight ship.' Without ceremony, he precedes them across a covered corridor into a weather-beaten timber shack built on wooden platforms over the water. There is something surreal about the transfer, reminding Venter of getting into an aeroplane. What he needs now to complete the effect is for a bored African immigration official to scrutinise his Green Mamba passport.

The inside of the shack is musty, cluttered with industrial items, twenty-gallon paraffin cans, tents shoved against the corner, bric-à-brac. Fenton removes blankets and cans of insect repellent from a rough table which is riveted to the floor like all pieces of furniture in the room, and invites Ralph and Venter to sit down across from him.

'Strella missiles.' He smiles, showing a row of white teeth, made whiter in contrast to his sun-tanned face. Even in the artificial light, the blue of his eyes is set off by his tan. Then he flags them to follow him. Fenton leads them to another part of the room, which is partitioned off. Gesturing that they sit down, he perches himself behind a large desk and forms a pyramid with his hands, his eyes on Venter, preparatory to delivering a lecture.

'You're intelligent men,' he says. 'Hugo has been in contact with Ralph. Ralph has advised us that you're to be trusted.' His eyes take in the room, their colour taking an aquamarine hue from the light. 'Trust is important, today more than ever before, in this vale of vipers. Everywhere there is betrayal. I'm from England, witness my name, but I know a brave and honourable tribe when I see it – and yours is the bravest – and most honourable – of all.'

Tribe? Venter experiences a dreamlike moment. What fucking

tribe? Whites are not a tribe; that's for *darkies!* He says nothing. Fenton clears his throat.

'Throughout time,' he says, 'we've stared at the face of death. We've been everywhere, and seen it all. Blacks have a tendency – a habit – to die like flies. Like all tendencies, this becomes something like an epidemic, starts to embroil white people. It's happened in the Congo, Uganda, you name it, and black deaths have also contaminated the whites. In your country, white people don't have a motherland; they cannot go back to Europe, they're stuck there. This means that the motherland must exist somewhere in the mind, in the viscera of men. Our intelligence tells us that you're all going to be sold down the river, army or no army, all that will fall into black hands.'

He rattles off a chronology that spells out how whites are being sold out. Last year, in 1983, the United Democratic Front was formed. 'And who are their patrons?' he asks. 'Nelson Mandela. Helen Joseph. Allan Boesak.' Fenton laughs mirthlessly.

'The very fact that the government allows this is the first shot at capitulation.' Fenton is in full flight now. 'From there it will be downhill, if my knowledge of communism is anything to go by. White people have to prepare. You are part of that preparation.'

The long and short of it was that Fenton's group, with the help of the military, would secrete arms inside the country. Some would be distributed among sympathetic black groups, just to sweeten the deal, but the rest would be kept in caches in specific parts of Natal. 'I know the Zulus,' he continues. 'Hell, one of my great-grandfathers was killed at Isandlwana in 1896. Those people are brave and they won't let communism anywhere near their children. They're our best hope.'

Venter knows little about the national make-up of the ANC or the Communist Party. But intelligence briefings commented on prominent Zulus at leadership level. The first president of the ANC was a Zulu. There are people like Moses Mabhida in Swaziland. Jacob Zuma. Luthuli was not only a Zulu, he was a chief, for Christ's sake! He stops himself from pointing out this little discrepancy. It also rankles that a *rooinek* has the gall to pre-scribe how their fight will be carried out. Since when is Britain so concerned about the welfare of the white tribe, when they closed the last century by decimating thousands of Afrikaner women and children in concentration camps?

The men are promised ordnance maps with co-ordinates of arms caches. But Fenton confides that an ideal location looks to be Upper Ngoza, near Bergville, a region of such internecine strife that security service dispatches have coded it Armageddon II. Venter is astounded at the cynicism. Knowing that for Fenton there is no dividing line between argument and a challenge to his massive ego, Venter swallows his misgivings. Soon enough a suddenly distracted Fenton ushers them out, smiling. Accompanied by Hugo, a Nubian foil to their blistered white-ness, Ralph and Venter leave. The latter has doubts that they'll ever contact him again.

They don't.

★   ★   ★

Now, looking for Momberg on the most unromantic night of the year, when rain dampened even the memories of colossal betrayals, Venter's stomach lurched. He had never felt afraid like this before. The curtain of darkness had been relieved somewhat, and he could make out ghostly shapes of trees, boughs and leaves flattening under the assaulting rain. Proceeding deeper into the woods, hoping that Momberg was playing the fool, he deter-mined to give the younger man a thorough dressing-down. Then he heard a sound, and whirled round. And something with clam-my fur climbed onto his back, damn near scaring him to death. Diving into the ground, rolling, he tried to disentangle himself from the imprisoning clasp. Then he started punching, flailing his arm, and keeping his weapon under his arm. It was then that he saw it was Blackie, Momberg's monkey.

'Jesus!' he cried, 'Blackie? What the fuck are you doing here?' Then, as if addressing a human being, he asked: 'Where's Momberg?'

The monkey chattered, biting its claws. Venter was sure he heard it saying, 'I don't know.' But then the monkey pointed into the deeper darkness. Then it stood up and thrashed into the undergrowth. Venter followed. Running, guided by the squishing slog of Blackie's footfalls in the mud, he cocked his gun, aiming at the waist level of whatever might emerge out of the dark. Sweat glistening on his face, he ran on and, for a moment, stopped when he thought he heard an inhuman scream of voices in the throes of abject terror. Knowing that darkness could induce auditory hallucinations, he trotted on, crouched, until the bush changed, almost miraculously, into a stretch of even ground, like a bald patch on a burred head. The glade was misty and smoky, as if the rain had disturbed the progress of a great brush fire. Then, his nostrils assailed by the smell of burning flesh, he saw Momberg sitting propped against a tree, the monkey no longer chattering but screaming so loudly that Venter almost shot it on the spot.

'Momberg?' he called, advancing carefully. He repeated, already knowing that Momberg was beyond hearing. Someone had sliced his throat and then propped him against the tree in a pose of eternal watchfulness. It was not so much the method of the killing as the deliberate arrangement of the corpse, which chilled Venter. He had seen many deaths, but they had happened in the heat of battle. And the majority of the dead were black. This was different. He had no doubt that this was the work of his kinsmen. Blacks killed people with atavistic glee, but maintained a certain abstract communion with their victims. Time had been taken planning this. Blacks didn't plan. They just acted. White people were practical, all deaths caused by them were usually for a higher purpose. What was the purpose here? To steer them off the trail of the guns?

Then the smell of burning flesh became more cloying, and Venter abandoned his slain colleague and rushed back to base, knowing even as he ran that it was too late. Under the cover of darkness and driving rain, someone familiar with fire had carefully isolated both the guardhouse office where the guns were stored and the holding cell with a score of blacks, and subjected everything to an incendiary device of intense heat. It was as if the bodies had been wheeled into a crematorium and then left lying in different stances of surprise. Gazing on the warped bodies and charred contraband, Venter reflected on the biblical observation about the wages of sin. The time was 0400. The carnage had taken exactly fifteen minutes.

Thirteen

The river was the first of all nature's creations to start the mourning process for the dying patriarch. One day it had been flowing, sometimes flattening the grasses and the bulrushes on the banks in its hunger for movement and, on the next, it was a mere trickle. Where the children had been yanked forcibly by their parents from playing near a roaring vastness of water, there now existed excited yelps as the young ones cavorted in the mud. Inside one week, all the vegetation succumbed to the ravages of the sun, becoming yellow, then brown and then disappearing into a yearned-for memory of green. The only structure – for that was what it was – which defied man and nature was the Humiliation Tree, which seemed to have pulled itself up to its full height, dark and imposing and infinitely mysterious. Its survival gave credence to of those who held that its roots were nurtured with blood.

It was at this moment that Johnny M decided to strike and show the villagers and the squatter community that he meant business when he asked for levies. In the morning the women woke up and filed to the communal tap, only to find that, overnight, someone had erected a latticework of reinforced iron bars around the tap. What was even more galling was that people could see the source of water, the tap dripping the life-giving liquid in slow, frustratingly regular trickles. Those who had come to draw water for household use discovered that they were suddenly very thirsty. Without access, they would have to trudge the two kilometres to cadge water from the despised believers in the New Jerusalem. It was humiliating.

'Something has to be done,' said MaNdlela, hitching her granddaughter on her back, tightening the straps of the rude cradle. Although addressing no-one in particular, her contralto voice, which had shouted not a few men into instant impotence, drew people to her like bees to honey. For the younger women, it was a reassuring voice that came out of a presence that had come to embody stability. MaNdlela was as permanent as a syringa tree. Zelda, who was fresh out of her teens but who had decided that frumpiness gave her protection against predatory men, had great admiration for MaNdlela, who was also her great-aunt.

'Why do you think he does this?' she asked. Everyone knew to whom she was referring.

'Because he's mad,' MaNdlela said. Madness for her was an intimate aberration, where the mind reflected on itself; it was a phenomenon which catapulted itself above and beyond love or sex – above and beyond primeval urges – or the sharing of body fluids between man and man, woman and man, woman and woman, mother and child. This madness had had the effrontery to excommunicate itself from the royal fellowship of sane human beings. She had seen it standing, strutting and clothed in its own uncomprehending garb – oblivious to the fact that it was the mind that had conjured it up in the first instance – curling its lips preparatory to activating the tongue to hurl an insult or a word or phrase gifted with the power to galvanise the soldiers and expel from their minds all vestiges of mercy. 'Anyway,' she went on, placing her bucket atop her head, 'let's ask the believers for some water.'

'Maybe', said Nosipho, who sometimes moonlighted in Nerissa's shebeen, 'we'll get old man Joshua and his bearded disciples to turn water into wine.'

'You've got alcohol in your blood and men in your brain,' MaNdlela said.

'So what?' Nosipho said. 'Have you ever had a beard tickle

your—'

She never got to finish the sentence, as the women's easy banter was cut short by a long shriek. Even the imperturbable
MaNdlela almost dropped her load in surprise. Their eyes sought
to locate the source of danger. When they saw who was doing
the screaming, it confirmed something that had always hovered
at the periphery of their minds: women – given that the world
has traditionally reserved a certain type of treatment for them –
understand screams and could write tomes on them. They can
invariably recognise the tonal range and almost instinctively
assign to it the immediate corresponding source. From the tone,
they could tell, from nameless peril to unspeakable ecstasy, each
scream had a register.

The screamer was Popolani, Nerissa's niece, a teenage girl
who still had to wrestle with the meaning of life; and also with
boys that grew into men at a disconcerting speed; and with the
magazine version of beauty and fashion which was the current
orthodoxy; and with being born in an unyielding part of the
country. When the women saw her – as they rushed to her, fearing that she had suffered a grievous injury – they concluded that
the men had struck again. Knowing that no amount of hurrying
would improve the harm already affecting the girl's frame of
mind, MaNdlela walked on stolidly until she caught up with her
breathless colleagues.

'Popolani,' Nosipho said, taking the girl by the shoulder,
'*Kwenzenjani* – What's happened?'

'*Izilwane*,' Popolani said, getting on her knees, stretching her
legs and lying on her back as if overcome by a heavy burden.
'*Izilwane*. – The animals.'

MaNdlela strode forward and knelt before the girl, simultaneously unhitching the baby from her back while handing the
bundle to Nosipho.

'What animals?'

Popolani looked up at the older women as if asking herself
why they found it so difficult to comprehend something so

patently simple. Coiling herself up, as if resisting the impulse to surrender to whatever was pulling her down, Popolani abruptly got onto her feet. As she started walking ahead of the women, she rearranged her dress, whose gingham fabric snagged on her ample, little-girl hips, outlining a promise of the future terror that awaited her at the hands of men.

The other women, who had at first stood stock still, now joined MaNdlela and Nosipho as they trailed behind the young woman, who now walked as if possessed. The unshod feet of this procession stamped on the parched land, avoided rancid sewage where the puddles furrowed the ground, and took a path which led to the outskirts of the Two Rivers squatter camp.

Laden with smoke, the morning air wafted over drying blades of maize whose stalks tilted such that the roots clutching the stony ground showed, like the skeletal fingers people would encounter in their dreams. The men who came out of doors to walk or ride their rickety bicycles to work were mostly rumpled and unwashed, with sleep riding their eyes, seeming more tired than when they went off to bed. Their flat, incurious eyes which surveyed the women had been surprised so often that nothing short of the Second Coming would ever elicit a flicker of genuine amazement.

There was a hush as the women walked on, broken by the sounds of the awakening day punctuated by MaNdlela's laboured breathing. The sun which had earlier risen in a red ball was now hidden behind a screen of wisps of lazily rolling nimbus cloud, the wind still, the insects silent as if shocked into muteness. The smell of dead and dying grassland and sterile maize fields was taken over by a strong, heady sickly-sweet odour of blood. While the women gagged, perhaps imagining that they were being assailed by a strange case of collective nosebleed, their eyes rested on the tangled mass of ruined flesh. Green flies the size of bumblebees swarmed around their heads, corroborating the incidence of death. The women's goats, hacked with edged instruments fashioned for bringing about sudden death, lay in destroyed heaps on the ground on which their blood had flowed. The eyes of the beasts, dull and accusing and infinitely alive in death, stared in lifeless incomprehension, speaking of the pain that had throbbed before the final gasp.

MaNdlela was aware of a whistling in her head, a circumstance that told her in eloquent and unmistakable terms that horror was upon her. In the land of the warlords in the Natal Midlands, where slaying had become so commonplace that in the mortuary the drunk police had the gall to refer to dead women as cows, she had dedicated her life to saving the lives of children. It didn't matter whose offspring they were, the children were sacred bequests, issues of loins once engorged with love and a straining and a final clenching in the coupling, for the seed to find fertile ground, a place of rest. In that township named KwaMagwaza – a place of stabbing – where men violated women and forced the bruised eyes of husbands and children to watch, violence took the form of more dead bodies lying in glades, mutilated in the pursuit of vital organs, ingredients that guaranteed the potency of *muthi* from the Natal Midlands.

Deciding to visit Baba Joshua's daughter was almost automatic; MaNdlela did not need to manufacture consensus. All the women, the young and the old, the drowners and the survivors, all agreed that something had to be done. It was an instinct borne of the realisation that men could not be trusted. Since they were a species whose very physical organisation could be a basis of self-esteem or -immolation, dealing with them needed the steady hand of a mining chemist, who could tell just when and how to go about delivering explosive compounds from one shaft to the other. 'But', Popolani demurred, as was her wont – just to shake things up a little bit – 'I hear she's snooty.'

MaNdlela knew that life was a grind and she wasn't about to suffer fools gladly. 'All of us, especially us women,' she said, 'are vulnerable.'

The women, bonded by their sense of power which came from their knowledge of the bullying that lay ahead, organised kindling and gathered twigs and wood. Popolani, the eternal emissary, was sent to find and come back with petrol or diesel. Understanding that the fuel had never been part of what the ancestors knew, MaNdlela accepted that they were sending the girl into a terrain that could never be smiled on by the ancestors. However, sporting a knowing smile, a bedraggled and flustered Popolani came back, obviously having been pawed by men at the garage, carrying a gallon of petrol. In a minute there was the smell of burning flesh. Then the women started the long walk to where the daughter of the dying man waited.

★   ★   ★

It is noon on 11 February 1991, one year after Mandela's release. A commemoration service celebrating a year of the great man's freedom is planned for that late Saturday afternoon, in the community centre which abuts a beerhall, a knot of shops, a struggling hair salon and an undertaker's parlour. Across the road, separated by railings and past a sidewalk strewn with hawkers' wares – from second- or third-hand car parts to beads and meretricious goods – minibus taxis ply their noisy trade, the touts shouting the route from KwaMagwaza to Shallcross, to Bulwer to Eshowe.

Supporting herself on a cane, one fist pressed against the small of her back, MaNdlela shuffles behind the would-be passengers waiting in the queue; she's on her way to Ngeleza to the revival. For the first time in her eighty-odd years, she looks forward to the service. There's a new priest from Stanger, whose fiery sermons have led to his being compared with Reverend Nicholas Bhengu, a gangster who had changed from his evil ways after being struck down by the blinding light of the Holy Ghost.

For a reason that had much to do with neglect than some preordained dispensation, KwaMagwaza became a commuter town. Everyone here seems to be in transit, or in flight. There are taxis of all shapes and sizes and of varying degrees of roadworthiness or decrepitude. When the Seven Day War between the comrades of the United Democratic Front and the warriors – *amabutho* – of Inkatha. Although there was evidence of burning, which was supported by graphic letters and images on the walls, which denounced leaders and elevated tyrants, KwaMagwaza seemed intact, mainly because it had already been so looted from within that any violence against it could be seen as a gratuitous act of malice. People, no matter how demented, took a dim view of someone torching an empty building.

The warring factions formed by the young against the old – whole families riven by political allegiances – finally represented the poorest and the most wretched of the country. The young comrades who had spent endless days and nights of love and war parrying blows and ducking bullets fired by armed Inkatha men, who were supported by the KwaZulu Police, vaguely understood that the struggle was about the purging of poverty. The traditionalists, many of whom were in Inkatha cohorts, also saw in the comrades an embodiment of corrosion, a bankrupting of their values. So the struggle continued. It went on until the sensible members of the contending forces facilitated a period of peace. During this period, which leads to the commemoration of one year of Mandela's release, tolerance holds sway. There is a lessening in incidences where men brandish guns and machetes. Today, men, women and children walk unhindered by expectations of the reports of guns, or the swish of a descending machete striking against yielding flesh. Or the screams that fractured the night into millions of shards. Or the smell of burning flesh. Or the sight of women swaying at the lip of a grave, sorrowing over yet another slaughter.

The afternoon, characterised by an absence of tears, is charged, the air holding the ominous smell of sulphur. The man who came from the corner – cradling the weapon under his arm – could have been anyone's brother, father or lover. He has a flat face, a flat nose and wears his clothes as a mere sop to propriety. The gun comes up, out of the plastic-bag carrier, and the muzzle searches for the face of the young man. The discharge is muffled, much like a colony of wasps loosened on an unsuspecting crowd of holidaymakers. A woman screams and MaNdlela dis-

covers that her tongue – in the face of terror – has been unteth-
ered.

The killing of the United Democratic Front's young leader
halts the peace process dead in its tracks. Suddenly the nocturnal
sounds are punctuated with bursts of sub-machine-gun fire, the
concentration of which tells the listener that it has zeroed in on
a target, not random. Those who fear being attacked, change
their patterns of sleeping; during the day they can be recognised
by their bloodshot eyes which hanker for a moment of rest.
Funerals are no longer held only during the weekends, because
the bodies pile up and threaten to engulf the mortuary. Living so
close to death, MaNdlela decides to collect whatever belongs to
her – which includes her nephews, nieces and grandchildren –
and flees to Ngoza. And now this.

★　　　★　　　★

'How can I help you?' Zodwa asked, taking in the accumulated
smells of old age, despair, and the proximity of the grave. Zodwa
was amazed though not surprised that the first word that leapt
into her mind was 'crucible'. She suddenly felt that the room was
preparing to whirl.

'We are aware', MaNdlela said, 'that we're catching you at a
very bad moment ...' The other members of the delegation, eyes
downcast, nodded and groaned. 'But your father is not dead.' She
raised her eyes and scanned Zodwa's face. 'But, even if he were –
and trust me, he was a dearly loved and respected man – we'd still
insist that the living must be given a chance to continue living.'

Zodwa was not lost to the tense used, but she shrugged this
off as one of the linguistic quirks of the neighbourhood. She had
meant to pay a visit to the women of New Rivers, but time had
not allowed. Now, surely, something of great urgency had
brought them there. Her law-student disposition, which dealt
with facts, merely wished that they quit beating about the bush
and got down to business.

'Yes. I hear you, MaNdlela. Please go on.'

MaNdlela started speaking, in measured tones, describing the shutting off of water. As soon as she touched on the issue of the slain stock, her voice failed her.

'Can I get you some water?' Zodwa offered, cursing herself for having chased Nozizwe from the meeting. *She* would know how to handle this: MaNdlela was the old sangoma's age-mate.

'No. I am fine.' She looked at Popolani. 'Maybe *you* continue with the story.' MaNdlela was suddenly very tired. 'You tell it, Popolani, you have the words of youth.'

Ouch!

Despite her outward appearance of giddiness, Popolani could tell a perfect story – perfect for its unconventionality, where the beginning was at the end, and the middle was scattered throughout the narrative, like bitter almonds on a bar of chocolate. 'We don't have any men,' she started, 'simply because we're the women who brought the trouble. Which was started by the bull-headedness of men in the first place. The men who were not killed – and many of them were mere boys who happened to wear the wrong T-shirt in the wrong area – those who weren't killed disappeared. We buried every day the good Lord brings down. Every day. Twelve, thirteen. After the Seven Days' War, we carted scores of our dead to be buried in other areas, because Inkatha and the KZP refused that we bury them at KwaMagwaza. They would contaminate the burial grounds, they said.' Popolani paused, struck by the immediacy of another memory. 'You remember that, in the past, it was the men who stood two or three on each of the four sides of the coffin, taking turns, making sure that the body was never left alone, was always accompanied by friends and comrades? That duty fell on the women's shoulders. We stood watch, witnessing. Sometimes, it happened that the KZP would come into the service and start shooting, sometimes upending the box, kicking the corpse, having fun. They were most dangerous when drunk. They shot at the old men who couldn't run, they shot the women, they shot the children.' She turned her eyes – which had been turned inwards – to Zodwa. 'Now, *this* man has slaughtered our livestock. It begins like that, with the livestock. The next step, it will be us.'

'Which man?' Zodwa asked.

'Which man?' MaNdlela had found her tongue. 'Which man? If you don't know, then you have no reason calling yourself Joshua's daughter!'

'If you know the identity of the perpetrator ...' Jesus, she thought simultaneously wishing for a cigarette and a large whisky, what bullshit am I talking? 'Look,' she rephrased her sentence, knowing that her authority was at stake, 'we have to have some kind of proof that this was done by Johnny M ...' As the name rang out, the women exchanged looks of triumph. Fucking squatter women, Zodwa thought savagely, suckering me into the oldest trap which any lawyer would have avoided; she was the one who had said – corroborated – that Johnny M was the perpetrator, her own word.

'In the past,' MaNdlela, magnanimous in victory, said, 'we would have seen the picture of the killer in the dead man's eyes. But with animals it's a little difficult. Moreover we burnt the carcasses.'

'You burnt ...' Zodwa wanted to add, '... the evidence?' but thought that the question itself would have added to the surreal nature of the discussion. Everything was out of reach of normality. She was aware, all the people were aware, that the violence in other parts of KwaZulu tended to affect areas that had never known strife. She knew, also, that there were many refugees here, some in her father's congregation, who'd fled and become integrated into the New Jerusalem settlement. She had regarded Johnny M as a cheap crook on the make, who was just too flashy to pose a serious threat when the chips were down. But the logic of the women, the survivors, located Johnny M within the ranks of warlords. Her father, who would have had insight into this conundrum posed by both the women and Johnny M, was out of the running. Nozizwe.

'Look,' she said. 'Go back to your places. I'll consult and get back to you quite soon.'

'With all due respect,' MaNdlela, who was also something of a mind-reader, put in. 'Even Nozizwe would tell you that the only way this matter could be cleared up, and Johnny M get his just deserts, would be for you to challenge him to the test of the Humiliation Tree.

'What test?'

'Nozizwe will know.' The old woman made to get up, the delegation following suit. 'She will tell you.' On her feet now, she favoured Zodwa with a look that was as full of cunning as it was compassionate. 'And one more thing, Joshua's daughter ...'

'Oh,' Zodwa asked sarcastically, 'is there still more?'

'Yes,' MaNdlela said levelly. 'Don't even dream of a drink between now and then. Else you won't survive.'

Zodwa was still formulating an appropriate response, the more cutting the better, when there was a commotion outside. She knew, even before she peered through the door, in that infinitesimal moment before the drawing of breath before a scream – before Naomi's heartrending wail – that Baba Joshua had joined the ancestors. Her sadness was superseded by an unspeaking rage, and she held Johnny M responsible, because it was his shenanigans which had drawn her away from her father's deathbed.

The mourners congregated, and looked at her. And their eyes said it all. Zodwa's sadness was compounded by a feeling of relief, as if a great load that had for ever rested on her shoulders had finally been laid down.

Fourteen

It was Reuben, making the last of his deliveries, who pointed out the miracle to Mpanza. 'Do you know that it's now three days that the old man died – and his corpse doesn't smell?'

'That's impossible,' Mpanza said, cursing himself for having not gone to pay his last respects. He gazed at the people milling about the tent which housed Joshua's body, all of them stunned, most of them – especially the women – weeping disconsolately. 'And unless they have the coffin rigged to some sophisticated refrigeration mechanism,' he went on, 'there's no way a body could stay fresh. Not in this heat.'

Even as he spoke, he felt the noonday heat burning the crown of his head. Heat and dust. It swirled, like a living thing, dry particles enveloping everything within range. Dust entered Mpanza's nostrils and mouth and set his teeth on edge. Two old men flanked the entrance of the tent, a bucket of purifying water placed between them, so that mourners formed two lines whose advance inside was interrupted when people stooped to rinse their hands. Knowing that he was no longer in touch with traditional rituals, he still wondered at this reversal, because he knew that hands were washed only after burial. Reuben said that all this was Nozizwe's doing. 'Sometimes, 'Reuben mused, 'I think she makes all these rules on the hoof.'

'Think we should go in?' Mpanza asked. He wanted to see the old man's body but needed the decision to be sanctioned from elsewhere. He didn't want to take responsibility by what he suspected he might feel. But Reuben wasn't about to let him off the hook.

'You do want to go in, don't you?' he asked, almost aggressively. 'I mean, you've talked about nothing else since Joshua died?'

'Am I that obvious?'

'You must sometimes take responsibility, Mshana,' Reuben said gently. 'As for being obvious, when I went on this delegation to Pretoria, there were all these high-powered fellows with pie charts and laser pointers. One of them kept on talking about how transparent the new government is. You know the type. Until Joshua cut him in mid-sentence, which was rare because he's such a gentle person. He said, "Excuse me, but you've told us nothing of substance since we arrived here except how transparent the government is. We are here to try and formalise our getting the land back. Don't treat us like children – we can see through that transparency of the government." Their reaction was instructive. Some people looked like they wanted to laugh, being read the Riot Act by a country bumpkin, others as if a polecat had been let loose in the room.' He shook his head. 'People are so full of bullshit, man, it makes you sick!'

Mpanza had never heard Reuben so upset, and he realised that he, like many people now, also reeled from slights by people who weren't worthy to kiss his feet. There was everywhere some incidence of one-upmanship, where, the more mediocre people were, the more likely they were to be empowered to inflict their incompetence and insecurities on others. He remembered that in the camps some comrades would make dreadful mistakes, and the next time you looked they were on the truck to Luanda, having landed a plum mission in the front areas. Those who were faithful to the cause, who broke their backs defending the Movement, were likely to be bypassed when it came to recognition or promotion. He shook his head, thinking, that's the way it is, children.

The day was hot. Dogs without pedigree, whose purpose in life was to give companionship to old men who had lost hope, lay curled under the shade, their tongues hanging out, neither barking nor glancing at the horse-drawn wagon clattering past. A knot of young boys, some of them recently returned from their parents' exile, played games, chasing one another, wrestling silently. The death had affected them, too, when they saw the reactions of the elders. They had a good idea that their world, now wrenched from its moorings, had changed, and that this change foretold strife. A few of the boys unleashed their anxiety on dumb animals, like dogs, tormenting them off the shade. They composed themselves, however, when Mpanza and Reuben alighted from the wagon.

The two men walked towards the tent, each considering the wisdom of the step they were taking. In Mpanza's mind roiled the images of death, where people he knew were transformed into unspeaking shells. Inured though he might have been to death, he hoped that the old man would not exhibit signs of having suffered. He recalled the transformation that came over bodies of comrades, the discoloration and bloating of the skin, the smells, liquefied eyeballs, teeth bared in a rictus of death. In two or three cases, when the reconnaissance platoon found the corpse, it was already decomposing, maggots milling about like live *kapenta* fish from a Lusaka market. He was therefore surprised – even though Reuben had prepared him for the sight – to enter the tent, which was full of villagers whose own body odour recalled an open grave, to find Baba Joshua looking fresh and rested, as if he were just taking an afternoon siesta. His coffin, a plain pine affair, rested atop a bier. There were no wreaths, except for a solitary white rose along the body's crossed hands. Two sweating boys with grim expressions fanned the corpse with crane feathers, managing to recycle the hot air in the tent. The old man looked like he was smiling in his sleep, undisturbed by anxious dreams.

His daughter, Zodwa, was conferring in hushed tones with two women, one wizened and as alert as a meerkat, the other, white, apprehensive, it seemed, to be alone in a tent so full of black people. Mpanza reasoned that it must have been the latter who had brought the rose. The sentimentality of that singularly futile gesture was not lost on him. When he looked up again, he saw that they had been joined by a young man dressed like a warrior about to do the Zulu *indlamu* dance. Zodwa was gazing at him. She was a big-boned woman with a clear, dark-brown complexion, with a small, somewhat flat nose. Her hair beneath the black *doek* spilled out in braids, coloured beads jiggling at the ends. Attired in a simply cut black dress and black heels, she seemed austere, her huge puffed eyes smouldering, accentuating her full lips, determined jaw and prominent cheekbones. Taller and thinner than he remembered – and even though death was not a dependable custodian of people's features – Zodwa bore a striking resemblance to the man in the casket. It was perhaps this likeness which evoked a constant chorus of sobbing from the mourners, who saw in her face a reflection of what had been snatched from them.

Many of the people who had returned to Ngoza had lost a family member, during the years of wandering among strangers. People realised, with a sense of alarm, that Joshua's death was the first since their return, and would offer them a possibility of conducting a series of traditional rites that would ensure the safe passage of his spirit. They had been forced to bury their dead in alien lands, where the rituals of transcendence had been different. In the cemeteries of the township, where every weekend was a time to bury the dead, funerals took place like a conveyor belt in a rubber factory. Those wishing to pay their respects and commune with the souls of the departed could only do so on weekdays after work. That was also dangerous, since cemeteries were haunts of bandits and body snatchers that crafted *muthi* out of parts of the cadavers. It was too high a price to pay for a simple sacramental act. The logic followed by most exiles in the townships, then, was that they had come to mourn, and not become substitutes for the rotting corpse six feet underground. Mpanza didn't know how he knew this; it could have sprung from primeval precepts buried deep in his mind, a knowledge imbibed with his mother's milk, like any African child not born into orphanage. Reuben had added some of the detail. While acquainted with the ways of the city, and certainly not a traditionalist, he still held that home was where the umbilical cord was buried.

Watching her from above the heads of mourners, he saw that she now had on a pair of dark glasses. Despite the canvas material of the tent, sunlight still filtered in brightly, bouncing off the tea or whatever liquid people were drinking from aluminium mugs, creating patterns on the white fabric. Her disguise threw him off because, he couldn't tell whether she was looking at him, although he had a fair idea. Fanning herself with something which looked like a funeral programme while sipping from a tall glass, Zodwa seemed lonely and out of place. Apropos of nothing, Mpanza reasoned that her mother must have been a very beautiful woman. Unaccountably – and for the first time since arriving in Ngoza – he felt afraid.

Although Zodwa was grateful for Benedita's companionship, she was a little irritated by her constant, solicitous chatter. She was tired. The past thirty-six hours had been spent in something of a daze. She first had to deal with the full impact of her father's death. Zodwa had known that this end was inevitable, but when it happened, it left her open, vulnerable. She hadn't known that she harboured within herself this great capacity to grieve. But all that would have to be deferred, since her father was a public man and the public wished to get a piece of him. While he had been a religious man, Joshua had been expected to govern over secular matters. In the eyes of the unbelievers, Joshua was their chief, a leader to whom they took even the most insignificant of problems. In his incarnation as a chief, then, he made decisions relating to public life and settled disputes between his subjects. Casting around in her mind, she recalled her earlier studies in law where they commented on the integrity of chieftaincy in ancient African society, which was under constant threat from both external attacks and the fragmentation caused by the political process itself. In the past, the threat had taken the form of raids for cattle, conflicts over grazing. Sometimes there would be a threat from a rival chieftaincy. But greed and the capacity for mischief occasioned the threat, which she knew existed today, from Johnny M's people. Leafing through her father's journal, she read of the earlier encounters, and how these remained unresolved. There was an entry that intrigued her, which simply read, *H. Trouble! And Grey – what does he want?* Nozizwe was patient enough to tell her that the village of Ngoza would not rest until people knew what Hodoba was up to. Zodwa knew Grey and of his corruption, which she had gleaned from snatches of conversations with Benedita.

'Your biggest threat, however,' Nozizwe tells her, 'is from the traditionalists.'

'How so?'

'Throughout history,' Nozizwe explains in formal Zulu, 'traditionalists have caused schisms in political formations. They take advantage whenever there is a lack of clarity, which gives rise to internal succession disputes. If, for instance, there isn't a recognisable heir due to the uncertainty about the identity of the great wife, this uncertainty trickles down and affects the eldest son. In your case, your father eschewed polygamy and took one wife, a Xhosa maiden. This was at the time when, although we do say, *induk'enhle igawulw'ezizweni* – choice wood is gathered in foreign lands – people here were not unanimous in welcoming her. There were many nubile women waiting to be chosen. But Baba Joshua was famous for following his heart rather than his head.' She pauses and sips from her mug of black tea. 'When Jonah was born,' she continues, 'all of us, except, of course, Hodoba, rejoiced. Jonah was the heir and would learn all the white man's laws and help us out of darkness. But Jonah chose to die, and that leaves you.'

The words, said in a laconic manner typical of village speech, twisted the knife in her heart. Jonah didn't choose to die, he was chosen for death. Knowing that any show of weakness would empower her enemies, Zodwa puts a brave face to it. Nozizwe tells her that the traditionalist cannot bear the idea of being ruled by a woman. Furthermore, they have allies among the women-folk, many of whom still haven't forgiven Zodwa for her dalliance with Horwitz. 'But', Nozizwe says, 'there are some of us among the elders who wield power, who want you to take over. You also have natural allies among the more politicised women in the New River squatter camp, who are fed up to the teeth with the way men have run roughshod over them.'

'But I haven't decided to take over from Baba,' Zodwa objects, thinking about her uncle, Mbongwa, the stultifying small-mindedness of the village. At the back of her mind is the knowledge that she wants to become a lawyer. Women lawyers are few and far between. But her biggest fear is the lack of acceptance she knows beats in the hearts of some of the powerful people. Being her father's daughter is not enough. Zodwa has never tasted rejection.

'That decision is no longer in your hands.' Nozizwe's brow furrowed in irritation. 'Your promise to Joshua on his deathbed was a promise to us all. Joshua was crafty,' she adds. 'He even got that poor white woman as a witness. I'm sorry, but you can't get out of it.'

'Why me?' Zodwa wails, 'I don't know the simplest thing about this place.'

'Consider the political leadership of this country,' Nozizwe says. 'They are more familiar with fighting in the bush. They were thrown into a situation where they have to run a country. All of them had never voted before, not even for the village dog-catcher, but now they spread knowledge about voting, and got us the new government.' She pauses to look out into the night, which spreads outside like a black veil. 'If anything goes wrong here, if people do not get running water and electricity, if the gangsters still victimise women – can you honestly say then that you did right by not giving your father's people – no, your people – a fighting chance? Will you hold your head high when you didn't take a chance and helped build schools, so that our children's children are also equipped to face the New World? Life', she adds fiercely, 'can only be lived when people take a chance to weave miracles out of nothing.'

Immediately on finishing her tea, Nozizwe gets to her feet. She brushes herself and then orders, 'Come with me.'

'Now?' Zodwa cries. 'Do you know what time it is?'

'Never mind the time, just follow me.'

Something about her tone convinces Zodwa that it wouldn't be wise to refuse. And then, as she tries to catch up with the old woman, something comes over Zodwa, beneath the vast sky, and her body is washed by an emotion she can only identify as shame. They pass the tent where the men take turns guarding Baba Joshua's body from scavengers and their two-legged cousins who are wont to mutilate it for purposes of sorcery. Even though people don't mention it, there is something of a village-style all points bulletin for Hodoba. Anyone who sees him should report to the Elders. She remembers a story Jonah told her about his meeting with a commander from the PAIGC, the liberation movement fighting Portuguese colonialism in Guinea-Bissau and Cape Verde. The man told Jonah that they had been marching for nights on end, from the forests of Guinea-Bissau into Sekou Toure's Guinea, whose capital was Conakry. Then one of the guerrillas had said he was tired. They stopped and rested and then the commander told the story.

'Once upon a time, I was a young man like you and was not really convinced that anything would come out of this struggle. The Portuguese were powerful, even if they were the poorest country in Western Europe and didn't even produce toy aeroplanes, they were still supported by NATO. And here we were, a ragtag army equipped with carbines against a force that boasted artillery, tanks and planes. I was sure that Amilcar Cabral was just full of shit. Then when we reached our camp, I was instructed to go back to Guinea-Bissau and tell the commander of the rear base that there was going to be an aerial attack on the neighbouring village. The Portuguese strafed villagers so that the people lost sympathy for the guerrillas. We had just marched all these miles, hungry and barely alive, and here I was supposed to go back. I thought about it, the journey on foot, not even a bicycle. Then I walked reluctantly, dragging my feet, telling myself that it was possible the intelligence information was a hoax. Also: if I returned to Conakry and disappeared in the big marketplace, how would they find me? I'd just be another deserter, or they'd conclude animals in the forest had savaged me. But, on the way, I saw women and children returning from the river with gourds and cooking-pots balanced on their heads. They were singing songs about the simple things of life. There was some poetry there, in their movements, in being part of the human race, vital, alive and optimistic. Then and there, all my doubts dissipated, because I knew then that even if I'd convinced myself that I owed society nothing, I owed the women and children across the border their lives.' Reaching the base, he raised the alarm and the village was evacuated. Zodwa muses over the generosity of common people like Nozizwe, who have spent all their lives sacrificing to improve the lot of others. What have I done for my people? she asks herself. The night doesn't answer.

★   ★   ★

Filled with a sense of *déjà vu* as she follows Nozizwe down the trail to the cave, Zodwa reflects on the regularity with which Jonah insinuates himself inside her head. She doesn't need to be a psychologist to accept that this comes from wrestling with an unresolved matter. What is extraordinary is that for her time hasn't healed the wounds. The older she gets the more urgently she yearns for an answer. Am I going mad? She asks herself; then she is jolted awake from her self-absorption by a branch raking across her cheek. She jumps. Nozizwe halts.

'What is it?' she asks.

'Nothing. I'm sorry,' Zodwa apologises. 'I thought a snake had bitten me.'

In the dark, she hears the smile in the old woman's voice. 'Don't they teach you anything in that big school of yours? The snakes here don't lunge at you from trees. They're most likely to pick you up from your sleep at night.'

Zodwa doesn't know what she means; then, she knows exactly what it means. They are now past the old cave, and Zodwa feels the temperature drop and hears the whisper of the stream. They follow it as it winds its way between bulrushes and flows into a slight gorge, some fifteen metres high. Their trail follows a path down the right-hand side of the gorge, where they find themselves amid stumps of dead trees. Then they walk left on the lip of the gorge. Some kind soul had erected a fence to stop walkers from falling off the sheer drop. Zodwa has never been here. She hears the water dropping and cascading into a wider river down below. Nozizwe, who can see in the dark, takes her hand and warns her to be careful. Guided by the old woman, Zodwa encounters a deeper darkness and can sense, from the sound of their footfalls, that they have entered a passage to a cave.

★   ★   ★

Nozizwe rummages in her bag and comes out with a box of matches. Rattling it, she strikes a light. By this time, Zodwa is cowering against an expected bombardment by bats. But nothing happens. Nozizwe lights a flare stuck into a wall recess and, as in the song, darkness flies away. The main entrance drops suddenly down to the bottom of the cave, which is some twenty metres below the surface. The chamber is long and seems to entrance the visitor with the play of light on underground lakes and vitreous rock. Everything about the cave speaks of enchantment: the dripstone formation, the large stalactites and their curtains, the limestone, as smooth as glass, formed atop the underlying dolomite rock. The quiet of the underground is eerie and yet, in a strange way, quite arousing, as if it were the last trysting place for ancient lovers fulfilling a suicide pact. Zodwa looks up, hearing the steady dripping of water which, over millions of years, carved these magical shapes.

'I brought you here,' Nozizwe says, 'so that you can be strengthened to deal with whatever comes your way.' Walking towards a fossil forming a rock table, she unslings her back and beckons for Zodwa to advance. Her voice sounds ghostly, profane and completely out of place in this cavern whose formations were calcified through innumerable ages by an amalgam of earth, rock fragments and bone material. It is a place that diminishes human beings, humbles them and deepens their understanding that they are but temporary sojourners on this earth.

When Nozizwe asks Zodwa to undress, the latter responds as if to the most natural request. She hears, as if for the first time, the hum of the cave's internal acoustics. Somewhere in the background, higher than her eyes can see, a barn owl hoots – a mating call – and is answered by a mate. Taking off her clothes, she feels the cool air blowing like feathers over her skin, caressing her body hair. She looks on as Nozizwe empties her bag on the table, scattering bones and phials containing dark powders. She then selects wood shavings and adds shredded twigs to make a small fire. Placing an aluminium mug on the flame, she scoops some water from the lake and mixes herbs and powder, allowing a pungent smell to waft over the younger woman. Then she isolates a blade and makes small twin incisions on Zodwa's face, first on the widow's peak, then where the jaw meets the neck. Then the arms, elbows, wrists, knees and ankles are subjected to Nozizwe's surgery. She gets to her feet and dips her fingers into the mug.

'This might hurt a little,' she murmurs, and Zodwa, remembering dentists lying before sticking a needle into your nerve, thinks, *Yeah, right!* The pain when Nozizwe rubs hot powder over the fresh wounds causes Zodwa to groan. But she soon gets used to it; by the time Nozizwe is dabbing powder on her lower limbs, the thrill of the pain is gone. Then Nozizwe takes a bone necklace from the scattered objects on the table. 'Put this on,' she commands, 'and never remove it. Not even for a lover.'

★   ★   ★

Not even for a lover, she thought as Benedita chattered on. Zodwa was tired, hot and felt like a drink. God, she thought, the woman would drive me to alcoholism. The sight of barefoot men, who had obviously travelled long distances, dressed in greatcoats, further heightened the effect of hotness. She prayed that they would take them off, knowing, also that these were much more than their security blankets. Men traditionally didn't lug blankets along, and taking long journeys meant facing the chill at night, especially near the Drakensberg Mountains, when temperatures sometimes dropped below zero. She understood, but still wished they would get a life and divest themselves of the coats. Then there were the traditionalists, men and women, turned out in a mix of Western clothes and traditional garb. However, the young warriors, *amabutho*, were decked from head to toe in Zulu national attire. Zodwa's eyes were drawn to one statuesque man who strutted in, a headband of leopard skin called *umqhele* crowning his head. Plugged into his ear lobes were cylindrical wooden discs, *iziqhaza*, decorated with blue, red, white, black, green and gold colours of the new South Africa. Around his massive neck was *umphapheni*, a necklace of intricate beadwork, usually worn on official occasions. Below this, was *ingcagcane*, a small rectangular bead choker, worn by men to wedding dances. Running from the hollow of the neck to the solar plexus was another flat bead matting, called *ulimi*, after the tongue of an ox. Around the biceps, above the elbow, below the knees and above the ankles, the man wore *ubusenga*, wire bracelets, which also acted as charms against evil. A strip of skin filigreed with bead patterns, *umgaxo*, hung crosswise from the shoulder to the hip, where it was fastened to *umbhijo*, a tangled beadwork waistband also worn by women. The loins were covered by *ibheshu*, made from tanned goatskin or cowhide, fastened to which on either side were *izinjobo*, tassels made from genet fur. Encasing his firm buttocks was *isinene*, also fashioned from cowhide. He carried a knobkierie in his hand, and, from his expression, looked ready to use it on any of Baba Joshua's ene-

226

mies. It took time for Zodwa to recognise Joachim, her father's faithful aide. He hadn't wasted time before throwing in his lot with the traditionalists, showing his true colours.

She caught his eye, and waved at him. He hesitated at first and then, shrugging his broad shoulders, he steadily wove his way through the crush of mourners. She watched his face as he apologised to people he gently edged aside, beads of perspiration on his brow, until he was before her. His eyes darted briefly to Benedita's face, and then back to Zodwa's. Extending his hand, he shook her hand.

'It's good to see you,' he said, 'although we can all say that we've had a bitch whelping inside the house.'

For a moment she was stumped. Bitch? She however quickly grasped the idiomatic expression for great misfortune. 'These things happen,' Zodwa said. 'What do people do in funerals?'

'I had a talk with some of the men,' he began. 'Some wanted a quiet affair, but others wanted pomp and ceremony.'

And I wasn't even consulted, Zodwa thought, the men don't have the simplest courtesy. 'And then, which faction won?' Zodwa noticed that Joachim was uncomfortable with talking to her. 'What is it? Are you keeping something from me, Joachim?'

Joachim glanced furtively around him, a gesture as incongruous with his attire as a Masai warrior in a cellular telephone advertisement. 'Please,' he whispered, 'don't call me Joachim. My name is now Jeqe. I was called Joachim according to Christian conversion. . .'

Zodwa suppressed an urge to laugh. 'And now, you've converted back, to what?'

'To my real self. An African man.'

'Tell me, then, African man – isn't *ujeqe* some kind of bread?' Her flippancy, she knew, could cost her potential allies. 'What have the men decided?'

'It's not everyone, really,' Jeqe explained. 'It's your uncle, Mbongwa. He's the one who wants to preside over the funeral, over the arrangements.'

'Is that why I wasn't told anything, because Mbongwa wants to be the chief?'

'That is correct.' Jeqe looked her straight in the eye. 'Can we talk privately?'

Although not understanding a word they were saying, Benedita could see that they needed privacy. Nodding at Zodwa, she sauntered off to another white face, which had entered the tent. Horwitz stood with a bunch of wilting dizzy lizzies in his hand. He looked lost, like someone who'd been stood up by a date and didn't know what to do with the flowers. Zodwa watched her, registering Horwitz's presence, shrugging it off. 'What's happening?'

Joachim cleared his throat. 'When Baba Joshua died,' he began, 'Mbongwa led a delegation of traditionalists to a meeting of the council of Elders. I was there as a scribe, also on sufferance because Nozizwe insisted that Baba Joshua had said that all council meetings should be recorded. Some of the men were not happy, but they relented, because they didn't want to cross Nozizwe.' He brightened up a bit. 'Do you know that she once pointed at a man who'd annoyed her, and a small penis grew on his forehead?'

'Poetic justice for a prick,' she said, half to herself. 'Go on.'

'First of all, Mbongwa declared that he should succeed Baba Joshua,' Jeqe said, 'and before people pointed out the little detail of the daughter, he said that under the Bantu Native Law, a woman is a perpetual minor and can never take over unless she's the first wife. But a brother-in-law could take over, first as a regent, and then be confirmed later.'

Zodwa thought: Why not let Mbongwa run this show? But then she remembered her father, and what she had promised. Nozizwe's words, also, rang clearly in her head. 'What's the situation if Mbongwa doesn't get what he wants?'

'There's a rumour that he's the only one who visits Hodoba. People are afraid. He's also friendly with Johnny M and Grey. People here cry for their lot to be improved. For all the things that Baba Joshua planned. Running water. Electricity. Schools. That simply can't happen with Mbongwa.' His troubled eyes sought hers. 'Having known Baba Joshua, and that the colours of a bull are brighter on the calf, I think you should become the chief.'

'But?' Zodwa prompted, 'there's a *but* somewhere in your tone …'

'If you take over,' Jeqe said, 'you must bear in mind that there are now guns here, and there is tension. People are preparing for war.'

'So,' Zodwa asked, 'you think my nomination could start a war?'

'Without a doubt.'

'I'm flattered,' she said, 'that a war can start on account of little old me.'

Throughout her exchange with Jeqe, she had been aware of someone's concentrated gaze on her. She had put on her dark glasses. The man was a head taller than Jeqe, his premature grey hair, instead of giving him a distinguished look, gave him an air of dissolution. But still, there was a certain quality about him, dignity perhaps, reflected in eyes that seemed to have seen everything and forgotten nothing. Each time she fixed him with a stare, he immediately turned and spoke with Reuben the Collector. She racked her head, reaching into the catacombs of memory, because she was sure she had seen that face somewhere. But where? 'Excuse me, Jeqe,' she said. 'We'll talk later.' As she started off towards where the man stood near the coffin, fingering Nozizwe's necklace beneath her dress, Zodwa concluded that the route to wise and effective reign started with knowing the names of all her subjects.

Fifteen

Benedita could still hear strains of the singing at the wake as she walked home. She had done her bit, and was sure in her heart, even if the recipient of her kindness wouldn't acknowlege it, that she had been there for Zodwa in her hour of need. It was late, around seven-thirty p m, but the evening air was invigorating, a good time for a leisurely stroll. She had no idea when Jannie would come back. Men and their official secrets, which were invariably public to all and sundry … The secrets industry of this country, like its prison walls, was as leaky as a loofah. But that didn't stop people pretending they were privy to matters whose disclosure could bring down the government. Knowledge, as someone had once said, was power. With Jannie, though, it wasn't just a simple matter of power. His preoccupation with Grey's downfall had taken on such proportions that Benedita had been forced to step in and prohibit the mere mention of the police chief's name in their house. If the name was banned from their lips, it was, however, for ever on their minds. It followed them into their bedroom where it soiled their lovemaking with its filthy fingers.

For her part, she had organised her mind in such a way that she could consign people neatly in their pigeonholes. That made it easier to deal with life; for her, then, there were no grey areas. Police Chief Grey, she believed, was not an inherently evil man, the way a Nazi would have been. But, like the ordinary Germans who wallowed in an atmosphere where evil was possible, he had taken a path that wouldn't be such a burden on his conscience, by electing to believe that whatever he was involved in was for the general good. She was sure that, were this mediocrity to be asked, *Whose good?* he would have answered, *Of the people.* Meaning white people. Here, she found herself reflecting on what bonded these disparate men. They hated each other, she was sure, implacably, and their mutual hatred had something to do with the presence of the black man in this country. Whites didn't hate blacks, for the simple reason that you cannot hate what is effectively at your mercy, in the same way that, no matter how much you might dislike a child, that antipathy never transcends into hate. But since hate was an emotion as useful as adrenaline, white people wasted no time finding each other. The history of the world, from the voyages of discovery, through slavery to apartheid, was not so much the slaughter of despised peoples as fallout from massive clashes among rulers. The powerless, unfortunately, preyed on the weak in the chain of existence. Her fear for Africans found a coherent channel, when she met Venter.

*   *   *

Benedita is in Johannesburg in the autumn of 1993, when the secretary-general of the communist party, Chris Hani is shot dead by an illegal Polish immigrant. She takes a keen interest in the assassination because it bears the swift, effective and surgical trademark of Mossad, a security service she knew worked closely with South Africa's security service. The capture of the blond Pole, Janusc Walus, is in itself a transcendental phenomenon, taking on board the Western world's ambiguous relationship to Poles. She watches on television as the bloodied body of a man no-one thought capable of dying was covered and carted away by singing men from Hani's Dawn Park home in Boksburg. Weeping uncontrollably on nation-wide television, Tokyo Sexwale is comforted by a matronly Gill Marcus. It is a poignant moment, where blacks live with the suspicion that one of theirs could have committed the crime – a suspicion given an ironic twist by their knowledge of the real beneficiaries of this murder. Nine days of mourning, and seventy-two deaths later, a state funeral is held for Chris Hani, at the First National Bank stadium, a few miles from Soweto. Benedita tells her hosts in the suburb of Norwood, of her intention to attend the funeral. Eva and Arthur Goodman, who are both retired broadcasters, explain gently – they know this country – why no sane white person would go anywhere near the stadium. Later, convinced that Benedita is one insane woman, Eva and Arthur throw her and their car goodbye kisses. As she drives off in their red Toyota sedan, Benedita is herself not sure she'll ever see them again.

The faces of black drivers who stare at her with eyes that wish her dead compound her sense of foreboding. Joining the Louis Botha Avenue, she struggles with minibus taxis from Alexandra Township, which careen as if they want to consign their passengers to the graveyard. These minibus taxi drivers stop in front of you without signalling, or change lanes as if there's no traffic behind them. Benedita, who since hitting Johannesburg has eschewed all ladylike conduct, curses the wall-eyed drivers or gives them the finger. Others find this amusing. One rolls down his window and peers down at her. 'Hey, baby,' he says in a whisky-scarred voice, giving her his penis-sized finger, 'how many fingers must I give you to make you satis?'

Despite herself, Benedita laughs around her indignation. The new democracy. It has introduced its own brand of rudeness, made in South Africa, boy, what a world! She turns into Harrow Road, having hooted twice – *Fuck you!* – Hoping he'd get the meaning. Satis. What would satisfy her is getting all these maniacs off the road. She's still thinking about this when, through peripheral vision, she sees in her side window a face covered in a balaclava. Panic hits her, a hijacker! There is a dull thud and she thinks she's hit him, this inexperienced fucking hijacker, only to see a bumper sticker affixed across the windshield, black lettering in a field of yellow with red-and-green margins, ELPOEP EHT FO OREH INAH SIRHC, Chris Hani hero of the people. White drivers pulling alongside at a traffic light, glance at the sticker and something happens to their faces.

The morning is a bit cold, but the air signifies a scorcher. Heat and violent death, the South African connection. And, of course, the necessary ingredient, poverty, to complete the effect. Men in different, no doubt rehearsed, stances of mendacity stand at inter-sections with cardboard signs on which their penury is written. Indifferent drivers speed on, and Benedita joins the concourse of haste. Nearer the industrial area of Booysens, the needy human traffic is replaced by hurrying, hard-faced men, young, wiry and agile in their trainers, whose eyes dart from car to car, predators looking for an opportunity to strike. As she heads westwards, gaping tracts of land turn into old mines, the disused shafts grow scraggly green bush on yellow soil, colours borrowed from Chris Hani's sticker. There are more of these now, so that, by the time she gets onto the Soweto highway, almost all cars exhibit stick-ers, banners and magazine covers sporting the face of the slain communist.

Even before she reaches the perimeters of the stadium, where the ground teemed with hundreds and hundreds of people, mainly the young, she sees the grey pavilions and hears the stamping of feet and the roar of voices. Suddenly people there are jogging alongside the car which now crawls at ten to fifteen k p h, Benedita trying to negotiate her way through the crowds, some asshole banging on the roof of the car. In her confusion, another face peers at her through the window, and a hand waves her on, someone shouting, 'Let her go, she's a comrade!' Her sav-iour is a young man in a khaki uniform and a black beret bear-ing a miniature ANC flag, black, green and gold.

No sooner has she smiled thank you at the young man, than her door is yanked open and strong hands pull her outside. She lands on the ground and, momentarily dazed, finds herself pinned to the ground with a big, sweating black man above her. She feels his hands groping for the fabric of her dress, trying to rip it off her whilst, simultaneously wedging her legs apart with a knee the size of a tree stump. Benedita's gaze is fixed on her assailant, taking in his foul breath, acne and the odour of a charged, unwashed body. Stinking black motherfucker, she thinks, hating him with every single fibre in her body, stinking depraved black son-of-a-bitch, you're not raping me! And jabs her stiffened fingers into his eyes whilst hitting the bridge of his nose with the edge of her hand. He howls, and drops of his black, stinking blood fall on her shirt, for fuck's sake, and he reaches into his back pocket, she knows, for a knife. The young man in khaki comes up from above them, behind her attacker and hits him with a large stone. The man gives a grunt and collapses on her. And then it all happens so quickly that Benedita can almost swear it didn't take place. The young man helps her into the car, closes the door and turns. Then he reaches behind as if trying to scratch his back, and sinks against the side of the car, palms flat on the roof. She hears the whine of the bullet as it smashes into her windscreen, leaving a small hole out of which radiates a striated network of cracks. Then she ducks, almost leaving the steering-wheel as the gun explodes right next to her head. She had seen people being shot in a film, where the audience enjoys the benefit of the camera's point of view, and there is music, even in the bloodiest of films. But, in real life, and especially when death happens near you, everything is so sudden, you only react to the aftermath of a shooting. Sometimes you don't actually see the gun, just the results. Through her window, she sees her would-be rapist waving a pistol and then going down under a hail of bullets.

Suddenly, she witnesses a running battle between the police, who have materialised suddenly, and the young township boys with stones. Her saviour, who's been leaning against the car, takes a few steps back and rolls onto the ground, his khaki jacket stained with blood in the front and back. The bullet has gone through his lean frame and through the windscreen. While stones fly, she stops the car and gets out and kneels above the wounded boy, for that is what he is – was – just a boy, and watches helplessly as blood froths in his mouth. Then his eyes roll back into their sockets, and Benedita hears a scream going like a steam engine. She finds out, when strong arms yank her from the ground and put pressure on her neck so that she is forced to walk with her knees bent, feeling the man's crotch on her buttocks, that the scream she had heard came from her.

'The boy –' she says to her new saviour, 'the boy. . . ?'

'Forget about him,' the voice behind her says, 'he's all right, just in shock. . . '

She registers confusion in terms of colour. Her borrowed car is red, the angry faces are black. The uniforms of marshals trying to maintain order are ochre. There is a widening swathe of blue of police uniforms and the deep blue of bullet-proof vests. Their faces cover the range from white through pink to black; the bulk of the black webbing, the ochre ground, green grass, and the crimson patches where the black man lies bleeding, become the colour of fear. Benedita takes in the bronze, hairy arms enveloping her, frog-marching her to the car, gets a whiff of a now-familiar odour, perspiration, fear, a smell of imminent death trapped within her nostrils and rendering her mouth dry.

The sticker flapping in the windscreen creates confusion in the youthful throngs, especially since both occupants of the car are white, and one is even an armed policeman. Another uniformed marshal waves them on, his conduct telling the policeman, we are in charge here, fuck your gun! The policeman urging her to drive on is also young, with a small ginger moustache and quick, alert eyes under the peaked cap. Benedita's foot alternates between the clutch and accelerator as they follow the line of cars edging to the massive gates of the stadium where 250 000 people, including Nelson Mandela, wait to bury a fallen hero. She shrugs off the policeman's offer to escort her to a safe place from where she could watch the proceedings. Still shaken, she climbs the steps and sits next to an Indian couple. They give her a nervous smile; smiling back, she notices a sprinkling of white people, and tries to imagine whether anyone would ever know the trouble they've seen.

The ceremony is a daylong catharsis. The crowds take turns

singing revolutionary songs, sometimes stamping on the concrete pavilion until it shook. There is a real threat that the accumulated angry weight will cause the blocks to crumble and send hundreds of bodies to their deaths in the scaffolding below. As people sing themselves into frenzy, Benedita gets a whiff of dagga, which is being smoked openly, defiantly in the back. One kid in dreadlocks sends a sheaf of pages flying, the *Sowetan's* special edition featuring a colour photograph of Chris Hani, the way leaders release white pigeons in a demonstration of their commitment to peace. There is a scramble as people snatch the pages, while the singing continues. In the centre of the stadium, on a dais, sit lines of political, trade union and civic leaders, who take turns speaking. Their voices snatched by the wind, they relate the journey Chris Hani took to fight for his country. They recount how he was a non-conformist, full of courage, how he fought against the combined might of South African and Rhodesian forces in Wankie and Sipolilo in 1968 and 1969. Peter Mokaba, the youth leader, chants a slogan which fires up the stadium, doing the swaying dance which was once banned.

Kill the boer, the farmer.

He chants, his voice rasping, managing to tell, in a disjointed but frighteningly coherent manner, the troubled history of his country and its people. Under the stammering sky, in the unrelieved heat, leader after leader exhorts the government of the day to set April next year as the date for the first democratic elections in South Africa. When Nelson Mandela, looking frail but speaking with a clear voice, echoes this call, there is a roar among the crowds, an affirmation rising out of the ashes of a blasphemed life, to bring about a new dispensation.

After Mandela has spoken, Benedita sees buses starting to move, heading towards the Soweto Highway. On the tops of the buses, people are stacked like baggage, shouting and thrusting their fists into the air. Farther up, she notices smoke billowing out of burning houses; the air smells of sulphur, a concentration of fear and anger. Following her instincts, she starts her own departure from the vale of hope and despair. She doesn't know how she made it to the car, but when she finally gets there, her knight in blue armour stands watching, his head cocked to the side, a small I-told-you-so smile on his face.

'So,' he asks, 'how was it?'

Benedita just shakes her head, still overcome by what she has seen. 'I don't know,' she answers, 'it's all so confusing.'

'That's right,' the policeman says. 'Next time you want to have a near-death experience, call me. I'm at the Pretoria police station, but I'll be in Hillbrow for a while, doing VIP protection. Just ask for Jannie Venter.'

On a whim, a week later, she picks up the phone and calls him.

*   *   *

She would agonise over why she got married to Venter. They were poles apart in every respect. Much as she didn't pretend to have an answer to what was plaguing the country, she knew at least that, in the eyes of many – black people and white English-speakers – Afrikaners or Boere in the parlance of township streets, were held responsible for what had happened. Although they hadn't originated the colour bar (that was as English as tea and scones in Dorset) they had certainly institutionalised a system of control that had few parallels on the planet. Venter had come to her, rough, unpolished, the archetype of all the things she was brought up to hate. In some corner of her mind, she admitted that the initial attraction had been as physical as her shock when she lay exposed on the ground. He hadn't disappointed her in bed. In moments of immodesty, whenever he brought her into new heights of pleasure, he would boast – invoking something he must have heard somewhere – that he was a savage in the sack. Her unacknowledged dependence on this side of him sent her mind dwelling on the visions of the civilisation to which she laid claim. A student of the Renaissance and a believer in the scribes that helped preserve the precepts of Greco-Roman and Judeo-Christian cultures, she found it strange that she was hitched up to a relic of the Stone Age.

There were moments of frustration, which were never relieved until she pored into her books, when she wished to bring him into the orbit of the world which had shaped her. She was almost in tears, one afternoon, reading of Augustine and how Virgil's *Aeneid* entranced him. She painted mental pictures of Aeneas's escape from burning Troy and how the tempestuous love affair with Dido, the queen of Carthage, who is won over by his story-telling skills. Benedita sought to create parallels between ancient lives and modern anxieties; much more, she wanted someone with whom to share these illuminations. She read him a line, *These are the tears of things, and the stuff of our mortality cuts us to the heart.* Stopping, the words on the page suddenly jumping like so many little black ants, she knew that she, like the Romans at the fall of their empire, was doomed to make do with a situation where she was beneath even the underdog.

More than two years later, here she was, switching on the kitchen lights, thinking about cooking, undecided. Although the kitchen was clean, her fingers encountered dust everywhere she touched. For a while she busied herself dusting and sweeping, raising a cloud of dust, totally disgusted with herself. Clearing out a corner where she kept her recipes, she extracted a dusty volume, *La Cuisine Provençale*. This might do the trick, she thought, reading on, hoping she had the ingredients. ... *de tomates, d'oignons, d'huile d'olive et d'herbes des collines: thym, origan, sarriette, romarin, basilic, fenouil* ... Oh, God! Giving up, she tossed the cookbook on the counter. No way I can rustle up a meal like that, she thinks, where the hell do you get herbs from the hills here? The decision to cook was taken out of her hands with the arrival of Reuben with a steaming pot of goat meat, courtesy of Zodwa. She thanked him and watched him climb into his wagon; the tall man she had seen earlier at the wake accompanied him. She put some potatoes on the stove to boil at low heat, and ran a scented bath.

Outside, the night had fallen, slowly, almost tenderly. Far, into the unseen mountains and valleys, caves and squatter camp units, whoever was there was also governed by the dictates of the night. The beasts and plants, which owned neither watches nor any means to measure time, knew, instinctively, that it was a period to sleep, and await the rays of the morning light.

Where was Jannie? Now, luxuriating naked in the bath, she saw her reflection in the misty room, her brown hair that fell before her like a curtain until she swished it back with a jerk of the head, and the brown eyes, which looked black in the gloom. Soaping herself, she felt her breasts for lumps – a dreaded exploration – and sighed, thanking her gods for the smoothness of her globes. Feeling her nipples harden, she wondered, whether Jannie would still find her desirable when her breasts started to sag. She consoled herself that something in him would have started to sag, too. But she knew the vanity of men, their horror of ageing. Arthur and Eva carried their years gracefully, companions, she knew, to the grave. They had been mildly put out when Benedita returned with the car, which seemed to have survived a war, but they had been relieved that she was safe. She'd held back on the more gruesome details, regaling them with stories of Mandela's dignified air, the menace which had hung over the stadium like a pall, and, of course, Jannie. Later, when she introduced him to them, they couldn't disguise their surprise and – of this she was sure – their disappointment. He had also sensed it, and tried to keep away from them, never attempting to endear himself to the couple. It was not a class thing, she comforted herself, and Jannie looked too rough a diamond, someone who might not have a future. This unstated disapprobation put a gulf between them, especially after they heard of Cynthia. As if Cynthia's voracious past would rub off on Benedita. The silences between visits became longer and longer, up until there was nothing more left to say.

I must get back to my cooking, she thought, feeling lazy. Then, she must have nodded off for a moment for, when she next looked at the mirror, her heart nearly stopped when she saw, in addition to her own face, another greyish face dominated by large eyes. It took her one heart-lurching moment to see that it was a monkey, and by then she was out of the bath. The monkey, startled by her reaction, climbed on the toiletry shelf, sending bottles and jars skittering on the tiled floor. Grabbing a jar of her expensive facial scrub from the Body Shop in London, she was about to throw it at the animal when Jannie called her. 'Skattie?' he said casually, 'is Momberg's monkey in there?' She looked at the jar in her hand and read the inscription as if for the first time. *Against animal testing*. Well, this animal was certainly testing her. 'Blackie?' Venter called again. 'Are you behaving yourself in there?'

Blackie? Who the fuck was Blackie – this monkey? What was a monkey doing in her bathroom, staring at her with those eyes. Wrapping a towel around herself – the monkey, Blackie, was giving her a knowing look – she left the bathroom and padded on the floor towards Jannie, more furious than she'd ever been in her life. She found him fixing himself a drink, the assault rifle propped up on the settee. 'What', she asked, 'is the big idea?' She was livid, and when in this state, she spoke in clichés.

'Don't yell at me,' he said.

'Don't yell at you?' Benedita couldn't believe the nerve. 'You disappear and then come back with a monkey on tow, and you tell me not to yell at you. . . '

Even as she spoke, she sensed that something was wrong. His face was marked with black splotches, like a kid who'd wallowed in cinders. Even from where she stood, with the scent of bath water still in her nostrils, she could smell from him burnt bone. As she found a chair and sunk into it, she wanted to throw up, for she knew that, whatever it was, it would disgust her, and spoil her evening.

Jannie Venter took a sip of his drink, grimaced, and told her the story.

★   ★   ★

A tired and thwarted Venter had driven back home from Upper

Ngoza. He had spent the entire day helping the Midlands police with their inquiries – police-speak for saying that he was the chief suspect – and fielding questions from the media. Christ, he hated them, the journalists and their notebooks and endless questions. Let me take you back to the scene of the crime, said one mealy-mouthed anchor from one of the South African Broadcasting Corporation's channels. Let me take you back to the killing fields, Sunshine, Venter wanted to say, and rub your fucking nose in bone ash and see how that tickles your tonsils. After the blinding flash of bulbs, the medical and forensic teams had arrived, followed by a bomb squad with sniffer dogs *nogal*. The medicos zipped Momberg up in a body bag and loaded him in the ambulance. Now Venter was driving back with a monkey on his back, literally.

Blackie had screamed like a banshee, spitting and clawing at anyone who approached him. The only living thing he trusted was Venter, jumping and perching on his shoulder, making near human sounds and faces. Someone suggested that they either radio the SPCA or shoot the damn thing on the spot. The latter suggestion was met with outrage, what was wrong with this guy – had he never seen a traumatised monkey before? No-one had ever seen a monkey in the throes of a post-traumatic stress disorder, and no-one could suggest a reliable animal psychiatrist. This was Upper Ngoza, not a Hollywood movie set where animal rights people routinely arranged for animals to have personal physicians. When the monkey demonstrated its affection for Venter, people heaved a sigh of relief. The matter was no longer in their hands.

'I don't want this monkey,' Venter remonstrated.

'Look, buddy,' one of the men said, 'be reasonable. It's obvious the monkey has taken a shine to you. Take it back home, then you can dump it in a zoo.'

'Jesus, what a grouch!' added one of the SABC journalists, a woman in outsize glasses, no doubt a producer because she'd never make a presenter. Thinking about it later, he should have presented her with Blackie. Just then, the mynas screeched inside his head and he knew he was in for a bad migraine, and there was no telling what he would do. He took a deep breath, suppressing an urge to empty a magazine on the assembled media corps and the medicos and the monkey. Talk about post-traumatic stress disorder – they were all out of order.

'What are we going to do?' Benedita asked now. 'I also don't want this monkey.'

'You're asking me?' Venter countered. 'You're the one who knows about pets.'

'Jannie,' Benedita wailed, 'I don't know anything about pets.'

Venter thought for a while. Then he snapped his fingers. 'Tell you what,' he said, brightening up, 'in the olden days, when a chief snuffed it, they killed a couple of men to accompany him.'

'Where did you hear such a ridiculous thing?'

'I saw it in a film, "Shaka Zulu".' He pondered for a minute, envisioning hapless men with broken necks being thrown into the grave. 'A monkey is as near as it gets to a Zulu.'

'I don't want that kind of talk.' Benedita listened, heard the monkey moving about in the kitchen. She worried about her dinner. 'Get that thing out of my house. Now!'

'Okay,' Venter said, crossing over to the kitchen, 'if that's what you want.'

She heard him calling the monkey, in surprisingly endearing tones. After a while he came into the lounge with Blackie on his shoulder. It dawned on her that beneath Venter's hard exterior was a little boy looking for a pet. But she still wasn't happy with the idea of the animal being made part of funeral rites. She knew that Zodwa might not agree to anything being buried with her father, but, then, they might not even tell her. What will the palaeontologists of the future say when they excavated monkey and homo sapiens remains fossilised in the same spot? They'll probably comment on some arcane sacrifices or sexual practices of this civilisation, getting it all wrong. Thinking of Zodwa, she remembered that the funeral would be tomorrow. She didn't know what to wear, and was afraid of asking Venter to come along. There was no telling what he would do, and, already he and Zodwa had started off on a bad footing. The monkey made a sound, like a cough, and Benedita saw how closely it resembled human beings. Killing it would be akin to murder. Even though she'd never owned a pet even as a child, and was frightened of animals, she didn't want this monkey's death on her conscience.

'Where are you taking him?' she asked.

'To the Zulus, where else?'

'Put that monkey down, this minute!'

Venter sighed and lowered Blackie to the floor. Benedita studied his face, looking for signs of shock after what he had experienced in the early hours of the day. She knew, even if he didn't, that Momberg had not been the target, he just got caught up in a spiral of events he didn't know about, had been, to be more exact, in the eye of someone's storm. She thought of the prisoners who had died a horrible death, burnt beyond recognition. She could smell them on his shirt and wished he would take it off and bathe and cleanse himself of horror. She went into the kitchen and set the table, even though she knew he wanted to eat in the lounge, where he could watch the cowboy films on television.

But he followed her into the kitchen and sat down. He commanded the monkey to sit still. Then he said grace and they started to eat. Benedita put an assortment of fruit in a side plate and set it before Blackie. Blackie noisily shoved an apple into his mouth.

'Didn't Momberg teach his pet some manners?' Benedita asked. 'See how he's gobbling his food.'

Venter shook his head. What did she expect with a monkey? He sat still for a moment, looking at Blackie. Still unsure of his ground, Blackie bobbed his head from side to side, like a spectator in a tennis match. Despite herself, Benedita started laughing. Men and their monkey business!

*　　　*　　　*

243

At dusk, Johnny M, Police Chief Grey and Mbongwa held a council of war in Johnny M's palatial home. They sat in the patio, looking at the dying embers of the barbecue fire. Johnny M had personally overseen the braai, standing over the cook's shoulders, instructing him on whether a piece of prime steak was done to order. Grey had preferred his medium rare. 'Can't say you're eating meat,' he had quipped, his syllables dripping with sexual innuendo, 'unless there's some to taste.' Mbongwa had settled for chicken, doctor's orders. Johnny M, still wearing the chef's hat, had loaded his plate with rump steak, well done, please, potatoes, salad, washing it all down with Pilsner Urquart, imported from Belgium. Behind them, in the sleek and modern kitchen, the battery of helpers washed dishes and prepared the dessert. Now and then a waiter in black-and-white and a black tie ambled over to freshen drinks and bring beer bottles beaded with condensation to the table. This was the life. Even Grey, who yearly pulled two hundred grand max, after deductions and including undeclared earnings – mainly from capers sponsored by tonight's host – was impressed. Darkies certainly knew how to live it up, that's why they bought imported shoes. Grey always glanced at a man's shoes before deciding whether to do business with him. By their shoes ye shall know them. What was that song by the big Negro – no, African–American – singer? 'All God's chillun got shoes'. This was the reason Grey hated barefooted people, especially barefoot burglars, disturbing the peace of shod white folks. Johnny M wore imported American wingtips, style in motion. Johnny M was a lover of anything American. His car, house furniture, all spoke of a great affectation for Uncle Sam. Unless he was extremely pissed off, he would quote Shakespeare with an American accent that he received from his prodigious library of video films. Johnny M was a connoisseur, a man of refinement who liked things in apple-pie order. That's why he was upset with Mbongwa and the police chief. They were taking too long to sort out the mess attending Joshua's burial. But he must have been in a convivial mood, because, using his familiar

Shakespearian banter, he enjoined Mbongwa to drink some more.

'Have another scotch,' Johnny M said, admiring the label on the squat Chivas Régal bottle. 'We'll teach you to drink deep ere you depart.'

'No,' Mbongwa said, 'I've had it. Furthermore this is the mourning period. I, more than anyone else, must be seen to be a model of abstinence.'

'Model of abstinence?' Grey cried, 'Give me a break. You mean those Elders still have a sense of smell? Jesus, they're so old you can hear their bones creaking!'

'They might be old,' Mbongwa snapped, 'but they're not dumb.' He didn't like Grey.

'Gentlemen, gentlemen,' Johnny M chided, raising his hand like a chairman of the board, 'we will proceed no further with this business of bickering.' He stared at both men for a minute. 'Ours is to plan, perhaps cry havoc and slip the dogs of war.'

Mbongwa didn't know what the hell Johnny M meant but, seeing Grey nodding his assent, he decided to follow suit. He had a feeling that his position, here and back at the settlement, was precarious. And when a man's business was precarious, vultures started hovering around, ready to descend and tear his flesh from bone. Mbongwa knew something about vultures. He needed allies, backers, and benefactors. If they got their kicks from talking gobbledegook, it was all right with him, as long as they put out the money to bribe people. Lots of money.

'Mbongwa?' Johnny M said, reading his mind, 'we'll solve your problem and put money in thy purse.' He paused and glanced at Grey. 'What about the little errand you wanted him to run?'

Grey came to life. 'You could help me with a little thing,' he said. 'A minor irritant.'

'What's that?' Mbongwa asked, knowing that whatever it was, the price would be too high to pay, but he was deep enough as it was. He listened as Grey outlined the plan. It was, of course, monstrous, but that was the shape of things.

He accepted the envelope from Johnny M. His helpers loaded a side of beef and two crates of beer into the boot of his car. As he drove off, he thought he distinctly heard the men laughing. Let them laugh, he thought savagely, they don't have my problems. As he drove, he tried to put the problems in some perspective, order or proportion. One, he did want to be chief. He had seen many opportunities, which his brother-in-law had missed. There were a number of consortiums that wished to develop Ngoza. Johnny M had worked out a plan for a casino; he had had discussions with a representative from Sun International, and the area of Two Rivers squatter camp was decidedly a prime location. The squatters and, to a large extent, the settlers in the New Jerusalem had to be induced to move. But there wasn't enough money around to compensate people. So, there had to be some disincentive for them to hang about the eyesore of a squatter camp, like a bad smell. The campaign to exact levies from the residents wasn't running smoothly. Johnny M was a good manager, and believed in the devolution of tasks. Or, more precisely, he was a democrat, and believed in the equitable redistribution of anxiety. To that extent, he had put Mbongwa in charge of Fakude, Sipho and whatever additional muscle they could muster. The second problem that Grey articulated – boy, did that man make his blood boil! – was how to convince the Elders to find an alternative burial plot for Joshua. The one the Elders had chosen would simply not do. Grey had official papers to the effect that it was military land. The military had not finished doing its experiments there when the Land Claims court ruled that people could return to their ancestral lands. It was late already, and Mbongwa knew that the gravediggers were already digging. That had to be stopped. He knew that the Elders, who didn't know their collective arse from a hole in the ground, would pose a problem, especially if Mbongwa invoked the power of the white man. Nozizwe – and his niece – were problematic. It was time to see Hodoba and the Vulture-Men.

'There goes Nero, to feed the lions,' Grey said, watching the red tail lights of Mbongwa's car winking until they disappeared in the dark. 'Think he'll do it?'

'He'll have to,' Johnny M said, suddenly bored with the white man. 'One of the things I learnt while working for your people was that every man has a price. Mbongwa wouldn't last a day in any other circumstance, so, it's to his advantage that he sorts things out.'

'If he fucks up on this one, we're in deep shit, Johnny, you understand that?'

'Look,' Johnny M said patiently, 'Mbongwa wants to be a leader, the head honcho. He wants unlimited access to village beauties, money and power. We'll provide him with all three, keep him sweet, until our deals have some kind of momentum. After that, we'll see.'

'What about our brave boy?'

'Mpanza?' Johnny M thought for a while. 'I'm paying him a visit later this evening. I've looked at the notes you gave me. Like all men looking for something, he also has his weak spot. I don't think he can afford Zodwa knowing that he killed her brother.'

'Yeah,' Grey said, 'but it was a set-up.'

'*Ja*,' Johnny M said carelessly, 'try explaining that to someone whose brother you've shot. People aren't that rational. You kill my brother, I do something very bad to you.' He looked at Grey. 'If I were you, I'd worry about Venter. I hear he escaped.'

'I'll sort that out. Don't you worry about it.'

But Grey worried about it. He knew Johnny M's connections, and the violence he could unleash when thwarted. He thought of Venter and Benedita, and grinned.

Sixteen

Without the singing, the night was eerie, and drove Mpanza into philosophical contemplation. Still as though accepting an inevitable death sentence, the sleepy settlement below was in darkness save for pinpoints of yellowish light. This was where gravediggers and the men guarding the old man's corpse needed warmth and light to fight the chill and darkness of the night. From the vantage point at the top of the hill where Reuben's house stood, Mpanza tried to make out Zodwa's lodgings, but the darkness was too stubborn. He then tried to imagine her asleep. Did she snore or talk in her sleep? After catching sight of her today, he felt an abiding need to meet her, even though he hadn't worked out in his mind whether the purpose would be to explain his role in her brother's death or something else. Knowing himself and his needs and capabilities and limitations – and his proclivity to procrastinate – he realised that making a confession would be very difficult. What was he going to do? To speak to her before her father was buried was out of the question; people in grief, he told himself, grasp neither the subtleties of military decisions nor the convoluted logic of betrayals. He couldn't add to her woes. On the other hand, after the funeral might be too late. He had finally confided in Reuben, only to find, from his reaction, that Reuben already knew what was weighing heavily in his heart. He was not a fool; he had probably checked out with Ntombi. If Reuben – whose chest could not bear too many secrets – knew this, then who else did?

He heard the purr of the engine long before he saw the twin

lights stabbing the darkness. Even in the dark, he thought he could see clouds of dust trailing the lights. By the time the darkness receded in direct proportion to the vehicle's advance, he wondered who this late visitor was. Instead of anxiety, he experienced the sweetened stab of a sudden spasm of vanity, in expectation of imminent temptation. In a blasphemous cast of mind, he puzzled over Christ's mental frame when Lucifer turned on the charm. The difference, though, was that, although Mpanza had spent forty days in Ngoza, he was well fed. Reuben, and his own culinary skills, had seen to that. Theology never having been his strong suit, he nevertheless questioned whether Christ hadn't in reality been seeing visions induced by extreme hunger, so that the desert *bosberaad* with the Devil could have been conjured up by a febrile mind. But, bearing in mind that this was Christ – and the creator of all – the whole encounter, including the response to the Evil One, could have been rehearsed long beforehand, so what was the fuss all about?

Ruminations over religious lore brought about a memory he couldn't block out, when he remembered his father. The old man had been a deacon in the Pentecostal Holiness Church. Faced with a wayward son, he had always warned Mpanza of the vengeful power of a thwarted God. And that Mpanza would see God's face on his deathbed. Mpanza certainly saw a face that blazed with an Inner Light, minutes before their convoy, from Cacuso to Dondo, was riddled with automatic fire. In that infinitesimal moment between the vehicles' careening off the road and the loud explosion, Mpanza saw his grandfather's face, smiling, almost mocking, telling him that he would not survive. The irony was that it was on his birthday, 18 December 1982. It was a lifetime ago.

*　　*　　*

Mpanza woke up in a *kórház* for the Hungarian and international political elite in Budapest. He couldn't remember how he got to the hospital, except for dim, pain-ridden snatches of being transported by an army ambulance to the TAAG airlines cargo plane in Luanda. Shot full of morphine, he was unconscious until the first things he was aware of were banks of snow the height of a Volkswagen, the foreign solicitous voices and the careful hands of nurses, before everything receded and died in a white light.

A month later, healed and disoriented, he is instructed by headquarters in Lusaka to enrol with the international institute for journalists, *Nemzetközi újságírás iskola*, run under the auspices of the International Organisation of Journalists, in Kapy Utca, by Mr Ferenc Németh and his assistants Szusza Zigány and László Magay. This is the Hungary of János Kádár and the Workers Party, where the country is straddling the difficult worlds of socialism and capitalism, or, as they say, socialism with a human face. This coinage is perplexing, for it implies that capitalism has a human face, which socialism must strive to emulate. The trainees, a score of them, are a Namibian, a South Yemeni, a South African, two Syrians, two Afghanis, two Indians, two Colombians, a Lebanese, two Iraqis (there were no Iranians because of the war), an Ethiopian, a Tanzanian, one Eritrean, two Nigerians and a Palestinian. Salim al Hamadi is a captain in the Palestinian Liberation Organisation's Fatah army. He has just returned from the seventy-seven day Israeli siege on Lebanon, where Israel tried to flush out the PLO. He and Mpanza become close, if mutually ruinous, friends. Salim, who understands Hungarian, having received his officer's training in Budapest, has a problem of concentration that manifests itself in disruptive behaviour. It is not unusual for him to stand up in class and shout, '*Szünet!*' – 'Break'. The instructors indulge him, much to the annoyance of other participants. Mpanza gets to understand that the Arabs, even if they come from the same Semitic tree, are not brothers. There are heated exchanges daily, especially between Adnan Yassin, who is Lebanese, and Salih Al Moufty, who is Iraqi. Arguments flare up and disturb classes following briefings by notables from the Arab resistance, such as Hanan Ashrawi or Nayeef Hawatmeh. Salim acts like a crazed man

250

when Hungarian television replays the assassination of Anwar Sadat, standing up and taking a firing position, going, 'Rat-a-tat-tat!' Mpanza pulls him down.

Mpanza enjoys the outings to the city's Turkish baths, taking in the sights of the most beautiful city he has ever seen. Sometimes, alone, he takes the Number Twelve bus to Batthyany square, where fashionable youngsters in Gucci and Christian Dior attire scowl at the official slogans extolling virtues of socialism on billboards. Here and there are memories of home, where hawkers peddle their fruit and vegetables in stalls along the underground station. The train takes him to Gellert Ter where he trades forints into dollars, thanks to Salim's Arab connections. Everywhere are signs that this country was once occupied by a succession of invaders. The statues and curlicued railings in inner courtyards speak of the Austro-Hungarian Empire. Tiberius first built the hot bathhouses inside the Gellert Hotel, and they can be seen in almost original splendour among the ruins of Aquincum. Taking a hike along the Szechenyi Bridge, Mpanza admires the parliament building, which seems to have risen out of the Danube. The river winds its way along the banks, a sinuous, liquid voluptuousness that complements the friendly, almost flirtatious disposition of the city dwellers. He is surprised at how quickly he adjusts to being called a néger, without any racist undertones, the way people comment on the colour of someone's hair. The winter, which was punishing by its northern strangeness, has given way to a short spring, and now it is summer. People emerge out of their dark, encumbering clothing, like butterflies out of chrysalises. Everywhere, Mpanza encounters smiles and greetings: *Szia!* or, with older people, *Jó napot kívanok!* It is hot, and people are in different degrees of undress near the water. A young woman, in a halter and shorts, sees him watching this overabundance of exposed flesh and, without hesitation, asks him, '*Míert napozik?*' – 'Why aren't you sunbathing?' He shakes his head and moves on, knowing that she was just being friendly, nothing to it.

If the Hungarians show no antipathy towards blacks, they exercise an excess of vigilance over Arabs and gypsies. He encounters here a reaction with which he was very familiar back home, the sudden disappearance of a smile and the face congealing with rage or becoming as blank as an empty page. Much later, Szusza tells him the reasons: the Arabs are disliked because the Hungarians still haven't got over their history of defeat by the Ottoman empire; much more, the Arabs lord it over them with their oil money. They accuse them of corrupting their youth, especially the women. In the middle of this lecture, Mpanza remembers that all the smooth-talking black-marketers around big hotels like Gellert or Buda Penta are Arabs. The gypsies? Well, he is told that is a long story.

It is in the summer when Budapest's Népstadion hosts a series of concerts by Western artists. Johnny Cash's craggy face is on posters everywhere. Salim, whose mysterious source supplies him with tickets to the most inaccessible events, organises a couple of tickets for Mpanza. Since Salim's taste in music is limited to the Egyptian diva Umm al-Khulthum and Algerian Khaled, he passes this one. Mpanza is accompanied by Rajabu and the Swapo participant, Angula, and a few other friends from the students' union in Buda. In a country where and when anything Western, no matter how mediocre, is celebrated, Johnny Cash is a hit. As the band plays and Cash sings, Mpanza listens for the saxophones, isolating them from a sound dominated by strings and drums. He hears from the tenor sounds that remind him of home, something closely resembling the broad and breathless syncopation associated with the *mbaqanga* beat. Enraptured, he notices through a haze a vaguely familiar, young Hungarian couple seating themselves next to him. The man, Richard Vas, is caught up in a time warp where hipness was once equivalent with rolling the thinnest joint and knowledge of lyrics of songs by Crosby, Stills, Nash & Young. His wife, Judit Szabó, is an interpreter with one of the many bureaux serving non-governmental organisations and embassies. It is through her unease that

252

Mpanza senses that this encounter is not purely accidental. After stilted greetings, the two get back to enjoying the music, Richard snapping his fingers and tapping his feet to the beat. During the first break, Richard looks at Mpanza; Judit concentrates on the emptying bandstand.

'What is it, Richard?' Mpanza asks. He wants to go for a drink, but curiosity gets the better of him. Some of the students are gesticulating to him that they are headed for the bar. Join you later, he mouths silently.

'I need someone with friends in Germany,' Richard says.

'He means *West* Germany,' Judit adds. There is a subtle impatience in her voice, as if something as simple as giving her husband an address in Germany could be lost on him. It is when she turns to address him that Mpanza is struck by how blue, and huge, her eyes are. Although her face is scarcely made up, her full lips are red and vulnerable, like someone who spends time worrying them with her teeth. She keeps her blonde hair imprisoned inside a Lakers baseball cap. To Mpanza she looks so Teutonic he resists advising Richard he should consult *her* on contacts in Germany.

'I might know of some people,' Mpanza replies, suddenly feeling uncomfortable. He casts around his head for names. There's Bernhard Mutter he met in Lusaka, from the Friedrich Ebert Foundation; then he remembers they had a serious fall-out over some obscure philosophical point. Then there's Theo Wiener, whose last address was Stuttgart, where he ran a small publishing house. He can't say that he's really close to Theo, but he knows the man thrives on intrigue. Rumour had it that he had helped the ANC identify South African security agents among the solidarity movement people in Bonn. Richard's case would be a test for Theo: his politics are social-democratic and he sympathises with revolutionary principles, but Mpanza suspects him of having a difficult relationship with socialism. Most people, even potential oppressors, don't have a problem with opposing apartheid, since it is tailor-made for condemnation. It is what happens after that which worries a number of people.

In any event, he gives them Theo's name and address and directs Richard to get in touch. Richard thanks him, and Judit gives Mpanza a look that convinces him she really doesn't care much for him. He leaves them.

On a Saturday afternoon, Themba and two Zimbabwean friends drop in on Mpanza. Themba, a South African student doing economics and history in one of the institutes in Budapest, is here to show off his car, a passably sleek Lada. As Mpanza is at a loose end, he accepts their invitation to go for a spin in Themba's car. They follow the route taken by Bus Number 12 to the city. Still suspicious of vehicles since his incident in Angola, Mpanza holds on to the door handle, thinking of landmines. The trauma, he knows, will live with him for a long time. Themba catches his eye in the rear-view mirror.

'Don't be scared,' he says. 'My driver's licence is the Real McCoy. Not your *mshanga* from the bantustan.' Turning to his companion in the passenger seat, he adds, 'Give him a drink, Jethro.'

Jethro turns to hand Mpanza an uncorked bottle of rum. 'Here,' he says, 'this will ease your pain.'

Even as he drinks, Mpanza knows that his pain will never be eased. Neither liquor nor esoteric narcotic can assuage his sense of having led a life that seems destined for endless loneliness. He watches the murals on the museum walls whizzing past, the colours mingling into an elongated splash of memory. The artist, whoever he or she might be – what would they think of him, once an artist himself – a musician – who has lost all inspiration, without a land or a flag, with a national anthem which still invoked the mercy of an unmerciful God?

Knowing that an excess of drink occasions thoughts of self-pity, he refuses another offer from the front seat, and looks on as the car speeds to the outskirts of town. They reach a leafy suburb, which reminds him of Johannesburg, where youths play handball inside a fenced-in enclosure the size of a tennis court.

They evince something innocent and carefree, these children who've never known trouble, that still burst with hormonal confusion. Time will tell, Mpanza thinks grimly, remembering his own stormy childhood.

The drive turns into a well-planned programme whose centrepiece was someone's farewell party. They enter the university complex, fronted by a statue commemorating one of Hungary's ancient war heroes. The summer light has changed and dusk approaches with the sureness of a mountain goat. Here and there are floodlights that will bathe the fountains come nightfall. The ancient buildings, whose beauty is almost breathtaking, speak of history and learning, of secrets that beat in the breasts of monks who scribbled on scrolls, preserving knowledge for the coming generations.

Beneficiaries of this age-old sacrifice down drinks and jive to hits by Sakhile, Hugh Masekela, Miriam Makeba and an assortment of South African music. Mpanza is aware of a throbbing bass and trumpets – and voices simultaneously sorrowful and joyous – which commingle with the smell of liquor and cigarettes, to become an instant slice of the home he hasn't seen in many years. There are sixteen, mainly young revellers in the flat owned by an African Studies lecturer. Hungarians, men and women, and South Africans and Cubans, men and women, dance, each nationality bringing out the rhythms that pulse in the bloods of its peoples.

Themba, Jethro and their silent companion soon disappear in the crowd. Mpanza walks over to a table laden with drinks and helps himself to a double of Scotch whisky. He listens to Miriam Makeba singing 'Gauteng', a song about the city of gold, Johannesburg, on whose mean streets, if not in the insatiable mines, many have perished. Mpanza has heard this track countless times, but it still evokes a curiously baffling question: How is it possible that a country that has spawned such evil can produce such golden talents? He hears the saxophonist breaking out in a bewildering solo, and the sadness of his own discarded calling envelops him. Taking another sip, he weaves through the bodies that are no longer gyrating, but holding tight, closely, spellbound by lyrics that are as much an invocation as an indictment.

A hand touches him and he jumps, nearly spilling his drink. He turns to find himself swallowed in the Great Lakes of Judit's eyes, whose appraisal of him is accompanied by a slightly mocking smile on her lips. 'Why so nervous?'

I'm not nervous, he thinks, just on edge. Feeling himself strangely drawn to this fragile woman with large wet eyes, he concludes that the drink is getting the better of him. But then, she has asked him a question. 'Don't know,' he lies. 'I suppose it's being in a strange place. Do you know,' he goes on, 'that this is the first time I've ever been inside a Hungarian's flat?'

'Is that very important for you,' Judit presses on, 'seeing where people live?'

'Back home,' Mpanza replies, feeling his tongue swelling in his mouth, 'we take strangers to our homes. It's not just …' He cannot quite find the words.

'African hospitality …?'

'Nothing as grand as all that.' He looks at her again, this time to ascertain whether she's being sarcastic. 'It's just the done thing. The way people behave.'

'Well,' Judit says, almost carelessly, 'look where all that got you.'

'What do you mean?'

'Simply this … open your doors to strangers and they take over the house.'

'Don't you ever open your doors to strangers?'

'All the time,' she says. 'Strangers can give us rare glimpses into familiar lives.'

It sounds to him like a quotation, from a poem, perhaps; stumped for an appropriate retort, he fumbles for a cigarette, lights up. Through the haze of blue smoke, he catches her glancing at a group that huddles in one corner, like a street gang debating the merits of casting their lot with their rivals, if only to gain access to their sisters, where the departing lecturer, their host, is holding court. His voice carries as he expounds on the meaning of madness. 'Men', he says, 'are completely mad. Some form of insanity has invaded all of us. Those that think themselves sane are candidates for an early entry into the nuthouse.'

'The great philosopher,' Judit murmurs, without irony, deepening the rancorous tone. Mpanza wonders if the two have a history together, a past where certain important businesses were left unfinished. 'I'm going outside,' she says.

The evening air is cool, blowing from the direction of the great river, the Danube. Mpanza can see the lights of the city girding the horizon; the powerful halogen lamps, which delineate the architecture of the American Embassy — a building whose catacombs spawn professionals practised in the art of darkness — cast a shimmering halo above a strip of skyline. In his pagan heart, he applauds the intellectualism of God, who must have been a very lonely or twisted guy to dream up all these obstacle courses. For what? Glory? The notion of the God who had the effrontery to use His only begotten Son as a bargaining chip against the pre-eminence of sin returns. Is there a difference between sin and evil? Why had God chosen the Jews? Or was that another imponderable, where the Almighty would have really preferred to designate pygmies or gypsies as His chosen? If, for instance … but this time more secular thoughts, engendered by the sight of the ginger-root colour of the illuminated sky bouncing off from Judit's locks, intrude. As he is just about to comment, he is distracted by the sound of voices raised in anger, followed, predictably enough, by glasses breaking. Then the door opens and Themba comes flying out and lands spread-eagled on the patio. '*And stay out!*' The host's voice thunders, threatening in that instant to shatter the glasses that survived God-only-knows whatever bedlam went on inside. Mpanza rushes to the aid of his friend, who is now slowly getting onto his feet. Nothing broken, only injured pride.

'Did you see what he did to me?' Themba asks, his indignation enabling his larynx to cover the tonal range from a deep bass growl, through a baritone, all the way up to a soprano screech that would catapult any aspiring diva to instant fame and glory. 'Fucking Hungarian racist motherfucker!' His voice, loaded with the accumulated rage and frustration from enduring centuries of violations, real or imagined, carries an urgency that galvanises Mpanza into action. Circling Themba's shoulders with his arm, Mpanza admonishes, 'Cool it, bro.'

'*Cool it?*' Themba is incredulous. 'What fucking cool it? Black people been cooling it for five fucking centuries, man, that's not the kinda message I wanta hear from a homeboy.' His gaze, brief, insolent and dismissive, rests on the pale white woman, Judit. 'Homie,' he says, aggrieved, a rabid dog whose master has just sanctioned that he be put down, '*you* not selling out to *these people?*' His voice breaks, and he sounds like a little boy. 'No sacrifice is worth all that. Not even white pussy.'

To Mpanza, the accusation that he's selling out – an assertion that agitated for an automatic death sentence way back home, where the self-defence units routinely executed anyone branded an informer – brings about a blinding spasm of rage. Knowing that he might strike the accuser down, he sidles back inside the party and gets, much later, stinking drunk.

He cannot remember how he got to the residence. He suspects that Judit and her compatriots had a hand in this. Fearing the embarrassment of meeting up with her, he avoids the haunts where Hungarians and foreign nationals converged. In his mind, he has had it with solidarity campaigns and their bouts of socialist carousal.

A few weeks pass, and the whole episode is forgotten until Moses Mabhida, the general secretary of the South African Communist Party, arrives on an official visit. He addresses a group of people from the Hungarian Socialist Workers Party in an hotel next to Keleti East railway station. Mabhida is a legend of the South African political struggle; he speaks forcefully, outlining the situation in the front areas and at home. Mpanza, looking at the man whose shock of white hair and a grey handlebar moustache contrast with his dark skin, feels a pang of nostalgia. What am I doing here, so far away from the arena of battle? he asks himself.

Mpanza is surprised to find that Judit is part of the Hungarian delegation with Mabhida; this must mean she has connections in high places. Later, during cocktails, she seeks him in the crowd. She looks different, in a navy-blue two-piece suit, a beige blouse whose collar is fastened with a brooch of ornate design, and black high heels. She looks different with her hair loosened, falling to her shoulders and framing her face. She smiles, peering at him from above the rim of her wine glass.

'Is this what they mean', he asks, 'by revolutionary transformation?'

For a moment her face registers confusion, and then comprehension spreads across her face. 'You mean the *ruházat*?' Judit asks, fingering her jacket. Her fingers are long and strong, like a pianist's, the nails cut severely close to the quick. 'I have to wear respectable for the whole official *retyerutya*.'

'It suits you,' he says, puzzling over why he's flirting with her, 'the *retyerutya*.'

She looks at him to see if he's making fun of her. He in turn smiles to show he means no offence. '*Kérem szépen*,' Judit asks, 'Could you please get me another glass of wine? Dry white.'

'All right,' Mpanza says. He takes the proffered glass and their fingers touch, briefly, and Mpanza experiences a jolt, like electricity cruising up his arm. Mistrusting the feeling, he wanders towards the bar, exchanges a few words with some comrades from the Polisario Front, gets their refills, and heads back. On the way, Themba, who seems to have a special radar for occasions where free booze and snacks are on offer, tells him that someone has promised them a party, somewhere in Pest. 'I'll pass, T-man,' Mpanza says. No more parties where we humiliate ourselves in front of Hungarians.

Themba drifts away into a throng whose larynxes were

already in full dress rehearsal for the real party.

It is when they are standing on the corner of the rapidly emptying room that he realises she hasn't said anything about Richard. He doesn't wish to ask her, knowing she'd tell him if she felt he needed to know. From where they stand, they can see the Danube below, now shining and glittering like scattered rhinestones from reflected lights crowning the parliament building, the bridge hanging as if without supports and the brighter illumination spilling out of some foreign Embassy. Some of the light catches her face in profile, the graceful curve of her neck, the nose, the lips sipping the wine, the hands holding the stem of the wineglass, tight, as if about to snap it into two. He hears, from a great distance his friends' murmured valedictions, and responds without turning, focused on the baubles of light dancing on her hair.

'I think it's time to go,' she says. She places her half-full glass on the sill. He empties his.

'Where do you live?' he asks as they move out of the lobby, towards the taxi rank. It is a balmy night with the merest suggestion of rain in the air.

It is not far. They walk, passing lovers huddled in streetcorners, some kissing like there is no tomorrow. As they walk silently, he discovers that, although Budapest is a small city and he has spent eight months here, he hardly knows it. He hardly knows its people who, despite rampant urbanisation, are still country folk, with ties to the land and relatives there. The city, he tells himself, can only be known by those who fear it, whose intimacy with danger gives them an incentive to study each corner, each topographical feature, so that they would never stumble into an ambush. The tourist or the student, who can never claim any real or visceral engagement with the city, survives its indefatigable strength by dint of innocence. It is only when the casual visitor encounters the unnameable that he or she can claim something resembling kinship, or even love. Desperadoes and the police, two sides of the same coin in many instances, know the city because it is their source of survival, and can also be their downfall. At night, the police of Budapest lose the bonhomie of the day. They cruise by in their squad cars, the legend *Rendőrség* stamped boldly and arrogantly across the side panels. Their peaked caps swerve from side to side, like beaks of bluebirds, scrutinising anything that moves, especially in the dark corners. Despite the incitement he has the potential of evoking, a big black man escorting a beautiful white woman, Mpanza finds the police presence and vigilance reassuring. It is not because they'd protect them from marauders – that item was never on the agenda of any police force anywhere on this globe – but simply because their behaviour reinforces his belief that the world hasn't been torn off its moorings. Were this woman to scream, he knows, the cops would react in a universal, time-tested manner and apply their nightsticks, handcuffs and abuse. It is very easy, in an untroubled environment, to think of the world as one endless Garden of Eden.

'Here we are,' Judit says, as they stop in front of wide glass doors leading into the high-rise apartment block. There is a moment of awkward silence while she rummages in her bag for her keys, not so much a moment as a cue whereby he'd make his escape, to facilitate another meeting another time, when they'd imagine the potential of unfulfilled promises. But she finds the key and leads him into a marbled lobby with a high ceiling. An old man sits on the other side of the counter watching wrestlers sweating on a black-and-white television screen. He gives them one look and turns back to his entertainment. They stride to the bank of elevators, where one is open. They enter, and Mpanza feels as if he has entered a cage. She presses a button and they go up, up and the door opens with a loud swish. This time, as they stand before her door, there is no fumbling with the keys. In a moment they are inside the apartment. On the wooden floor are slippers and boots. Three coats, one small, hang from a brass hook. 'Judit?' he says.

'Shh,' she warns him, placing a finger across his lips. It is the first time she's intentionally touched him. 'We mustn't wake up Richard.'

'Richard?'

'My son.' Judit says. 'He's seven years old.'

'Oh.'

'My father is here, too,' she says, 'and he's not asleep. He never sleeps.'

Judit leaves him standing in the hallway and disappears, he thinks, to check on her boy. Somewhere in the house, a toilet flushes, the water gurgling inordinately long. Then he hears her moving about. She must have taken off her shoes because she is almost on him, gliding like a ghost on stocking feet, carrying a bottle of *pálinka* cherry brandy and two glasses on a tray. She has also changed into a long, flowing robe that might or might not be her night-dress. Allowing him to take the tray from her and preceding him into the lounge, she leaves in her wake the scent of wild flowers.

It is a simple lounge, but everywhere there are signs of taste, travel and a preoccupation with history. There are batik prints on the wall, tapestries he recognises as Zimbabwean draped over a low settee. In the middle squats a coffee-table supporting an array of expensive-looking hardbacks. Throw cushions are arranged with studied carelessness all over the lounge. Placing the tray on the table, Mpanza walks across the wooden floor covered with a wide, rectangular grass mat, and studies a framed picture hanging on the wall. A print by Gerard Sekoto, it shows a squad of black workers digging a road while their hatted, pipe-smoking white overseer looks on. Meanwhile, Judit measures their drinks and, taking a small, ladylike sip of hers, places his glass on a coaster. Folding her legs under her, giving Mpanza a glimpse of olive thighs, she sits back on the settee.

'*Gyere ide!*' Judit orders playfully, patting a space next to her, 'come here. That way I don't shout.'

Seated next to her, sipping the sweet-smelling brandy, he determines not to look at her. She speaks, telling him that

Richard, the Richard, is safe in Germany. Instead of hearing the sense of what she is saying, his mind registers the tone, the cadence of her speech, the parts of her – her throat, her tongue, her lips and her breath – which harmonise towards the articulation of the spoken word. It is as if, although not touching her, he can gauge her body temperature, the rise and fall of her respiration, the speed with which her blood pumps an endless cycle from her heart to her brain and through her body.

'... you're not listening ...'

'No,' he says, turning, a mistake, because she is looking at him, once-blue eyes now misty cobalt-grey, the mouth forming words no longer a vehicle for speech or sipping drinks, the teeth, the tongue. Lost in that gaze, taken over and enfolded in it, he places his hand behind her head, and, feeling the silkiness of her hair, smelling it now, his lips brush hers and he tastes brandy, and the taste, borne on the nodes of a mobile tongue, empties his head of all thoughts but this. The lights seem to move, the earth making an imperceptible shift from its axis, and the fingers, as if sighted, bunch around the fabric of her robe, pull and claim a space on her back and linger on the soft roundness of her breasts, feeling the mysterious nipples and sending a message to his mouth. Somewhere in the distance, he hears her speaking in a foreign tongue, chiding, goading, cajoling, her breath coming out in short gasps; he tasting the hardened flesh, her tongue now searing his neck, trailing and burning, he hiking the encumbering cloth up her thighs to her soft belly the colour of cream, holding her hip, feeling the smoothness of her buttocks. Suspended above her as in that moment between salvation and damnation, she, beneath him, opening up like a flower, he descends as if from a great height, and lowers himself, feeling her catch her breath, and is inside her. And out again, leaving her empty, and then he's sliding along her breasts, down to her belly, nibbling the belly-button, brushing his lips along the thatch of hair, taking in the odour of must and mint, he hears her begin to protest, licks her down there, she, murmuring, feeling her flesh cleaving, *I heard*

263

that African men don't … and, as he caresses the inside of her thighs, *Oh, Jesus* … his tongue inside, probing, licking, she starts to scream and he, easing himself up, up, until he enters her now, with long strokes, and she starts to wail, and the two of them, entwined, start working towards an explosion that leaves them rocked and spent.

★　　★　　★

She shows him the city, taking him to cultural houses, like the national Széchényi library, which, she tells him, contains more than two million books and more than double the amount of documents. They walk, sometimes hand in hand, on the cobbled streets, drinking coffee and eating sandwiches in pavement bistros. Sometimes, when the rain catches them during a walk, they duck into an art gallery, or museum, like the National History Museum, where they stand awed by the savage beauty of the paintings by 19th-century artists such as Mihály Munkácsy or Viktor Madarász. In the same summer, she takes him to a riding school. He is scared, never having been on a horse before, but she coaches him. Atop of the huge beast, Mpanza is told to clench his legs, hold the reins between the little finger and the thumb, and dig the balls of his feet into the stirrups, heels pointed downwards. 'All horses are Leftists,' Judit says, 'that's why you have to mount the beast from the left.' He feels out of control, the horse not being a car but an animal capable of thought and volition. In two weeks, they ride all the way to a small village outside Budapest, where the horses fly above cherry plums from which pálinka is made. Later, he meets Mr Szábo, her father who never sleeps. The old man was once a close friend of János Kádár and his predecessor, Imre Nagy. During the 1956 revolt, as a member of the writers union, he joined Hungarian students who demonstrated against compulsory courses in Russian and Marxism–Leninism. At some stage, Mr Szábo shared a cell with Nagy before the latter's release to take over from Premier Hegediüs. Judit's father was released, after he had been beaten and tortured. When Mpanza sees him, the unspeaking, unsleeping man's face shows intelligence. But Mr Szábo is a shell of his former self.

'I'm still a communist,' Judit says, fiercely, 'and I'll probably die a communist. But I'll never forgive Kádár, not so much for what they did as what they could have done for people like my father. It is not a cliché that the revolution eats its own children. I just hope that you never have that experience in your own country.'

Judit phones Mpanza at the institute, exactly on the day the group embarks on a study tour of the Soviet Union. She is tearful, telling him that her father has died. 'I need you,' she says.

'I have to go,' he says. Outside, the taxi hoots; the other participants are impatient.

'I need you,' Judit says again, and he can hear she's been crying. 'I love my country, but I love you. I can come with you. I won't be a nuisance in Africa.'

He hangs up on her. I can't deal with this. Replacing the receiver and rushing to the airport taxi, he knows that, whatever he does – and wherever he is – Judit will always remember Mpanza as a living example of man's depthless capacity for betrayal.

★   ★   ★

The car wove its way up the hill and stopped some ten metres from where he was seated. In spite of himself, Mpanza admired the practicality of the car's steel and chrome majesty, the harmonious shape of the pink Cadillac Brougham, not so much a car as a fiery chariot, a bird to glide through the wind. Johnny M got out and strode purposely to Mpanza. He had in his hands a six-pack of beer. 'Thought you might appreciate some libation,' he said, and then sighed: 'So foul and fair a day I have not seen.'

'Thanks,' Mpanza said, popping the can open. 'What can I do for you?'

'I've been thinking,' Johnny M said, 'since our last conversation. I am more than sure that you're going to help.'

'Come on, Johnny,' Mpanza said, 'your men can collect money without my help.'

'*Ja,*' Johnny M said. 'They can do that, all right. I've also got them primed to scare the living daylights out of the squatters. Just to prove a point.'

'But they don't have anywhere to go?'

Johnny M got to his feet. He brushed the seat of his trousers. 'I gave them a chance, asked them to contribute to the development of this place. But they're still in the eighties, when your Oliver Tambo asked people to render this country ungovernable. Now, they just believe they can get away with anything. But I'm no longer asking for their money, no, sir, more's on the way. I want them to move, make room for real development.'

'You mean as in casinos and suchlike?'

'Yep,' Johnny M said. 'Liven up the place a little, bring in some big bucks.'

'And Grey reported them?'

'I made Grey, Mpanza,' Johnny M said. 'I made Mbongwa.'

Mpanza looked at Johnny M. He had a feeling that they were having a dialogue that skirted what was being said. '*Ja,*' Mpanza said, 'but what does that have to do with me?'

'How do you feel about Zodwa?' Johnny M asked in lieu of an answer.

'I don't know much about her.'

'But how do you feel about her?'

This was ridiculous. 'Why don't you say what's on your mind, instead of this quiz show?'

'Okay,' Johnny M seemed to think. 'Tell you what. What would you say if I asked you to help me get her out of here?'

'I'd say, "Good luck, Sport," that's what I'd say.'

'Even if it meant her death?'

'You mean you'd kill her?'

'Not me. I wouldn't touch her.'

'One of your men would kill her,' Mpanza asked. 'Is that it?'

'Now, who's the quiz show host?' Johnny M was enjoying himself. 'You've never been a credible defender of womanhood, Mpanza. Just to let you know what I know: your wife, Khethiwe,

266

lives on 29A Martinez Street, Norwood. It's a three-bedroom house; since your departure, she shares her bed with her kids – your kids – nice little poopsies who cuddle up with mumsy at night. There's a reading lamp on the table next to the bed. As a military man you should know there is such a thing as an explosion. I don't handle such things, too unreliable.' Then he laughed, genuinely tickled. 'Truth will come to light; murder cannot be hid long. But before Zodwa goes, she will know that you killed her brother. And your wife will also know you killed her and the children.'

Khethiwe, Mpanza thought. The kids. 'Why do you want to bring my family into this?'

'To make you understand that I'm serious.' Johnny M sounded serious. 'I made you an offer to work with me, which you refused. I'm not used to being spurned. Now, I'm giving you an order. Convince Zodwa to let everything be. Go to that law practice in Jo'burg and leave the running of things to the men.'

This town's too small for the two of us. This thought came to Mpanza, unsummoned, like a revelation. It was as if all his training in Angola and elsewhere had prepared him for this moment. In all the years he had worked in the underground of the political struggle, the law that ruled was how to preserve himself. How to survive. Even as commander of the two-man unit that assassinated Jonah, he'd never had to worry about his comrade's survival. Now, things were different. If he acted against Zodwa – he still couldn't think how to approach her – he was damned, eternally in her eyes, an unpalatable option. If he didn't, he'd consign his family to a horrible death. Accepting that Johnny M was serious, Mpanza also knew that he was getting weary of flight. He would kill Johnny M with joy.

'I'm serious about running this place.' He glanced at his gold wristwatch. 'Time's ten p m. See what happens at midnight.' And, without waiting for a response, Johnny M walked back to his car. 'Enjoy the beers,' he said.

Mpanza watched the car's smooth departure, feeling drained,

impotent and angry. Reuben found him standing outside the house, contemplating a course of action.

'Reubén?' Mpanza asked. 'Where can I find a phone?'

'This time of the night?' Reuben answered. He shrugged. 'Nowhere.' Then he said: 'Why don't you try that lady, Benedita, who was in the tent today?'

'Do you think she's still awake?'

'It depends on how urgent it is.' Reuben studied Mpanza's face. 'It's urgent, is it?'

'Very,' Mpanza said. He disappeared inside the house and came back with his address book. Then, into his waistband, he shoved a pistol. 'Let's go.'

Seventeen

Although David Horwitz was a little tight by the time he left the tent, his mind was lucid enough to register something that shook him to his vitals. He had been watching the mourners streaming out, noticing that, like himself, most were unsteady on their feet. Drinking was a *sine qua non* of comprehensive mourning. He had been steadily sipping his brandy and coke, helping the men make the final arrangements, getting the pallbearers to rehearse their moves, when he looked at Baba's face and saw the smile. He nearly dropped his glass. What the hell is happening? He looked round for someone to confide in, someone who would not dismiss him and tell him to grow up.

Naomi was crying softly in the corner as she collected Baba Joshua's clothes and piled them into a bundle. These would either accompany the old man into the grave or be consigned to a bonfire. Obliquely, he thought about the poor people in the squatter camp and concluded that they wouldn't appreciate these clothes. The poor of the land might have been needy, but they were not without taste. This observation made him laugh, causing Naomi to give him a quick, perplexed look, before returning to her chores. Maybe he should tell Zodwa that some weird thing was happening with Baba Joshua. Firstly, people had remarked on the fact that the body didn't smell, and now it was smiling!

Naomi's gestures indicated that she had finished and was preparing to go; she went past the coffin and rearranged the flower across Baba Joshua's breast, and then waved goodbye to the men. She was about to step out of the tent when she paused in the manner of someone who had forgotten to switch off the stove before going to a theatre. She hurried to the coffin, edging the men aside, took a look, and screamed. Uh-oh, Horwitz thought, the penny has dropped. Hastening to the coffin, he discovered that it wasn't only the smile that had caused the reaction from Naomi. The white rose, instead of wilting under the heat, had developed a series of green buds along a growing stem. How was this possible? Either someone, a prankster, perhaps, had switched the flowers or something very strange was happening here. He had to tell Zodwa. Having spoilt his chances with her, he hoped that reporting this development would reinstate him in her good books. He wouldn't blow it this time. He would stop drinking and carrying on like a buffoon. Using signs, he asked Naomi to accompany him to Zodwa's place. She shook her head. 'I think we should keep this knowledge to ourselves,' she said. By the time it dawned on him that she had actually spoken – itself another miracle – it was too late.

★　★　★

After parking the car, Mbongwa had been walking for three-quarters of an hour, his progress curbed by the darkness and the heavy meat and beers on the wheelbarrow. The evening air was redolent of wood-smoke and bitter herbs. Nozizwe must be cooking up her mischief somewhere in some distant dark. The sky above was like a deep-blue ceiling, starless and moonless, the dead rays of the sun hanging in strips on the western horizon. Something disturbed the dry stalks of the tall savannah grass. An animal, perhaps, or someone watching. Mbongwa felt eyes on him, but shook the feeling away. Cowardice, especially at this late hour, paid no percentage. He smiled, thinking that Johnny M's effect on him was disturbing. He was beginning to think of life in purely economic terms.

He hoped Hodoba and the Vulture-Men wouldn't mind getting their dinner this late, but they also had to understand that they were not exactly located in accessible surroundings.

Although he knew why these outcasts lived in a cave, he still did not welcome the idea of visiting them. They'd been getting quite restive of late, and there was no telling what they might do. He rested for a while and felt for his pistol in his waistband. Although he knew that the puny .38 Police Special wouldn't help him much if the gang attacked him, it still felt reassuring to be armed, much like a man with a toothache comfortable with a supply of aspirins in his medicine cabinet.

Finally, he reached the entrance of the cave and dragged his haul inside, carefully balancing the meat in the burlap bag under one crooked arm and the crate of beer under the other. He would send one of the men for the remaining crate. He was here to feed them, not demonstrate that he was a Hercules.

Passing the shrine where Nozizwe performed her mumbo-jumbo, he looked at the ancient fossils and rock formations, feeling the cold chill his bones. Hodoba had told him of Zodwa and Nozizwe's visit here a day ago. Did they think a mere necklace would stop Hodoba? He shook his head. Going down to a chamber below, he sloshed on the water, cursing the dead Baba Joshua and his ambitious daughter. Why had he died before he, Mbongwa, had made all the necessary arrangements? It wasn't fair.

Almost slipping on wet ground, he released a loud oath. The entrance to Hodoba's cave was dark, did they expect him to feel his way inside or what? Suddenly, his skin crawled when he heard the sound of laughter, no different from hyenas'. He had heard from Hodoba that some changes had come over the men, caused by some root they had eaten, which had accelerated the process of mutation, but he hadn't expected the timbre of their voices to be so alien. 'Hey,' he cried, 'someone give us a light. This place is like a tomb.' He stepped inside the cavern.

Off, in the dark, a voice countered: 'It is a tomb, in case you'd forgotten Mbongwa!' There was some muttering. 'Where in hell is that matches?' Someone struck a match, and Mbongwa almost dropped his load and bolted. Sitting in a semicircle were four

271

Vulture-Men. In a dislocated moment, he remembered the curse that some prelate had cast on a hapless jackdaw which had stolen his ring. He had also seen 'The Elephant Man', with Jack Goldblum and Rowan Atkinson: the Vulture-Men were a composite of the two disparate images, men whose upper jaws had lengthened into a semblance of a beak; their eyes were hooded, like those of predatory birds. Hirsute as bears, it was not clear whether or not they were clothed, so covered were they with coarse coir-like fur. Their fingers ended in curved talons. The only features which still joined them to the royal fellowship of the human race were their language and speech patterns, which were modern and peppered with allusions to popular culture. Mbongwa attributed this to the magazines which stood in a grey pile in the corner of the dank cave. When had this transformation taken place? The last time he saw them, they were showing signs of changing, but this was dramatic. How do you hold a conversation with such … things?

'Hi, guys,' he said airily.

They stared back at him. Like dogs, they could sense fear oozing out of him like vapour. One of the Vulture-Men stood up. 'What have you got for us today?'

Another piped in. 'I hope', he said, 'it's not donkey meat again. We're tired of donkey meat.'

Mbongwa threw the bundle on the floor. 'This is prime beef,' he said. 'And I've got some beers for you.'

'We're tired of all this,' complained the first man. 'When last did we have a treat?'

'You mean human flesh,' Mbongwa asked, 'don't you?'

'Of course a human being,' the Vulture-Man answered. 'What do you think? You're the one who gave us a taste for human flesh.'

'Yeah, boys,' Mbongwa said, feeling like someone in the middle of a nightmare, 'but it's off season now for that little delicacy.'

'Yes, but you told us that we're Nero's lions, chomping on

Christians.' The first Vulture-Man, evidently their spokesperson, said, pointing with a leg. 'And this sure doesn't taste anything like a Christian.'

The third man, who had not spoken, cleared his throat. 'I could have told you, boys,' he said, 'that Mbongwa was giving us a line.' He seemed to ponder. 'Nero's lions, fellows, they almost died of heartburn. Is it true that Christians give you heartburn?'

'If eaten in excess, yes.'

'It figures,' the second man said. 'You would feel a little uncomfortable after eating someone who believes that the meek shall inherit the earth.'

'Certainly gives a new meaning,' Mbongwa said, trying to lighten things up, 'to turning the other cheek.' He laughed, nervously, ha, ha, ha.

The fourth man was not amused. 'You're cracking jokes,' he roared, 'and it's not so funny, Mbongwa. For your information, you've become mighty unpopular around here, do you know that?'

The four men surrounded Mbongwa. It was like being hemmed in by four glowering hillocks. 'What do you think', the first man asked, 'we should do so that you take us seriously? Shake things up a bit? Maybe cut a piece off your backside? That would be funny.'

'Yup,' agreed the third man. 'Sprinkle a bit of salt 'n pepper.'

This was fast getting out of hand. 'Okay, you've made your point,' Mbongwa said. 'Look, fellows, there's an old man who's just kicked the bucket ...'

'*Yuck!*'

'We want young juicy meat. Preferably a virgin.'

'I might provide someone,' Mbongwa said, 'but I can't guarantee she's a virgin. That species is rare, nearing extinction as it is. But she's pretty ...'

'We don't eat dogs, you know?'

'... like a picture, with the right vital statistics ...'

'You're not palming us off with a Goodyear blimp, Mbongwa,

are you, now?'

'No, fellows, true's God she's what people call a stunner ...'

'Do you have a picture of this ... this stunner?'

'Funny you should ask that,' Mbongwa said, reaching into his inside-jacket pocket and taking out a folded copy of *Penthouse* magazine. 'What do you think?'

The Vulture-Men turned the pages furiously. The first man looked up. 'Hey,' he said, 'there's nothing here but naked white women ...' His eyes landed on a vacuous African–American model. 'Ah, ha!' he said. 'Look at this boys. Real meat.'

Seeing that they were engrossed, drooling over the images in the magazine, Mbongwa started backing out of the cave. The second man looked up. 'Mbongwa?' he called.

'Yes?'

'This democracy,' the man asked, 'this new dispensation of yours ... does it mean that Mandela will now let us have white women for dinner?'

Mbongwa scratched his head. 'I'm not so sure about that. I'd have to ask him.'

'We wouldn't want white people to feel they're victims of reverse racism ...'

'Yup,' added the second man, 'nothing beats diversity in diet ...'

Beating a hasty retreat, Mbongwa was soon outside in the invigorating air. He left the beer on the wheelbarrow and ran to his car. Mbongwa stopped to mop his brow, thinking, bloody bastard vultures. Cannibals. Driving away, he wondered why Hodoba was not among the men. Something had to be done, and soon. The Vulture-Men were getting way out of hand. Zodwa my dear, he thought, wait until you meet these fellows!

★   ★   ★

David Horwitz looked at his wristwatch and saw that the time was nine forty-five p m. He had walked to his house, a room really, about five-hundred metres from where Baba Joshua's body lay in the coffin. Then he had poured himself a shot of brandy, telling himself this was his last one. From tomorrow on, he was going to be a clean man, no booze. Even as he drank, he had puzzled over today's events, the surprises and, even for his befuddled brain, small miracles. First, the old man smiling, then the flower blooming almost in front of his eyes. Then, here he shook his head, Naomi surprising him like that. Naomi. She looked ripe, the loose shift not concealing the swell of her ample hips, tightening at the region of her breasts which, beneath the shift, seemed as hard as mangoes. Thinking about her, feeling his genitals burning, swelling, he reflected on whether the relationship with Baba Joshua had been all that innocent. She had been the only one who hadn't looked at him as if he were a pariah, after he had made fool of himself with Zodwa. Suddenly, Zodwa became a distant memory, a fantasy representing unenforceable ideals. She was unattainable; Naomi, perhaps, was. It was worth investigating, nothing ventured, nothing gained.

He stepped out into the cool night and heard the insects chirping, the sound relaxing, complementing the sense of well-being deriving from the drink in his hand. A hundred metres to the left, past the water pump, he heard the sound of men walking towards the burial ground, their implements clashing, their clanking reverberating in the air. These must be gravediggers, Horwitz thought. Naomi's place was a short distance from the graveyard. He quickly drained his drink and gave a satisfied belch. Life wasn't so bad after all. Locking the door, he trekked towards Naomi's place, via the graveyard. He wasn't going to try and trick her; he would state his need as clearly as possible. There was a chance she would understand.

*　　*　　*

The two gravediggers, Zondo and Khumalo, were the Tweedledee and Tweedledum of the burial circuit. Zondo was tall and big, almost six feet, with a scarred face and a shaven head. Khumalo was thin and short, with a full head of hair and an untidy beard. But despite the difference in their physical appearance, the men operated like twins, and one had come to be associated with the other to such an extent that if people saw Zondo in a fight, they knew that Khumalo, if not there already, would soon make an appearance and fight his friend's corner. Fuelled by alcohol, they fought frequently, winning some, losing some, but, mainly, they fought among themselves. This evening presented another opportunity for their frequent discord.

Zondo sent the pick whistling into the ground. 'Another grave,' he said, 'another body …'

Khumalo said: 'Another delectable feast for the worms.' He stopped digging with a spade. 'How come is it', he asked, 'that we only bury black people?'

'Because,' Zondo replied, 'whites haven't made dying their favourite pastime …'

Khumalo pondered this. 'Used to work for an undertaker … called himself a mortician …'

Zondo cut in. '*Ja*, and your wife ran away because you used to bring your work home …'

'Used to brood over', Khumalo went on, ignoring the interruption, 'how worms gnawed through wood into the body. Came across something used to shake me.'

'What was that?'

'We all have our worms inside us, waiting for the moment of death.'

'That's a lot of horseshit.' Zondo sounded unreasoningly angry. '*You* might have worms crawling inside you, I don't.'

'Oh, yes, you do!'

Zondo took a deep breath. 'Look,' he said, 'this is beginning to irritate me. If you're worried about worms, why don't you go and see Nozizwe? She'll give you some medicine?'

'I'm not worried, you are. I'm comfortable with my worms.'

'If you don't shut up,' Zondo threatened, hefting the handle, 'I'm going to hit you with this pick. Give your worms an early Christmas treat.'

Khumalo decided that he was here to arrange accommodation for a corpse; he had no intention of becoming a substitute for one. 'Okay, whatever you say, Boss.'

'That's right,' Zondo said, 'leave the worms to birds and fishermen.'

Working hard and fast, their practised familiarity with the task helping them make good time where others might have been slowed down, they chanted their work song.

We-S'gubh' we-S'gubh'
Thelan'amanzi!
Abafazi bamabhun'abasazali,
Mabezala bazal'amagundwane,

they sang. The two men stopped, suddenly when they heard the sound of a scuffle. From where they were, Khumalo already waist-deep in the hole, they saw shadows moving quickly, urgently, dark men in dark clothes, their faces masked, converging on the white man who walked as if drunk.

★   ★   ★

Blackie had settled in smoothly as a new member of the Venter household. Venter, not knowing anything about providing accommodation for apes, had nailed together some masonite boards and stapled cardboard boxes into a passably comfortable monkey-house. With Benedita's aid, he had covered the floor with two or three old duvets and an odd cushion. He had scattered around a couple of branches from the mango tree, hoping the monkey would appreciate the arboreal touch. Scattered randomly on the floor was a choice of ripe fruit: mangoes, bananas, peaches and guavas, which Benedita had gone into much trouble collecting. To ensure that Blackie didn't inconvenience himself quenching his thirst from the outside water-tap, they set an aluminium dish of water. They didn't know what monkeys used for the toilet and hoped that Blackie would at least have the decency to do his business in the bush. Venter had to dissuade Benedita from factoring a set of toilet rolls into the arrangement. Maybe, when Blackie was really house-trained, they'd give him toilet training. Flushing the toilet wouldn't be a problem since monkeys were always yanking at something. They remarked on the possibility of Blackie's being lonely. Perhaps, they joked, they should place an ad in the classifieds: 'Virile monkey looking for a white mate with a black face. A snapshot will be appreciated. Successful applicant must be of clean, sober habits, smokers need not apply.' Venter and Benedita almost killed themselves laughing. The couple studied their handiwork and agreed that the place looked fit for the king of the apes. The trick, now, was getting Blackie inside his new lodgings. Venter hoped the monkey was not too finicky.

Which was a problem, because Blackie refused adamantly to go anywhere near the new house. He made it known, in no uncertain terms, that he wanted to be inside the main house, not some box tied to a mango tree. By nine p m, Venter and Benedita decided that, to preserve their sanity, it was best that they complied with the monkey. Even Benedita, who had been Blackie's main supporter, was beginning to think that sending him to the Zulus might not be such a bad idea after all. A grumbling Venter removed the duvets and transferred them to the garage. Against Benedita's protests, he locked the monkey inside. Hope he chokes on petrol fumes, Venter thought vindictively.

Venter and Benedita had just watched the ten o'clock news and were getting ready for bed when there was a knock on the door. As Venter padded to the door, the phone rang, shrilly. Must be the headquarters asking about progress with Momberg and the bombing. He then took the phone and, with his hand over the mouthpiece, called Benedita. '*Skattie?*' he said, 'will you get the door?'

Benedita said *Shit!* under her breath and walked to the door, passing Venter on the phone in the hallway. Zodwa's people, she thought, probably wanting their pot back. She opened the door, heard Venter say, 'Hello?'

'Hello?' Venter said, 'can I help you?' He heard the sound of a man breathing over the static. Must be a wrong number or some fucking practical joker. Then, as if watching a film in slow motion, he saw Benedita at the door, two men with faces covered in balaclavas, throwing a grey blanket over her, lifting her off the ground and disappearing in the dark. He was so shocked he was immobile, before his brain flashed a red light, galvanising him into action. Dropping the phone, he rushed into the bedroom and retrieved his AK-47 assault rifle from where it lay under the bed. As he started out of the house, he saw the taillights of the car trailing off into the dark, on the way to the cemetery. He rushed to the garage and started the van. Blackie, roused from a restless sleep, sprang to life, clambering onto the tailgate.

He was pulling out of the gate, when his way was blocked by a rattle-trap wagon driven by an old man with grey hair. A younger, taller version of the driver sat on the side. '*Die Here weet*,' cursed Venter, '*wat gaan aan, nou?*'

'Thank God someone's here,' said Reuben the Collector. Somehow, he couldn't understand why Benedita's husband looked so agitated. Then Reuben and Mpanza raised their hands when they saw the white man pointing a gun at them. 'Get out of that *verdomde wa*,' Venter ordered, 'and keep those hands in the air.'

Slowly, Reuben and Mpanza alighted from the wagon.

'We come in peace,' Reuben said. 'We need to use your telephone.'

'Fuck peace,' Venter said.

'If you're worried about that car,' Reuben said, 'we know exactly where it parks ...'

'Fuck the car,' Venter snorted, 'those men have my wife in there ...'

'We'll find them,' Reuben insisted, 'don't worry about it.'

'When?'

'Soon's you let us use the phone.'

* * *

Zondo recognised Horwitz. Horwitz started running, panting, then he fell to the ground. The shadows picked him up and started punching him, the wet crunch of breaking cartilage loud and ominous. Somehow Horwitz broke free and started running, screaming. Zondo saw one man pulling a gun, taking aim. He saw the fire spitting out of the muzzle before hearing the loud explosion. Next to him, Khumalo gave a short grunt, and the next thing Zondo saw was that he was covered in sticky blood and brain tissue. As Khumalo dropped, another report split the night. The running man seemed to hesitate and then the momentum of the bullet carried him along one or two yards, and then he flipped over, like a swimmer executing a complicated stroke, and flopped inside the grave. For one stunned moment, Zondo looked at the two men whose sightless eyes were fixed on the sky.

'Jesus!' Zondo cried, and then he was running, running, out of the grave, scrambling over old graves, hearing another shot, the bullet whizzing past his head, like a mosquito, going thunk! into a tree, running faster than any bullet, until he slammed into a tree, and all lights went out.

*   *   *

'Hello?'

'Khethiwe?'

'Who's this?' A pause. 'Mpanza?'

'Khethiwe? Listen to me —'

'You've got a nerve calling me at this time. Do you know what time it is?'

'Khethiwe.' Calmly. 'Listen. I want you to do something for me …'

'Are you drinking where you are? Is that why you sound so … strange?'

'Khethiwe. Please get yourself and the kids out of the house. Now.'

'What?'

'Get out of the house. Now.'

Venter was impatient. He had a wife to rescue, if, indeed it wasn't too late. He tapped his wristwatch. 'Hurry!'

'Stop arguing, Khethiwe,' Mpanza pleaded. 'Get out of the

house.'

'Mpanza?'

'Yes?'

'Drop dead.' And slammed the phone down.

*   *   *

As the three men dashed to Venter's van, Mpanza had a moment to focus on the exact moment when love turned to hate. Khethiwe's valediction had been so laden with malevolence he concluded that he must have really hurt her. He felt a distant, despairing twinge of regret, realising that the mess he had made of his life – their lives – had now touched his children. He imagined the bedroom going up in flames, the kids confused in their sleep, being overcome by smoke, dying with incomprehension in their eyes.

When the shots went off, his mind going into operational mode, he prayed it wasn't the white fellow's wife – what was her name? Benedita – because even though the man tried to keep cool, it was clear he was nearing the edge. Mpanza had disliked him the minute he laid eyes on him, marking him as a racist, witness the monkey in the back. But now, the two of them were bonded by a fear of some totally ruthless people out there. Mpanza had lived a life of illusions. Now he told himself that he had to expect the worst. In his mind's eye his wife and children were dead. Another woman had been kidnapped, and there was no telling what her fate would be; the shots had not been reassuring. Zodwa was in danger. He had led to her brother's murder, in fact, he had pulled the trigger. Beside him, the man who introduced himself as Venter, kept on mumbling one name. Grey. That was Johnny M's crony. Mpanza hoped that Reuben was not kidding when he reassured Venter about the whereabouts of the car that had taken his wife away.

Venter gunned the van over the corrugated road, causing the monkey to hold tight as the van bounced as it hit potholes. Venter had heard the gunshots. He was also armed. The sound, which had come from the direction of the cemetery, was now gone, stolen by the whims of the wind. But it still echoed in his mind, visual and real, like an after-image of sniper fire. He could feel the hardness of the pistol of the black man beside him as the van bounced and rattled, its lights off. It was in this darkness, which he claimed and which he knew as intimately as the contours of a lover, that he felt alive. His first day of birth.

Eighteen

Nerissa's shebeen was abuzz with activity. About twenty customers, mostly men, were drinking and pontificating on the state of the nation. A group sat with its eyes glued to the television set rigged overhead, watching a soccer match. One of the punters – a loser called Virgin because no woman wanted him – kept yelling, asking for Nerissa to change the channel, because he wanted to see the news at ten. Virgin was shouted down and was now sulking as he took another shot of vodka. When Nerissa came around with a tray to collect empties, he fixed her with a drunken stare.

'Why,' he asked, 'aren't people interested in things that really matter?'

Nerissa had had a long day. 'I don't know, Virgin,' she said. 'Maybe because not many things matter nowadays?'

'I beg to differ,' Virgin said. 'Look. The Congress of South African Trade Unions has just celebrated its first decade. Don't you think that's important?'

'Honey,' Nerissa said sweetly, loading the tray, 'when Cosatu came into power, I was in this shithole. Ten years later, I'm still in the same shithole, so, who cares?'

Virgin watched her exchange words with other punters. He shook his head because he couldn't believe that people could be so apathetic. The drinkers were satisfied with their condition. It was in drink that they could more profoundly express and extend themselves and maintain an illusion of power and control. He thought it ironic that he was harbouring these observations, he who was a living example of failed dreams.

In the kitchen, Nerissa thought about Virgin's question. She also wanted to know why things no longer mattered. For her, the importance of everyday reality went away the day she enslaved herself to Johnny M. On occasions she looked in the mirror; what stared back was not a once-proud and beautiful woman, but the sum total of body parts that empowered men to call themselves men. After Johnny M had used her, he enjoined the gang members to drink their fill of her. Johnny M insisted that they occupy her every orifice except her mouth; that was his domain. What sickened her was her acceptance that this was an expected form of behaviour on the part of the men. Her own reactions surprised and shocked her, for instance when Johnny M looked at another woman, and remarked: 'What a pretty mouth. Think she'd like my condensed milk?' Could jealousy or an inability to countenance the possibility of another woman sharing her destiny have informed her reaction? She didn't know, but admitted that it could have been a little bit of both. Nerissa had come across women who held that their partners' abuse was an attestation of their love for them, the way, perhaps – she had seen this programme on TV – some hostages formed a bond with their abductors.

She immediately snapped out of her reflective mode when she heard the car pulling up outside. From the way the doors banged shut, she could tell he was in a foul mood. Quickly opening a bottle from his special cache of Pilsner, she poured the amber liquid in a tall glass, put it on a tray and went to intercept him in the lounge. Sipho and a recent acquisition, Colin, preceded him. He was a strapping lad, almost six feet tall, with broad shoulders and a strutting walk that was a mark of his masculinity. But it was this insistence on maleness that enhanced his effeminacy. His leather jacket, jeans and heavy shoes could not hide the nakedness in his eyes. Nerissa was sure that Colin's recruitment had as much to do with villainy as warming Johnny M's bed. She felt a deep, distant pity for him, the way people react to an arrogant juvenile hurtling towards a calamity. The men looked at her and through her, as though what weighed on their minds was much more important than memories of carnal pleasures she could provide. Even Johnny M, who ordinarily would have given her an acknowledging little hug, accepted the glass of beer absent-mindedly and surveyed the roomful of drinkers.

Dressed in black from head to toe, Johnny M looked like an emissary of death. The other two gang members, also as sombre as executioners, seemed to await an important announcement. Their stillness in the smoke-filled room started slowly to unnerve those drinkers who hadn't yet reached the state of reckless inebriety. Virgin looked up, met Colin's unwavering gaze, and concentrated on the wet rings formed by the bottom of his glass on the table. Eventually the sound which dominated the room came from the TV, where someone had just scored a goal, and the crowd at the FNB stadium was going wild, the commentator yelling a stretched out, '*Laduma!*' None of the patrons risked glancing at the flickering action on the screen. Just to make sure he had everyone's attention, Johnny M stretched his hand above the men's heads and punched the OFF/ON button.

'I will begin with a question,' Johnny M said, addressing himself to no particular person. 'The question is: do you like this shebeen?'

There was a general murmur, with none of the men wishing to volunteer an answer, people suspecting a trap. Other people looked one another in the eyes and then looked away, because the eyes of people could convey, in the most graphic style, what kind of trouble they could be in. A number of men, who had been warned against patronising shebeens, now regretted not heeding the warnings. They had come here for recreation; they hadn't bargained for philosophical discourses with gangsters. Nerissa looked at Virgin, and from where she stood, she could almost smell the funk of fear. Distractedly, she envisioned herself scrubbing the carpet again. Johnny M's men stood, like pillars, their menacing posture controlling the bladders of drinkers who wanted to pee.

'Seems like I have to repeat myself,' Johnny M said. Then, following Nerissa's gaze, he zeroed in on Virgin. 'Stand up, sir,' he called. He was extremely reasonable.

'Me?' Virgin said.

Johnny M laughed. 'Why is it', he asked, as genial as a talk-show host, 'that whenever you call people, they react by asking you that question? *Me?* Frankly, this kind of response to important issues bores me.' He pointed at Virgin. 'Yes, I mean you. *Up!*'

An instantly sober Virgin got to his feet. Johnny M approached him and stood a pace behind him. 'Now,' Johnny M said, 'we're all reasonable people here, wouldn't you say?'

Virgin nodded.

'Speak up,' Johnny M said, 'let the house hear you.'

'Yes,' Virgin said, 'we're all reasonable people.'

'So,' Johnny M asked laconically, 'why do you make me a *mampara* when I call you?'

'Me?'

'Me?' Johnny M echoed. 'That word again? *Me?*' Turning, he looked at the men, drawing them inside his orbit and asking them to see what he, a reasonable man, had to deal with.

The other drinkers mentally cursed Virgin for repeating himself, he was beginning to sound like a stuck record. Furthermore, they had come here for a quiet social drink and the soccer match. They didn't want to be bothered with Johnny M and his thugs, and this pathetic man who was obviously shitting himself. They were relieved, however, that Johnny M had singled Virgin out. It could have been any one of them.

'What', Johnny M asked, 'do you think we should do to bring back respect into our community?'

Nerissa, who knew what was happening, looked away and sought to break the tension. 'Can I get you a drink, anyone?' Johnny M gave her a look. 'Sorry,' she said. 'Just asking.'

'What do you think we should do?' Johnny M asked again.

Virgin knew he was condemned. 'I really don't know.' Let's get on with it.

'We are all products of tradition,' Johnny M said. 'In the past,' he went on, 'whenever men had a problem, they solved it with sticks. People formed a ring around them and they duelled. The winner was vindicated, and the loser admitted he was wrong. Since the white man came and took away our sticks, or banned cultural weapons, we have to sort this out in a gentlemanly fashion.'

'I don't want to fight you, Johnny M,' Virgin said.

'Who said anything about a fight?' Johnny M looked around for someone to contradict him. 'I said sort out problems that's what I said. So, since we don't have sticks, why don't we use gloves?' He smiled. 'Nerissa, dear,' he said. 'Bring us the gloves.'

Virgin had actually been a good boxer during his high school days. But he knew even as he took off his jacket and let Sipho put the gloves on him, that this was a lost cause. Where Virgin was taller and had a reach advantage, Johnny M was heavier and more muscular. Moreover, the fight was on his territory and decidedly on his own terms.

As the two men sized each other up, Sipho came in the middle and gave the regular refereeing instructions. No butting. No clinching. 'No biting,' he added, remembering one legendary heavyweight match.

Johnny M had stripped to his black T-shirt; circling, bobbing and weaving, he looked like someone out to enjoy working up a little sweat, get rid of unwanted flab. But his adversary, angry and stung by humiliation, was fighting for his life, perhaps to get out of this shebeen and never return. For him, the moment of fear and pumping adrenalin was the only moment he could think of. He dredged the bottom of his memory for tricks that had saved him in the past, in his schooldays, but drew a blank. Time had seen to the effacing of what had almost been second nature. So, Virgin squared up, his gloves close to the head, looking at the man who was no longer the genial sportsman but a beast with a wolf-like grin on his face. As Virgin feinted, jabbed, trying to summon the poetry of Muhammad Ali, shuffling on his trainers, he heard, from outside the sweating arena, the drinkers placing bets. Someone said: 'He hasn't got a prayer.' He knew that meant him. Say a prayer for me, he thought.

The assault was as sudden as it was vicious. Johnny M connected with a straight right to Virgin's chin, rocked him back to the tables, where the furniture had been arranged into a hollow square. To the outside observer, the punch had looked harmless, and didn't carry much weight behind it. But to Virgin, it felt as if someone had hit him with a concrete block. Someone, namely Johnny M, had hit him with a glove weighted with concrete. Johnny M had hit on this idea when Larry Stokes was disqualified for exactly the same form of cheating. Dazed, feeling his knees buckle, Virgin determined to avoid any punch. But the punches came, straight, unerring, crashing into his jaw. Then he knew that the best way out of it was to feign being knocked out. Another right caught him flush against the jaw, and he actually heard the loud crack as his jaw broke, and he felt himself sinking, Say a prayer for me, he thought, his last.

Johnny M, his red gloves spattered with blood, pulled Virgin from where he lay on the carpet and, supporting his back with the left arm, continued to pummel him with the right. The drinkers watched as Virgin's face broke open, as if it had been attacked with a can-opener, the cartilage breaking with a crunch, the mouth, pulped, spitting out stained teeth like grains from a maize cob. Something – human consciousness – threatened to push the men into the artificial ring and pull Johnny M from the man that was beginning to gag on his own blood. But something else – fear – stayed them. They knew – they had to know – that Johnny M's punishment of the man had nothing to do with Virgin. It was a message to them, to know now, and in the future, that they had to obey Johnny M, whatever it took. They knew without knowing that they were now accessories to murder.

It was Nerissa, who had watched similar scenes before, who

went forth and, with a loud ringing voice, commanded: 'Johnny. Stop!'

Johnny M looked around with wild eyes. For one long moment, the men, bonded by cowardice, expected the lethal gloves to swerve and connect with her jaw. But he smiled, shook the perspiration from his face, looked at the bloody man on the floor who had shed so much blood. He took off his one glove, leaving the bloody one on, and threw it on the table. Turning his eyes to the spectators, he hardened his voice.

'That', Johnny M said, his eyes scanning each face and filing away the details for future reference, 'could have been you or you or you.' Pointing with the bloody glove. He knew the psychology of fear, that it was better to bring cowards together and put the fear of God in them, as part of a tremulous, quivering mass. Perhaps he had sensed that Virgin was not a coward and could have put up some resistance, or had ideas that ran counter to his. But he knew that, by making Virgin an example, by showing the people what could also happen to them, he had won the first round.

'Today,' he went on, 'we find ourselves compromising with people who are sent to rule over us. We have to ask ourselves the question, When last did we choose our own leaders? Baba Joshua was a good man, and he led with wisdom and probity. Now, he has died and his daughter, who knows nothing, the little bitch who sleeps with white boys, is sent to become our leader. The question I have to ask is: are we going to allow this?'

The drinkers were getting dizzy from all these questions which they knew were purely rhetorical. They also knew that he was referring to Zodwa, of whom they knew little; they didn't care if she slept with Martians, as long as her nocturnal habits didn't interfere with their access to alcohol. If, perhaps, Johnny M had said she came with a special brief from some Muslim republic, where you could get flogged for drinking, well, then, they would certainly give her a thumbs-down. Furthermore, on this question of sleeping with boys, some had heard of certain very highly-placed men, present company included, who were partial to boys. But the drinkers knew that Johnny M wasn't too enamoured of Zodwa, which, in the scheme of things, meant they certainly couldn't guarantee her reaching a ripe old age where she would tell bedtime stories to her grandchildren. Since Johnny M had the upper hand – reinforced with concrete, as it were – and since they weren't suicidal, they nodded, silently saying, You're the boss. But a boss wasn't just a boss in a vacuum. He had to use his status to give orders. They waited for the order.

'From here,' Johnny M said, 'you're all going to your homes. You'll get your wives and your children and you'll march to where the bitch lives. You are all part of civil society and marching is part of your democratic right. My men will be around, watching the slackers, all those who'll just skulk away and sleep. I assure you, what happened to Virgin will look like a Christmas party. To be or not to be is not the question.'

As the men scrambled out, some already trying to remember the houses of their relatives outside Ngoza, Johnny M raised his bloody glove. 'Wait,' he said.

They waited. What now – another series of questions?

'You must remember,' Johnny M said, 'wherever you might go, you'll be watched. You might think you're saving your skins, running away elsewhere. Remember this. We'll not only track you down, we'll also kill off all your relatives, children, wives. If you thought the range wars in Upper Ngoza are grim, consider what will happen to you and your families. It will be a hundred times worse. The only way you can get out of this one, is by making sure that not only your families march but your neighbours.'

One of the men, Nzuza, raised his hand for permission to speak. Johnny M nodded.

'If Joshua's daughter isn't going to be the chief,' Nzuza asked, 'then who is?'

'I'm glad you asked that question,' Johnny M said. 'The man who has your interest at heart is Mbongwa.'

There was a stunned silence, followed by a generalised groan. *Mbongwa?* Then Nzuza, emboldened by his initial question, asked: 'But, with all due respect, Mbongwa … Mbongwa has nobody's interest at heart.'

'He has now,' Johnny M said. He was tired of backing what were evidently very unpopular people. 'He will take care of you, I'll see to it.' He glanced at Colin and his face softened. 'Just to wrap everything up, I want you to demand that Mbongwa is installed as your chief.' Gazing at the assembly of drinkers, Johnny M hoped that they knew that he had their interest at heart. 'Now, go.'

As her customers scrambled out, Nerissa became more and more fascinated with this woman Zodwa who had such a dramatic effect on Johnny M. She had heard and seen everything. The fatal assault on Virgin had resulted in instilling unquestioning loyalty in the patrons of her shebeen. It was a brand of loyalty that would endure for as long as people still feared Johnny M. It was not based on a sober assessment of his qualities, where people could reach informed conclusions that he was indeed worthy of being followed. In her life in this world, she had seen people forced into accepting the unacceptable. But she had also seen how time, the final equaliser, had worked on former despots and diminished them in the eyes of people who once feared and obeyed them. Nerissa was also aware of a singularly important point in the dicey game of power. She knew that, when the people started questioning the orders, when, in the loneliness of the midnight hour, they came to a conclusion that what had been done to Virgin was wrong, then Johnny M's support base would end, unless it were to be sustained by more violence. But then, she knew, at some stage, people became tired of turmoil, especially when it justified defending an obscenity.

She, Nerissa, was a woman. She didn't have anything. This shebeen in the New Rivers squatter camp was her sole source of subsistence. In these times, she said to herself, there is no future in such enterprises, especially if they were based on whims of unstable men. She saw herself old, owning nothing, a laughing stock of the settlement. Because, she knew, Johnny M, like most men, was loyal only to the stirring in his loins. He was undependable even in the sexual arena; his predilection for boys simply meant that, in due course when homosexuality wouldn't be frowned upon, another shebeen queen, equipped with a penis and a pair of balls, would take over from her.

She watched Sipho and Colin lifting Virgin's lifeless body. Johnny M instructed them to put it in the boot of the car. Johnny M told her to stay put. 'Interesting things will happen tonight,' he said. Then he looked at the carpet on which the blood had turned black. He gave her a long look, as if trying to examine what was going on inside her head.

'I might be back later,' he said, another way of holding her prisoner.

'I'll clean up,' she said. She watched him get into his car. Then they were gone, with a corpse that would be dumped only God-knew-where. The thought of the corpse connected with her earlier analysis on women and abusive men, the sempiternal connection. In the television programme, she remembered now, they had called it the Stockholm syndrome, whatever that meant. Women like Zodwa would never have the Stockholm syndrome. They would never give love or comfort to a kidnapper. Suddenly indignant, Nerissa remembered her childhood home, her brothers and sisters, who had treated her like a princess, and who had thought she would become somebody and do them proud. Look at me, she said half to herself, in an onrush of self-pity. I'm destined to be someone's whore, a willing victim. She sat on the kitchen chair and looked at the pile of empty bottles, overflowing ashtrays, a pile of dishes on the sink, the story of her life. Tears welling down her cheeks, burning, and tasting of salt, Nerissa determined to change her luck. Deciding then and there to go and see Zodwa, she started plotting against being forced to love an abductor.

Nineteen

It was the way they were at ease with her, which told Benedita that they meant to kill her. She recalled a conversation she'd had with a New York cabby, who could tell if a fare was going to try and stiff him. 'Paying customers,' he said, 'always have their eyes glued on the meter. The guy who'll try and pull a fast one on you, he hardly glances at the meter. It don't mean squat to him. You might clock forty, fifty bucks, and he's there contemplating his navel. Watch out for the welsher who doesn't bother with the meter.' In her case, Benedita concluded, her two black abductors had long since discounted the idea that her taxi of life possessed a functioning meter. Her clock had stopped the minute they knocked her out and bundled her into the car.

She had a dim recollection of the episode, it had happened so quickly. She remembered the surprise in Jannie's face, and then they covered her with the blanket. They must have sprayed her with some noxious gas which knocked her out. When she came to in the moving car, with one of her guardians sharing the back seat with her, her body was sore, as if she had first been bundled into the boot and bounced up and down over all those potholes. For one panicked moment, she had thought that she'd been raped, but could now dismiss the notion. Sexual assault of any kind was not these men's brief. They were too detached; although she understood that sexual attraction and rape were not linked, when they addressed her, there wasn't even the merest suggestion that they found her possessing qualities characteristic of other human beings. She cast around in her mind, trying to

293

imagine how others saw her. Tall, red-haired, freckled, brown eyes, a nose she sometimes felt uncomfortable about, squarish face, dimples when she smiled. A satisfactory bosom, a nice ass. At least that's what Jannie had said and he should know. The two men had introduced themselves to her. The driver was Fakude and her guard was Bhiza. The very fact that they had disclosed their identities meant that they didn't expect her to live long enough to expose them to the police Or the police were also in on this. *Grey*, she thought. Where had he got these men, who certainly didn't resemble any police she knew? Ignoring her completely, they were arguing about music and politics. Fakude had just remarked that today's kids didn't know anything about how music had played a part in dismantling apartheid.

'What do you mean, "dismantle apartheid"?' Fakude asked. 'If apartheid has been dismantled, then why are we living in Two Rivers while white people live in Central?'

'You're wrong, *chumza*,' Bhiza said. 'Darkies are in Central. Johnny M, for instance.'

'*Ja?*' Fakude said, his tone was laced with scepticism. 'How come I don't seem to hear the pattering of feet of little white children playing in the squatter camp?'

'No white kids in the ghetto,' Bhiza said, 'but it's only a matter of time before we have white neighbours there, too. Mixing it in the mud. Also,' he added with felt optimism, 'you now see a couple of white beggars on street-corners.'

Benedita had also never seen white kids in the squatter camp. But she had also seen white beggars exhibiting their cardboard placards with messages of their destitution. Under normal circumstances, she regarded herself as a moderate, or, within the South African context, a neo-conservative-liberal; she had imbibed good values from her mother, and knew right from wrong. People who knew her sometimes found her frustratingly practical, a tailor-made party-pooper. But one thing guaranteed to get her irrationally boiling mad was the sight of white people begging. Every time she saw one of these pathetic wretches getting crisped like bacon under the broiling sun, she had to summon all her powers of restraint from rolling down her window and letting loose a fusillade of invective. It had amazed her to see people who, despite having the deck stacked in their favour for five decades, still managed this demonstration of astounding ineptitude. The apartheid state had done everything for them, from job reservation to compulsory education: only they themselves were responsible for their graceless descent into mediocrity.

Looking out the window into the darkness, she found herself reluctantly agreeing with Fakude. She studied him: the skin mottled with ancient acne, a shaven dome and dark glasses even at night. His deep, bass voice rose up and down whenever he was excited. 'I remember when people went to the elections,' he said. 'All those queues. I asked myself what people meant when they said that Chris Hani had given us the elections.'

Benedita knew how Chris Hani had given South Africa the elections. After his assassination, which had almost plunged the whole country into an inferno, the only course that could avert the approaching explosion was the agreement of the National Party that April 1994 would be the time for elections. She felt an urge to tell them this, to explain, but instead felt the soreness of her body and remembered that she had been kidnapped. Benedita asked: 'Where are you taking me?'

Bhiza glanced at her, amazed she still possessed the power of speech. He looked at Fakude, who adjusted the rear-view mirror to zero in on her eyes. 'Afraid we can't tell you anything. We're just the Indians, Madam. Chief sent us to get you, and we got you.'

Madam. She had read a newspaper article where Gillian Slovo wrote about a white woman who was hijacked in Johannesburg. A couple of blocks down, the robbers discovered the woman's high-heel shoes on the floor. Reversing to the shaken barefooted victim, one of the robbers rolled down the window and tossed shoes on the pavement. 'Madam,' he said. 'Your shoes.' It was the memory of the incident, coupled with the solicitousness of her kidnappers, which brought home to Benedita that not only might she get killed, but also she was probably going to die a slow, agonising death. Even though she wasn't tied up, the thought of escaping never entered her mind. The smell of the gas they had used on her lingered in the car. Benedita pondered the hit-or-miss nature of death in South Africa, where you could become a casualty of a drunken driver, a stray bullet or some armed psycho wishing for company to the gates of Hell. Now she was to become a statistic, courtesy of a police chief, an epitome of reason, a pillar of society.

She thought she heard the sound of shots, far off in the dark, someone focusing on a target, but it could have been kids who'd laid their hands on firecrackers. It was December, a month when people found a reason to celebrate. Remembering Zodwa, she thought of Joshua and the funeral. Zodwa had no reason to celebrate. Benedita already knew of the intrigues generated by Johnny M and Mbongwa and of course Grey. Where did these people in the car fit in the scheme of things? She watched the settlements shooting past, dark shadows in a deeper darkness leavened by a flash of yellow light, people making cooking fires. They passed another settlement, shacks of tin and cardboard; the little children who still played outside at this late hour looked like a collection of sticks. A ripe smell of faecal matter entered the car before they rode up to a marshland, which, in the darkness, looked alive with the industry of malarial mosquitoes.

Then the road led them to a part of Ngoza she had never been to before, a suburb of rambling townhouses, also fenced-in, where she could see past the hedges floodlit tennis courts and swimming-pools. Most of the houses were painted white or yellow, like company houses oppressed by the convention to uniformity. Grey's place was in an elegant section of Central. As she got out of the car, Benedita saw the paved streets and more townhouses with iron gates and windows fronted by burglar bars.

She was convinced that an unasked question in her mind – why kidnap her instead of the prime enemy: Venter – would be answered when she was shepherded up the driveway onto the threshold of the house. The door was ajar. Fakude nodded at her and gave her a slight push into the hallway. Then he joined the other shadows hovering outside. Inside the lounge, a radio was playing a selection of classical music. Most of the pieces of furniture were covered with sheets of grey canvas, as if the owner were either decorating, preparatory to moving in or enhancing the value of the estate before vacating the place. Dressed formally in a black suit, white shirt and a tie, Grey stood in the middle of the room with a glass of whisky in his hand. An old lampshade, either snapped up in a flea market or bought from an exclusive antique shop, screened the yellow light from an equally old lamp with a polished mahogany base. The weak lighting gave the lounge an effect of a dwelling recently vacated by restless spirits. Leather settees took up most of the room. On the glass-topped coffee table were scattered selections of pornographic magazines, women in various poses of stylised passion. Looking up from the pictures, Benedita's eyes found the police chief's eyes burning into hers, communicating a lust that was overpowering in its abject desperation.

'Do you want a drink?' Grey asked. He still hadn't moved.

'What I want', Benedita said, 'is to know what the fuck you think you're doing?'

Grey pretended to stagger, clutching his breast as if her words had sent a dagger into his heart. 'You wound me with your words,' he said, pointing at the settee. 'Please sit down.'

'I'm all right,' she said. 'What do you want from me?'

'I SAID SIT DOWN!'

Benedita had meant to stand her ground, whatever happened, but the violence behind the order shook her to acquiescence, and she sank into the settee. She realised that she had knuckled under an old police tactic of shouting the suspect down and bombarding them with the sheer volume of threats. Suddenly feeling naked in the flimsy gown, she felt the coolness of leather against the back of her thighs. She knew she had lost the round when she looked into Grey's face, stolid in its triumph, as he approached and stood behind her, his manicured fingers gripping the backrest and smelling faintly of cologne. She flinched as he brought his face past her shoulder and round to look at her, his breath holding the odour of recycled malt.

'I'm sorry I yelled,' he cooed, trailing a forefinger along the strap on her shoulders. 'I merely wanted to conduct an adult conversation with you.'

'Please don't,' Benedita said, wondering whether silence wouldn't be a better weapon.

'But I want to,' Grey murmured, removing his hand and circling the settee until he was sitting next to her. When he shoved his hand up her gown, she started and made to stand up. Agilely, with his one hand, Grey imprisoned both her wrists against the backrest. Without any seeming effort, he then slapped her twice, thrice across the face, all the time his face betraying no visible emotion. She tasted her own blood and hoped that none of the teeth were loose. She had closed her eyes during the assault; when she opened them, looking past him, she focussed on the opened thighs of the woman in the magazine, *Oh, God!* Having ascertained that she wouldn't be offering resistance, Grey then resumed his illegal search into her flesh with his fingers, poking and alternately bringing them under his nose. Awash with shame, Benedita remembered that she and Jannie had been about to make love before the series of interruptions, and now *this*.

As though from another world, the sound of the radio broadcasting classical music carried through, where she could separate the strings from the horns. It was when she heard the woman singing in a foreign tongue, possibly about love and all the qualities that differentiate men from beasts, that the problem that was Grey solved itself, like pieces of a jigsaw puzzle falling into place to complete a coherent picture. She suddenly imagined Cynthia with this man of bizarre appetites and found a place in her heart for pity. Because, whatever had happened between them had less to do with desire or the imperatives of the flesh than a hysterical hatred, which translated into terror, for Cynthia's erstwhile husband. Like a serial masturbator for whom sexual intercourse resided in the evocation of images of others' couplings, Grey had passed Cynthia on to other men, extending himself through them, shuddering in vicarious ecstasy. Now that Venter had extricated himself from Grey's sphere of influence, and had changed the rules of the game by refusing to be destroyed by Grey's ploys, the sins of the men would be visited on the women.

Twenty

The runner came and breathlessly told her that Horwitz had been shot. Nerissa, who related what had taken place in the she-been, followed him. She pleaded to stay with Zodwa, if only until morning. Zodwa summoned Nozizwe, and the three women walked to the tent. Ordering the sentinels to leave, they sat watching over the body, talking in muted tones, planning. They knew that the time for peace would only come after some blood had been shed. Zodwa, Nozizwe and Nerissa determined that not a drop of blood of the innocent would be spilt. As the ancient clock on the belfry tower chimed the hour of midnight, they heard the first explosions. It was time.

Twenty One

It was the dogs that had the first intuition of tension. The mongrels of the Two Rivers squatter camp heard the men plotting, and before they acted, the dogs sent out an infernal howling, a telegraphic message that carried across the drying riverbed onto the terrain of their hungry brothers, sisters and cousins in the settlement of the New Jerusalem. If Johnny M's advance patrols heard the howling, they didn't let it dissuade them from the task in hand. They moved from door to door, calling people out, arming them with cudgels, pick handles, axes, machetes, knives and spears. For more than three-and-a-half years, the people hadn't marched. Among them, there were those who had marched from pure instinct. If people had a problem about water, they had enjoined others to march. As happened with people who hadn't ridden bicycles for years, once they laid their hands on handlebars, they immediately knew what had to be done.

A considerable section of the marchers didn't have the faintest idea why they were marching, but since it was in their bloods, they followed the leaders, who were mostly following some thug who had another agenda. They left the comfort of hearth and home, took the proffered weapons, and walked.

As they marched, this mob swelled from a hundred to two hundred; by the time they came to the outermost section called Katanga, the marchers were more than five hundred strong. Since it was a balmy night, which occasioned flights of imagination, the people imagined that they were going to confront an implacable enemy. Since no march was complete without a battle hymn, Johnny M's men composed crude songs about what they were going to do with choice bits of Zodwa's anatomy. This ran against the grain with women from the Two Rivers Women's Collective, but they were aware that a march was not an arena to raise gender issues. They were marching on Zodwa so that they would air *their* grievances. They needed plots of land to cultivate crops. Johnny M had already subdivided their plots and this made life difficult. But still, they took up the rhythm of the dancing feet, chanted their own lyrics and followed.

Two old men who were either tired or drunk, or just contrary, defied the order to come out of their respective houses. Johnny M's men wasted no time. They doused the shacks with petrol and set them alight. As the flames devoured the fragile cardboard and cooked the zinc walls, people stood, watched and then started chanting, egging the flames on, drowning the screams of the people, including women and children, trapped inside. The smell of burning flesh. Since there was something greedily fascinating with fire, some of the marchers torched the empty shacks of those who had fled earlier. In no time the Two Rivers squatter camp resembled a battle zone.

After this, most of those who had been marching out of ignorance suddenly knew that it was actually fear that motivated them to march. Other assaults were taking place ahead, where people who complained of tiredness were clubbed to the ground and kicked. Since a mob depended on coherence, the malingerers were denounced as Zodwa's spies who wanted the women of Ngoza to be fucked by white men. It didn't matter that most of the people didn't know who Zodwa was, and even less how she would facilitate this inter-racial debauchery. But since someone who sounded quite indignant had raised it, it started having the dimensions of a monumental iniquity, which required them to redress.

When the throng, moving as if to the pulse of one heartbeat, chanted and danced its way to New Jerusalem, some of the leaders decided that they should detour and trek towards town.

Many of the residents of Two Rivers had not been to town in a long time. They had avoided it because it was here that they were faced with the reality of their unemployment and poverty. Town meant unaffordable goods behind plate glass. It was the domain of white people and the few black people who ate well. They stayed in the squatter camp and developed an alternative existence, which satisfied almost all their everyday needs. If you wanted a suit for a wedding or a funeral, you could get one cheaply in the squatter camp. Even musicians needing instruments found them in the squatter camp, sometimes still in their original packaging.

But the word *town* sent a ripple of excitement, evoking memories when people could still find connection with the displayed goods, when things were cheap. For others, the reasons were more complex, such as when a person remembering an old toothache passed by a dentist's surgery. In the way a whisper develops into a scream, the march graduated into a riot. The explosive charges that Johnny M's men had laid in choice locations in Two Rivers went off, creating more excitement. That they exploded at midnight meant that this was the last day that people were going to be taken for granted.

'Town!' the angry man said. He had a raucous, whisky-scarred voice that had been trained in church choirs and in funerals where he sang for the dead. It carried across the crowds, reverberating against the walls of the burning shacks, and was finally taken up by more and more celebrants.

'*Town! Town! Town!*' The people shouted, hoarse with expectation. This cry was heard as far as the New Jerusalem settlement – sounding to them like *Down, down, down!* – where the believers also waited for the hordes of Satan come to disturb the peace of their eminent dead.

★   ★   ★

'I'm sure,' Venter said to himself, 'that Benedita will hold out, wherever she is, until I arrive.' Mpanza and Reuben knew that this was the closest Venter had come to saying a prayer. They had driven to the police station where the desk sergeant had told them that, no, Grey hadn't been there the whole day. Mpanza had looked at the man's black sweating face and decided against asking about where to find Johnny M. He hadn't trusted the police in the city, there was no reason to trust them in town. But the cop had volunteered information.

'Chief Grey could be at Mr Johnny M's,' the cop had said.

'Do you know where that is?' Venter had asked, using his cop's voice. When the man seemed to hesitate, Venter snapped his fingers, '*Kom, kom, kom, kom!*'

'I don't know,' said the cop. His eyes had suddenly reached deep down within themselves and discovered a spring of hostility.

'You *don't* know? How long have you been in this town?'

'Twenty years.'

'And you don't know where Johnny M lives?'

The cop's demeanour said that he'd had enough. 'Look, mister,' he said, his mountain accent deepening, 'I don't know whether it's me you want, asking all these damnfool questions. I don't know where Mr Johnny M lives and, what's more, I don't want to know.' He gave the two black men a strange look, which said, *What're you fellows doing with this turkey?* 'Now,' he added, 'if you'll excuse me, I have work to do.'

But Venter, who was a healthy, stomping kind of fellow, and who could recognise insubordination – that's the word that came quickly into his mind – from a *munt*, no less, decided that he had to put his stamp on this sleepy little police station, once and for all. Balling his hand into a fist, he was preparing to lunge at the policeman and pummel him to obedience when he heard two simultaneous clicks of guns being cocked, and found himself staring into the black muzzle of the policeman's pistol. Likewise when he turned to look behind him: Mpanza had also drawn his gun.

'You mean,' he asked the cop, 'that you'd actually shoot *me*, a brother officer?'

'You're not my brother,' the cop said. Holstering his pistol, he addressed himself to Mpanza. 'Perhaps', he suggested, 'you'd better advise *your* brother that people are very nervous around here, there's so much evil stuff going on. Everything's falling apart, farmers are crying for rain, nerves are frayed, so it helps to keep a cool head.'

'Are you keeping *your* head cool by threatening *me* with a gun?' Venter had to find a way of salving his punctured pride.

'I'd probably have gone to jail,' the cop said laconically, 'but *your* head would be cool for sure. Permanently.'

Venter and the cop stared at each other for a minute, across a great, unbridgeable gulf. Sensing the tension, Blackie the monkey, who has throughout the evening been like Venter's shadow, clambered up its owner's back to perch on his shoulder. Mpanza suppressed a laugh when he looked into the cop's sweating black face, which somehow seemed to expect the monkey to stick its thumbs into the ears, make a face and say, *Nyah, nyah, nyah, nyah!*

Outside the police station, Reuben, realising that he might have drawn a blank, suggested that they visit the settlement of the New Jerusalem and ask questions there.

'Do you have a particular person who might give us a lead there?' Mpanza asked in a voice that betrayed his doubt.

'Zodwa is the chief now,' Reuben put in stubbornly. 'She's supposed to know what's going on in her realm.'

'Zodwa's too busy grieving over her father,' Mpanza said. 'She knows nothing,' he added in a tone that made Reuben give him a quick look.

'Why are you so sure?' Venter had asked. To him every lead had to be followed. There was also a certain resentment that the black man had taken over the investigation and, true to form, it was going to be a shambles. He had established that Mpanza was an ex-guerrilla, an ex-enemy, if there was anything of that sort. But then he remembered that this wasn't any routine investigation. His wife had been snatched, and he could use any help he could get, but he still smarted over the humiliation inside the police station and felt combative.

'Because', Mpanza had replied, 'it makes no sense.'

That had made sense. Then they had gone back into the van. A few metres from the police station, it had conked out. Venter had gone out and kicked the wheels of his vehicle, cursing that he had forgotten to fill up with petrol. The three men and the monkey stood, thinking of the next course of action, when Reuben said that Johnny M owned horses nearby. Mpanza had felt a stab of pain in the region of his heart when he recalled Judit and their frolics in the cherry-plum orchards of Budapest.

The urgency of the situation had not allowed for sentimentality. Reuben had led them down the path skirting the police station and the mortuary. Johnny M's stables were guarded by a stereotype of a night-watchman, a big man in an outsize greatcoat armed with a knobkierie with a formidable head, his ear lobes stoppered with ear-plugs and his big feet in rubber-tyre sandals. Although the situation was desperate, they had time for mischief. Finding the night-watchman asleep in his upended beer crate, his chin balanced on the head of his knobkierie, they had debated whether to hit him with the butt of Venter's AK-47 or merely try to steal away with the horses, hoping that he would not wake up. It was Reuben who suggested otherwise.

While Mpanza and Venter had inched stealthily towards the stables, Reuben had taken Blackie along to where the night-watchman slept. When a yard away, he had thrown a stone at the crate and the loud crack had woken the man. Opening his eyes and wiping spittle from the corner of his mouth with the sleeve of his coat, he had taken one look at Blackie who was gazing at him with great haunted eyes and had concluded that he had woken up to a nightmare. Mouthing an oath, he dropped his weapon, upsetting the crate in his haste, and took to his heels, yelling, '*Umhlola! Umhlola!*' As Mpanza jimmied the stable doors open, hearing hasp and shooter pieces clattering on the floor, he had to agree with the running man that there was indeed something spooky about waking up to a monkey giving you the evil eye. Having saddled up, Mpanza and Venter had come riding two horses, a third one cantering alongside. On an impulse, Mpanza had gone back to the stable where he released all the horses, among them the thoroughbred Johnny M had ridden the other day. '*Hyai!*' he shouted, clapping his hands and then watching with satisfaction as the animals cantered out and then galloped off into the dark. Then they had all ridden to the van where Venter retrieved his army knapsack.

Reuben had directed them to Nerissa's shebeen, which they found deserted. As they rode out, Mpanza calmed his horse when he heard what sounded like distant artillery fire. Then the three men had heard the chants and oaths of marchers. Knowing that they were probably in the path of someone's military march, they steered the horses into a nearby bush where they stood in knee-high savannah grass and waited. Outlined against the eastern horizon, they could see the smoke-edged flames and hear the crackle of a ravenous fire.

The first wave of the marchers approached, moving slowly but in an excited manner of revellers. The horses, sensing danger, reared and neighed and had to be calmed, the men stroking their great heads and murmuring assurances. Behind the screen of mimosa trees, Reuben could make out faces he recognised. He also heard the chants and their messages of doom directed at Zodwa.

'I think', he said, 'we must go to the settlement.'

'Why?' Venter asked. 'What about Benedita? Are they saying anything about her?'

'No,' Reuben said. 'Those are Johnny M's men and they are leading people to Zodwa. I think she's in great danger.'

'What about my wife?'

Mounting his horse, Reuben looked at the white man. 'My feeling'. he said, 'is that we might get the answers there.'

'Wait one minute,' Venter said. Reaching into his bag, he took out a small tin of polish. Working quickly, he blackened his face and hands, leaving the palms free. Replacing the tin into the bag, he found a floppy bush hat; before putting it on, he rolled his hair into a knot and piled it on top of his head. Putting the hat on, looking up at the mounted black men, grinning self-consciously. 'How do I look?' he asked.

Mpanza at first suppressed an urge to laugh. Then he remembered how this camouflage had succeeded against his own comrades when the Special Forces launched the cross-border raids in Mozambique, Lesotho and Botswana. To him, Venter looked exactly like a white man in blackface, but this was not the time for a treatise on cosmetics. 'Like one of my uncles,' he said.

'But,' Reuben said, 'you've got only one uncle – me?'

'That's right,' Mpanza said.

The three men laughed and guided the horses along the flat terrain before they came up to a series of koppies, above the arid pasture-land running parallel to the riverbed, forming an unofficial border between Two Rivers and the New Jerusalem settlements. It was as they rode that the first moon rose, and with it a column of dust which set their teeth on edge. A drove of cattle came from the north, herded by boys who wore nothing but oversized shirts that came to just above the ankles. The horses reared again at the sight of the horn spreads of the oxen, causing the three men to detour and follow a path that skirted the koppies. From there, they could see the settlement spread out, tents looking startlingly white in the moonlight.

As they inched down the hill in Indian file, the path changed from sandy to stony, where they could hear the clatter of the hooves on the surface. The explosions behind them told Venter that whoever it was had used industrial explosives, for even at this distance, the earth registered a sight tremor, shivering as if in its own metamorphic thrill. The report of the explosion mingled, momentarily, with a different singing that was taking place in the settlement of the holy believers. Jeqe, who had sounded the alarm, had roused hundreds of people, men, women and children from sleep. When they saw the three riders, Jeqe, still in his regalia, stepped forward.

'Who are you?' he asked. Then he seemed to recognise someone. 'Reuben? Is that you?'

Reuben motioned for Mpanza and Venter to dismount. They led the horses to the assembled people. Reuben explained quickly what had happened. Joachim preceded the three men to the tent. Mpanza felt a knot of fear settling in the pit of his stomach. I've put this off so long, he thought, now what I was afraid of is upon me. There was no way he could back out of this now. He thought of getting on the horse and bolting away, but he knew that the armed believers would make mincemeat of him. There was something wild in their eyes, a holy rage, and he couldn't possibly overpower them all, not with a 9-mm pistol. Furthermore, he felt such a great weariness, like a traveller who had thought he had reached his destination, only to find that his journey was just beginning. My flight, he thought, started in winter in Budapest, now summer is here and I still cannot find any rest. Knowing that he had to claim his own resting-place and make a mark on it, he allowed the proud young man to lead them into the tent where the women waited and watched.

Twenty Two

Although in the company of the two women, Zodwa had felt utterly alone. Nduli, her confidante, was still somewhere in the Eastern Cape. Nozizwe and Nerissa were in a huddle, reminiscing about Mthunzini, where, it transpired, Nozizwe knew Nerissa's family. Horwitz was dead; she had not known that his death would affect her this much. The men, led by Joachim or Jeqe, had brought the two dead men, Horwitz and Khumalo, on stretchers and laid them in the corner of the tent. The tent of death. Baba Joshua, she had thought bitterly, now has other spirits to accompany him to the grave. She wondered about Horwitz, who had no known relatives, whether he would have wished to have a Jewish burial. She had read somewhere that Jews buried their dead as quickly as possible. They had their own rites and rituals of transcendence, where they had a rabbi, and where special people washed the body. We are a democracy, she lamented silently, but when one of us dies, we use different routes to intercede for their spirit. How does God ever make sense out of this confused cacophony of tongues?

Zodwa felt a spasm of resentment over Ngoza and the responsibility that had been thrust on her shoulders. Baba was wrong to die, she reasoned; he could at least have chosen someone to replace him long before. Grimly, she pondered that chieftaincy needed a comprehensive cadre policy, where people wouldn't be thrown into confusion with the death of a chief. Jonah. Despite his subsequent dissolution, Zodwa was certain, he would have provided leadership. Jonah had reminded her of a horse unwilling to accept a rider. This rebellious quality endeared him to women. He had quizzical eyebrows that strove to meet in the middle, almost dividing his face into equal parts, deep-set eyes, which shone with humour or passion, and wide nostrils that breathed his anger or derision. In his last days she had worried about him; his erratic behaviour culminated in irrational bursts of anger. He had found the series of massacres in neighbouring countries totally unforgivable, as were the collaborators, some of whom had been suborned into perfidy with a pair of Levi's jeans. Some of the white troopers, he had told her, wore helmets with signs of the swastika stencilled on them, and with their faces painted black.

Her mind idling, she thought she was seeing things – that Jonah's visions had come to life – when Joachim or Jeqe entered followed by Rueben and his friend she had seen earlier in the day, and a white man with his face painted black. Instantly refocusing, she saw it was Benedita's husband, Venter. A monkey leapt off his shoulder and landed on the ground, moving its head from side to side in a parody of the monkey which believed no evil.

Joachim or Jeqe tried to bow and hurry inside at the same time, managing to look like a Zulu warrior eager to prostrate himself at the feet of a leader. 'Nkosazana,' he said, 'these men bring bad news.'

It's a season of bad news, Zodwa thought, so what else is new? Part of what Joachim or Jeqe recounted corroborated Nerissa's apocalyptic tale. Johnny M and Grey – and Mbongwa, *surprise, surprise!* – were certainly out to destroy her. She could hear the controlled clamour of the believers outside and ruled out their capability to mount an effective resistance. There would be slaughter, of this she was sure. Two men were dead, a woman had been kidnapped, and an armed, fired-up mob was marching towards the settlement. She had been passive all along, and now it was time to lead. She beckoned for Nozizwe and Nerissa to join her in the discussions with the men. She looked at them, at the corpses in the corner. What a shambles, she thought. Quite a weird Praetorian Guard, with a monkey to tell the story when all had been reduced to dust.

'Why', she asked Venter, 'do you think Benedita was kidnapped?'

Venter didn't know. He thought back on the time it happened. He was the target, but they had taken his wife instead. Feeling silly, he turned to Mpanza. 'What do you think?'

'Well,' Mpanza said carefully, 'if you've been a thorn in Grey's side as I think you've been, then he's certainly hit on an irregular but effective way of getting at you. What's puzzling, though, is why they don't want Baba Joshua buried here.'

Nerissa raised her hand, like a school-girl requesting permission to speak. 'After people were removed from here,' she said, speaking hesitantly, 'this place was used for a few years for military activity. I remember trucks and armoured vehicles trundling past Two Rivers, with men in combat uniform. Then there would be explosions, especially at night, and we were not allowed beyond the perimeter fence. What I heard later, from Johnny – Mr Johnny M – was that some weapons, guns and things, were buried somewhere here. Johnny said that Police Chief Grey is in charge of the weapons.'

'Perhaps', Nozizwe suggested, 'he wants to find out from her how much you know?'

'That might be the case.' Venter had never discussed his wife with such a motley crew. 'But while we're wrapped up in Twenty Questions, Benedita is fast running out of time.'

Zodwa looked at Mpanza. 'What do you think?' She couldn't get over the notion that she had met him somewhere before. 'Split into search parties? Dig up the graves and raise Cain with the traditionalists?'

Mpanza's eyes had been focused everywhere but Zodwa's face. He now returned the look. 'I can volunteer to the graves detail,' he said. 'During the days of Umkhonto We Sizwe, we were taught of the likely terrain for DLB's. What I wouldn't know is the condition of the guns, or if there is ammunition.' He paused. 'But, since time is running out, I'll need a lot of manpower. We might just hold out against Johnny M's people. Just.'

'Nerissa,' Venter asked, 'do you know Grey's place?'

'Do I, now?' Nerissa asked. 'Of course. I'll be more than willing to show you.'

Throughout the discussion, Reuben had been unable to keep his eyes away from Nerissa. 'Can I join you?'

'Of course,' Nerissa was emboldened by visions of sweet revenge. 'The more the merrier.'

Nozizwe watched them going out, 'A white man, a black woman and a monkey,' she said tonelessly. 'Heavens above, what a night!'

There was a long silence punctuated by the sound of muffled explosions in the distance. The believers sang their religious songs and Mpanza lamented the absence of miracles as happened in the Bible when Joshua …

Joshua.

Mpanza could barely contain his excitement. 'Zodwa?' he called.

'Yes?' she answered.

'I have an idea.' Then he told her what he had in mind.

'No,' Zodwa said. 'Out of the question.'

Nozizwe took her by the hand. 'Zodwa, my child,' she said with great tenderness, 'this is one of the few instances when you'll have to follow your head and lock your heart inside a vault, to be opened when all this is over.'

'But', Zodwa protested, 'it's sacrilege!'

'It is necessary.'

Twenty Three

Johnny M waited on the bed for Colin to come out of the bathroom. They had made love earlier, and it had been an astonishing experience. Although the boy still showed rough edges, Johnny M was certain he would polish him as he would a precious stone, his black diamond. He couldn't remember the last time he felt this way. That fight in Nerissa's shebeen – *his* shebeen – had whetted his appetite. Colin had stilled the fire if momentarily.

He heard the toilet flushing. Then the door opened and a naked Colin headed for his clothes that hung over a chair. Johnny M was surprised if not a bit disappointed, as he had a couple of nifty moves to show the kid.

'Hey, baby,' he asked, 'what's this? What's with the clothes?'

Colin put on his T-shirt, giving Johnny M a full view of his naked splendour. 'I'd like some fresh air,' Colin said. He put on his shorts.

'Fresh air?' Johnny M cried. 'What's this? Come back to bed. Come back to papa.' Tapping the space next to him on the bed. Johnny M knew that this was going to be another sting, nothing he couldn't sort out with well-phrased promises.

Colin picked up his shoes and sat on the bed with his back to Johnny M. 'People call me a faggot,' he said sullenly.

Johnny M felt rage enveloping him like a suffocating shawl. 'Which people?' he demanded. 'Tell me which people and I'll go out now and sort them out.'

Silence.

'Was it Sipho? Fakude? Who?'

Colin sniffled and turned his face to Johnny M. 'I'm tired of this life, Johnny,' he said. 'I'm twenty-six years old and nothing to show for it.'

So, Johnny M thought, this is it, at twenty-six the boy is anxious over a retirement plan. He didn't think that this was unreasonable; under the same circumstances, *he* would be concerned about his future. Johnny M regarded himself a reasonable man, who pushed frontiers for the youth. He was rich, sure, richer than all his tribe, but he was not a *moegoe*, no one was going to pull wool over his eyes. Getting off the bed, he watched himself in the mirror, the full head of black hair with strands of grey at the temples. A smooth face unlined by age, and no one not even his mother, God bless her soul, would say he would hit forty-eight next January. Flexing his muscles and sucking in his stomach, he admired himself, thanked his good health and was suddenly hit by a spasm of magnanimity. Relationships were never without their downside, and it all had something to do with property, but that was human nature. Relationships were fraught with insecurity. He wanted Colin to feel secure, after all, the boy could have been his son.

'What is it that you want, Colin?' Johnny M asked. 'A car?' A BMW 3M series, he thought, trying to second-guess the kid. No problem: he'd assign Sipho or Fakude to hijack one in Johannesburg. Bring it to the kid in a box.

'I want a horse,' Colin said simply.

All the fun went out. 'What?'

'I said I want a horse,' Colin repeated.

'You don't want a *horse?*'

'You know a horse. You've got loads in the stable.'

'Boy,' Johnny M said, relenting, 'you sure drive a hard bargain.'

'Yes,' Colin said. 'I've always wanted one since I was a kid.'

       ★   ★   ★

Police Chief Grey had been warming to the delectable task of humiliating Benedita Venter when she pressed her own hand against his, as if urging him deeper into her flesh. While he had thought that he had long established who was boss, he had still expected some form of struggle, the anticipation of which had heightened his resolve and accelerated his desire. When she started responding, participating in what was usually a one-sided operation, he was briefly thrown off, and he gazed at her face for signs of deception. But Benedita's eyes were closed. Still, he wished to corroborate his triumph.

'What is it?' he asked. The room was quiet now.

'The other men,' Benedita whispered. 'Can they see us?'

Fuck the black men, Grey thought savagely. Frankly, he didn't give a damn. He didn't even know whether they were around or in some township chasing black cunt. But then he had never had a classy woman up here before, and somewhere in the back of his mind developed resentment against Johnny M's men seeing Benedita's nakedness, who was the nearest thing to a white woman. Even though he kept his girlie magazines displayed openly, he always felt a twinge of hostility whenever he caught a man poring over them. Conceding Benedita's point, he asked: 'What do you have in mind?'

'There must be a bedroom somewhere?' Benedita asked tentatively. 'You must sleep sometime?'

Grey laughed, hearing the words but missing their meaning. 'Of course,' he said. 'I do have a bedroom.' Breaking from her, he stood up and took her hand, helping her up as if readying them for the next dance and then, impatiently, he pulled her. The momentum of the tug brought her flush against him. 'Heavens to Betsy!' Benedita said in her most girlish voice and trailed her fingers along the back of his neck. 'You should get a haircut.'

Grey laughed again, happy in her company, entranced by the old-fashioned expression. It occurred to him that he was a little drunk, but he was known across the length and breadth of Ngoza as a man who could hold his liquor. It was realising that he might not be in total control which made him think back on the tone she had used, and found himself puzzling over the deep-

316

er meaning of her words. But this passed, like a shadow, and he led her past the covered furniture, along the hallway banked by closed doors.

The night hummed its own unknowable tune, now and then sending into the huge house the sound of firecrackers, out there in the distance of another world. A refrigerator belched in the stomach of the house, and Benedita suddenly felt hungry. This surprised even herself for, throughout the evening, her heart had been threatening to jump out of her mouth. When she told Grey, he replied that it was not a problem, he'd fix them something quick in the kitchen. As if fearing to lose her, in a way continuing to imprison her, he steered her gently across the wooden floor into the tiled kitchen. The floor felt cool against the soles of her feet, bringing back to her the reality of her predicament. Much as she had earlier thought of screaming, she knew now, as she watched him slice the bread, his fingers which had been inside her now working as if independently of their owners, any journey from the kitchen would be a descent into Hell.

'Tell me about Cynthia,' she said, not knowing why she felt so bold, fearing to upset the equilibrium. Perhaps it was her tone, but he shot her a quick look, and went on placing cheese and tomato slices on the bread. Placing the sandwiches on side plates, he bent to open the cupboard, possibly to look for a tray. Slowly but with agonising haste, Benedita slid the top drawer of the kitchen cabinet open, praying to her gods, to Christ, Yahweh, Allah, ancestors of Baba Joshua, *don't let me down, not now!*

Her fingers closed around an object with a chrome handle. *What if I end up with an egg-lifter?* She closed her eyes, drawing it out, and opened them to see her hand retracting a carving-fork with two long tines, *thank heavens for the lovers of red meat!* As stealthily, she slid the drawer as far back in as she could without a give-away sound.

Standing above him – *stick him in the small of his back, paralyse the fucker!* – Benedita calculated that she might just hit the belt, then she would be in real shit. Slipping the handle into the elas-

317

tic of her panties, she could feel the sharp points puncturing the side of her thigh.

When he straightened, she was looking at him, expecting an answer. He was again uncomfortable with the domesticity of the scene. It was not in the script, but then, he nodded to himself, the script will only stop changing once the movie is completed. He had not had a woman in the kitchen in a long while, and he had heard from somewhere that women were most ferocious there, in their domain. He glanced at the knife block, doing a quick mental inventory and found that he could account for all his edged weapons.

Opening the cabinet, he removed two glasses and a half-bottle of Dimple Haig. He placed these items in her hands and picked up the tray and preceded her into the bedroom. He walked confidently inside the spacious room, which, though furnished to taste, appeared bereft of a female touch. The bed was there, a white duvet weft with intricate aquamarine doily lace designs along the edges, looking now as bare and as lonely as its owner.

Grey kicked off his shoes and unbuckled his belt. Benedita noticed that he wore polka-dot shorts, which was really a great pity because she had intended buying Venter a pair for Christmas. Pouring them both two fingers each of whisky into the glasses, Grey took a quick sip of his. 'Have a drink,' he said, taking off his jacket and hanging it over the chair in front of the mirror. She noticed the holster and the gun, a slash of black against the pristine whiteness of his shirt. He undid the cuff-links and jerked the tie off in one uninterrupted move. Standing in his shirt, shorts and stockings, Grey could have been anyone's favourite uncle. It was only his eyes, blue, smoky and distant as if they strove to unearth the mystery of their own creation, that shattered any avuncular illusions. Without seeming to think about the motion, he stowed the gun under the pillow.

'You wanted to know about Cynthia,' he said. 'Why?'

She was wondering if she had overplayed her hand for, as she searched in her mind for a reason, she concluded that she really didn't want to know anything about Cynthia. 'Nothing,' she said, amazed at her own capacity for dissimulation, *Joe Nhlanhla should give me a job,* 'just that she must have meant so much to you.'

Grey's eyebrows rose in a moment of surprise. 'Your perceptiveness astounds me,' he said, laughing. Then, seriously, *in memoriam,* 'Men don't really know much about women,' he said, sitting down on the bed as if overcome by the discovery of his own wisdom. 'Cynthia was … what?' He groped for the word, '… a sex machine, a voluptuary of unequalled appetites. She helped a lot of us understand that we knew nothing. Each day with her was a discovery of something dark, possibly sordid about the physical aspect of sex, or, if you'll pardon my French, of *fucking.*' Taking off his shirt, he stretched his arm and grabbed his glass. Sipping, looking up at her from below the rim of the glass, he smiled. 'Cynthia taught us that we need not be ashamed of extending the sensations that our bodies were capable of feeling.' He seemed to tire. 'Does that make sense?'

The gospel according to Saint Cynthia, the suction pump. Benedita knew, now, that this was the time to act, or she'd be dead. Slowly shrugging the night gown down her shoulders, she advanced to the bed and knelt before him. She heard rather than saw him stiffening against the fabric of his shorts, in anticipation of the pleasures – and pain, she was sure – Cynthia administered with a social worker's resourcefulness.

When she began, fear and a need to survive this brute had motivated her. As she went on, kneading him, sending him teetering on the threshold of his own precipice, she found that another self had taken over, Cynthia's alter ego, perhaps, that strove to excel in this one department where she was a novice. Surprised at herself, she found herself nibbling and nuzzling him with her teeth, getting a faint taste of urine, the smell of desire kept too long in check. She was participating in all this while at the same time outside it, beyond it, conscious of how her own back must thrust out, an invitation for his probing fingers. She could feel the teeth of the fork gouging into her flesh, drawing blood, *it's that time of the month, dear*, probing into his anus with her finger, grateful for her clipped nails, getting a whiff of rectal gas, breathing beyond it, conjuring up inoffensive smells. Her eyes closed, she could hear him groaning and mouthing incoherent words of endearment or impiety as Grey clenched and unclenched his inner thighs. She laboured on hearing above it all the faint sound like paper-bags popping, the clip-clop of horses in the area immediately outside her shame. Feeling with astounding tenderness the vulnerable spot where the urethra joined the scrotum, she hefted the fork, brought it up, in, once, and pushed it with all her might, heard him scream, *The monkey! the monkey!* and he came, semen and blood spurting all over her hair, face and breasts.

Grey howled and jumped to his feet, the fork forming a tail or a second penis, his eyes glazing as he looked at Blackie, who stood amazed at the things human beings were capable of doing. As he grabbed a handful of blood-soaked duvet and scrabbled for his gun under the pillow, a sober comprehension of reality overtook his pained expression, a man who had stumbled on that rare, epiphanic moment when all of life's experiences finally congealed into the answers to the time when, the people who, the places where and the reason why. The only question that remained unanswered as he pitched forward and rested in a pose conducive to prayer, was *how* it had all happened. Venter came in when an hysterical Benedita was trying to wipe the stickiness off her face, unaware that Grey had attained the supreme form of rapture that existed only in male fantasies.

In her shocked state, Benedita could offer no word of protest as Reuben and Nerissa helped Venter remove the two dead black men who had brought her here. She dully noticed that they both had holes in their foreheads and that their skulls and brains were splattered all over the front seat. Venter kept slapping Blackie's paw away from the gore. She was dimly aware of three horses, one riderless, that cantered gracefully alongside the moving car;

they looked like horses seen through a windscreen with two bullet holes out of which radiated a network of cracks reminiscent of her window the day she drove to Chris Hani's funeral. Chris Hani, she remembered them talking about him. Had they been there at the funeral? Had they been there, and understood the delicate contouring of this country, they perhaps would not have ended up with holes in their heads and their brains oozing onto the choice upholstery of this fine car.

Twenty Four

Mpanza was waist-deep in the hole when the pick scraped an iron surface. Sweating men who looked ghostly in the dark heaved until they pulled the first heavy trunk out of its burial place. Using the tip of the pick, he quickly snapped the padlocks open. Inside, covered in oilskin, were arranged rows of dozens of AKM assault rifles with steel folding stocks alongside hundreds of boxes of 7.62-mm ammunition. He would have to inspect the ammunition for tracers. Magnesium flares, F1 defensive and RGD5 offensive grenades completed the haul. Instead of elation, Mpanza felt curiously let down, as if the suspicion he had always harboured of the destructive nature of man had been corroborated once more. He reasoned that whoever had buried the arms here must have used a mechanical digger, because the contiguous area was characterised by hard rock. He had held his breath against their digging up old graves and alienating the community. Carefully inspecting the oilskin-covered hoard for wires that might indicate booby-traps, Mpanza passed on the first trunk of six. They must have deployed a full platoon to bury the arms, for each trunk could be carried by no fewer than six men. It was a strange unearthing, like an exhumation, since it happened in a place – and time – when people needed to bury their dead. The men laid the boxes inside the spill of light outside the big tent. Working under a poor light made the task more difficult but provided the advantage of keeping the enterprise as private as possible.

It was 12.45 a m. The volume of the singing and chanting

increased as the marchers crossed the dry riverbed and drew nearer the territory of the New Jerusalem.

The march had been delayed when an old woman suffered a heart attack. The people had waited, and Johnny M had decided to wait, also, so as not to split his forces. The momentum, however, was not broken. The night was suddenly alive with the sound of chickens, which had broken out of their runs. The herd-boys, who were meant to spend the night in the veld, returned with their droves, the horns of the oxen shining like lances under the moonlight. The dogs, which had taken a breather since the initial clue from relatives across in Two Rivers, resumed their howling. Man and beast, as if bewitched by an ineffable power, slowly gravitated towards the main tent.

Zodwa came out of the tent and looked up from the boxes at Mpanza who was busy reading the labels on the sticks of flares. 'So,' she began, 'you were in MK?'

Mpanza, stripped down to the waist, squatted on his haunches, stopped his work for a minute. Then he nodded. 'Yes,' he said, not wishing to talk, 'but that was long ago.'

'When was that?'

'Why do you ask?'

'Why are you so evasive?' Zodwa was genuinely irritated by his attitude. 'We're in the new South Africa, now. Secrets are supposed to have died with the past.'

'That is,' he said gravely, 'if the past is really dead.'

Zodwa seemed to think this over. 'You've got me there, mister,' she said. 'I suppose I'm one of the most immediate examples of the past standing in the path of development.'

Her ready admission that the whole system of chiefs was an anachronism surprised him. Then he remembered that she was just fresh from university, and, from Tsepo's analysis, wished to join a law firm. 'But', she said, 'whether we believe it or not, we have to engage in these traditional forms of governance, don't you think so?'

'During our history lessons,' Mpanza said, 'we learnt of transitions, how one social formation is supplanted by the other. Feudalism. Capitalism. Socialism. That knowledge was further developed in political-economy classes in the camps, under a tree.'

'When I started at the university,' Zodwa said, 'I was into the humanities, pure and simple. I took English, History, Philosophy and Political Science. I'd meant to graduate and become one of those lecturers we admired so much at Fort Hare. There was Ralph Peteni, who took us in English Lit. There was Miss Verschoor and Miss Henley who drummed into us the sanctity of the word. My first disenchantment came with Professor Green, whose real name was Groenewald, who believed you had to have an *English* name to be an English professor. I think he must have had a problem. He would come into a lecture room and tell us that only six of us, out of a class of, say, thirty, would pass *his* English. He was so sure we'd fail that I made a special effort, just to prove him wrong. I've never really hated people, finding hate a waste of useful emotion, but Green or Groenewald made me so bitter I knew I would eventually choke on this kind of hostility. So I left. Took Law.'

'You don't strike me', Mpanza said, 'as someone who easily throws in the towel.'

'It wasn't that,' Zodwa said defensively. 'I already knew then that if I had to feed my hate, it must be in a worthwhile cause, not wasted on some anal professor.'

'So,' he asked, knowing the answer, 'what do you feed your hate on now?'

'People who killed my brother,' she said, so readily that the answer must have been rehearsed numberless times in her mind. 'It's not so much the act itself, or the activity of dying on his part. It's the not knowing which kills me.'

'Not knowing what?'

'There's the truth and reconciliation process,' Zodwa said. Then she paused. 'Do you have a cigarette?'

Mpanza took out a packet and tapped it on the palm of his

hand. Offering her one, he lit up for both of them. He watched her sending twin columns of smoke from her nostrils. 'The TRC,' he prompted, 'go on.'

'Yes, the TRC,' Zodwa said, nodding. 'The ANC made its submission. Accepted culpability for some of the mistakes where agents of the regime branded innocent people informers. My brother was one of those casualties.' She gazed at him through the smoke, her gesture asking the question. 'But my problem is that there were many people, for whom the ANC has apologised, who *were* informers, and whose deaths, if we operate on the morality of struggle, could be justified. My problem, my *pain* is whether Jonah was one of those people.'

Just then, Nerissa and Reuben arrived on horseback. From the way Reuben gingerly helped Nerissa dismount, his grip staying inordinately long on her waist, it was clear they had struck some rapport wherever they had been. Seemingly out of breath, they interrupted each other in their eagerness to relate the story of Benedita, Grey, Venter and the monkey. Mpanza watched Zodwa's face as she listened, and saw it crack into an admiring grin. 'Wow!' she said, 'that's one lady who knows what to do with *her* hate.'

Mpanza took a puzzled Reuben aside and briefed him on what needed to be done. Zodwa stood smoking, the glow of the cigarette reflecting in her eyes, making them seem more mysterious than the darkness surrounding them. 'I have a feeling you're uncomfortable around me,' she said. She searched his face. 'Am I right?'

'You can't blame me for that,' Mpanza asked, surprised by his vehemence. 'Can you?'

'Why?'

'I don't know,' he said. 'I'm possibly uncomfortable around royalty.'

'That's not funny.'

Perching on a box containing destruction to fuel months of mayhem, Mpanza looked her in the eye for possibly the first time since their encounter. 'I wasn't meaning it to poke fun,' he said. 'I'm dead serious.'

'Unfortunately,' she said, 'I've always had to put up with people calling me Princess.'

Mpanza seemed to concentrate on the tip of the burning cigarette, the smoke swirling, creating patterns that recalled nightclubs, heat, bodies gyrating on the dance floor. 'Someone once said all Africans are descendants of kings.'

'What a crackpot of an idea,' Zodwa scoffed. 'I suppose it must have been some royalist.'

'It was actually someone in the camps.' Mpanza paused. 'That thought somehow stayed with me all the time we were playing in different places with Amandla.'

*   *   *

Amandla Cultural Ensemble have finished their run at the Hackney Empire in London. Group members have been distributed to different boarding houses, hotels and private accommodation. Mpanza is lucky to be bunked in a maisonette flat in Islington, on the border with Stoke Newington. Although he has learnt his way around the city, it is not Budapest; he knows no one here except the members of the group, who are themselves dealing with the sneaky beast of loneliness. From the South African exiles who depress him even more, he can gather that this city has elevated many to the dizzying heights and also consigned not a few to the threshing-floor. Looking out the window in the morning, he sees snatches of life. A black man of indeterminate age walks stiffly on, a carrier bag in his hand. The man fascinates him. Each time Mpanza sees him, he appears to have sloughed off a possible connection with humanity. Even from the distance of the window, he looks the worse for wear. As the sun climbs, he retreats to a bench in Clissold Park with his draughts of Thunderbird wine chased down with strong Kestrel lager. Mpanza knows it is only a matter of time before the man disappears completely from the Islington landscape.

He watches a riot of twelve- and thirteen-year-olds who

throng the street corner. Their pastime, it seems, is sniffing the azaleas and yellow crocuses that grow unattended outside the undertaker's. The children walk along the street unmindful of the cars. The drivers, mainly Turkish-Cypriots, stick their heads through the windows and let loose with imprecations heavy with Mediterranean accents.

On this one evening, Mpanza feels the walls and ceiling closing down on him. Putting on his jacket, he goes out. On the landing downstairs, he meets the Chilean exiles, tenants of the flat below his. They exchange greetings and Mpanza, after disgracing himself again by responding in Portuguese to their Spanish felicitations, notices that César and Demetria are once again costumed for a party.

Life goes on. Night-time people head for places of enchantment. Young women, already dressed for going out, strut like cowboys bound for a sunset shoot-out. Lights from oncoming traffic blind them. Bonded by an anarchic sisterhood, they shriek in feigned terror, causing older citizens to regard them with reproachful envy. A young man with a blond mane revs his sports car, a Dalmatian in the back seat nodding as if to the rhythm of the soul music issuing out of the boom-box.

A policeman passes. Mpanza feels an urge to tell him that things are hotting up in South Africa. But the look the policeman gives him communicates that the police, worldwide, are not in the business of getting into rhapsodies over anything that does not affect them directly. Here and there, unloved, unloving and unlovable knots of people in the mandatory funereal black are collected by black taxis to celebrate the ascendancy to power or mediocrity in the West End. Groups of black and white people walk on the stone pavements, listening to the silences.

On the right, as he walks, Clissold Park is in darkness. Farther up, a tower block rises to the sky, grey in the gloom of the approaching night. Curtains are parted as an old couple peer at the street below, looking for something that can confirm that they are still part of the human race. Mpanza has already heard

327

the stories about the estates: the dark corridors, playgrounds, lifts, corners: everything sprayed with the graffiti of rage, the smell of piss, vomit and despair wafting over all like poison gas. How, he wonders, can people bring up children here?

But the children are survivors. He can hear them playing in a darkened courtyard, their voices conquering the stench and squalor which conspire to stunt lives. A man and a woman pass, the man placatory while his partner berates him: 'You're just a disgrace, Pete. A *disfuckingrace!*' The children, whose ears are attuned to such information, snicker and repeat the newly coined obscenity.

Entering the Manor House underground railway station, he buys a ticket from the machine. As he goes down the escalator, looking at the intense people recently disgorged by the south-bound train, Mpanza is struck by the absurdity of life. Here we are, he muses, hurrying, *hurrying*, all the time trying to make some change. For what? To buy sports cars so that our Dalmatians could sit in comfort and listen to Arthur Conley? The overhead display flashes the imminent arrival of a train bound for Heathrow Airport. More people escaping.

The giant snake roars into the underground cavern. Mpanza finds a window seat. Across him, wearing a head dress of rainbow colours is a young black woman. Beneath a beige raincoat she has a caftan on, and carries a raffia handbag. Everything about her speaks of Africa. The words return to him, *All Africans are descendants of kings*. He reflects on whether this woman knows that, in some people's eyes, she's a princess. He feels like engaging her in a conversation, but shrugs off the impulse. You don't approach women like that in London, they'll think you're trying to hit on them.

The other black people in the coach could not, he judges, be descendants of kings. Something about their dress and the way they carry themselves, the cadences of their speech, defy any connection with Africa. The men are in leather jackets with zips and iron studs; their jeans are so tight, they might have slipped them on with the aid of a lubricant. Their eyes are watchful. These are eyes of people who have seen what it is like to be despised. The women, softer version of their companions, wear boots, black stockings, short skirts and, yet again, black leather jackets that hug the waist like a basque. Their eyes reflect something which a country, a civilisation, like England, would one day have to confront. These are women who would refuse to be in anyone's kitchen on terms other than their own. The men would not, on pain of death, carry drinks or food trays unless they were entertaining. Their eyes stubbornly said: *Even if monarchs cannot claim us, we arrogate to ourselves the right to be princes and princesses of the city. Beyond all that, fuck you!*

The train rolls on. At Finsbury Park, a young black man in a woollen coat enters holding a Styrofoam cut. Having cleared his throat, he sings with a voice of trombone timbre a selection from Pachelbel's *Canon*, his eyes closed in narcissistic rapture behind glasses. When done, he bows. There are cheers followed by a plop and tinkle of coins. Back home, Mpanza thinks, alms are for those bereft of crutches.

But the colours of creation bouncing against the sepia velvet of the black woman's skin force his eyes back on her. She looks at him fleetingly and their eyes lock. He smiles, trying to show he means well. But her expression betrays uneasiness. In her eyes, Mpanza knows, he is perhaps a drunk, someone to be avoided. Abruptly getting to her feet, she stands by the door, leaving Mpanza feeling like a prize idiot. He has a feeling that he might have spoilt her evening or reinforced her attitude towards men. She gets off at Arsenal.

'Did you want to hit on her?' Zodwa asked.

Mpanza mulled over this, the woman's face was no different from Zodwa's. 'No,' he said. 'I don't think so.'

'Why not?' There was a mischievous smile in her voice. 'Spread some knowledge of Africa to the children of the Diaspora?'

'I'm not good with women in the conversation department.'

Mpanza saw that she was still looking at him. 'I get scared.'

'In what way?'

He laughed a small, embarrassed laugh. 'I always suspect that they can read my mind.'

'What would they read?'

'Perhaps that I'd like to make love to them.'

Zodwa reared her head and hooted. '*Woo!*' she said, 'what a line! Is that what they teach all guerrillas in the camps? Sneak up on a woman with a long cockamamie story like that?'

'What I'm telling you is true,' Mpanza said quietly. 'It's not bullshit.'

Zodwa threw away her cigarette stub. 'So,' she asked, 'you're uncomfortable with me because you might find yourself telling me you'd like to make love to me?'

'Yes.'

She gave him another one of her long looks. 'Would you, though?'

'Would I what?'

'Like to make love to me?'

'No.'

'You bastard!' She started moving towards the tent. 'Who's this dreamer who told you about Africans and kings?'

'The dreamer was Jonah,' Mpanza said. 'I think he missed you a lot.'

Twenty Five

When Johnny M found all the horses gone, he went berserk. Pulling out his pistol, he fired into the stables, emptying the whole magazine. He reloaded, now with the intention of loosing a fusillade into the negligent chest of the night-watchman. The intended victim probably realised that, with the horses gone – on account of a monkey – his longevity was no longer guaranteed. He had also taken off with the sole intent of leading a less calamitous life in the villages of Upper Ngoza. Johnny M was so incensed he started shooting at the empty space recently vacated by the hapless night-watchman, until Colin had to restrain him.

'Cool it, Johnny,' Colin said. 'No need to waste ammo like that.'

'My horses,' Johnny M cried, 'my horses.'

Colin wanted to recite: *A horse! a horse! my kingdom for a horse!* But he took one look at Johnny M's contorted features and decided against it. *Might end up getting myself shot.* He had wanted a horse, had actually seen the one he would have liked, but now the horses were gone, which, in the scheme of things, meant that Johnny M had broken his covenant. So, he concluded, there was nothing more to do in this sleepy town with religious fanatics, smiling dead men and ageing faggots. Colin was also seeing a weak and flabby side of Johnny M he hadn't known before. He had a feeling that his patron was soon developing into a potential victim. It started with small things like someone stealing your horses, no telling what's next. Colin had no desire to be embroiled in situations where he had to prove anything. That was for old geezers. His was to provide comfort and pleasure, take some where he could; it was nowhere written that he had to chaperon a sure-fire loser. The racing-track metaphor was not lost on him. He was an educated boy and, since he could also swing both ways and women liked him, the future was his for the taking. He had to haul ass. He smiled, liking that phrase: *haul ass*.

As if reading his mind, Johnny M asked, 'What are we going to do, Colin?'

We? Colin thought, what motherfucking *we*? 'I really don't know …'

Johnny M gave him a sidelong glance. 'You're not thinking of running out on me, are you, Colin?'

Which was exactly what was on Colin's mind. *Take the car from Fakude, shoot if needs be, off to Durban …*

Colin was still trying to conjure up a pleasant, idyllic image of Durban and its white beaches when Johnny M shot him at point-blank range in the face. He looked at Colin's ruined face and something choked up inside him. 'I humbly do beseech you of your pardon,' he said solemnly, 'for too much loving you.'

At the head of the march, Sipho had heard the gunshots. Hurrying the throng on, he was the first to find Johnny M squatting over a lifeless Colin, weeping like a child. Sipho helped him to his feet. 'What happened, boss?'

'I'd sent Colin over to check the horses,' Johnny M said, 'when I came here … *this* …' Gesturing with the gun, embracing the barrenness of the stables, the absent night-watchman, Colin's blood gurgling into a drain. With bloodshot eyes he looked at Sipho. 'What do you think I should do to these people, Sipho?' he asked.

Sipho didn't know which people Johnny M was referring to. But he was not a fool. Looking around he saw only one car, Johnny M's, and he knew that Colin hated walking, and would not be caught dead near the stable alone at twelve midnight. He knew a lover's tiff gone fatally sour when he saw one, but it was not for him to verbalise that. Johnny M had to sort it out.

'It doesn't look too good, boss,' he said.

'You don't believe I killed him, do you?'

'The thought never entered my mind, boss.' Sipho was aware that a couple of hundred eyes were watching them, waiting for direction. 'Tell you what,' he volunteered, 'let me get Colin into a … more appropriate location. In the meantime, carry on with the march. I'll join you later.'

'Thanks, kid,' Johnny M said, touching his arm. 'You're a star.'

'Get a move on,' Sipho said harshly. 'It's late as it is.'

'Sure, kid.'

If the marchers perceived the subtle but irrevocable shift in power relations, they didn't let on. They knew they had just witnessed the aftermath of a murder, and that the little palaver between the two gangsters was for their consumption. Since the beginning of the march, about two hours ago, seven people they could account for had been killed: the two men and their women and children in the burning shacks. Colin's death was different, because, whatever had happened, it meant that a cog in the wheel grinding to unseat Zodwa had been disabled. While the incident heightened their anger and sharpened their resentment, it also commented on their own vulnerability. It was while they were marching, wondering whether they weren't falling within the radius of an ancient curse, that someone deep in the belly of the march remarked on the fact that Baba Joshua's body had defied all laws of nature by not putrefying five days after death. Others spoke about the smile. It was a rare smile of good health, which seemed to have been carved in a corner of a man's heart where smiles were manufactured. Then, of course, the flower still blooming, the last they'd heard, in the dead man's hands. The whisper was passed on from ear to ear and – true to the dynamic qualities of rumours – had become exaggerated almost beyond recognition by the time it reached the penultimate *ear*. Having had a first-hand experience of people actually shooting the messenger, the owner of *this* ear didn't think it prudent to repeat to Johnny M's ear – the terminal station for the proverbial buck – that people suspected that Baba Joshua might possibly be still alive. And that they feared Nozizwe's sorcery. They were also getting mightily resentful that the chief-in-waiting, Mbongwa, was nowhere in sight.

★   ★   ★

Hodoba and the Vulture-Men were not happy with Mbongwa either. He had been late bringing their dinner and offered an excuse that he had been delayed by planning the march with Johnny M. The men didn't want to hear that. Johnny M, and Mbongwa, come to think of it, ate their dinner in time. Hodoba and the men had run the little errand for Mbongwa, collaring that white boy, Horwitz. The plan had been that Horwitz would be taken back to the cave and the men could do with him as they pleased. Then he had escaped through no fault of theirs. Mbongwa had shot him. He had also shot Khumalo, who was a good fellow, really, who happened to be digging a grave for a dead chief whose daughter was a thorn in Mbongwa's side. Now Mbongwa wanted them to be grateful for bringing their dinner so late!

Hodoba and the Vulture-Men were believers in peaceful co-existence. They could even be said to be adherents of the philosophy of non-violence, but their patience was being stretched beyond endurance. Hence this dinner, eaten in a smouldering, hostile silence. Finishing their food, they cracked the beers open. The beers were warm, *Jesus!* And there was Mbongwa sitting like a knot on the wall, watching them.

'How was the food?' Mbongwa asked. He was always uneasy around silence. Hodoba just clicked his tongue and looked away disgustedly. The Vulture-Man nearest to Mbongwa raised his eyes off the bones on the floor and pointedly studied his bottle of beer.

'The food was lousy,' he said candidly, 'and the beer's like warm piss.'

Mbongwa grinned sheepishly. 'Sorry about that,' he said. 'Problems with refrigeration.'

The man put the beer down. 'Mbongwa?' he asked, 'how come is it that, from the first time we met you, you've done nothing but apologise?'

This seemed to strike a resonant chord with the others, except Hodoba, who had his back to Mbongwa. 'Yes,' another man supplied, 'you sound like a second-hand car salesman. If it's not this particular thing going wrong, it's another one. What kind of leader are you going to make?'

Mbongwa had to say something. 'I promise —' he started.

'*Don't promise!*' Hodoba hissed, cutting him off in mid-sentence. '*Just do!*'

'Okay,' Mbongwa said. 'You've got me there. Truth is, *I'm* doing something already.'

'Like what?' Hodoba's loathing was bottomless. 'Getting fat? Farting with your fucking mouth?'

'I'm *organising* the march!'

Hodoba rolled his eyes and sighed. 'The march.'

The third man spoke. 'Tell us about this march,' he said in a helpful manner. 'What will it achieve?'

Mbongwa was on more reliable territory now. 'People are marching as we sit here,' he said, 'and they're going to Zodwa in New Jerusalem, where they'll demand that I take over as chief.'

'But why,' the man asked, still being helpful, 'do you need people to march? Why not just go there, kill the fucking bitch and start running the business?'

'It's not that simple,' Mbongwa said.

'Is it a long story?' the man persisted.

'Another long story,' the first man said.

'Like the long story,' the second man said, 'why we don't have a radio or a TV set.'

Mbongwa had promised them a radio and TV but had hit a snag over a generator. Something about the dankness in the cave and the lakes. He couldn't remember the actual details, the men were confusing him. 'Look,' he pleaded, 'I'm here to ask you to join the march.'

'What for?' This was Hodoba.

'For my investiture.'

'For his what?' asked the third man.

'His *in-vest-i-ture*,' Hodoba explained patiently. 'It's a word the highbrows use for when you're crowned king or some such ridiculous thing.'

'Is Mbongwa going to be a king?'

'Fuck knows.'

Mbongwa had had enough. He stood up. 'I'm leaving, now,' he said, surprised at the petulance of his tone. 'What this means is that we'll all forget about the promises I made about houses, women, booze, TV and VCRs and all the other goodies. We'll kiss all that goodbye.'

'Mbongwa?' Hodoba said, 'don't get so bloody dramatic.' He paused, reflecting. 'Say we agree to go with you now to your … investiture, then what happens?'

'I take over,' Mbongwa said quickly, 'and by tomorrow …' he looked at his watch, 'no … by today, this morning, I'll set the wheels in motion for you boys.'

'You promise?'

'Of course,' Mbongwa said. 'I promise.'

'And if you can't keep your promise?'

'You can do whatever you like.'

Hodoba consulted his men. 'Did you hear that, *madoda*?' he asked. 'Mbongwa says we can do whatever we like with him.' He studied Mbongwa's face. 'Are you sure?'

'My word is my bond.' Mbongwa was eager to leave. 'Let's get a move on.'

★　　★　　★

Johnny M's pace quickened when he saw, some twenty yards away, the pinpoints of lights, which indicated that the believers in the New Jerusalem were also up, and would perhaps put up a fight. Feeling all juiced up, he commanded his army, a latter-day

Macbeth or Richard the Third, out to restore order through wreaking havoc. That's how it was done in the past, he thought, and that's how it will be done now. He felt the stones through the soles of his brogues, but this temporary discomfort was a necessary sacrifice. His pale Brooks Bros. suit was a little dirty, the turn-ups of his trousers having come into contact with the invincible dust of Ngoza. Come next February, he dreamed, all this will be gone, the same way the dinosaurs perished under the megaton detonation from a giant meteorite. From the crater, he would build a new empire of concrete, glass, steel and chrome. He could already see in his mind's eye the winking red neon, the name *Johnny's* illuminated in such a way you would see it from outer space, like the Great Wall of China.

He envisioned cabaret shows, clean-shaven, well-dressed croupiers with severe haircuts, doormen and greeters in their livery, preternaturally beautiful, long-legged women who'd do their rounds, catering to the most select clientele. Captains of industry, politicians, film producers and stars, a cornucopia of celebrity, a surfeit of style, all waiting for a word, a nod, from him. He lamented that Colin wouldn't be there to help him choose the most distinguished evening suit, but that's the way the cookie crumbles, he consoled himself. The world was full of hungry young men, more beautiful than the models parading on Elsa Klensch's show on CNN. He would not be a ruler; that was for dunderheads like Mbongwa. He would preside over an empire. That was his attitude to power.

He had seen the pitfalls of power and determined not to become another monument to failure. Politicians, like rulers, surrounded themselves with accoutrements of office – *his sceptre shows the force of temporal power* – whereas he believed that real power derived from controlling its representatives. He thought of the battery of sharp lawyers and accountants he would recruit from top companies. He would outstrip Cyril Ramaphosa and cause Don Ncube to eat crow.

The lights ahead shone brighter now and he could see

beyond them a small tent whose front flaps covered a yard's depth of a raised stage. The believers were about two yards away, their candles, lanterns and flares held above their heads, creating shadows under their eyes and foreshortening their features. A wind as rare as rain had started blowing, from the Mveli mountains, bringing with it the odour of drought. Las Vegas, he thought, is built on a desert, so drought is good for development. Look at the Lost City, in a fucking dust bowl!

The believers, he realised, were all dressed in robes, their leader a tall woman ... *fuck's sake, it's Zodwa!* She had a nerve venturing out here when she had to know that she was in trouble. With him. He waved his own followers to stop, *let's hear what she's got to say.*

Zodwa put up a hand and the believers stopped. She looked past Johnny M, cancelling him out, and addressed herself to the mainly unseen faces behind him, in the dark.

'I'm very happy', she said, 'that you've all come out in such large numbers to help us bury Baba Joshua.' She turned and the believers cleaved like Moses' sea and she proceeded to head a train that moved with a dignified slowness towards the stage. Johnny M found himself following, his own mob no longer behind him but actually shoving to see what was taking place on and around the stage.

From where he stood, now pushed to the twelfth row, Johnny M could see that the stage had been constructed from long, community-hall benches pushed side by side and fastened together with ropes that looped below and above the timber. A man crossed the stage from left to right and helped Zodwa climb the metre-high platform and steered her to the centre. Mpanza. What's he doing here? After threatening him like that? He expected the man to be on his way to Johannesburg to secure his family.

Zodwa made a sign and the flaps opened, like a curtain raised in a theatre There was a stunned silence among the spectators, followed by a sharp intake of breath. Moving quickly, Zodwa

338

removed the hood from the figure in the centre. There was a loud gasp as Zodwa brushed back her father's grey hair. Somewhere in the throng a woman was choked by a sob; failing to be controlled, it rose in loudness, a lonely sound of someone descending steadily into hysterics. Johnny M heard feet shuffling and the crying woman was taken away. The light on Baba Joshua's face seemed to originate from a power source inside himself. In the gloom, he was the light.

'This man', Zodwa said tonelessly, 'is my father. Some of you knew him, some didn't. Many of you loved and admired him and, like any man born of woman, some hated him with the most implacable hatred.'

Suddenly feeling his skin prickle, Johnny M deduced that the other shrouded body on the left must belong to that boy Horwitz; the one on the right, perhaps the unknown grave-digger. Khumalo. All dead people. But he wasn't taken in by this smoke-and-mirrors performance. *The sleeping and the dead are but as pictures; 'tis the eye of childhood that fears a painted devil.* Around Johnny M, the concentrated gaze of the marchers and believers was fixed on the theatre of the dead. This was where the lamps scattered around the stage floor flickered, the unseasonable wind now blowing stronger. The shadows playing on Baba Joshua's face, the grim and stammering light, animated the corpse, giving it the vitality it had perhaps lacked when Baba Joshua still trudged the dusty trails of Ngoza.

On the western horizon, the blue-black sky was suddenly suffused with russet hues as if the sun strove to reverse the natural cycle and rise. Cottony clouds, like black smoke, scudded across the rusty tint, momentarily plunging Ngoza into an instant of something imminent, prophetic. Replacing her father's hood, Zodwa spoke to the people, her voice almost breaking, as she told them what she had witnessed.

'When we were removed from here,' she began, 'all light vanished from my father's eyes. As for my mother, she began a long journey into her own special form of death. After she died, Baba suddenly began to see visions which simply directed him to get his people back to this place. This is where the bones of our forefathers are buried. For many of us, it is where our umbilical cord is buried but, much more importantly, this place is the repository of our collective memory.'

A gust of wind blew out all the lamps, leaving the whole area in pitch darkness. Joachim or Jeqe and another young man scrambled onto the stage, lighting the lamps one by one. Zodwa thanked them and turned to the assembly. 'But', she said, 'what is clear now is that some people – and some of them are in your midst – wish to turn Baba Joshua's holy dream into a blasphemy.'

From somewhere in the depth of the crowd, a raucous voice screamed: '*Get out of there, you bitch*. We want Mbongwa!' Those are my boys, Johnny M thought. Pump up the volume.

There was a titter of nervous laughter from people used to outbursts by drunkards. One or two other voices echoed the exhortation for Zodwa to vacate the stage. A sizeable section of the listeners were not amused. 'Why don't you go and sleep it off, you fool?' shouted someone who sounded very angry. 'People are serious, here.'

'Who are you calling a fool, you idiot?'

'You! Who else?'

Zodwa raised her hand. Admonishing the last speaker, she said, 'Don't call people fools for wanting their choice of leader.' She paused, letting the words sink in. 'We are a peace-loving people,' she said.

'*We are sick and tired of peace*,' the irate voice boomed again, '*We've got to do something!*'

A look of great sadness flashed across Zodwa's face. She raised her hand, a superfluous gesture, really, because the crowd's response to the outburst exhorting people to do something had been to turn its eyes to her. As she looked down on the agitated mass of humanity below, it became clear to her that, even in times of strife, people tended to gravitate towards measures to build rather than destroy. She knew that most conflagrations

were caused by a minority. As a student who sometimes partic-
ipated in strikes and sit-ins, she was familiar with the power of
demagoguery. There were student leaders who strove to change
what needed to be changed, but it was her experience that,
towards final exams, those students who suspected that they had
done badly in the year tended to be more vociferous about a
need for disruptive action.

*   *   *

In her mind's eye she sees the graduation ceremony where some
of the rabble-rousers sit on the terraces of the great hall. The procession of sombre men and women, the honoured guests led by
the university chancellor, Nelson Mandela, who looks frail and
grim in a black suit beneath the academic robes and the tasselled
mortar-board crown topping his hoary head, moves slowly and
silently to the platform. The vice-chancellor, Mbulelo Mzamane,
his goatee now peppered with grey, shepherds them to the chairs
that resemble thrones, at an institution of higher learning in one
of the poorest provinces of the country. There is education minister Sibusiso Bengu looking drawn from the strain of cohering
an education system in a country which hadn't made provisions
for the majority of its darker children. The choir conductor
waves a hand holding an invisible baton while the pianist who
sits higher than the highest hits a note that trills throughout the
packed hall, reducing all conversation to silence. Then the
singing starts, conveyed by voices trained in church choirs,
school assemblies, weddings, celebrations of new-born babies,
funerals and baptisms. The song rolls like a wave, cascading not
so much as an evocation as an expression of the surging forth of
collective memory and experience. The choir, which once sang
to accompany the spirit of Chris Hani and Oliver Tambo – and
many more patriots – to their eternal resting place, now sways,
as much to the beat as to blood doing penance in primeval
rhythms that have never found expression in such exalted places.
A woman soloist in a yellow robe hits a high note of such pure
clarity her lithe body could have been a vessel assigned to artic-

341

ulate to the world the unknowable language of morning dew. Her voice resonates within the hall and thunders against the high ceiling and goes out to the world, causing the dignitaries, faculty members and students to murmur with an appreciation characteristic of pilgrims finally reaching a place of worship after years of wandering in the wilderness. It is in this murmuring that Zodwa glances at Ayesha and sees tears in her friend's eyes; the hall becomes clouded and, as Zodwa blinks, tears drop on the polished toes of her black shoes.

★   ★   ★

'We're tired of peace,' Zodwa said, echoing the speaker, seeming to agree with him. 'We want an alternative to peace.' She paused as though groping for something in her own internal darkness. 'Those are words that must have been spoken by warlords and warmongers who have reduced Africa to one continental begging bowl. Informing any man who talks like you is a need to profit from strife. I am a young woman. In the eyes of many of you, I am a sinner. I went out with a white man who is now sitting dead behind me. He was a Jew and must have descended from people who paid a heavy price because some people were tired of peace. In my dictionary, the word sin does not exist. Evil does.' Then she dropped her bombshell.

'MaNdlela came to me,' she said, 'and advised me to challenge Johnny M to the test of the Humiliation Tree. After spending time thinking about this, I've decided that this is the right thing to do.'

There was a gasp, which rippled like waves, settling atop a head and wandering off to another member of the audience. 'What did she say?' someone asked.

'She's challenging Johnny M to the Humiliation Tree!'

'Oh, God,' someone cries. 'Does she understand what she's up against … ?'

'Shush.'

No one was more surprised by Zodwa's challenge than Nozizwe. She stood stock-still, hearing the words envelop her

342

like a blanket that alternated between hot and cold, a harbinger of a debilitating fever. She had given Zodwa charms and amulets to ward off evil, but had never once thought of preparing her for a journey to the mysterious enfolding arms of the Humiliation Tree. She knew its dangers, which were flavoured with the sweet seductiveness of nectar, since they throve on the vanity of those who entered the domain of the tree, which had proven fatal to almost all the people who had engaged with it. She knew that Johnny M had been strengthened by a sorcerer who had learnt the art of midnight death at the feet of Khotso Sethuntsa, the legendary inyanga who had administered even to leaders such as the late Hendrik Verwoerd, the architect of apartheid. The challenge itself was therefore judged by Nozizwe to be foolhardy and motivated by a stubborn pride, which might yet prove fatal to the young woman. But traditional protocol precluded any gesture from her, not now. Zodwa was on her own.

A spiral of intense incandescence suddenly illuminated the field, whirling like a fluorescent dervish, before people grasped that they were in the maw of a thunderstorm. This unexpected display of nature's hidden powers was followed by a darkened moment of silence — where the marchers and the occupants of the New Jerusalem later swore they could almost hear each other's thoughts — as if the spirits themselves were paying tribute to their own dead. Then the sky was lit by thunder flashes, lightning zigzagging and crashing in the peaks of Mveli mountains, the forest trees afire. The darkness which had been dispelled by the agency of torches and hurricane lamps at once deepened as the sky scowled and became suffused with even darker clouds that proceeded to open up and unleash a savage downpour.

During the roaring interplay of darkness and light, Johnny M's spiritual guides administered the necessary *intelezi*, having stripped the man naked; the rubber elastic bands holding the *muthi* around his biceps seemed ready to snap from the pressurising bulging of muscles. When Nozizwe approached Zodwa, preparatory to taking something out of her satchel, Zodwa made an imperceptible movement with her head, demurring yet acknowledging the older woman's intentions. Zodwe however succumbed to the treatment, where, naked, she was daubed with ochre, from the brow to the toes, the silent women working furiously quickly under Nozizwe's watchful eye. From where he stood, Mpanza caught a glimpse of Zodwa's wet nakedness, the breasts glistening like over-ripe mangoes, the curvature of her spine, the wide hips and the long legs that flowed into thighs which had a rendezvous with a dark triangle beneath a flat belly, wherein lay promises of unattainable pleasures. Distractedly, he ruminated on their earlier exchange, the flirting, which he knew was more a demonstration of the stealthy cunning of loneliness than a manifestation of desire, and despaired at his own dark secrets. Without consciously understanding how he had reached this conclusion, Mpanza knew that Zodwa was no mere woman; she belonged to the land of the spirits.

The rain seemed to let up a little, degenerating into a steady drizzle, allowing the moon to show its face. It was also a signal for the insects, which had been holding their breath, to come out and celebrate whatever their senses were capable of celebrating. Sleepless birds chirped and feasted on maggots and worms and beetles that had dared break the surface. All these sounds commingled into a great and palpable silence. She was aware of walking inside it, this silence, like a traveller suddenly finding himself inside an ancient cavern that told tales in the tongues of the dumb. Knowing that the silence around her spoke of a more profound silence inside herself. It was a silence that came from not being able to come to terms with some of the more cataclysmic events of her life. Her mother Nomonde, whom she had not really known; her brother who had been snatched at a time when she could have started understanding the demons that roiled and thrashed within his blood. Now her father was also gone. Silence was the most appropriate weapon to combat what lay outside her powers of comprehension. *If I don't come back*, she said to herself, *then it means I don't belong here in the first place.*

She was aware that Nozizwe was among the throng trailing them as they walked towards the river. Johnny M, walking some two paces ahead, was purposeful, confident, comfortable with his nakedness. Zodwa was conscious of the breeze that drove the drizzle which had all but washed her of the ochre coating. The moonlight, instead of reassuring her, cast threatening shadows. The sleeping village, the sleeping squatter camp, the eerily white tents of the believers – all conspired to conjure up something unsleeping, with eyes unclosed, which waited for her in every shadow. The shadows themselves moved, animated by the moonlight glancing off the mountain peaks on which the lightning had danced, bringing about a memory of another thunderstorm waiting in the wings. The air was cool; somewhere in the distance she heard a chatter and surmised that it must be a troop of insomniac monkeys. Mosquitoes descended on her and whined around her head: she chose to let them feast, knowing that whatever ravages they wrought on her face, there was no lover for whom she had to adorn herself. She walked on, remembering the words of a visiting Ghanaian professor that if you feared something, walk towards it, embrace it, love it, and own it.

The water was cool, stretching like a sheet of black glass, now and then the surface shimmering like onyx. This is it, she thought, hearing Johnny M splashing somewhere to her left in the dark. She walked in, keeping her eyes away from the silhouette of the sensuous, magnificent tree of terror. The sand beneath her feet was slippery, and she wondered if she wouldn't stumble, if it were possible to stumble in water, into a mire, a whirlpool. *If that happened*, she told herself, *then I'm not supposed to be here*. The sand gave way to pebbles and then she stubbed her toe on a sharp rock and felt the sting of water entering the fresh wound. She imagined her blood discolouring the water, adding to all the tints and hues that had given the water its colouring throughout the millennia. Risen now to a level just below her breasts, the water became colder. She felt her nipples stiffening. The darkness cast by the shadow of the mountain, as if a curtain has been drawn, started to claim the river, but still, and aided by peripheral vision, she was aware of the tree's presence and stayed on course. Now that she was a few metres from the tree, she saw how huge it was, like those baobabs her brother had told her about, in which you could build a perfect dwelling. Its branches spread out, like huge arms of a giant, presiding over the water swirling around the trunk, the water, as if driven by a centrifugal force, whirling and whirling, and she watched this in the dark – when she heard a crack. As she looked up something delivered with a lot of power behind it smashed against her jaw – and the lights were bright once again, but now, they had turned into individual stars. As she started her fall, tasting the rusty tang of blood, she smiled and shook her head at human folly. She sank, taking in the taste of water mixed with her own blood, and let herself sink, knowing – understanding – that struggle was futile, *Every time we say goodbye*, she sang to herself, keeping close to Ella Fitzgerald's rendition of the Cole Porter ballad, intrigued that she was not thinking about one powerful, defiant and valedictory liberation song. I'm a sell-out, she thought, and as laughter bubbled inside her, she blacked out, momentarily, and came to, underwater, where she felt herself propelled forwards and downwards to the river bed, by a force – it could have been a raft of anonymous hands – she couldn't see.

Her lungs screaming for relief, she headed towards an opening in a wall that was covered with lichen and found herself in a channel that stretched for almost forty metres. Above her, the sound of water pressed down on the walls of the channel, thrumming like blood in the veins.

Zodwa was still trembling when she became aware of many eyes watching behind the screen of darkness. She was not even sure on what kind of surface she was treading, because what she had taken to be a room, had broadened and stretched out into a field; she thought she could see the tops of huts, silhouetted against a charcoal-grey sky. But the eyes were there, penetrating the dark, scrutinising her. The music – or whatever the sound could have been – she had heard had stopped, to be superseded by a steady drumming that seemed to originate from distant hills. At that moment, Zodwa was hit by a need to take stock, and find her moorings. What was the date? It was Monday, 9 December 1996.

Her need to locate herself and thereby retain her sanity was disturbed by a booming voice, which – in shattering the darkness – simultaneously seemed to have ignited hundreds of torches that flickered at first and then merged to form one unit of blazing light. A thin, wiry man whose dress was similar to Jeqe's traditional attire, stepped out of the circle of light, an assegai and a shield held in either hand, in an attitude preparatory to attack. Zodwa was suddenly surrounded by men, warriors, who danced around her more to instil fear in her than to harm her. '*Imani madoda.*' said the deep voice. 'Who are you, my dear?'

The owner of the voice, a big, pot-bellied man who carried himself with the self-assurance of ancient monarchs, advanced, his hands empty, a dead leopard grinning above the crown of his head, seeming more alive as the play of light and shadow continued. 'Whose daughter are you?'

'My father is Joshua of the Ngubane clan.' Zodwa realised that she was talking to Dingane. This was the wiliest of the Zulu kings, who had slain his half-brother, Shaka, and challenged the settlers. How long ago was that? She ran a few dates in her mind, and then remembered February 1838, when Dingane made short shrift of Piet Retief and his party of land-hungry Boers.

'Is this how the maidens of the amaBomvu clan dress nowadays?' Dingane asked, a mischievous twinkle in his eye. As if on cue, one of the warriors broke out in a lusty song:

> *EmaBomvini kwakhal' inkomo*
> *Kwakhal' imbuzi*

And then the chorus: *Yash' imizi.*

The leader continued: *Bangakanani?*

Chorus, which now included women singers, soprano, alto, tenor and bass:

347

> *Bengangotshani!*
> *Bengakanani?*
> Chorus: *Bengangoboya benyathi*
> *Esayigwaz' egcekeni …*

A praise singer, his blood fired with memories of ancient victories, leapt out of the shadows, a knobkierie slashing the air, flying dangerously close to Zodwa's head. He started with Dingane's praise song:

> *Uvezi unonyanda umgabadeli*
> *Owagabadela inkundla yakwaBulawayo —*

Dingane roared: 'Enough! We have to clothe the young woman.'

Since leaving the settlement, Zodwa had been totally oblivious of her nakedness. She wondered, fighting a rising panic that came from disorientation, whether it were possible to be violated by apparitions; these looked mightily real, hale and hearty – possessed of bulging muscles and attitudes where they seemed eager to engage in combat any enemy that would oblige them the opportunity. From his avuncular utterances and placatory mien Zodwa was assured that carnal thoughts were farthest from Dingane's mind. This was leadership in action. The young women, her own age-mates, quickly surrounded her and began dressing her. It was a labour punctuated by giggles and admonitions, since the women were mostly well-fed and Zodwa was, in their estimation, a survivor of severe famine. She was then covered modestly in beads and skins and tassels and a headband made of a skin which the women insisted was worn exclusively by women from the royal house.

The long-dead king of the Zulus appeared very much alive. His cheeks, under the yellowing light of the flares, were quivering with suppressed mirth over some remembered juvenile mischief. He had enjoined her to sit with him in his *idlangala*, a makeshift hut for peripatetic herdsmen,

'I suppose', he said, 'that you'd like a comment on how I'm supposed to have been instrumental to the dissolution of the

Zulu kingdom.'

'The thought did occur to me,' Zodwa said, honestly, 'but I felt it was above my station to raise such issues.'

'Shaka', Dingane said, 'did a lot of good, not so much for the Zulu kingdom as for introducing a new way of fighting, which earned us our self-respect. From kwaSoshangane, which I hear you now call Mozambique, farther south-east to Mzilikazi's land, which was called Rhodesia and then Zimbabwe, all the way down to eKapa, the land of the Xhosa and those short yellow people, the hunters – all that was wrought by my brother's restlessness. But it all served to shape an African identity.'

'But', she asked, thinking about Johnny M, 'should the shaping of the African identity be achieved at such a cost?'

'All change, is usually preceded', Dingane said, 'by a cataclysm. Simply put, that means bloodshed.'

Dingane then told Zodwa how Piet Retief and the platoon under his command helped him regain his cattle, which had been stolen by Sikonyela, a rogue whose pastime was rustling. Dingane had been intrigued by the whitemen's weapons of war, the stick they used, which spewed fire and left men dead. But, much more – the handcuffs with which they had tricked Sikonyela, who had thought they were enchanting silver bracelets. 'Then,' he said, reflecting, going back in his mind to scenes he certainly would have liked to push to the farthest recesses of memory, 'there was the little story of land. We had a covenant with the Boers: bring back my cattle and I'll grant you land. They did return the cattle, that I can't deny, but the swath of land they needed, to accommodate a thousand wagons, hundreds of families, men, women and children – and their own livestock, gained only Mvelinqangi knows through what subterfuge – 'how', he asked, his eyes boring into Zodwa's, 'do you deal with such people?'

'You kill them,' a voice said, signalling the entry of Mkabayi ka Jama, the Lucrezia Borgia of the ancient Zulu royal family. She was much smaller than Zodwa had imagined, with alert eyes

349

that never seemed to stay focused on any one object: the restlessness of the eyes, Zodwa concluded, spoke of a voracious appetite to conquer, to own and subjugate whatever was within this formidable woman's orbit. How old could Mkabayi have been? She must have been around thirty-seven/eight when she joined that dynasty in the sky, but her facial features expressed the journey, a range from the virginal, sweet innocence of adolescence through the era of discovery of fleshly needs and its concomitant of sensual perils, all the way to an acceptance of age and its imperatives.

'Shaka', she said, 'had become a river in flood.' Mkabayi paused. 'It was a river that had routinely given sustenance to the crops. Our land burgeoned and all the homesteads went to sleep knowing that there was a monarch who was building something immense, that would add to their glory. But he became too ambitious. Power. We had to put a stop to it, especially after he went to attack the Swazis and was chasing after Mzilikazi. He didn't know, he couldn't have known, that men were defecting to Mzilikazi's army, and these became the spies whose information led to a long-drawn campaign that denuded us of our self-respect.'

'And the Boers', Zodwa asked, 'couldn't they be conscripted against Mzilikazi? Later?

'It was too late by then. Retief and his followers were already in the stomachs of the vultures.'

'Maybe', Zodwa offered, 'it was a bad move to kill Retief.'

'Have you ever led people?' Mkabayi asked.

'No.'

'You will find', she said, 'that you have to make decisions – life and death decisions – and you won't have the time or the luxury of weighing things up. Do you trust your instincts?'

'Sometimes.'

'Do you trust us?'

'I don't know you long enough to form a basis for judgement.'

A vulture fluttered into the hut; it trained its eyes on Zodwa, looking, strangely enough, like a person trying to ascertain the identity of a newcomer in a party. Its hooded eyes were surprisingly omniscient, as if in its travels it had partaken of festivals where all types of flesh had been on offer. Mkabayi gave the bird scraps of left-over chicken, at which the vulture pecked without enthusiasm. Zodwa felt her gorge rise. She was about to stand up and bid the apparitions goodbye when Mkabayi caught her eye.

'Come here,' she said. Mkabayi had effectively taken over. 'Come with me.'

Dingane, who had been displaced from centre-stage, glanced at the women as they departed, and continued with the task of ministering to the vulture. Zodwa noticed that the floor, which echoed their footfalls, was bestrewn with small objects which clanged when she stubbed her foot against one. As she bent to pick it up, Mkabayi pulled her back, brusquely, and said: 'Don't worry yourself, dear. There's more where that came from.'

And she led Zodwa along another passage into a chamber where the arrangement was not unlike in the cave where the villagers had stored their treasures and totems, on the day they were removed from Ngoza. The temperature in the chamber, which had been quite balmy and stuffy, suddenly dropped at the same time that Zodwa's eyes conquered the gloom and adjusted themselves to the tableau. She gasped, feeling her skin prickling, as she saw layers upon layers of skull-bones arrayed as if for a surreal modernistic exhibition in a municipal museum. For the first time since entering the eerie world whose portals were the Humiliation Tree, she accepted that, here, she was out of her league. *Ngisemasimbeni la* – I'm in shit.

Apropos of nothing, Mkabayi said: 'There's something ironic – and humbling – about death. For Dingane, killing people served a certain utilitarian purpose. Whenever he started enjoying it, something intruded, and reminded him that the people he was butchering were no different from him, were, in fact, moulded in the same clay. That always stayed his hand, where he let

351

weakness overcome him and dictate the course of action or, in most cases, inaction.'

During this macabre sighting compounded by Mkabayi's laconic recital, Zodwa was aware of the changes that were coming over Mkabayi. She had added inches to her height and pounds to her weight, seeming, in that instant of recognition, to have ballooned out and become a dominant feature in the chamber of bones. 'These bones', Mkabayi went on, 'were the enemy. It was an enemy that lacked judgement, which is why they are all displayed here, dead. Their spirits are somewhere in the world, most probably here, and they look to people like you to help them find rest.' She gave Zodwa a sidelong glance. 'Are you going to liberate them?'

'Me?'

'Yes, you.'

'I'm very sorry,' Zodwa said, really meaning it. 'I'm just here to continue my father's legacy. To discover what could be discovered and get back to the community.'

'But', Mkabayi said, 'you don't have a choice. You want to become a leader, you don't want to deal with the by-products of leadership, especially when it comes to a place like KwaZulu-Natal. You're hard, but then your hardness is compromised by a core of softness.' Mkabayi seemed to wrestle with a major puzzle in her head. 'The new government, under that Xhosa,' she said, 'has made it hard to prosecute criminals. Do you agree? You're a lawyer after all.'

'What do you mean – prosecute?' You fucking bitch, you and Dingane murdered Shaka – would you be comfortable standing trial?

As if reading her mind, and responding to Zodwa's animosity, Mkabayi smiled. 'Would you still admire Shaka if you knew that he couldn't abide any manifestation of weakness? Cripples, diseased people, were all sent to the hill of destiny, *kwagoqanyawo*, clubbed or speared to death. Even Mpande, his own half-brother, who was somewhat of a retard, was destined for execution, until

I intervened. The supreme irony is that, Shaka — do you know that the name derives from a skin disease, *ishaka*, what you'd call eczema today? — didn't know that the thumb and forefinger, which belong to *umlom'ongathethi manga* — also pointed to him; he despised the folks who were his mirror image.

'The bones —'

'Let's forget about the bones for one second,' Zodwa said, interrupting Mkabayi. 'What I want to know is, what kind of covenant Johnny M made with you? Why was he so confident about delving into these depths?

'Ah,' Mkabayi said, 'I understand.' She clapped her hands, twice, thrice and was immediately rewarded with the eager presence of warriors, who sniffed the air like setters. But these were different, pale, like condemned people who had spent endless days in the dungeon. '*Izinsila zami lezi*,' Mkabayi said, 'and they accompanied me to the grave.'

Zodwa knew that where the world of the spirits merged with reality there was a need for precipitate action. She knew, now, that Johnny M had been communing with these wretches, *via* his own spiritual mediums, who must decidedly be the strongest sorcerers in the region. Taking off her new garments, she flung them at the group — and ran. She heard Mkabayi shout something and forged ahead, taking in the darkness, knowing that she could do serious injury to herself were she to fall into a ravine. But she ran, hearing the men panting like hunting dogs behind, and realised that, since they were already dead, they had no footfalls.

Zodwa felt the ground give beneath her feet and, for a long minute, she was suspended in the air — and then she hit the water. The impact knocked the wind out of her, but she determined not to pass out. Knowing that Johnny M must have promised Mkabayi and her group illimitable bushels of blood, she knew that her own capture would be a mammoth betrayal of her father's people.

Still reeling from the experience, she broke the surface and realised that she had swum beyond the Humiliation Tree, which stood imposingly behind her. I don't want to see that tree, ever again, she thought. In a haze, she became aware of arms pulling her out of the water, and then gave in to the sense that she must learn to let go.

*　　*　　*

Later, refreshed but still feeling sore, Zodwa recounted her experiences from the podium, feeling the presence of more reassuring ghosts behind her. Her father and Horwitz. She could have used their counsel now. As the people listened agog, she returned to her earlier speech, as if the journey to the Humiliation Tree had never intervened. As she spoke, there was a slight disturbance at the back of the throng; Johnny M hadn't wasted time. He was back and garbed in his characteristic cream suit. But, Zodwa knew, she was now on the threshold of a new revelation and a new beginning – which would be the beginning for her people.

'I speak of the evil of men like your champion Mbongwa,' she said, 'who has never lifted a finger to help a single person. I speak of Johnny M here, standing before you, leading you to ruin. What has he done for you? I ask you all these questions, not because I have any great wish to be your chief. There are many good men and women, most of them in Two Rivers, who have the experience and the courage to lead. There are people like MaNdlela; there's Nduli in the Eastern Cape, whose heartstrings are tied to the pain all of us feel here.' She swallowed something which must have tasted of bile. 'There is nothing here, people are poor,' she went on, 'but in this poverty I have come across demonstrations of great generosity. As Africans, especially now that we have our own government, we have to be generous without being foolish. We have to strive for peace and democracy.'

Someone in the back clapped, a sound that was swallowed up in a throaty roar of applause. Seeing his plans being dashed by the oratory of a woman who was once a child of silence, Johnny M couldn't contain himself any longer. 'Democracy?' he cried.

354

'What fucking democracy? Who chose *you* to be the chief?' As he spoke, he was making his way to the front, pushing and shoving, glaring down any show of protest.

'*I am the one*', said the voice belonging to Baba Joshua, '*who chose her.*'

All hell broke loose. Another stronger gust of wind caused the lights to flicker. Some of the people who had heard the rumour that Baba Joshua might not be dead pushed to the front, almost crushing the front row against the edge of the stage. From somewhere in the back a magnesium flare whooshed up into the sky, spreading a constellation of purplish sparks, illuminating a wide area of the New Jerusalem. Somehow, this visual display seemed to complement the earlier mystical occurrence of someone speaking from beyond the grave. But the confusion also played into the hands of Johnny M, a man who thrived on turbulence. Balancing on two people's shoulders, he levered himself onto the stage. As he advanced towards Zodwa, in that rolling toe-to-heel strut of Sixties' *tsotsis*, his jacket flapped open to expose the pistol stuck into his waistband. On his face was written the depth of his anger and frustration, and what he intended doing to this woman who presented an obstacle.

Johnny M was about four or five feet from Zodwa when he drew the gun and aimed. Mpanza, who had been watching everything from the wings, came charging, yelling, 'Johnny!' As he crashed into Zodwa's body, sending her sprawling on the wooden floor of the stage, he first felt a numbing pain on the side of the head before his ears were nearly shattered by the loud report of the gun. All motion slowed down as in an instant replay of a television soccer match. He saw Johnny M getting ready to fire again, but this time swerving his body so that he was near the feet of the shrouded corpses on the chairs, raising his arm, snapping off two shots at the figure of Joshua in the middle. All the time shouting, '*Die! die! die!*'

The shot had taken off Mpanza's left earlobe. He was surprised that such an innocuous part of his body could bleed so much. Fighting nausea and the restraining hands of Joachim or Jeqe and other believers, he crawled to where Johnny M was crouched with the smoking gun in his hand. Mpanza was mystified at the sight of a sobbing Johnny M, the man who had struck fear into every heart in Ngoza.

'Did you have to shoot the corpse?' Mpanza asked. By this time the stage was a hive of activity, as in the aftermath of a boxing match where an unpopular champion has lost to a local lad.

Zodwa produced a towel which she pressed against Mpanza's head to staunch the bleeding. As he took it, their fingers touched briefly, their second contact in a space of ten minutes, and Mpanza felt something welling up in him. He closed his eyes the better to keep from staring into hers. He knew he was in for a bad headache, but he had to do this one thing. Her fingers gripped him at the forearm, and she forced him to look at her.

'Are you going to be all right?' Zodwa asked.

'Well,' Mpanza replied, 'I won't be able to scale the heights of fashion where you need an earring.'

'Don't worry,' she said, smiling for the first time, 'we'll get you a replacement from somewhere.' Still studying his face, she asked. 'What do we do with him?' Pointing at Johnny M who was flanked by two burly men in traditional garb.

'Perhaps', Mpanza suggested, 'he should see the extent of his damage.'

They took Johnny M and walked him to the corpse he had shot. Joachim took off the hood. Mpanza studied Johnny M's reaction. There was a silence which conveyed itself all the way to the last person in the New Jerusalem settlement. It touched the chickens in their runs, where they stopped clucking. It was felt by the dogs which had already lost contact with their compatriots. The dray animals felt it and stopped lowing. Even the night sounded as if it wished to hunker down and rest. The silence was broken by a hoarse, inhuman wailing, so lost in its wretchedness that, for a moment, Mpanza felt it possible to pity him.

Police Chief Grey's dead eyes stared out at Johnny M as if

looking for an answer which would provide one last piece in a perplexing jigsaw puzzle. But before Johnny allowed himself to be escorted by the warriors, curiosity had the better of him.

'How did you do it?' he asked. Perhaps it was a knowledge he would use to spice prison conversations.

'There was nothing to it,' Mpanza told him. 'Whenever the light changed, we shuffled the corpses around.' Mpanza was reluctant to talk. 'I was very young when my father died,' he said. 'At his funeral service, the children sat in the front pews in the church. It was a large church with intimidating figures of Christ and pictures of holy people. Windows decorated with mosaic. The light spilled from up above, filling certain sections of my father's coffin with brilliance. Every time people filed past, viewing the body, their moving reflections on the glass under that dancing light, made me believe, for one moment, that my father was still alive, and I didn't know what he was doing laid out like that under glass.' He laughed. 'I'm not sure whether that memory was behind the presentation here today.' Looking at Johnny M, he added: 'But, as you well know, people are willing to believe anything once it happens around death.'

'And Baba Joshua's voice?' Johnny M persisted. 'That *was* convincing.'

'Yes?' Zodwa asked. 'Who was that?'

'That was Reuben,' Mpanza replied. 'He knows something about throwing voices.'

Nozizwe who had been standing watching everything as if from a distance, cleared her throat. They all turned to look at her. 'I've got news for you,' she said. 'Throughout the whole thing, Reuben was in the other tent. With Nerissa.'

Zodwa and Mpanza looked at Nozizwe. 'Who was it, then?' they both asked.

'Baba Joshua,' Nozizwe said simply. She turned and joined the men carting Johnny M to the only cell in the settlement of believers called the New Jerusalem. As Mpanza and Zodwa watched Nozizwe's slight frame, there was a loud thunderclap, then the air was full of sulphur. And then the rain came down.

As Johnny M was led away, he stopped and looked at Zodwa. 'I wish you a very long life,' he said. 'Especially since you'll be cohabiting with the man who murdered your brother.'

Zodwa stood rooted for a long minute, hearing the words, shaking her head, imagining that she were still in the land of the spirits. 'What does he mean?'

'Let me explain,' Mpanza began.

'There's nothing to explain,' Zodwa said, 'except to tell me whether you did or didn't kill Jonah?'

'We killed Jonah —'

'*We?*' Zodwa cried. 'What fucking we?'

'We the Movement,' Mpanza explained.

'Oh,' Zodwa said, 'so that's supposed to explain everything?'

'Hey!' someone shouted, 'there's Mbongwa running away— !'

'Don't worry about him,' Nozizwe said. 'Before the beginning of tomorrow, he'll be lying heavy in the bellies of his own vultures.' She looked at the man and the woman, who had seemed destined to build something together, but who were now separated by a screaming chasm of blood, family and history. 'I suggest', she said, 'that we all get inside and talk this thing over.'

'There's nothing more to say,' Zodwa said, turning her back on Mpanza. 'This man killed my brother, for whatever reason, and I want him out of this place.'

Mpanza stood his ground until Nozizwe led him into the house. Zodwa stood looking at him, her mind replaying the image where Johnny M, his mouth twisted in derision, told her about Mpanza and Jonah, and that she was consorting with the killer of her own flesh and blood. Swallowing this humiliating piece of news, she felt tears of rage burning her eyes.

Then, he came to her house carrying his remorse. He looked at her once and instantly knew that whatever he had planned had been blasphemed by words. Mpanza tried to explain, but all she could do was pummel him on the chest, tears streaming down her eyes, and ask the unanswerable question, *Why?*

A sliver of light had cut through the parting of the curtain and skewered his face, bronzing it and rendering it irretrievably cruel. In that light, she understood that he would forever remain unknowable, an eternal stranger. His tired eyes, which had seen everything on the surface and on the edges of the world, spoke of a bottomless longing, a quest for a moment's rest.

'I watch our world deluding itself that it knows the battle-field,' Mpanza said. 'I see leaders composing words that might be articulating factual events but are as far from the truth as is light from darkness and night from day. We left our homes and went into these kingdoms where we tasted what it meant to be despised. Coming out of a country where to look like us was akin to being cursed, we found a home in the political struggle, where we were made aware of our humanity. We then learnt how to confront all those who had denied us this quality and in looking at the enemy, we were sometimes shocked to see how much he looked like us. Because, if you study the configurations of this country, and its process towards self-discovery, you'll realise that, without the enemy within, the enemy outside would never have managed to penetrate our armour. Political theory taught us what was paraphrased by James Baldwin, that the mistake we make is in thinking that, since all our brothers are black, then all blacks are our brothers. If you look at the number of casualties of the struggle, through the ages, an alarming percentage is black. White people who died in the struggle are almost negligible compared to the nightly vigils and burials and wailings attending the lives of black folks. Why? Because, however elegantly we put this in obscuring political language, to be black and to betray was the greatest, most unforgivable sin in our eyes. It was in this spirit that we justified within ourselves why Jonah had to die. With him, so we thought, it was even more unacceptable that he had been a stalwart of our movement, a cadre of impeccable credentials. We accepted the order from Rosie, a supreme irony, since Rosie took his orders from past-masters of intrigue in Pretoria. Once the order had been given, we, the soldiers, had to execute it. With hindsight, now, how they must have laughed, watching our bungled attempts to follow him. How they must have carried one another on their shoulders as they shadowed Stan and me to all those places where we trailed Jonah. After shooting him, I managed to escape; Stan didn't – and he was hanged. All of us, then, were marked for death. I wanted to die when the truth finally came out. Through all these years of wandering, of pretending to live, I have been trying to atone for Jonah's death, exposing myself to danger, hoping to die. When I lunged at Johnny M – even though, seeing you, knowing you for that briefest moment had given me a reason for living – I still hoped to die, to make sure that I never endured this moment when all is revealed.'

He wept. Zodwa realised that what she had taken to be her own private sorrow, actually belonged to more people than she would know. Strangers, then, were part of the murmuring of her own blood. Mpanza missed Jonah for the camaraderie and the shared experiences in the camps. For him, the killing was the closest thing to suicide. Incapable of taking his own life, he now spent his time staring into space, trying to recreate a time when people had been bonded by an impulse, an ideal of struggle. In a strange way, then, when she finally made love with him, Jonah's face superimposed itself on Mpanza's, giving the act a curious quality of incest.

Twenty Six

Thirty days after the funeral, at the end of the mourning period, Ngoza was green, fecund, the long drought a mere memory, like the distant memory of a toothache. Looking at the growing things, marvelling at the many disguises nature sometimes wore to introduce herself to the living world, Zodwa found that the memories were the most constant features of her people's lives. They were there, changing all the time, as unreliable as a lover, but they would never escape from you, nor, she realised, could you ever escape from them. Memory had sustained her kinsmen, who were now more relaxed in their religious beliefs, holding on to some ancient orthodoxy but opening the door to other influences.

⋆   ⋆   ⋆

She lamented the passing away of Horwitz, whom, she admitted to herself, she hadn't really known. She had assigned Ayesha and friends in legal institutions to go over their records, do research and find out about one David Horwitz, but they had drawn a blank.

⋆   ⋆   ⋆

Mpanza took Zodwa along to meet his wife and children. Even though she hadn't yet slept with Mpanza – 'I didn't *want* to make love to you,' he told her later, 'I *ached* to make love to you'– she was surprised at her own depth of feeling when she met Khethiwe. She was beautiful, poised and had taken special care to present herself in the most glamorous light, as if saying to Mpanza, *Just take a look at what you're missing*. It was perhaps the

361

fact that Mpanza treated Khethiwe with the greatest courtesy, the way we treat strangers with whom we have nothing in common, which pointed to Khethiwe that she was actually the loser. This realisation, to which women are attuned from birth, brought out the harridan in her. During a disastrous dinner at a restaurant in Norwood, Khethiwe strove to catch Mpanza on the wrong foot, and failed. It was unbearable to watch her reaction to the fact that Mpanza had stopped drinking; here, she felt judged a failure because liquor had been so much a part of their discord that she couldn't imagine him not inflicting himself and his bad habits on another woman. The fact that the other woman found him almost without weaknesses was insupportable. It was in Khethiwe's eyes that Zodwa saw how much she hated them. They never saw the kids since, Khethiwe said, Mpanza hadn't warned her he was coming and the kids had made arrangements with friends. Which was just as well, Zodwa had thought.

★   ★   ★

On a whim she had gone to visit Johnny M in Modderbee prison. He had been surprised at this gesture and had been understandably suspicious. Prison had changed him and hardened him, such that Zodwa saw an old man who exercised obsessively to maintain a physical condition that would empower him to wrest from the strongest jaws what he wanted and, in the same way, repulse enemy attacks. If everything in him had been burnt out, the hate still gleamed in his eyes. Although he didn't confide in Zodwa, she knew that it was this hate fuelling the inner furnace which kept him alive. As Zodwa was about to replace the receiver through which she had been communicating to Johnny M across the dividing glass, he told her what had been stored in his heart, something he knew would clutch her heart as if with steel fingers. His mouth twisted in derision, he told her about Mpanza and Jonah, and that she was consorting with the killer of her own flesh and blood. Swallowing this humiliating piece of news, she left the prison with tears of rage burning her eyes. She avoided Mpanza for a week.

Then, Mpanza had come to her house carrying his saxophone. He looked at her once and instantly knew that whatever he had planned had been blasphemed by words. Mpanza tried to explain, but all she could do was pummel him on the chest, tears streaming down her eyes, and ask the unanswerable question, Why?

A sliver of light had cut through the parting of the curtain and skewered his face, bronzing it and rendering it irretrievably cruel. In that light, she understood that he would forever remain unknowable, an eternal stranger. His tired eyes, which had seen everything on the surface and on the edges of the world, spoke of a bottomless longing, a quest for a moment's rest. I watch our world deluding itself that it knows the battlefield, Mpanza said. I see leaders composing words that might be articulating factual events but are as far from the truth as is light to darkness and night to day.

We left our homes and went into these kingdoms where we tasted what it meant to be despised. Coming out of a country where to look like us was akin to being cursed, we found a home in the political struggle, where we were made aware of our humanity. We then learnt how to confront all those who had denied us this quality and in looking at the enemy, we were sometimes shocked to see how much he looked like us. Because, if you study the configurations of this country, and its process towards self-discovery, you'll realise that, without the enemy within, the enemy outside would never have managed to penetrate our armour. Political theory taught us what was paraphrased by James Baldwin, that the mistake we make is in thinking that, since all our brothers are black, then all blacks are our brothers. If you look at the number of casualties of the struggle, through the ages, an alarming percentage is black. White people who died in the struggle are almost negligible compared to the nightly vigils and burials and wailing attending the lives of black folks. Why? Because, however elegantly we put this in obscuring political language, to be black and to betray was the greatest, most unforgivable sin in our eyes.

It was in this spirit that we justified within ourselves why Jonah had to die. With him, so we thought, it was even more unacceptable that he had been a stalwart of our movement, a cadre of impeccable credentials. We accepted the order from Rosie, a supreme irony, since Rosie took his orders from past-masters of intrigue in Pretoria. Once the order had been given we, the soldiers, had to execute it. With hindsight, now, how they must have laughed, watching our bungled attempts to follow him. How they must have carried one another on their shoulders as they shadowed Stan and me to all those places where we trailed Jonah. After shooting him, I managed to escape; Stan did-n't – and he was hanged. All of us, then, were marked for death. I wanted to die when the truth finally came out. Through all these years of wandering, of pretending to live, I have been tying to atone for Jonah's death, exposing myself to danger, hoping to die. When I lunged at Johnny M – even though, seeing you, knowing you for that briefest moment had given me a reason for living – I still hoped to die, to make sure that I never endured this moment when all is revealed.

He wept. Zodwa realised that what she had taken to be her own private sorrow, actually belonged to more people than she would know. Strangers, then, were part of the murmuring of her own blood. Mpanza missed Jonah for the camaraderie and the shared experiences in the camps. For him, the killing was the closest thing to suicide. Incapable of taking his own life, he now spent his time staring into space, trying to recreate a time when people had been bonded by an impulse, an ideal of struggle. In a strange way, then, when she finally made love with him, Jonah's face superimposed itself on Mpanza's, giving the act a curious quality of incest.

*   *   *

But there were other important things. The women's co-opera-tives needed her advice on how to create food gardens. She knew nothing about agriculture but was in power and therefore had access to experts who ran reconstruction and development programmes. The media had heard about her, and for a while some badly dressed journalist would camp in her guest house, asking questions. *How does it feel being a woman chief?* Why, it feels just fine. She slew them with her insistence on banalities. Journalists, she had long realised, only printed what had long been in their minds in the first place, and merely needed interlocutors to validate their conclusions.

*   *   *

Benedita had left Venter. She had written from Crete, and twice from London: *I'm beginning to be like Steve.* Every time news reports featured the random bomb or John Major's slide into political obscurity, Zodwa wondered where Benedita was in all that madness. Nozizwe reassured her that Benedita would return; she was just at the beginning of her journey. She also needed to recover from the ugliness she had seen in South Africa, and what it had forced her to become. *I was black in London*, Benedita wrote, *and became white in South Africa, only to realise that I'm back to the consciousness of blackness that only London can evoke. Love.*

*   *   *

Political people sometimes came to visit. They would invariably appeal to her vanity, saying how much she would be an asset in national politics. The journey from Ngoza through KwaMashu, to Fort Hare and back, was helping to break the cycle. Power, she knew, was very seductive, but she was satisfied with her lot. This much she expressed to the joint SANDF and National Intelligence Agency delegation which included Tsepo. They voiced unhappiness with Mpanza, suspecting that he had filched some of the arms.

*   *   *

In her bathroom mirror, she would see strands of grey in her hair. She had plucked them out in the past. Now she cherished them. Sometimes, Mpanza would interrupt his composition of a blues poem to Zodwa and come up behind her and gather her in his arms. They would take long walks to the caves where discoveries of prehistoric fossils were being made, it seemed, weekly. They would look at the ancient formations and rejoice that they were part of the living world. Exulting, kissing him, tasting his awful tobacco, Zodwa would know that time would pass and transform them. Perhaps when their graves were dug up in some future millennium, the palaeontologists would comment on their primitive state. But these experts would have had no access to the enduring power of memory.